The Ministry for Ignoring Climate Change

David Millar

Melting Tundra Publishing, Cochrane, AB, Canada
www.meltingtundra.com

ISBN 978-0-9938321-2-3 (paperback)
ISBN 978-0-9938321-3-0 (ebook)

‘Canada is now a world leader in the fight against climate change.’

Canada Government website, December 2017

Canada now ranks 51st out of the world’s worst 57 carbon-emitting countries in terms of their efforts to combat climate change.

Climate Change Performance Index 2020
Germanwatch, Bonn

Contents

CHAPTER 1

The Ministry for Climate Change

'Eddington? He's what you might call pale green,' said Paul Hawthorne quietly, wrinkling his nose and tipping his head slightly towards the man at the end of the room. His colleague Adam Winter looked puzzled.

'Environmentally aware but a political realist. Take last month for example; he attended a rally for polar bears, and then voted to support a new oil pipeline the same afternoon.'

Winter blinked. 'Polar bears? At a rally?'

Hawthorne stared at him. 'Not *at* the rally, no,' he hissed. 'It was a rally in *support* of polar bears. To raise awareness of the shrinking sea ice they hunt on.'

'Oh…' It was Monday morning. He was feeling a bit slow.

The two men were standing at the back of a staff meeting convened to announce the appointment of the new Minister for Climate Change, the Honourable Nigel Eddington, a fortysomething MP getting his first cabinet position, and their new boss. Well, Hawthorne's boss. Winter was further down the pecking order.

'Anyway, he wants to meet with both of us right after this. Apparently he has some new ideas he wants to share.'

'Hmm…' frowned Winter, before smiling broadly and clapping enthusiastically and with complete insincerity as Eddington stepped up to speak.

Hawthorne might have his doubts but for now Eddington looked like a refreshing change from his predecessor, a man who appeared to regard climate change as more of a personal affront to his political career than a crisis for the rest of the planet. 'MinCC' was widely regarded as the kiss of death to any political career, unpopular with most of the electorate and near-impossible to show any results in less than several electoral cycles.

If Eddington was pale green, Winter was greener—he'd only been in the department six months. He wasn't even Canadian. Lanky and in his early thirties, he was a self-confessed climate nerd. he had been working at the Department of Energy and Climate Change in London as part of a team coming up with ways to reduce carbon emissions, and this overseas posting was a significant opportunity for him. He had been seconded to the Canadians for two years on a UN initiative to share best practices on climate change policies.

Things had not been going well.

On the face of it his secondment made good sense. Canada had one of the worst records on the planet when it came to tackling climate change—fifty-first out of the world's fifty-seven most carbon-emitting countries, whereas the UK ranked fourth, just a few places below saintly Sweden. So the idea was that he could give them some pointers on how it was done, assuming of course they wanted to listen.

The problem was, he was increasingly convinced

that they didn't. He had decided that the role of the Ministry was not to take action on climate change at all, but to provide a smoke-screen for inaction, to generate a steady stream of nice-sounding initiatives and press releases that gave the impression the government was doing something, whilst actually doing nothing at all. In other words, to ignore climate change rather than to fix it. Hence his hope that the arrival of a new, younger, greener Minister could only be a Good Thing.

He would therefore have been disappointed if he had known that Eddington himself didn't identify as an environmentalist at all, but more as a manager and a problem-solver. His primary motivation was not to help the planet but his career, and he cannily saw the recent upsurge in voter interest in the environment as a way of achieving that.

Before moving into politics he'd been a management consultant and was hoping that he could bring some out-of-the-box thinking to the challenges of climate change and reducing CO2 emissions, then use that to demonstrate his skills for bigger jobs—defence, foreign affairs, maybe even finance. Nigel Eddington was ambitious and full of ideas. His critics felt he should sometimes focus more on the quality rather than just quantity.

Hawthorne was the most senior civil servant in the department—the Ministerial Permanent Secretary, in effect the Minister's deputy. He was the one who could get things done—the one with the finely-tuned political antennae, someone who knew the right moment to pitch an idea to his Minister to get it accepted, or to discretely introduce doubts that would sink an undesirable one.

When he had first arrived Hawthorne had spent

several weeks briefing Winter on the department's activities, a process which had left Adam with a grudging respect for Hawthorne's skills. What he still couldn't decide was whether the lack of real results was down to the hard line taken by the prairie provinces, as Hawthorne claimed, or to skilful foot-dragging by Hawthorne himself.

Overall Winter feared it was going to be an uphill struggle to actually achieve anything. He hoped that the new Minister would prove him wrong.

- - -

Thirty minutes later the new Minister swept into the meeting room and enthusiastically shook their hands before dropping a handful of coloured pens and Post-Its on the table, taking a seat and waving for them to join him.

'Winter. That's rather appropriate, isn't it?' he grinned.

Adam gave him a weak smile. 'Believe me, I've heard them all, sir.'

'I was going to say you've brought the weather with you too, but you've probably heard that one. Anyway, I hear you're from London---they've certainly got their act together on climate change. Remarkable progress on actually reducing emissions, down by forty percent in the last thirty years. Hopefully you can show us how they did it and how it can be applied here, eh?'

Without waiting for a response he swivelled towards Hawthorne and continued: 'Now, the reason the PM has asked me to take over the department is that he wants to see progress on climate change, a fresh approach. The public perception is that too little is happening. He wants to see real progress in reducing carbon dioxide emissions. Most importantly, people need to see that the Carbon Tax is delivering.'

He beamed at them. 'Plus of course we need to pay more attention now that schoolchildren are starting to become politically active on climate.'

Hawthorne nodded sympathetically. 'We all need to be thoughtful about the next generation, Minister.'

'Absolutely! Absolutely!' Eddington grinned mischievously. 'After all, they get the vote at eighteen!' he laughed. 'Anyway, I'm looking to the two of you for some fresh ideas so let's get the facts on the table, give me the inside scoop—hash out some ideas together.' He rubbed his hands together enthusiastically and Winter started to feel more optimistic.

'How about we start with the national emissions target that was agreed with the IPCC in Paris: we don't seem to be making much progress on meeting it do we, so what can we do to fix that?'

'Well, to start with the basics,' began Hawthorne, flashing them both a reassuring smile, 'the biggest issue is the target number itself. At the Paris Agreement three years ago your predecessor committed this country to reducing greenhouse gas emissions thirty percent by 2030. In my opinion he got in over his head, it became a stupid macho thing, and he committed us all to something that's virtually impossible to achieve.'

Eddington seemed taken aback by Hawthorne's bluntness. 'I know it's traditional to blame your predecessor but that's a bit below the belt isn't it? It doesn't sound macho to me, just that he was trying to set high standards.'

Hawthorne pulled a face. 'That's one way of looking at it, Minister. But in a sense this is a numbers game. You've inherited a tough target. If there were a way of lowering that target, you'd have a much better chance of meeting it. It could be the difference between being seen as a success rather than as a failure.'

Eddington looked thoughtful. 'But surely the target is based on the science?'

'You would think so, but no. It was just a negotiation, a number. Canada accounts for only one and a half percent of global emissions. Whatever we do will not make any difference in the big picture. If our target was, say, twenty percent less, it's much more likely we would achieve it, and that would in turn give a big moral encouragement to people to try harder.'

'I guess that's one way of looking at it.' Eddington seemed unconvinced, although he was clearly considering Hawthorne's point.

Hawthorne leaned forward. 'The thing is, Minister, your predecessor got into a kind of, well, a pissing match with the Danish delegation. He was trying to impress this particular woman on their team. The EU was going for a forty percent reduction and she more or less agreed to go to bed with him if he could get Canada to match it. She was daring him that he didn't have the authority to commit to it. There is no scientific logic to the target. Only a…psychological one.'

'You're not serious?!' laughed Eddington, incredulous.

'Oh, the Nordic countries are just brutal at these climate negotiations, they'll do anything—I remember there was this Norwegian girl at the Doha meeting…' began Winter, before thinking better of it.

'Consider this,' continued Hawthorne. 'We're an arctic country, covered in snow five months of the year, temperatures down to minus twenty for weeks on end. Even with good insulation it takes a lot of energy to keep homes warm. More to the point almost eighty percent of our electricity already comes from non-fossil fuel sources, we simply don't have that much scope for burning less gas or coal. Thirty percent just made no sense—even our own scientific advisors were against it, and they're usually the ones pushing for more ambitious numbers.'

Eddington shrugged. 'Okay, it might be a stretch but it's still good for the planet though isn't it? I mean, ideally we'd have a one hundred percent cut in human CO2 emissions, wouldn't we?'

Winter looked alarmed. 'Ah, not really Minister...a complete ban on man-made emissions might suit the rainforests and plant life, but it would be pretty detrimental for humans, obviously.'

Eddington seemed surprised. 'Oh?'

'We breathe out carbon dioxide, Minister. A *complete* ban would mean we could only ever breathe in, never out.'

'Serious?'

Was Eddington pulling his leg, or had he somehow skipped basic biology at school? He really wasn't sure. 'Plants absorb CO2 and emit oxygen. Animals—including us humans—inhale oxygen and exhale CO2.'

Eddington nodded sombrely as if Winter had just imparted some deep scientific secret to him.

'Actually its cattle that are more of the problem,' continued Winter. 'The average cow emits around a hundred kilos of methane per year, but methane is twenty times more potent as a greenhouse gas than CO2. So eating beef is actually really bad for the environment, not just the methane they produce but the fact that in order to make cattle ranches they often cut down carbon-absorbing forests. It's a sort of double whammy.'

'Cows emit methane? Really? How?'

Winter wondered if he was pulling his leg. Evidently biology was not the new Minister's strong suit.

'They, er, fart it, Minister.'

'Oh, yes of course...', he grinned sheepishly. 'Maybe we could reach our emissions target simply by banning cattle?' He tapped the table thoughtfully with his pen. 'Or...how about if we replace all those cattle ranches in Alberta with solar panel farms? The farmers would still be farmers— technically anyway—but solar panels instead of cattle.' He looked pleased with himself. 'What do you think of that?'

Hawthorne looked thoughtful. 'Well, Minister, it might take a while to persuade the country to go vegetarian...you know how people love their steak, not to mention cream in their coffee.'

'And I suspect it takes a lot less people to look after a field of solar panels than of cattle, if you include the whole field-to-table food-chain,' added Winter. 'You might be inadvertently creating an unemployment problem.'

Eddington nodded thoughtfully and then scribbled 'Cattle farms → Solar farms' on one of his Post-its and stuck it on the whiteboard behind his head. 'Let's park that one for the moment. The main thing I'm concerned about right now is that our emissions are going up not down. We need to bring in some quick targeted pieces of legislation to cut emissions in factories, promote the switch to electric vehicles, phase-out coal-fired power stations. Get things moving.'

Hawthorne smirked as if about to explain the cruel

realities of life to a teenager proudly clutching their first pay cheque and naively thinking it was all theirs.

'Admirable thoughts, Minister, but the challenge is that you're the Minister for Climate Change—not for Industry, or Transport, or Energy. You can't just legislate in another Minister's portfolio.'

'No, of course not, but the cabinet are on the same page on this. We just need to plant the seeds, show them what to do. Ask for their cooperation.'

Hawthorne smiled again. 'Are you *sure* they're on the same page, Minister?' He glanced at Winter. 'Do you have any idea how long it would take the Minister for Energy to get approval to flood a valley to construct a new hydro dam, for example? It can be decades—not to mention the amount of public abuse and aggravation he's going to get in the process. It would literally be a suicide mission for him to do what's really required to meet the emissions targets.'

'Suicide mission? Isn't that a bit strong?'

'Political suicide, I didn't mean it literally,' replied Hawthorne grumpily.

'Actually you did say 'literally',' pointed out Winter, immediately wishing he hadn't. Hawthorne glared at him.

Eddington stood up and drew a rough outline of Canada on his whiteboard. 'Bit of a digression, but I've got an idea about that I'd like to run up the flagpole with you guys and see if you salute it, so to speak. The arctic coastline is the part of Canada most affected by climate change, right? Rising sea levels are flooding Inuit villages, the shrinking sea ice means polar bears are starving, and thawing permafrost threatens to release gigatons of methane into the atmosphere.' The other two nodded. 'So why not turn all that to our advantage and build a massive combined solar-wind energy farm up there? In the summer you have twenty-four hour daylight so it's ideal for solar, and in the winter it's more windy so ideal for turbines. And it'll be dark so no one will notice they're there.'

He drew what looked like a line of daisies stretching across the top of Nunavut. 'We put them all along the coast—almost no one up there to complain but anyway they should be sympathetic so it's easier to get public approval. Ten thousand wind turbines all along the arctic coast. Mission accomplished!' He put the marker pen down with a flourish.

Winter and Hawthorne looked at one another. It was hard to know if this was the musings of a genius or just hopelessly naïve. Probably the first daydreams of laying a transatlantic cable or putting a man on the moon had started the same way, so maybe they shouldn't be too harsh.

'It's certainly ambitious,' replied Hawthorne cautiously. 'It would be a huge engineering project of course. You'd be talking tens of billions of dollars and decades to complete. But in principle, if it could be done, it would indeed be a tremendous achievement. A bold and career-defining act for sure.'

'And it would solve the problem of Inuit unemployment at a stroke,' grinned Eddington.

'As long as they had a head for heights,' replied Winter dryly.

'What's more, we could use the Carbon Tax to pay for it,' continued the Minister, on a roll. 'How's that going by the way? Is it persuading people to live low-carbon lifestyles?'

Winter winced. This was what he'd spent most of the last week studying. 'Yes and no. There's been an increase in sales of low-energy lightbulbs, but that's because the old thermoluminescent ones were banned. And roof insulation and double-glazing too, but again that's mostly because the cost is subsidized—in effect you pay people to buy them.'

'But at least people are switching,' replied Eddington. 'How about electric vehicles?'

Hawthorne nodded. 'Sales are doubling every year, but it's still early days—still fewer than half of one percent of all new cars sold are electric.'

'Which might not sound a lot, but at that rate they'll account for more than half of all new vehicles sold within ten years,' chipped in Winter encouragingly.

'Excellent! And the revenue raised? Can we point to some good things it's being spent on?'

'It generates about ten billion dollars a year—although of course it's not intended as a *source* of revenue, its function is simply to deter people from burning fossil fuels,' said Hawthorne cautiously.

Eddington persisted. 'But all the same…'

Hawthorne looked evasive and chose his words carefully. Winter had learnt that when Hawthorne wanted not to say something he used longer and more convoluted sentences.

'Well, parliament took a multi-faceted approach to determining the metrics by which provincial governments decide how Carbon Tax funds are deployed. In principle it could be lots of things… developing carbon-capture technology, improved public transportation, education about carbon tax objectives, initiatives to motivate carbon-light lifestyles, and so on.'

'Okay, but what's it *actually* been spent on?'

Hawthorne looked increasingly uncomfortable. 'Er, well, the main deployment avenue so far has been to return it to taxpayers in the form of rebates.'

Eddington raised his eyebrows. 'We're raising taxes simply to give it back? How does that help solve climate change?'

'The refunds are remitted to different socio-economic groups within the contributor spectrum.'

'Sorry?'

'You take from the rich and give to the poor,' explained Winter, becoming equally frustrated with Hawthorne's evasiveness. 'Which sounds a bit odd, but offering rebates makes the Carbon Tax far more acceptable to the public—even though most people have no idea how much they're getting back. It creates a sort of feel-good factor.'

Eddington rolled his eyes. 'Okay, okay…but what else is it spent on? Are there any projects that actually reduce emissions?'

'Green infrastructure and energy-efficiency initiatives,' replied Hawthorne smoothly.

Eddington still looked puzzled.

'Better public transport and LED streetlights,' translated Winter.

'So the Carbon Tax is just a convoluted way to encourage people to take the bus?'

'That would be a bit of an over-simplification,' winced Hawthorne, disappointed by this dumbing down of his elaborate explanation. 'But I guess some people might see it that way.'

'So if we were to phase out the rebates, or get the Min of Transport to pay for the buses, we should be able to afford the 'northern power project'?'

Hawthorne nodded slowly. 'I suppose it might help dispel the bad press the Carbon Tax has gotten so far. People would see they were getting something concrete for their money. They could watch as their millions were steadily poured into it.'

'Absolutely!' enthused Eddington, missing Hawthorne's sarcasm completely.

'I guess it would be more concrete than some of the projects that have been suggested,' added Winter, hoping Hawthorne would appreciate his continuing the joke.

'Oh yes?'

'Oh, giant space shades, genetically-engineered cattle that fart oxygen instead of methane, spraying white paint on the sea ice, seeding the oceans with iron filings to make them more productive—there's no end to the wild ideas people have come up with. Just look on the internet!'

'Really?' Eddington leaned forward and Winter realized with alarm that he'd inadvertently piqued his interest.

'Needless to say they're all non-starters,' he added quickly. 'Completely bonkers, most of them.'

Eddington looked at him thoughtfully before looking again at his sketch on the whiteboard. He stood up and walked around the table and stared out of the window, thinking.

'Okay. I take your earlier point about the emissions target being arbitrary, and in an ideal world we'd push to have it lowered, but what's done is done. We need to focus on policies that give at least the appearance of being able to meet them within the lifetime of the next parliament.'

'The *appearance?*,' interjected Winter in alarm.

'Poor choice of words. We need policies that could, in theory, achieve the goal. All due respect but we won't get there fast enough by increasing electric vehicle sales by a couple of percent per year. We need something bold that could, if successful, be a true game-changer. A policy that we can all confidently get behind and defend.'

Confused, Winter glanced at Hawthorne who, ever the professional civil servant, had a serene expression on his face.

'That bold vision is going to be the Northern Power Project, NorPow. Adam, I want you to run the calculations on how much our carbon emissions would be reduced if we built ten thousand combination wind and solar farms along the coast. If my gut is right that should just about supply the country's energy needs, in which case the problem is solved, right?'

Winter realized he'd been wrong-footed.

'Wait, what? Solved?'

'Of course! If we can actually make it government policy to switch from coal and gas to arctic wind and solar, then CO2 levels will reduce and climate change will be eliminated.'

'Well, maybe, eventually…'

Eddington gave him a supercilious smile. 'That's the great thing about our system in Canada, Adam. Once its government policy you know it will happen.'

'But making it policy doesn't in itself mean it will actually happen, does it, Minister?' interjected Hawthorne, apparently also alarmed.

'I don't understand you,' replied Eddington, frowning. 'It will be policy, and therefore under our control. If it's under our control we can ensure it happens.'

'But what I mean is there's no guarantee that even if we build all this that it will actually *work*, is there?' repeated Winter, feeling a little panic-stricken at the prospect. 'I mean that by switching our energy generation one hundred percent to this…' he waved at the board, 'northern power project, that it will actually reduce CO2 levels!'

Eddington cocked his head on one side, that slightly condescending smile again. 'Don't you have faith in the models Adam? Are you telling me the science is wrong?'

'Well, no, but…'

'So if the models are correct and we build the thing then carbon levels will drop, won't they? It's commonsense.'

Winter thought it was far from commonsense, but he didn't say so.

'Look, we're reducing an uncontrollable problem—the climate—to a controllable one, government policy,' continued the Minister. 'If its policy then it will happen, it *must* happen.' He sighed, clearly a little exasperated that his underlings did not see his point. 'In effect, by creating a policy which the science and the models say will reduce CO2 emissions, we will control the climate. No if's or but's.'

He looked at the two of them. 'Well I think this has been very productive,' he concluded, rising from his chair. 'I'm having lunch with the PM next week so I shall float some of these ideas past him. Now if you'll excuse me…'

Back in Hawthorne's office a few minutes later Winter looked at Hawthorne.

'Oh God, he's like a child! We should have tried harder to discourage him. Knocked his ideas down and kept him on the straight and narrow. Now he's convinced he's got a magic bullet that can solve climate change. We both know that's impossible.'

'Not at all,' smiled Hawthorne winking mischievously. 'I think we should give him all the encouragement he needs. This country needs a bold vision. Besides, it'll distract him from the *real* agenda, eh?'

Not for the first time, Winter had the feeling that things at the Ministry were not all that they appeared.

CHAPTER 2

Unwelcome Discovery

'Don't get me wrong, I'm not in denial. I just don't believe it.' The two figures walking along the beach appeared deeply engrossed in conversation, although it was the woman who was doing all the talking. 'Not the fact that it exists of course, I'm not questioning *that*—just whether it's too late to do anything about it. Am I living on borrowed time? That's the question.'

Although the topic of conversation appeared rather morbid, their surroundings were unquestionably uplifting. The beach at Balancing Stone Bay was five kilometres long, an arc of white sand sheltered by tall pine trees on the landward side with the rocky foreshore and sparkling waters of the channel on the other. Across the other side of the channel the hazy outlines of mountains were like a Chinese painting.

The perfectly balanced mass of the Balancing Stone, the objective for their walk, was still some distance in front of them—a huge boulder left on the beach by a retreating glacier thousands of years before, looking for all the world as though a good shove would send it slowly rolling into the water. Other than the rustle of two hundred year-old pines swaying gently in the afternoon breeze and the lap of the water all was silent, and not a single person in sight. Later the sun would set into the sea, orange and gold. The islands of the Echelon Quartet group, off Canada's magnificent western coast, were a magical and ancient place.

The woman, in her seventies but slim and clearly in good shape, shook her head in frustration. 'The whole thing is like some mad riddle. Our salmon have disappeared because of climate change caused by cowboys in Texas driving big trucks and factories in China spewing out carbon dioxide, and the solution is supposed to be for me to eat less beef, put a solar panel on the roof, and buy a Tesla—except that I'm practically vegetarian, it rains endlessly here, and I've never owned a car in my life.'

Her companion looked at her sympathetically but said nothing.

'I tell you Duncan, it all sounds very fishy to me.'

At the mention of his name her companion finally gave up the pretence of listening to the conversation, barked, and tore off down the beach towards the balancing rock where he proceeded to bark some more and jump up and down next to a dark object that he'd found at the base of the rock, tail wagging furiously.

Aurora Jones walked on in silence, worrying about the world and her community like the school teacher she was, or had been until she had retired four years previously. It was in her nature to care about the children she had taught. She looked up and saw she was only a hundred metres from the rock. What had Duncan found now? Some sack of garbage? It was probably something unmentionable. As she peered more closely a small wave lifted the black mass and a long pale object floated out from beneath it.

A few steps further on a pulse of adrenaline flooded her chest. A human body lay face down in the water at the base of the rock, its hair moving back and forth like a clump of seaweed as the tide washed gently over it, a single outstretched arm beckoning her attention.

They were a long way from help. Echelon was one of the most remote places along the sparsely inhabited Canadian west coast, four elongated islands like the fingers of a hand placed in the northwest Pacific a hundred kilometres off British Columbia, the edge of the world. It was a cold but bright September day and the sandy beach she had walked along stretched back unbroken towards Edenshaw, the island's main settlement, now hidden behind the trees and the curve of the coastline.

As dead as it appeared, she decided that her first responsibility was to check that the person wasn't actually alive. Maybe they'd just fallen out of a boat and swam ashore, exhausted. Perhaps it was even someone she knew. Aurora approached closer and could see the person more clearly now. it looked like one of the local First Nation lads, late teens, long bedraggled hair, jeans and a denim jacket, black leather boots. His face was mostly obscured and she thought transiently about rolling him over, but decided against it.

Then a crab crawled out of the corner of his mouth and she knew for sure that he was dead.

Realizing that the water was washing over her shoes she stepped back and cursed, then pulled out her cell-phone and dialed 911. She was lucky to even get a signal this far from the village. Even so, the connection kept cutting out momentarily.

'Hello? Can you hear me? Is that the RCMP? I need to report a dead body.'

After reassuring the operator that no, she was not

herself in any danger and no, she hadn't killed the person she was calling about, she explained where she was.

'Okay hold on, I'm going to put you through to the RCMP station there.' There was a ten second pause before the terse and slightly annoyed voice of Officer Alan Michaels answered, the senior RCMP officer who'd arrived in Edenshaw the year before.

Aurora had always found Michaels a slightly prickly character. Generally cheerful and courteous, he could nonetheless be quite abrupt sometimes. She also found that he had a bit of a tendency for coming up with a complex explanation when a simpler one would have done equally well. She remembered a conversation they had had once about the assassination of JFK, and his reasons why Lee Harvey Oswald had to have had at least two accomplices to account for all the shots. But to give him his due he was pretty good at keeping order in Edenshaw.

'Hello Alan, this is Aurora Jones. Listen, I'm out walking my dog on Balancing Stone beach and I've just found a dead body. A young lad, I think, right next to the big rock. Face down in the water.'

There was a pause before Michaels answered. 'Seriously? This isn't some joke to get me to drive out there just so you can get a lift back is it? Cos I'm not falling for that one again.'

Aurora sighed. 'That wasn't me, Alan. Unlike some folks around here I can tell the difference between a Japanese sex doll and a real person, believe me!'

'Hmm. It's not a sack of rubbish or something? They can look awful deceptive sometimes.'

Aurora assured him it wasn't and described the crumpled heap, the hands, feet, hair. 'I can try sending you a photo if you like, but honest to God this is a real dead person. And the tide's coming in.'

'Okay, okay, we're on our way. Can you stay until we get there? I'll need a statement from you anyway.'

She looked at the incoming water and then at her watch. 'Sure, but then you really will need to give me a ride back otherwise I'll get caught by the tide.'

Aurora called Duncan and then walked up the beach to where a stranded tree trunk provided shelter and still had sight of the body, and then took her shoes off to let her socks dry. This part of the beach was littered with the bleached bones of massive trees a metre or two in diameter, piled up chaotically as though someone had emptied a giant box of matches. Most were decades old, escapees from the logging barges as they hauled their harvest south to the sawmills, their bark stripped by the waves and salt water.

She leaned back and made herself comfortable against the tree and tried to forget about the corpse a few metres away. The idea that Officer Michaels clearly thought she was just some crazy old lady who didn't know what a sex doll looked like made her smile. She closed her eyes and listened to the lap of the water against the rocks, trying to decide whether it was getting any closer.

It was only a few minutes before the sound of the RCMP truck coming along the beach intruded into her thoughts. She got up and started walking back down to the big rock. The vehicle slowed to a halt a few metres away and Duncan started barking again, defending his find from intruders. Michaels jumped out, frowning as he always seemed to. Late-fifties, lean, wiry hair, slightly below average height, his eyes were already looking beyond Aurora towards the dark mass at the base of the large stone.

He indicated his younger colleague climbing out of the passenger seat. 'Constable Harrison. He joined me just recently but he's from here originally—so I guess you probably know one another?'

Aurora nodded. 'Of course, George was one of my pupils. Haven't seen you for a while.'

George stepped forward with a big smile to give her a bear hug. 'Great to see you again Miss Jones.' He was a well-built lad, tall, more muscular than the wiry Michaels. He glanced at the corpse and Aurora wondered transiently if this was his first dead body. He was probably only recently out of police college.

Michaels walked down just far enough to see the body. 'Tide's coming in,' he observed gloomily. 'Come on, George, get the stretcher and give me a hand.' It only took the two men a couple of minutes to retrieve the corpse and carry it up to the back of their truck on a stretcher where Michaels began to examine it more closely. Aurora could see that apart from being sodden it was relatively unmarked, but that the limbs were stiff.

'Rigor mortis present so dead between four and forty-eight hours, which puts the time of death sometime last night.' Michaels used a pen to move the hair back from the man's mouth and lower face. 'Smooth skin for a guy,' he remarked. 'Full lips too.'

Everyone peered more closely at the face. The body had broad shoulders and a narrow waist giving it a superficially masculine appearance, but now that they could see the face and her chest there was no doubt that he was a she. The woman had an almost Asiatic face with high cheek bones, perhaps First Nation, feminine lips and eyes, and a smooth skin.

'It's a girl,' stated Harrison factually. Michaels cocked his head and then nodded sheepishly in agreement.

'Oh, poor thing!' exclaimed Aurora. 'I wouldn't think she's more than mid-twenties!'

'Either of you recognize her?'

Harrison shook his head. 'No, not from around here. I know everyone my age.'

'She does look vaguely familiar,' replied Aurora slowly. 'She's not from Esh, but I have seen her before.' She hesitated. 'Maybe in the Co-op?'

Michaels took a towel and cleared the mud from her face and swept her hair clear. As he did so he revealed a large circular wound about an inch in diameter, high on her forehead, almost at the hairline.

'Bloody hell! She's been shot!' he exclaimed, visible shaken.

He gingerly held her hair back so that the others could see. Blood was matted into her hair and small fragments of bone protruded from around the wound. Harrison leaned forward to study the wound and looked thoughtful.

'Looks like this was no accident,' said Michaels grimly. 'Bullet to the head, she's been whacked! Classic drug gang execution.' He stood up and grinned as though the matter was solved. 'We used to see this all the time back East.'

'Except that Esh doesn't have a drug problem,' remarked Aurora slowly, wondering if he really had to do all this here on the beach with the tide coming in. Tragic though it was, the girl was dead now. Couldn't he just take her to the morgue and do everything there? It was getting cold.

'We don't have any dealers on the island, that's for sure. Those that do use get it by mail order,' commented Harrison.

Michaels glared at him. 'Let's see if she's got any ID on her.'

He pulled open the jacket and slipped his hand into the sodden inside pocket before trying the other one and then the trouser pockets, pulling a cellphone out of one and a plastic wallet with some cards in it out of the other, from which he extracted a driving license.

'Judith Altmann. So not First Nation then. Twenty-five, Saskatchewan address. Long way from home.' He handed the wallet to Harrison. 'There's some of her business cards there, describes herself as a Photo-journalist and Climate Change Activist—she's even got a website.' He rolled his eyes as though the latter indicated some kind of artistic affectation.

Aurora nodded thoughtfully. 'You say she can't be First Nation, but she certainly looks it and with a first name like that she actually might have come from around here originally.'

Michaels looked puzzled. 'How?'

'Esh is famous for its biblical first names.'

Seeing him continue to look blank she glanced at George and continued. 'You can blame my father,' she explained. 'He was the village rector here until the late sixties and pretty full-on with his faith. He believed that all children should have biblical names and he could be quite persuasive with first-time parents, so a lot of children from the forties onwards had biblical names. He went through the alphabet quite a few times.'

'But she's too young.'

'Ah, but folk here also keep names in the family, naming their kids after parents and grandparents.'

'I see.' Michaels stood up. 'So how come you escaped, eh? Aurora—that's not biblical.'

Aurora shrugged. 'Apparently the night I was born

there was a spectacular display of the northern lights, so my mother insisted I be named 'aurora'. I think she also found the family surname a bit dull and wanted to add some colour. It was a bit unusual when I was a child but of course later on, in the sixties, it wasn't so bad. Everyone thought it was very hip.'

'Huh,' grunted George, looking up from his phone. 'At least you didn't have a Beatles fanatic for a dad.'

Aurora laughed and George gave a rueful smile. 'You know, if she died last night and ended up here, then I'd bet she went into the water somewhere around the village or a bit further over,' he continued. 'The current at night brings things up here and the distance is about right.'

Michaels shook his head firmly. 'But we know she was shot, we can see the wound, and we know she wasn't from around here, so she was most likely killed elsewhere and dumped at sea.'

'Assuming it *is* a gunshot wound…it looks too big to me, and there's no exit wound. Maybe she just fell and hit her head?'

Michaels gave him a withering look. 'They're not all neat little bullet holes like you see on TV, son. They're usually messy—believe me that's a gunshot wound alright.'

George frowned and looked like he was going to argue about it, but then shrugged and continued fiddling with Judith Altmann's phone instead.

Michaels knelt down and tried to straighten the girl's clothes so that she didn't look so bedraggled, a task made more awkward by them being sodden. Then he noticed something on one of her arms and pulled up the right-hand jacket sleeve again. There was a red and black tattoo on her forearm—a leaping salmon with the words "Sea Warriors" below it in a Gothic font.

'Any idea what "Sea Warriors" means? Some kind of environmental group?'

Not getting a response from either of them he shrugged and pushed the sleeve down again and stepped back. 'We had quite a few Altmanns in Saskatoon when I was there, German immigrants, didn't look much like this girl though. She really looks First Nation, doesn't she? I reckon she was adopted.'

He continued to stare at the body before shaking his head, as though he was blaming her for dying on his patch. 'There's virtually no way we'll ever know for sure how she got here though, let alone why she was here.'

'She was here to investigate the link between climate change and the salmon,' replied Harrison.

The more senior man sighed heavily. 'Well you *say* that because she's a journalist, but you're just speculating.'

Harrison held up the girl's phone. 'No sir, I'm quoting her own words. Her last blog entry is about coming to Esh. She says "Off to the west coast to investigate why their salmon are disappearing! Hope to get a chance to check out my own history too."'

'Give me that!' Michaels grabbed his colleague's phone and read for a moment before tossing it back to him. 'Fair enough, we'll look into that but I'm not sure how much we should rely on it. It could have been faked after her death for all we know, and it doesn't help us with *how* she was killed.' He scratched his head.

Hope to get a chance to check out my own history too. As Aurora looked at the young girl lying on the stretcher between them: an awful possibility occurred to her.

She had carried a secret for over fifty years. Many

years before she had given up a baby daughter for adoption. She had only been nineteen at the time, first year at university, completely out of her depth, couldn't bring up the child on her own, couldn't tell her puritanical parents—so she had reluctantly done what she felt was best for the girl and had given her up. She still believed it had been the right decision, but that had never stopped it from being an extremely painful one. That daughter would be in her early fifties now. Michaels' comment about the girl most likely being adopted was about the only sensible thing he'd said since he'd arrived, arguably now supported by the girl's blog.

This girl was far too young to be her daughter, but she was exactly the right age to be her grand-daughter. Perhaps she or her mother had managed to find out where she had come from? It was a long shot but as she looked down at the girl who might be her own flesh and blood she knew it wasn't something she could ignore. Was that her nose? The long dark hair reminded her of her mother's at that age.

George had been trying to remove a piece of wet card out of the wallet without tearing it and was now studying it. She saw his eyebrows lift in surprise.

'Sir, you should look at this.' He handed him a beer mat which had been torn in half. Michaels looked at it and also raised his eyebrows before turning awkwardly to Aurora.

'You're absolutely sure you don't know her?'

Aurora nodded. 'Know her? No, of course not. Like I said she looks vaguely familiar, but only like someone who passed me in the street maybe. And I'm also sure she didn't grow up here—anyone her age I would have taught.'

'So...how do you explain this?'

He handed her the scrap of card. Written in ballpoint pen was something that even in the bizarre world of Michaels' elaborate explanations simply should not be there.

It was her own name and address.

CHAPTER 3

The Daughter Who Wasn't

In the small flat above their shop on Edenshaw's main street Gaia and Wolf were having an argument. Or, as Gaia preferred to call it, a sharing of opinions in a constructive and mutually respectful atmosphere.

As the island's resident environmentalist Gaia Thompson dressed unlike anyone else on Esh, a sort of backwoods-meets-Boho-chic with a bit of latter-day hippie thrown in, all rough fabrics and earth-tones and beads in her hair. She had rich wavy shoulder-length mahogany hair and striking eyes.

University-educated middle-class white kids in their late twenties, she and her partner Wolf had arrived two summers previously and had taken over an empty shop near the harbour from which they'd started selling an eclectic mix of native art and crafts, homemade soap, and wooden furniture that Zebedee Moongazer—their landlord and village Mr Fixit—had assured them were Indian antiques. He hadn't explained specifically which Indians though so Gaia still blissfully tried to peddle them to tourists as locally made, although perhaps the fact that Esh didn't have any furniture makers should have raised her suspicions by now.

Unfortunately the shop didn't have many customers, targeting as it did a tourist industry that barely existed anymore. Until fairly recently there had been a moderate number of tourists coming every summer for sport fishing, basing themselves in the Edenshaw Hotel and consuming plenty, but with the collapse of the annual salmon run that had dried up.

To try and offset the lack of shop traffic Wolf had started to offer 'back-to-nature' tours from a website called Echelon Escapes, mostly mountain-biking and horse-riding trips with a couple of nights camping under the stars. They didn't actually possess bikes or horses, but as Wolf had breezily explained to Aurora one day, as though she wouldn't understand, they had outsourced those aspects of the business and would procure them as required. He said it was called 'just-in-time' management, although she had privately thought 'in-your-dreams' management would have been more appropriate. They had yet to secure their first booking.

Of course a few tourists did still come to Esh, but mostly just in July and August on sailing holidays from which they only stepped ashore for a few hours, not requiring accommodation or meals. Or soap, or furniture. In the meantime Gaia happily filled her days hiking and exploring the island and blogging about her zero-carbon lifestyle. Wolf on the other hand had become increasingly concerned about their dwindling finances. Today things had come to a head.

'All my life I've just been a bystander, watching helplessly as our planet is ravaged by mankind's rampant consumerism and pollution, with factories belching out more and more suffocating carbon dioxide. I've never been able to do anything actively against it, but living here I actually play a part in getting out the message and showing people how it can be done. I've got to do this Wolf!'

'Sure hon, but we have to eat too! I know living here is cheap but we have almost no money coming in. We can afford about another three month's rent, after that we'll need to do something desperate—and I *really* don't want to have to borrow from your father again.'

But the truth was that Gaia had never felt more alive. When they'd lived in Toronto they'd gone to environmental debates and meetings every week, hung out with people who shared their views—she'd felt part of the scene. Before they knew it they had talked themselves into a situation where living the lifestyle, true dedication to the cause, was inescapable. Gaia had first suggested Echelon as a joke, somewhere so far off the map they literally could go no further, but after they visited on a whim they were hooked, and moved within a month. To symbolize the commitment she had changed her name from Gail to Gaia the moment she stepped off the ferry. Gaia, from the theory that the planet is a self-regulating organism that heals itself, and the Greek name for Mother Earth. She liked it.

Moving to Esh had given her a new perspective. Since they'd stepped back from the Toronto 'green scene' and got some perspective she'd started to feel that the whole climate change movement wasn't really going anywhere. Most of the organizations and sites didn't actually do much other than point out how little progress was being made, like they thought it was enough to just raise the issue and hope that someone could somehow fix it. She'd even begun to wonder if the whole recycling eco-lifestyle thing was a smokescreen promoted by the oil companies to deflect people from doing something more drastic—like not buying their oil anymore.

To her alarm she'd recently discovered that all the stuff they told people to do—recycling their plastic, switching to LED lights and not flying—wasn't going to be enough. That all those economies combined, even if everyone on the planet actually did them, would contribute barely one percent to the reduction in CO2 emissions required to keep global warming under control.

Wolf saw himself as the pragmatic one in the relationship. He was quietly sceptical that mankind was capable of reversing the damage it had already caused. In his view relentless population growth meant that the planet would inevitably consume more resources and generate more waste and pollution, people couldn't help themselves. So while he went along with Gaia's passion, and sincerely felt that a cleaner planet was a good thing, he no longer believed that mankind had the will or the time to change the outcome.

His main interest now was more practical. He wanted to see if he could make a go of the tour business, something which he found intellectually stimulating in a life that was otherwise largely unchallenging. Once he'd figured out how to do it profitably he was going to suggest they move somewhere less isolated and run it on a more commercial scale. Nova Scotia maybe.

But for the time being he kept those thoughts to himself because he knew she wouldn't move anywhere yet, and he also knew who wore the trousers in the relationship. Even his name was her idea; she'd never warmed to Walter, his birth name, and had started calling him Wolf as a sort of joke on a camping trip. When they moved here and she had started calling herself Gaia he just decided to use it all the time. It was kind of cool, and it went with his new ponytail—the natural progression from the trendy man-bun that he'd sported in Toronto.

'Look, we both know there aren't enough tourists coming here right now to support us, but the answer isn't to give up and leave. The answer is to publicize the place and attract a new kind of tourist—not sport fishermen but people who are going to value it and respect like we do. People who are going to want to hike into the back-country and buy stuff to remember it by.'

She put a hand on his shoulder. 'Have faith, Wolf. We're doing all the right things, I get lots of interest on the web, people saying they want to visit, we just need to stick with it.' Seeing his despondency she continued. 'Okay, I'll admit that maybe we need to fine tune things a bit. Maybe the furniture was a mistake, maybe we need more stuff that people can take away.'

They were interrupted by the tinkle of the shop bell below them. Gaia stood up to go downstairs, then turned back to face him. 'I'm not giving up now Wolf.' As usual in their mutually respectful sharing of opinions, hers was final.

Their first (and only) customer of the day was Aurora Jones.

'Aurora! I heard the news about you finding the body on the beach. It must have been awful!' To Aurora's surprise Gaia gave her an impromptu hug.

'Oh! Well, it wasn't that bad. It wasn't me that was dead after all, or anyone that I knew. Some poor girl from Saskatoon.'

'But all the same, it can't have been nice. Was she…you know, cut up or anything?' Gaia gave an exaggerated squirm. 'I heard they found a body with its face cut off by a boat propeller a couple of years ago. It's brain was hanging out where it's eyes were supposed to be.'

Why was it that people always wanted the gory details? She sighed.

'No, it wasn't like that at all. All in one piece, just very wet, hair all down over her face. I was mainly concerned that I was going to get stuck by the tide, actually, what with waiting for the RCMP. She was an environmental journalist actually. But Michaels thinks she was murdered—there was a hole in her head he claims is a bullet hole, although it looked too big for that to me.'

'Seriously? Murdered? What was her name?'

'Judith Altmann.'

Gaia looked thoughtful. 'Wasn't she the one who did an exposé of the pipeline companies a while back? Or am I getting her mixed up?'

'I'm not sure but it sounds like her sort of thing. She had a tattoo of a leaping salmon and the words "Sea Warriors" on her arm. We were wondering whether it's an environmental group or something. Have you heard of them?'

Gaia laughed. 'The Sea Warriors? Wow, it's been a while since I heard of them! Yes, I remember them from Toronto, a pretty hardcore bunch. They blame big business for the pollution of the seas and damage to fisheries, they used to organize actions like dumping dead fish in company foyers.'

'So maybe she was here because of them.'

'Except we don't have any big industry here. Anyway I haven't heard of them doing anything for ages, I'd assumed they'd disbanded to be honest. And like I say, their thing was more disrupting investor meetings, they never left the big cities much.'

Aurora shrugged. 'Maybe that was something old then. She has a blog where she said she was coming to Esh to investigate where our salmon went to.'

'Not much to investigate about that, it's common knowledge where they went,' replied Gaia slightly indignantly. 'Thanks to climate change warmer waters drove them north.'

'Hmm.'

Aurora saw a display of soap and moved towards it. 'Anyway, I came in for some soap. I've run out and thought I'd try one of your fancy ones. Buy local and all that.'

Gaia started to explain the relative benefits of seaweed soap and soap with ground pine needles for exfoliating the skin, both homemade products. 'Ground pine needles are so much better for the planet than the plastic microbeads most soap manufacturers use. And they're Esh pine needles too.'

Aurora started to smell the different soaps, but the image of the girl and the question of what had brought her to Esh came back into her head. 'So you think anything can be done about it—the salmon I mean?'

Gaia shrugged. 'They might just come back by chance, but I wouldn't count on it. Most likely it's going to stay that way, although some people have suggested man-made solutions.' She reached over and picked up a magazine from the desk behind her, a mess of paperwork and half-wrapped soap packets. 'This article I was reading by some prof in Montreal argues that you might be able to boost fish stocks by creating an artificial plankton bloom through spraying iron sulphate onto the ocean.' She was flipping through to find the article. 'Oh, here it is—it's called iron fertilization. Dr Langara Renouf, "Climate Change Solutions Don't Have To Cost the Earth".'

Aurora froze. 'Could I see that?' she asked, and almost snatched the magazine from Gaia's hand without waiting for an answer.

'It's a surprisingly simple idea actually,' continued Gaia as Aurora stared at the magazine. 'You dump a few hundred tons of the stuff in the ocean way offshore, it boosts the plankton population, and that attracts the fish. Sort of like sprinkling fertilizer on your lawn to make it green, it's a quick one-season fix. You're not reversing climate change, but you're reversing its effects. Assuming it works…'

Aurora was squinting at a photo of the author on a boat. '*If* it works?'

'Well, it's only a theory at the moment. The idea has been around for a while, but she's done some research that suggests it's more likely to work than people thought. She's also making the general point that there are things people can do to try and fix the situation, instead of just complaining about CO2 emissions going up, so she's pushing people to try it—instead of just sitting around moaning.'

Aurora was still scanning the article but Gaia carried on summarizing it for her anyway. 'Of course people have had all kinds of crazy ideas, like covering the ice sheets with tin foil to insulate them, but in this case it has some credibility because it actually happens naturally sometimes. There have been several cases where volcanic eruptions deposited iron-rich dust on the ocean surface and what they call 'blooms' of plankton formed, and in a couple of cases there were good fishing years afterwards.'

'That sounds interesting. Could I borrow this?'

Gaia nodded. 'Sure, but don't get your hopes up about it happening here. I think you'd need millions to do it on a large scale—you'd need a proper research vessel, a few hundred tons of iron sulphate, satellite data to tell you where to put it, oceanographers to interpret it all,' she scowled. 'But nobody will do it because it would be much cheaper to pay the islanders to stay unemployed.'

Aurora nodded thoughtfully. She wasn't so keen on the soaps, they were a bit too strongly scented for her liking, but having been in the shop ten minutes she felt obliged to buy something. 'This purple one's lavender?'

'Yes, and all completely natural ingredients.'

'I'll take it then.'

Outside it was a beautiful autumn day and as she turned towards home she stopped by the harbour wall and watched two boys working on a boat—Eddie and Jack Manyshots, both had been her pupils in her final year teaching at the school a few years back. She regarded them as successes because despite coming from a family whose parents had become too dependent on social security to be motivated to do much, both the boys had jobs…usually. Eddie waved to her and she returned the greeting.

There were four fishing trawlers based in Edenshaw these days, and she remembered that Eddie had told her once they could carry twenty-five tons of fish in the hold. That was a hundred tons right there. She turned towards home with a new purpose in her step.

As she moved away from the harbour wall she discretely dropped her paper bag of lavender soap into the water. It was just too smelly, and the good thing about Gaia's stuff was that it was good for the environment, right?

- - -

Aurora was halfway home when George Harrison passed her in the RCMP truck and pulled over. She was so lost in thought he had to pip the horn to get her attention.

'Miss Jones? Do you want a ride?' He seemed in a particularly good mood.

Aurora climbed in and George continued as they moved off.

'Guess what? Our Ms Altmann wasn't thrown off a boat after all, she had been staying right here in Edenshaw for at least three days before she died, checked in at Mike's B&B on Third Ave. So we were able to look through her stuff.'

'Does your boss still think she was murdered?'

George smiled. 'Not so much. The preliminary autopsy says it's not a gunshot wound, too shallow.' He winked. 'By 'preliminary autopsy' I mean that at the morgue the first thing the doc did was prod the wound. That hole's messy but it's only half an inch deep. It cracked her skull badly, but no penetration.'

Aurora grimaced.

'So something more mundane like falling off the harbour wall, perhaps?'

'That's definitely looking more possible, but she could still have been attacked with something like a hammer—or she could just have fallen onto a particularly pointy rock. But the other good news is we have more info on *why* she was here.'

'Oh?'

'She had a laptop in the B&B. Turns out someone had emailed her about Esh's climate problems and encouraged her to come here and investigate.'

'But she was just here because of the salmon, right? Doesn't sound like anything that anyone would have killed her over.'

'No, and I can't remember the last time we had a fatality as a result of a mugging. Or a mugging, come to that.'

Aurora frowned. 'Maybe it was just a ruse to get her here? Perhaps she met whoever emailed her and they had an argument? Was it someone here on Esh?'

They had reached her house and George pulled up and stopped the truck. He looked a bit uncomfortable. 'Er, not as far as we know. Anyway, here's your place.'

'But you know who it was?'

'Not really.' He hesitated and Aurora realized he felt he'd already said too much. 'It was a junk email address, but there was a document with it which was the real reason she came.'

'Oh?'

George hesitated again. 'Look, I just wanted to let you know we were working on it, but I shouldn't discuss too much of the specifics. Sorry.'

Aurora smiled reassuringly. 'I won't tell anyone George, I promise. I'm just curious. I did find her, after all.'

'Yes, I know, but…'

'Okay, okay. But at least tell me what the document was *about!*'

George winced. She knew he was honest and found it difficult to lie. 'Er, it was a government report. That's all I can say.' He glanced self-consciously at the back seat of the truck. Aurora followed his gaze. There was a laptop lying there.

'Is that it? Her laptop?'

He nodded unhappily.

'Oh.'

Aurora didn't get out of the vehicle. Her curiosity about who Judith Altmann was and how she died wasn't going away, and this email sounded key.

'Couldn't you just show it to me? I won't tell Michaels. I might even spot something useful—I used to have to read quite a few of those government reports when I was still a teacher,' she lied.

George shook his head more firmly. 'I'm sorry, really not. It's sensitive.'

Sensitive? Now she was even more curious.

Aurora sighed. 'George, I don't mean to be difficult here, but I really want to see it. I need to know why she was here.' She paused. 'Probably as much as you would really like the fact that I caught you and some others smoking marijuana behind the school in your last year to stay between us. It was still a criminal offence back then…'

George stared at her in alarm. 'I, I really don't think that matters, does it?'

Aurora shrugged. 'I don't know. Not to me, but you know how Officer Michaels is. If I happened to mention how well you'd turned out, given your earlier failings, he might just laugh it off—or maybe he'd want to know what those failings were, and then feel obliged to write it on your record. He is a bit of a stickler for procedure, isn't he?'

George stared glumly at the steering wheel for a few seconds. He remembered his schooldays and how vicious Miss Aurora Jones could be when she wanted something. Roarer Jones they'd called her, like a tigress.

'Okay, okay, I'll show it to you, but you mustn't mention it to him. Or the other thing.'

'Of course.' She smiled. 'Perhaps we should step

inside?'

In her front room George turned on the laptop, found the email, opened the attachment, and turned the screen towards Aurora so she could read. It was an internal government memo, marked confidential, the report of a meeting about the impact of climate change on the islands off western Canada. She read in silence for thirty seconds.

'It doesn't seem that sensitive. They're just talking about the fact that our economy has been trashed by loss of the salmon, that it's caused high unemployment and a lot of younger folk to leave, and that climate change is the likely cause.'

'Yeah, but keep going.'

She read on while George stood awkwardly behind her.

'Well, this is interesting.' She pointed at the fourth paragraph. 'They're basically concluding that they can't do anything about climate change, that the loss of salmon is irreversible, and that there's unlikely to be any other industries that would be viable here. Their recommended strategy is to encourage emigration to the mainland, discourage further investment on the island, and that when the population reaches about half what it is today to start to withdraw government services such as Canada Post and the RCMP station. And eventually to recommend abandonment and re-development as an oil terminal.'

She sat back from the screen. 'It's actually quite outrageous. It's documentary proof of what a lot of islanders have suspected for years, that the government has little interest in preserving the way of life here and are just going to let things slide until abandonment became inevitable.'

George moved forwards to take back the laptop.

'Oh, I think that's Duncan at the door, could you let him in?'

He hesitated and went to the door, returning a minute later and shaking his head. 'No dog.'

'Sorry, must have been my imagination.' She closed the laptop and stood up. 'Anyway, thanks for showing it to me. Don't worry I won't mention it to a soul.' George picked up the computer and slid it back into its case.

'Was there anything else? Any indication of how she knew me, for instance?'

'No. Well, not really.' He looked guilty and miserable at the same time.

Aurora raised an eyebrow, questioning, then made a small gesture as though she was smoking an imaginary cigarette.

'Look, we agreed…' he looked embarrassed. 'Well, it's just a small thing. In her Outlook calendar for the evening she died she'd written "EIS?", which we're thinking might be the initials of someone she was meeting.' He shrugged. 'But it could have been something completely innocent, like a reminder to pay something, or someone she had to call. Anyway there's no one in Esh with those initials so it doesn't really get us any further.'

EIS…that rang a distant bell. Where did she remember that from?

She continued to try and glean what information she could from him. 'Had she been here long? It's a small place, she must have talked to someone.'

'Only a couple of days according to Mike at the B&B, and she was only booked in for one more night. It looks like it was just a quick trip.'

She nodded slowly, and George edged towards the door.

'Nothing from the adoption angle?'

George shook his head. 'No.'

'So did you track down her next of kin?'

'Saskatoon RCMP are on it. A lot of Altmanns over there apparently.'

She smiled reassuringly. 'Oh by the way, you can tell your boss that Gaia knows who the Sea Warriors are. They used to be an environmental group focused on holding big business accountable for marine pollution, but she thinks they're no longer active. So that also fits, although it's probably just something from her past.'

'Okay, thanks.' He continued moving towards the door and made his escape.

After George had gone she turned on her own laptop and went to Judith's website. She was struck by how lucid and passionate Judith was, and not for the first time wished that they'd met under better circumstances. It was a long shot that she was her granddaughter, but if she was then she would have been proud of her. She picked up the magazine Gaia had given her. If Dr Renouf was right, she might have the solution to Judith's investigation right there. Maybe she should do something with the government memo? She opened her email and found the copy that she'd surreptitiously forwarded to herself from Judith's laptop while George was checking the door, and smiled.

She sat back and tried to get her thoughts straight. Admittedly it was a stretch to think the girl might be her granddaughter merely because she was the right age and had said something about finding her roots, but it was kind of bugging her nonetheless. The only way to know for sure was when the RCMP had traced her family, so not much she could do there.

The angle she might be able to get somewhere with was how and where she'd died, since Michaels was clearly not looking into it, having made up his mind that she was bumped off by some non-existent drug gang. The trouble was there simply weren't that many places you could *fall* into the sea—most of the coastline was gravel beach, there were no high cliffs. There were a few private jetties of course, but they were rarely more than a metre or two above the water, just rickety affairs for small fishing boats.

Aurora gazed out of the window and tried to visualize in her mind the coastline around the town, but still couldn't think of anywhere that you could fall onto rocks or where there was a long drop into the water. It wasn't as though there were many buildings or places outside of town anymore; a couple of warehouses about a kilometre east, one owned by the roads department and the other by Zebedee Moongazer, but they were both well back from the coast, on the road. Not like the old days when there had been more industry, the boatyard, a big chandlery, the cannery. Time was when half the town worked there, fishing boats coming in all the time to unload their catch...

'Oh you idiot!' she said loudly, and slapped her forehead.

CHAPTER 4

Deadly Curiosity

Overlooking Edenshaw on a tree-covered escarpment called Tor Hill was a small crag, a discrete lookout currently occupied by two First Nations girls in their late teens sharing a cigarette.

It was a hot afternoon for autumn and from their perch they could see a long stretch of the village high street, people coming and going from the Co-op, the boats in the harbour and some of the houses. From up here one of the most striking things about Edenshaw was how silent it was—no sounds of industry, no traffic noise, no hum of civilization. When there was a noise, such as a few minutes of hammering from the garage, or someone cutting some logs with a chainsaw, it was quite noticeable, but generally there was just silence.

Both girls were unmistakably First Nation kids, broad faces, long dark hair, slightly shorter and stockier than their white contemporaries. Since finishing school two years previously they had hung out together almost all the time, working through their personal challenges. Aiyana lived mostly with her grandmother, who had taught her about her heritage—the legends of the island, the native language, ways of harvesting food and cooking—she was the artistic one, but had also been a bit of a wild-child at school, always getting in trouble. Julie lived with her father and was more practical in outlook, wanted to do something with her mind rather than her hands, knew that would be impossible in Esh—but shared Aiyana's love of the island and didn't want to live anywhere else. They leaned back against the rock face, hidden from below, and looked down on the village, unseen.

They had known one another since the age of four when they started school together but only become friends in their final year, sharing a determination to do something more worthwhile than their parents, something they felt should not be too difficult but which was nonetheless proving elusive. Julie's dad Johnny owned and operated two fishing boats and even employed a couple of crews sometimes, so by that measure was successful, but the fishing was sporadic and in Julie's view he didn't appear to be doing anything more than keeping his head above water. Her mother had died in an accident when Julie was quite young.

Aiyana's family provided less inspiration—her mother was an alcoholic and her father had left them when she was six and had not been heard of since. Both girls were sure they could do better with their lives but had struggled to come up with any real plan. They already had jobs, in fact pretty much the best jobs that Esh could offer them, namely working part-time in the supermarket, but that would never lead anywhere—for that they would need to leave Esh and head to a city, but that would be tough. So they were trapped between a rock and a hard place.

'Some fucker at the Co-op asked if I was 'First

Nation' today,' said Aiyana.

'Tourist?'

'American.'

'Worse. What'd you say?'

'I told him I was OC.'

Julie raised an eyebrow.

'Original Canadian. I just made it up.'

She smiled. 'Nice one. I'm going to use that.'

Below them the silence was broken by the angry buzz of a trail bike, one of the local kids tearing down the street. The disturbance lasted for almost a minute as it approached, passed beneath them and then faded again. 'Bloody Jack,' muttered Julie. 'Why's he always in such a hurry?'

Aiyana shrugged. 'I feel like a raven,' she said contentedly. 'Looking down on humanity.'

'Dregs of humanity, more like.'

They laughed and Julie passed the cigarette.

Aiyana shielded her eyes with her hand and looked out towards the horizon. 'It's hazy again today. I always love the way the mountains rise one behind the other, it makes Esh seem more mysterious, like there's a hidden world behind them. Gran says Esh used to be known as the 'land of the ocean haze' because a lot of the time in the summer it couldn't be seen from the mainland and in the winter it was hidden by the sea mist, just a silhouette that was sometimes there and sometimes wasn't. People on the mainland thought it was mythical, inhabited by spirits.'

She picked up a pebble and flicked it down the rock face, watching it bounce in bigger and bigger jumps. 'So…what are we going to do? Live with our families forever? And when are we going to tell them?'

'Shall we stay or shall we go, that's the question.

Find something better here or take our chances in Gastown? Except there's nothing here and we don't know what to do in Vancouver. I don't even know anyone we could crash with to get started.'

'I don't want to leave here Jules, it's who I am. No way I want to end up in Vancouver and neither do you, I've heard so many stories about girls that go there and end up in a bad way. We can't live anywhere else, you know that.'

Julie nodded, knowing she was right.

They watched as a bald eagle soared effortlessly past on the morning air current, taking big lazy circles around them before settling with a few flaps on the top of a spruce a couple of hundred metres away. With its two-metre wingspan and fierce white head it was a magnificent creature; as if on cue it turned and looked at them. 'You know when I was small I saw a dragon once, flying past those peaks on the other side of Edenshaw Sound. It was big and fat with very large wings and flew very slowly. My gran says when her dad was a boy he used to hike in the mountains and once he found a dragon's nest on the other side of Stoker's Peak, with eggs the size of footballs.'

'Yeah right.' Aiyana's gran had a bit of a reputation for her vivid imagination, she called it 'being in touch with my spiritual side'. Esh had a myriad of wildlife including several bird and animal species unique to the islands, as well as some of the largest eagles in North America, but so far no confirmed sightings of dragons.

'I keep telling you, we should set up our own business,' continued Aiyana. 'I mean, people do it. Look at that couple with the soap shop. They just came here and opened a shop, and they obviously had no experience of doing that before.'

'My dad says they can't be making any money from it considering the rent they're paying Zeb. He reckons they're living off savings, won't be here for long.'

'Okay, but you know what I mean. Your granddad must have some place he can lend us to get started, so if we're not paying for the shop our costs will be minimal. What else can we do? There's no jobs around here for girls.'

Julie shrugged and looked at the ground.

'No seriously, what else are we going to do?' continued Aiyana. 'Make babies or go to the big city, those are the only two options for girls here. And I'm not going to be doing either anytime soon.'

'We could try our own small business,' said Julie cautiously, 'if we could think of something to sell or do…it's just the risks I'm worried about. We can't afford to blow our savings.'

'That restaurant idea we talked about! There's nowhere decent to eat here, I love to cook and you're good at organizing and could get people in. There's no risk to it, well not much so long as we have a cheap place to get started in.'

With several big flaps of its wings the eagle launched itself into the air and lifted off the tree, gliding downslope towards the water. Julie looked at the distant peaks again, their tree-covered sides obscured by the haze.

'You see the way the haze forms curtains over the landscape? Remember that legend I told you about the guardians of the Islands of the Haze? We could be like that! A restaurant called The Haze Guardians serving my Gran's traditional recipes and using local produce, keeping our heritage alive. We stay here, work together, help make Esh a better place to be. What do you think?'

Julie looked down on the village and out across the channel beyond it. She knew she needed to take a Big Decision, but did she have the courage? Her dad got by but never seemed to get ahead and her brother wasn't much of an inspiration either, whatever it was he was up to in Vancouver. He claimed to be working for a company installing solar panels, but it seemed pretty seasonal and she knew he'd been working on a building site for at least some of the time.

Aiyana was right, unless you made your own future there were no better jobs to be had than what they were doing already. They just had to think of something that would be worthwhile and successful. What did they say? Four out of five new businesses failed within the first year? They needed something that was low-risk, cheap to start and that people needed—a 'must have' rather than a 'nice to have'. Some kind of café would fit the bill, although perishable food could be a problem...but she was allowing herself to be distracted by details again. It certainly sounded more convincing than the home-sewing business they'd talked about before.

Maybe a café not a restaurant, easier to run, less financial risk. Focusing on traditional recipes would give them something unique, they could emphasize the native culture with the name and maybe sell some local produce as well. The secret would be to quickly build repeat customers, people that came every day. Maybe open early and do a really good breakfast…?

'You're right, that's totally dope!' she grinned. 'Decision made. Let's make it happen!' The girls smiled, did a fist bump, and hugged. Julie felt momentarily elated, as though a great burden had been lifted from her—a feeling that was immediately replaced by one of apprehension for the work that lay ahead.

- - -

'Come on, George! Just an hour. Where's your spirit of adventure! What harm can it do?'

Constable Harrison felt very uncomfortable. He bitterly regretted offering Aurora Jones a lift a few days before. The old witch was getting her claws into him deeper and deeper.

'A lot of harm if Michaels finds out!' he replied miserably.

'You're supposed to make patrols, right? Just make one out towards he old factory and give me a lift. And then we can do a quick recce when we get there. I have a hunch it'll be worth it.'

Harrison knew he wasn't going to win, she had him over a barrel.

'Fine, I'll come by around five. But no more than fifteen minutes.'

Aurora smiled. 'You'll thank me later, really you will. You can take the credit for whatever we find, I promise.'

The old cannery had been Echelon's primary source of employment for thirty years until it had closed a decade earlier and the building had stood derelict ever since, a large warehouse with corrugated iron walls about seven or eight kilometres south of the village, slowly rusting. One side faced the water, with a large jetty and loading area for landing the catches. Inside were conveyor belts and dozens of long tables for gutting and filleting the fish, and then the cannery itself beyond that. The owners had committed to remove it of course, but had put the company into receivership and then quietly forgotten about their promises. They had fenced it off and left it.

From the road Aurora and George could see the weed-filled car park and the metal walls with its peeling paint.

Aurora picked up her torch and opened the passenger door. 'Looks like someone's cut the fence over there, let's start there.'

George followed her, still reluctant but his interest piqued by the hole in the fence, a big slash four or five feet high. He passed by here every few days and he hadn't noticed that before.

'I would say this has been cut recently, wouldn't you? The ends of the pieces of wire are still shiny. Can you hold it apart for me? I'm going to squeeze through.'

'You know this is trespass, don't you?' replied George. 'Technically I should arrest you for this.'

'Don't be such a wuss George! Someone's been here recently and I'll bet you it was our mysterious Ms Altmann. We're going to go in and check it out, now come on!'

They both squeezed through the fence and walked across the parking lot to the nearest door, which was locked. George turned away as if that was the end of the matter.

'We'll walk around until we find a way in,' said Aurora firmly. 'Come on.' It only took them a few minutes to find a side door near the loading dock which someone had conveniently kicked in. They both had to get on hands and knees to crawl through the broken door panel. Inside it was dingy and poorly lit.

'I remember coming here as a kid,' commented

George, looking around. 'My mom used to fillet fish on those tables. Half the women in the village did. We used to call it the 'ice' factory. For years I thought 'ice' was spelled 'eis'.'

'I bet they never realized those were going to be the good times, when most people still had jobs.'

George grimaced. 'So what are we looking for?'

'I don't honestly know,' replied Aurora candidly. 'Anything to indicate Judith Altmann was here I guess.'

'But why here? I don't get it.'

Aurora looked at him patiently. 'Still not? Who's the detective here? What was the last entry in her Outlook calendar?'

'EIS, question mark.'

'And what did this place used to be called, years back?'

'The old…oh! The Echelon Islands Salmon Company, the EIS.'

'Exactly! This is where Esh's economy died, it has to be connected to the plans in that memo. I bet you this is where she came on the last evening she was alive. Maybe she met someone here or was just photographing it for posterity, I don't know. I'm just hoping we'll find some clue.'

They wandered up and down the old gutting tables for a few minutes before George gave a shout and triumphantly held up a small backpack.

'This could be something! It was under the table here.' He lifted it onto the table and started emptying the contents. 'There's a camera and some gloves, a teeshirt, what looks like a hat.' He started to fiddle with the camera. 'It's still working. There's photos of the village, but nothing taken in here.'

'It was probably too dark. The calendar said evening, a couple of hours later than now, remember? Anything with her name on it?'

'Not that I can see, not enough light. I'll be able to see more in the office.' He looked back under the table and after a moment picked up a waterproof jacket. 'There's this too.' He held it up to look at it, then stuffed it into the backpack and slung it around his shoulder.

'Excellent! That proves she was here, but let's keep looking.'

It took them another ten minutes to check the rest of the building, but without any further discoveries. The factory had been stripped of any usable equipment when the owners had closed it, so apart from underneath the long tables bolted to the floor there weren't many places to hide things.

'I'm going to check the loading area outside, then we'll call it a day,' said Aurora. 'There's some kind of supervisor's office at the end of the jetty. That's probably the only other place there might be something.'

She crawled back through the broken door and started across the wooden loading area, originally built with thick railway sleepers but showing signs of decay. It was getting gloomy but she could see that a few were missing, others heavily rotted. At one time you could presumably have driven a truck across it, but that would be a risky venture now. She walked carefully.

At the far edge was a small wooden shed, presumably some kind of control post or supervisor's office for when they were receiving loads of fish. With some effort she pulled the door open and started to step into the gloom inside when she felt her arm grabbed sharply and pulled back. It was George—she hadn't even realized that he had followed her out and was so close behind her.

'Look out! There's no floor!'

Aurora looked, he was right. It wasn't an office at all but a structure protecting a wooden staircase going down to beneath the loading dock, except the stairs had fallen away. There was absolutely nothing between her and the water ten metres below than a few broken planks.

'Thanks. I owe you one,' she said quietly. 'I knew there was a good reason you were so keen you come with me,' she grinned sheepishly.

She was about to turn away when she had a thought and flicked on the torch and examined the remains of the collapsed staircase. After a few seconds she let out an exclamation.

'Look down there, where the light is, about two metres down. You see that bolt?'

George squeezed into the doorway beside her and looked down. There was a line of bolts fixing the broken remains of a metal ladder to the wooden framework, some of them protruding as much as a couple of inches from the surface.

'Yeah.'

'Does that look like blood on it?'

He took the torch from her and lay flat so that he could get a better look. 'Could be. I can't really tell if its blood but there's definitely something dark smeared on it.'

Aurora looked triumphant. 'How about this scenario? Altmann hears about this place, comes out here one evening—she pokes around, probably hoping to take some photos but realizes it's too dark and leaves the camera in the bag. Then she decides to check out the loading dock and does exactly what I almost did, she comes to this shed and steps inside. Pitches forward, whacks her head on that protruding bolt, and then continues down into the water. At eight o'clock the tide would be fairly full, her unconscious or dead body floats around for a bit and then goes out with the tide, until it ends up where I found it on the beach a few kilometres west.'

George nodded. 'I'd buy that. We should be able to prove it's her camera and clothes when we get a proper look.'

'And her blood on that bolt.'

George nodded soberly and picked up the backpack. 'I'll come back with Officer Michaels tomorrow and we'll get a sample and run DNA.'

'Don't forget to tell him it was you who found the backpack,' grinned Aurora. 'And I promise not to tell that it was me that dragged you out here in the first place. You'll be a detective yet.'

Somehow Aurora found the idea that Judith's death had been an accident reassuring.

CHAPTER 5

Motivating Zebedee

It took a couple of weeks for Michaels to get the blood analysed and check the serial number on the camera to prove that it was really Altmann's before the coroner officially closed the case as an accidental death.

Saskatoon RCMP traced her parents who duly came out to take their daughter's body home. Aurora spent some time with them showing them where she had died and where she was found. It turned out that the reason Judith looked First Nation and thought she was from Esh was that her great-grandmother had been from southern BC, backed up by a DNA test which suggested she was twenty percent Native. However there was no possibility that she was related to Aurora and her parents had no idea how she'd got Aurora's name.

None of that diminished Aurora's curiosity about what Judith had been trying to investigate when she died though, especially given her own interest in the subject. She thought about what, if anything, she should do about the document she'd been sent. More to the point, now that she had strong evidence that Esh's economic slide would continue without any prospect of government help, she wondered whether there was anything she could do to actually fix the problem.

The more she thought about it, she was loath to publish the document. Apart from not having any proof it was genuine, she could imagine it leading to a host of problems—both for her if she was identified as the leaker, but also that its publication could backfire and even accelerate Esh's demise—so she decided to keep that as a last resort.

Instead, she focused on the root cause of the salmon disappearance. Right from the start she knew what she had to do, but after a week she had a plan on how to achieve it. And when you had a plan that needed community support in Esh, you went see The Man.

- - -

Zebedee Moongazer had been the final direct casualty of the Reverend Jones's one-man campaign for biblical first names, his father (a fisherman) having been persuaded that the name would be particularly appropriate. Zebedee—the fisherman who saw the light, followed the Lord and achieved eternal salvation.

Ironically Zeb, as he was universally known, didn't grow up to become a fisherman after all, although he did possess a trawler—acquired as collateral from a business deal gone wrong. Although he ran the garage his speciality was what he called 'free enterprise'; if you wanted anything the Co-op didn't stock, a DVD player without regional restrictions, a load of cheap coal, or perhaps a haunch of deer for that special occasion, Zeb was your man. His paunch, droopy moustache and ponytail gave him the appearance of a First Nation version of Asterix the Gaul.

More importantly for Aurora, he was the close friend and business associate of the grumpy Saul Davidson, long-time Mayor of Edenshaw and owner of the Edenshaw Hotel and bar, and as such was the best person to bounce ideas off to see if Saul was likely to accept them or not. Not much happened in Edenshaw without Saul's approval, and if what she had been thinking about for the last few days was going to work then she would need his blessing.

Getting to Zeb's place meant walking pretty much the length of the village. Aurora still lived near the school, which she was proud of having left with a new roof and as many books as she'd been able to get her hands on, although she was a little disappointed that the new schoolteacher (a goofy white kid from out east who spent most of her weekends in Vancouver) seemed to take it all for granted. She was careful not to interfere or give advice though, and in fact hadn't stepped foot in the place for a couple of years now. There was nothing worse than someone who doesn't know when to quit. After the school there was a long line of dilapidated single-storey wooden houses facing out to the bay. It was not a bad place really, it actually looked pretty decent in the bright September sunshine. Nothing extravagant though—just functional.

Three doors down she stopped to say hello to Jack Manyshots who was squatting down working on his motorbike on the driveway. Despite being academic failures she had a soft spot for him and his elder brother. Unlike some who just gave up, they were always trying to find something to do, if not full-time employment then at least doing odd jobs. She'd had them clean up her garden a couple of times.

‘Hey Jack. Problems?’

‘Oh hi Miss Jones. Just trying to clean it, keeps misfiring. Eddie said I need to clean the plugs.’

Aurora nodded. ‘So how are you doing? I saw you down by the harbour. Working for Johnny again?’

‘Yeah, a bit here and there, about one day a week. We were just cleaning up yesterday. He says not enough catch this month to be worth taking her out, maybe next month.’

‘But you still get the social, right?’

He grinned sheepishly through crooked teeth. ‘Yeah, that’s one thing we can rely on.’

‘Anything else? I heard there was a new logging crew started up. D’you manage to get some work there?’

‘Eddie’s gone to talk to them.’

‘Fingers crossed then. I guess there’ll be less work around in the winter. What do most people do this time of year. Vancouver?’

He shifted his weight without getting up. ‘I guess so. Don’t seem many around so I guess that’s where they’ve gone. Usually just for a month or so. After that they get fussy about wanting your social number, but then you lose your benefits so it isn’t really worth it.’ He shrugged as if this was a failing of the employment system.

‘It’s good you’re able to find a few jobs around here,’ agreed Aurora. ‘If you don’t mind me asking, how many of your school year are still in Esh?’

He screwed up his face as though thinking hard. ‘About half maybe.’

‘And the rest all left to work on the mainland?’

‘Yeah.’

‘You keep in touch?’

Jack frowned. 'I see some of them on Instagram sometimes. Lot of them just disappeared, some are settled in Vancouver. Couple are travelling around, gone down to the States doing construction, fruit picking, that kind of thing.'

'I see. You think they'll come back?'

'Nope.'

Jack had turned back to his bike, apparently trying to figure out where the spark-plugs might be found.

'Well, you take care. Hope you fix your bike.'

Half of Jack's generation leaving permanently was more than she'd realized. From the couple of houses that no longer seemed permanently occupied she'd had the impression that the population was dwindling, but it was difficult to know if it was just seasonal—people had always gone away for weeks and months fishing, logging and summer work on the mainland farms, but half? At that rate the village itself would be in danger of becoming unviable in not too many years. She wondered how many pupils the school still had.

After the houses there was a group of half a dozen shops arranged around a central parking area which formed the village centre. Of these the Co-op and Canada Post office were well-maintained, but the parking lot itself was neglected and deeply potholed, the result of a failure of the shop owners to agree on how to share the cost of fixing it. Opposite the shops was the harbour and off to one side was the Edenshaw Hotel, and then a hundred metres further to Zeb's garage, or to be more accurate combination garage, counselling centre for mechanical and legal matters, pawn shop, and social club.

Aurora pushed open the office door and walked in. Zeb was reading a week-old newspaper, his feet up on his desk.

'Morning Zeb, how's business?'

Zeb lowered his newspaper and smiled. 'Not bad, it's been quiet.'

That seemed a bit of a contradiction but she didn't dwell on it.

'I have something I want to run past you. It's a sort of business proposition for the village.'

Zeb folded the newspaper and dropped it neatly into his waste bin. 'You've come to the right man then, you know I always like business propositions,' he grinned.

There were a pair of ancient wicker chairs in front of Zeb's desk so Aurora picked the one with fewer oil stains and sat down.

'This village is dying, the young people are leaving. I just talked to Jack Manyshots and he reckons about half his generation have gone already. Most of the kids I taught have no job and almost all are depressed. Hell, *I'm* depressed after spending my time teaching them stuff they never had a chance to use. Now I'm past seventy and I don't want to go to my grave knowing that life here never got any better.'

Zeb shrugged. 'You and the rest of us. Can't roll back history though, and there ain't no good jobs here anymore, you know that. Not much we can do about it.'

'Well that's where I think you might be wrong. I got to thinking this morning: what did this place used to live off?'

'Salmon.'

'So what if we had plenty of salmon again, the cannery reopened, and fishing tourists stayed in the hotel and hired boats from here again?'

'Then we'd all be rich my friend. Tell me when you've talked to the salmon.' He started sorting out the junk mail on his desk, sensing a fruitless conversation.

Aurora leant closer to get his attention again, gently removing an envelope from his hand to get his attention. 'I know it's an open question, and until a few days ago I was a bit of a sceptic too, but there's good reason to think its climate change that causing the salmon not to come here anymore. The air's warmer and that's changed the currents offshore and the salmon find it harder to migrate back here. They're probably still out there, lurking, but not in enough numbers, or maybe the current takes them further up the coast these days.'

Zeb shrugged, not in the mood to argue.

'What if there was a way to attract them back?' she persisted.

He squirmed in his chair with the awkwardness of someone who doesn't want to buy something sensing the inevitability of being persuaded.

'I've done some research and discovered that there's a scientist in Montreal who's been working on a technique called iron fertilization which might help bring our salmon back.' She looked him in the eye. 'And if that doesn't motivate you then I think the village could make some money out of it—we could apply for government grants, or maybe persuade them to come here and do research. Even if the salmon didn't come back we could still get government money out of it.'

Zeb stopped fiddling with his mail. 'Now you're talking my language,' he smiled.

Having finally caught his interest Aurora explained her proposal.

'Gaia Thompson knows about this sort of stuff, right? She thinks it would cost millions and take resources we don't have, but I've done some research on it and I'm not so sure. Basically all you have to do is dump this iron powder in the sea in the right place. You'd probably need a couple of hundred tons, but that's only two trips out for our fishing fleet. It's something we could do ourselves.'

'Fleet?' grinned Zeb. 'We have four rusty old boats! And one of them doesn't even have a working engine.'

'All you have to do is take a hold-full of this stuff out and throw it overboard. It's quite harmless, it's even used in lawn fertilizer.' She shrugged. 'Heck, you could even do some fishing while you're out there and bring fish back. It would cost you nothing to do.'

Zeb continued to look sceptical. 'How would we know where to put it? I'm guessing it needs to be near the salmon in order to work?'

'That's the one part where we would definitely need outside help. It needs to be done at just the right time and place to attract the salmon, so we'd need the guidance of a professional oceanographer. But I'm hoping we can persuade this scientist to do this for free or at minimal cost—it would fit in with their research anyway.'

'And you also said something about government grants?'

'Ah, yes. You've heard of the Ministry for Climate Change?'

He shook his head.

'Well you must have heard of the Carbon Tax?'

'I don't pay tax.'

Aurora rolled her eyes. 'Not directly maybe, but this is a new tax they've put on all forms of energy—

gasoline, your electric bill, gas, diesel, all that kind of stuff.' Not getting a reaction she continued. 'Anyway, there is this tax and it goes to this new government Ministry which is supposed to spend it on projects to combat climate change. I reckon we could easily apply to them for some money to try this. I've looked up the price of iron sulphate on EBay and we're probably talking ten or fifteen grand for a hundred tons—it should be easy to get that sort of money, plus something for the use of the boats, and anything else you can think of.'

'Bloat,' replied Zeb, thoughtfully.

'Sorry?'

'Bloat. That's what we call it when you add all kinds of unnecessary extra costs to something. Like fuel costs, fuel delivery charges, admin fees, manpower, cost of internet, paint, overtime, whatever…'

'Now you're getting it,' smiled Aurora. 'I bet if we applied for say fifty grand and it cost us ten grand for the iron sulphate they're not going to be looking too closely where the rest goes. All the Ministry is going to want to know is that it went on testing some idea that might have helped reverse climate change and bring our salmon back.'

'So they'd just see it as some kind of experiment that doesn't need to work?'

Aurora nodded. 'That's the beauty of an experiment, it tells you something even if it doesn't work. Whatever happens, it will be all good as far as they're concerned.' She leaned forward again. 'I used to apply for school grants and believe me anything to do with small native communities they just love, it enables them to check their boxes to say they've helped indigenous communities, remote areas, climate change, the environment—checks all the boxes for them!'

Zeb smiled. 'Sounds like a winner to me.' As he was to summarize it later, they might not be able to influence where the salmon went, but they could influence where the government money did.

Although she'd told Zeb that her motivation for the scheme was to bring back Esh's salmon and jobs, Aurora had no idea what the chance of success was. What she didn't tell Zeb was that she didn't care. She had an entirely different agenda.

- - -

As it happened Aurora was not the first person to concern themselves with how to bring the salmon back to Esh. Zeb's neighbour, Edwin Reid, had been thinking about it a lot lately. The difference was that Edwin already knew exactly what the problem was and how to solve it. At ninety-five years old he'd seen it all before, and it didn't have anything to do with changing climate. He knew for a fact that it was because people didn't throw their salmon bones back into the sea anymore.

Edwin was in all probability the oldest person on Esh—he even remembered Aurora's parents arriving. He remembered his own grandfather talking about the devastation of the population from smallpox in the mid-nineteenth century when the missionaries had first arrived, an event so horrific the visions had scarred him for life. But he also remembered the good times in his own boyhood when the entire village lived off the salmon harvest. He had been taught the ways of the land as well as its legends, the accumulation of thousands of years of human knowledge from life on the islands at the edge of the world. Above all he knew about the animal spirits.

As a boy he had spent months with his father climbing the steep tree-covered peaks, had explored every cliff and cove, knew where the spirit bears lived and which rivers the salmon came to and when. All of life depended on the salmon—not just humans but the bears, the sea eagles, the seals and the herons. And he knew that they all had life thanks to the benevolence of the Salmon People, a tribe of hybrid salmon-human creatures whose home was beyond the horizon far to the west, and who ruled over the salmon themselves.

Legend had it that long ago there had been no salmon around Esh, although they were found at other places along the coast, and consequently people on Esh often went hungry. One day four brothers were sent to find the salmon and to persuade them to visit Esh. First they had to persuade the Sun, who could see where everyone lived, to tell them where the Salmon People lived. The Sun told them of some islands far to the west where they lived, and also instructed them to prepare some medicine of herbs to take as a gift.

They paddled westwards for many days in their canoes until they reached the Salmon People's islands, and after giving the chief a gift of medicine were invited to a feast of roast salmon. He told them they could eat as much as they wanted, but on one condition: they must not throw away any of the bones but keep them all, even the smallest, so that they could be returned to the sea.

They did as they were told, and at the end of the meal the bones were gathered up and thrown back into the sea, whereupon they were immediately reborn as new salmon.

After staying with the Salmon People and feasting like this for many days they prepared to leave, and asked the chief if he would allow the salmon to visit Esh—which he agreed on the condition that every time they ate a salmon, they gather up the bones and throw them into the sea so that they would rejuvenate as new salmon.

Edwin also knew that the salmon had other places they had to visit, meaning that some years not as many of them were able to come to Esh, but above all he knew the importance of throwing the bones back, something which to his irritation many villagers didn't bother with anymore, despite his reminding them at every available opportunity.

He felt that people had no respect for the wisdom of old people anymore, and that upset him too. The more he discussed these issues with them, the less attention they paid to him, which was even more distressing. How hard was it to understand that if you threw away the bones in a plastic garbage bag and dropped it in the landfill outside town the salmon were never going to be able to get back to the sea to be reborn? No wonder their numbers were dwindling.

Fortunately, his youngest son Edward was also an enthusiast for Esh's legends and history, and so Edwin knew that he would pass it all on. Edward had even written down some of the stories for the local museum. He was a smart boy and Edwin was proud of him; he'd gone to university in Victoria and still worked there as an engineer, but he came back often, usually once a month.

Edward had studied the archaeology of the island too, and tried to match up the oral legends he'd learned from his father with old village sites and artefacts that archaeologists had found amongst the trees. That didn't mean much to Edwin, he didn't doubt these places existed even if he couldn't find them, but it seemed to give added credibility to others hearing the legends, particularly outsiders. So he rested easy knowing that one day they would find the island of the Salmon People and that Edward would make sure everyone knew the story of how the salmon came to Esh, and how they could be brought back.

- - -

That evening two of the people who hadn't paid much attention to Edwin's warnings sat on upturned crates in the wheelhouse of Zeb's fishing trawler *Spirit Bear*. Zeb and Saul swigged cans of Molson and watched a small boat coming up the channel, returning from checking lobster pots. If the fishing was no longer what it was, at least the changing climate seemed to favour lobster and shrimp catches, which had become a useful source of extra income for some.

Simultaneously feared and revered, Saul was the most respected and influential of the village elders—a white-haired man with a wide mouth and leathery skin who had managed to run a profitable business through good times and bad, largely through never wasting a dime on unnecessary maintenance. His hotel, of which these days only the bar was busy (the upper floor of ten rooms having never reopened after their annual winter closure five years previously), was dingy and dark, something which Saul claimed gave it 'character'. His village store across the street boasted metal shelving salvaged from a paint store that had gone out of business a decade earlier and lino flooring which was cracked and held down with Duck tape. So much tape in fact that the local children even played a game of hopping through the store without treading on the tape, which was harder than one might imagine.

'So if we do this right we'll all benefit,' Zeb summarized. 'Her idea is to apply for government grants, which she knows how to do from when she was running the school, and then just claim things against it—boat leases, equipment, man-hours, admin, whatever we can think of. All we actually have to do is dump this stuff out at sea but if the Ministry wants to send people to check then you can rent out hotel rooms as well. You can probably even get them to pay for a renovation before you rent it out.'

'Well I ain't paying for no renovation!' muttered Saul indignantly.

'That's what I'm saying, this would be a way to get someone else to pay! Hell, if you played your cards right you might even get them to put in AC for you. Aurora says the Government needs to show they're doing something about climate change but don't care what so there's plenty of cash available. Those two little words 'climate change' are gold, my friend, gold. You think all those big corporations who advertise so much about how green they are do it from the goodness of their hearts? No, I bet they all get grants for it. Everyone's at it!'

Saul swigged his beer. 'I don't dispute the weather's changing—tides are higher than they used to be, wetter warmer winters—but what the hell's it got to do with carbon dioxide? Isn't that the stuff they put in fire extinguishers? I mean, I just don't know where she gets these daft ideas from…and the woman's crazier than a sea otter at spring thaw if she thinks fire extinguisher gas will bring the salmon back. They've gone their own way, found a better place to spawn, and nobody's gonna convince them to come back to Esh until they're good and ready. So I wouldn't waste a dime of my money on some madcap 'fertilization' scheme—*but* if she's got a way we can actually make money out of it then I'll support that.'

Saul watched the lobster boat as it passed them. 'Any way of getting money out of the government is good with me, they've neglected us since forever and it was our money to start with. Count me in.'

Zeb grinned and slapped him on the back. 'This'll put Esh on the map my friend! People'll come here from all over. We'll be famous.'

'I don't want to be famous,' replied Saul. 'I just want the money.'

CHAPTER 6

The Proposal

Nigel Eddington on the other hand, definitely did want to be famous. At least that was the only logical explanation Winter could think of for his continued insistence on exploring his vision of a line of solar farms and wind turbines along Canada's arctic coast-line, which Eddington now insisted on referring to by the acronym NorPow.

Since he'd originally dreamt up the idea he'd ordered Winter to commission a study using departmental resources and outside experts. Winter set up a committee to study it but their view was unanimous: solar panels were out because they would continually be covered by drifting snow. And even ignoring the technical challenges of constructing turbine towers on thawing permafrost and operating them in temperatures of -40°C and below when maintenance would be almost impossible for half the year, the location was so far from centres of habitation that almost half the power would be lost in line transmission getting it to where it was needed. It would be like trying to fill your kitchen sink from a well at the far end of a long field using a very leaky bucket. In other words, both ideas were non-starters.

Any rational person would have given up at this point, but not the Minister. He pointed out that Winter had only considered where the centres of population were *now*. What if a warming climate led to cities being built further north than today? What if the arctic winter climate warmed from -40°C to -20°C? And had they considered the beneficial social and economic effects of increased Inuit employment that would flow from the construction and maintenance work? Winter had been instructed to discuss further with the engineers. Today he was due to present his findings.

'The committee looked again at the issues you raised, Minister, but I'm afraid it really doesn't change their conclusions much.'

Eddington raised his hand as though about to interrupt, but thought better of it and waved Winter to continue.

'Going through your suggestions in order, if cities were further north than today the power transmission losses would of course be less, but according to all the authorities we've consulted it really isn't very likely that any new Canadian cities would be built further north because there's simply no economic incentive to do so. Our main market is and always will be the United States. Moving cities further from that market would be counter-productive.'

'But our wheat fields will have to move north, surely? Crops need a specific temperature range to grow, and if the climate warms up that range will be found further north. People will have to follow.'

Winter frowned. 'Not many. Very few people work in agriculture these days, less than two percent of the Canadian population, of which only a few percent might ever migrate northwards over the coming decades—you're talking a couple of tens of thousands of people, max. Anyway, many farms are quite remote and have their own diesel generators, in fact a lot are not connected to the grid at all.'

Trying to avoid giving Eddington any more opportunity to challenge him he moved swiftly on. 'Second item, what if the operating temperature were twenty degrees warmer? The most pessimistic forecasts for the climate in Nunavut don't get even close to a twenty degree rise even over the next hundred years. The lifespan of a wind turbine is about twenty-five years. So, yes, maintenance would become easier, but any wind turbines we construct today would be long gone by the time the climate warmed that much.'

'Finally, the benefit of increased Inuit employment. The committee agrees with you that of course there would be a significant need for people living in the north to monitor and maintain these facilities, but you have to get the numbers into perspective. How many people do you think this might affect?'

Eddington shrugged.

'Or to ask a simpler question, what's the Inuit population in the north?'

'Er, I'm guessing around a million maybe?'

Then, seeing Winter shake his head he added 'Less?'

'Fifty thousand. There are fifty thousand Inuit in the whole of Canada. Of those I would guess only a few percent would have the educational skills for this type of technology work. So you'd doubtless create some local jobs, but probably only a few hundred at most. So overall I'm afraid these considerations don't change the overall picture. Placing wind turbines in the far north to supply power to our existing population centres would be expensive, costly to maintain, and above all highly inefficient.'

There was silence for a few moments while Eddington absorbed all this, his head down gazing at his desk. Eventually Hawthorne felt he should say something.

'Minister, we all appreciate your passion to make this work and for it to be your legacy, and I agree it's a very innovative idea, but there's a huge risk it would be a white elephant. It may well not work and even if it does the economics are just not there. It's simply too far from consumers.'

Eddington sighed heavily. 'I know, Hawthorne, I know, but it would just be so *neat* if we could move all our power generation to the part of the country no one—almost no one—lives in. Don't you think?' He paced around his office for a while as Hawthorne and Winter looked at one another in awkward silence.

'Let's go there!'

'Excuse me?'

'Let's go and have a look. None of us know the area, we probably have all kind of misconceptions. Let's make a field trip and that will help us decide on NorPow's viability.'

Winter didn't think there was much left to decide, and wasn't overly keen on travel. He'd recently signed up for an evening class in curling and didn't want to miss the first one. 'Er, okay, we could do, I guess,' he ventured cautiously. 'Where did you have in mind?'

'What's the capital of Nunavut?' asked Eddington, striding over to a map on his wall to answer his own question. 'Iqaluit. Must have an airport, let's go there!'

'But it's already November,' said Hawthorne with genuine alarm. 'It'll be cold.'

'Then we'll see it at its worst and be able to understand the true challenges. Hawthorne, set it up!'

He turned and pointed dramatically at the ceiling. 'Gentlemen, we're going to the Far North!'

- - -

Later that same evening another meeting was getting underway. Edenshaw Village Council was about to hear a proposal from Aurora Jones—a rather more modest one than Nigel Eddington's grand vision, but one which unknown to anyone in the room would actually achieve much more.

To prepare for the process, and to maximize their personal benefit from it, Saul and Zeb had divided up what they saw as the likely commercial opportunities to provide the range of services that they imagined a government-funded research project might need—accommodation, transport, catering, construction services and so forth. This was of course a speculative list since neither of them had any prior experience of such projects but nonetheless they were generous in their distribution of the work to their friends and relatives.

Saul's son Johnny would supply boats and handle any construction needed. Two of Zeb's daughters would provide meals and his wife the laundry services. A friend of Johnny could get satellite phones and knew how to rig up computers if needed. The list developed a life of its own, unencumbered by reality. Their assumption was that it would all be billed whether or not it was needed. Applying for government grants was a tricky one. Saul, as Mayor, felt that it should have his name on it but had no idea what to apply for or how.

After careful thought they decided to delegate that task to Aurora in her capacity as Secretary of the Village Council.

Eventually they could get no further and decided to call a village meeting to present the proposal and ask the villagers for a mandate to proceed. So one evening sixty Edenshaw residents gathered in the Community Centre to formally discuss what had become known as 'the salmon experiment'.

Aurora knew almost everyone in the room. Apart from herself, Gaia and Wolf, there were only a handful of other white folk, including Charles and Mary Abbott who had moved to the island twenty years ago to run the post office. The husband had always struck her as a frustrated and rather angry soul. It was no secret that as representative of the most visible government agency in Edenshaw he felt that he should also be leader of the community, and had taken it as an affront when it became obvious to him that he was not and never would be. He'd stood to be Mayor in the last election but only got a handful of votes, Saul sweeping the board with ninety percent. As usual with these things it had all been decided in advance over beers in his bar.

Saul chaired today's meeting, explaining with his usual stiffness at such occasions that a proposal had been made by Miss Jones for a project aimed at restoring the salmon population of the Echelon Islands, and that since it would require official representations by the village council in order to bring it to fruition he was seeking input from the community and their mandate to proceed. There would be a vote at the end of the discussion to authorize the Council to go forwards. With that he handed over to Aurora and asked her to explain her proposal.

‘Thank you Saul, friends,’ she started. ‘When I was a child this community was a thriving one. Almost everyone was busy and almost everyone depended one way or the other on the salmon for their livelihood. It was a happy place to live. But in the last ten years all of that has changed. Salmon numbers are a tenth of what they used to be and fishing is barely viable anymore. The cannery has closed. Many small businesses that supported the fishing have closed. We don’t have a boat repair yard or a chandler anymore. Our young people—the young people that I educated for the world of work—have no jobs and no prospect of one unless they leave. I was told recently that about half our youngsters now leave Esh to find work. It might be my imagination but the tides in the harbour are slowly moving higher. I find all of this very sad. It’s not what I worked my whole life for.’

Many of the older folk nodded in acknowledgement.

‘Now I don’t want to be alarmist, but I think we’ve reached the point where just carrying on as we are and hoping the salmon come back is no longer an option. Our population is declining, and there’s going to come a point where we lose essential services because they become too expensive for so few people—and once that happens the emigration will accelerate. And that tipping point might only be another ten years away.’ She wasn’t going to alarm people by telling them she had good evidence to back up her theory, she didn’t need to—looking around the room people looked suitably despondent.

‘So what can we do about it? I’m getting old now and frankly I don’t want to die knowing that my community is dying too, because if young people keep leaving at the rate they are we risk not having enough people here for the village to be viable. We might even find that we lose the Co-op or our post office as has happened in other communities.

'We've tried all kind of things over the years, the government tried to promote tourism here for a while, but that didn't work out too well. We have some logging and quarrying and we could probably do more of that, but it destroys the very things we hold most precious about our islands. However we've never tackled the root cause, the fact that the salmon no longer come here to spawn.'

She explained how Gaia had told her about iron fertilization and Dr Renouf's recent article promoting the concept, and how the Ministry for Climate Change had money to fund such projects, and her previous experience of applying for grants for the school.

'So my proposal is that we take the initiative as a community to organize a trial and try and get the government to fund it, and that's basically what Saul wants you to vote on later—to give the Council approval to investigate further, to apply for any available grants, and ultimately to run an experimental project.

'If successful it would increase our salmon numbers which ultimately would enhance our fishery and benefit the whole community. But even if it doesn't work it should provide short term work for some which would hopefully be funded by the government. I'm prepared to help with approaching Dr Renouf and applying for funding, and our Mayor here has offered to help organize local businesses to participate.'

She looked around the room at the faces. Most looked hopeful, optimistic even. 'That's all I have to say. It's a simple idea. I think we should talk about it and see if people think it's worth investing a bit of time to look into it further.'

There was some polite clapping, but no rush to speak. It seemed like no one wanted to be first until it was clearer which way the mood was going, but after a few seconds Gaia stood up and broke the silence.

'I'd like to support Aurora's proposal. As most of you know I'm a big enthusiast for protecting our environment here on Esh, it's why I live here, and I've also studied the marine environment quite a bit. Personally I have no doubt that the changes Esh has seen are caused by man-made climate change and I believe we can do something about it. The method she is proposing, although it's unproven, has a solid scientific basis to it and I think has a fair chance of success. And I guess since the problem of climate change is definitely man-made I feel it's only right that we should try and find a man-made solution.'

With that she sat down and Charles Abbott, who had been looking rather exasperated on the front row, sprang to his feet. 'I'm sorry folks but this is all just BS! There is no such thing as climate change. No scientist has ever proved it, no measurement has ever shown it. The reason why the salmon numbers have gone down is real simple, and has nothing to do with so-called climate change: they've been overfished! I'm sorry to say it but you folks caused the problem yourselves. You've overfished the salmon and they've done exactly what you'd expect them to do, they've gone someplace else.' Having got it out of his system he sat down, muttering something to his wife as he did so.

Gaia jumped right back up again. 'How can you deny that global warming is man-made, Charles! The scientific case is overwhelming—almost all of the world's governments have accepted that it is extremely likely that human influence is the dominant cause of climate change. It's one of the few things ninety-five percent of scientists are agreed on, which is precisely why those governments are taking combined action to reduce the world's CO2 emissions.'

'Stop lying!' shouted Charles without bothering to stand up again. 'It's been proven that NASA has falsified all this! There ain't no such thing as climate change! When will you people get it into your heads? Have you seen it get warmer around here, cos I sure ain't! NASA has cooked this whole thing up to enable them to get funding from the US Government for their ridiculous so-called science projects, and there's absolutely no connection with your goddamn salmon. They've just been overfished, plain and simple!' He looked around the room. 'This whole meeting is a waste of time!' he declared. 'Come on Mary, we're leaving,' and he angrily kicked his chair back and headed for the door.

There was silence as the two of them marched to the exit and banged the door behind them.

'I think Mr Abbott just demonstrated that climate change is a hot topic,' commented Aurora, to nervous laughter.

Attempting to reassert his control of the meeting Saul quickly asked what other views there were, and gave the floor to Edwin Reid. He spoke slowly but with determination.

'We should not forget the old ways folks. I don't pretend to understand this climate change and your see-oh-too, but our land and the surrounding oceans have taken care of themselves since time immemorial.

When our ancestors came here the land was covered in ice. The sea has moved in and out—I remember when it was further out than it is now. But always it takes care of itself and provides for us.' He looked around the room, watching people's faces. 'Obviously the weather is wetter and warmer every year, we can all see and feel that. The spring comes earlier, animals come out of hibernation earlier, up north there's less sea ice. But that's not the real reason—our legends tell us why the salmon don't come back: it's because we don't throw their bones back into the sea. If more of us did that then they could regenerate and more salmon would come back each year.'

There was general nodding at Edwin's comment and for a moment Aurora worried that he would divert attention from her proposal by finally succeeding in convincing the villagers that the solution lay in adhering to the old traditions.

'However, above all it's important that we are respectful to the salmon and offer them gifts, so I think Miss Jones's plan would be a good first step to winning back their favour. That and throwing back the bones.' With that he sat down.

One of the white retirees rose hesitantly.

'I'm with Edwin,' he began, 'and I don't see that we have much to lose, although I don't understand all this science stuff either. But I just got one question: if we want to attract the salmon back, couldn't we just put out some fish food?'

'Fish food?' asked Saul.

'Yeah. Salmon must need something to eat. Maybe we could like, put our garbage into the ocean and they would be attracted here to eat it.'

There was an embarrassed silence.

'That's pretty much what Aurora is suggesting,' replied Gaia, speaking slowly as if to a child. 'Fish eat plankton and small creatures in the sea, and what Aurora is suggesting is food for the plankton. So it would basically create a large amount of food for the salmon offshore on their way back here, and that would help them to make it back here to lay their eggs.'

The man smiled. 'Oh well, that's very clever. Genius! I want to support the project then!' And with that he sat down too.

People talked among themselves for a few moments until another elder in a waistcoat got up to speak. 'We should not try to interfere with nature, the salmon will come back when they're ready. Long ago the sea was much further away and legend says people could walk from Esh to the mainland, and maybe this is going to happen again and the salmon know it. The fish and the birds know a lot more than we do, they have great wisdom. We should not rush into changing the planet, we should let it heal itself in its own time. Maybe there is a reason why the weather is milder and the seas are rising, and we will know it when the time comes.'

People appeared to reflect on his words, showing respect by nodding thoughtfully, even though fewer believed in spirits and the wisdom of fish anymore in a literal sense. Aurora knew he was right about sea levels having been lower thousands of years ago and he might be right about the future, but they didn't have thousands of years to wait for a solution.

It seemed as though most of the village wanted to have their say, and a smiling middle-aged Filipino man was next. Aurora thought she recognized him from the cafeteria on the ferry. 'My name is Norman, and my grandfather had to move to this country because he accidentally hit a policeman in Manila with his tuba.' He looked around the room as if expecting some applause before continuing. 'During a parade... Anyway we need more fish in this world and I like salmon, especially on bagels which is a great Canadian invention, so I am voting for the motion. And I think this is a very big motion.'

When he sat down and the room tried to make sense of his comments, a timid-looking woman in the middle put her hand up. 'Are we sure we wouldn't be breaking the law? I mean, I just think there's going to be a law against us putting chemicals into the sea. There's laws against pretty much everything else. Just about whatever I want to do turns out to be illegal.'

'I won't ask what it is you like to do!' joked Aurora. 'But seriously, I think this is one of the reasons why we need some guidance from an expert before we go too far. I'm not thinking fancy consultants here, I'm thinking we simply approach Dr Renouf herself to see if she'd like to work with us to test out her theory. Being an experienced oceanographer she will probably be able to advise us on the legal dos and don'ts too.'

Saul looked thoughtful. 'Good point, we need to be sure whatever we do is done properly. But we're getting ahead of ourselves. We seem to be agreed that the most likely cause for the drop in salmon numbers is the changing climate, and we also hear a lot from the new government about what they're doing to tackle the climate issue and their new approach, it's supposed to be a big priority for them. Maybe next we should ask our MP to tell us what they're planning to do about it?' Then apparently as an afterthought 'And we can also ask him whether he'd support funding applications at the same time.'

Its human nature that everyone needs to have their say even when they agree with what's already been said, so the meeting went on for a while longer. Given the rather optimistic scenario that Aurora had painted of someone else paying for it, the choice presented was between not doing the project and definitely having no salmon, or doing it and have a small chance there might be salmon at someone else's expense, so at the end of the evening the room voted almost unanimously to proceed. The next action item for the Council was to see if they could hear from their MP, something which Saul promised to look into.

Charles Abbott didn't get to vote since he'd left and the only other vote against was from a lady who insisted that the real reason for the lack of salmon was that they were being enslaved in fish farms by the Japanese, on account of their well-known proclivity for sushi and 'what they did to the whales'.

CHAPTER 7

Parental Misguidance

'Dad? You want me to be happy and successful in life, right?'

'Yes, of course,' replied Johnny without thinking, realizing too late that Julie's question would have an ulterior motive. It wasn't like her to start a conversation like this without a good reason.

'So if I had a plan that would achieve that you'd want to help me?'

'Y-e-ss, I guess so.'

'Don't worry,' she smiled, 'I'm not asking you for money. But I do have a business plan that I want to discuss with you, that I'd like your support on. Some parental guidance, if you will.'

He turned off the TV and gave her his full attention. Julie had been working part-time at the Co-op since she'd finished school two years previously and the subject of what she would do longer term was one that had increasingly been concerning him the last few months. Apart from his dropping a few hints that he'd be willing to support her to go to college they hadn't yet been able to have a productive conversation on the subject. He was hoping she would follow her elder brother and go to college in Vancouver to get a qualification that she could get a better-paid job with, but she was reluctant to leave Esh and gentle hints had so far been ignored.

'I'm all ears. Tell me about it.'

Julie took a deep breath. 'Obviously I don't want to spend my life working at the Co-op, but it has given me time to think about what I really want to do. Not working behind a check-out for starters,' she smiled, 'but it also helped me realize how important Esh is to me. It's a big part of who I am and I'd drown in a big city. I also think Esh is a place with a lot of potential, its future could be a lot brighter than its past—and I want to help make that happen.'

Johnny nodded non-committally. He wanted to hear her out before saying anything.

'So I've been thinking of things I could do that might be a part of that, something that would also provide me with a reliable income, as well as something I'm going to have some passion about. What I decided I want to do is to open a café or café/restaurant in Edenshaw—firstly because I think there's a demand for it, and secondly because it will become a focal point for younger people interested in reviving our village and culture. There's a lot of kids like me that want to do something but don't know what to do or how to get started, and I think if they had a place to get together and kick around ideas then some of them might actually get somewhere.'

She looked at him for some sign of approval or acknowledgement.

'Okay…carry on, I want to hear you out before commenting.'

Julie placed a document on the table between them. 'I know what you're thinking, it will just lose money, so

I've made a business plan and looked at different options. Eighty percent of new businesses lose money and over half fail completely in their first year, so I want to have a really conservative approach, make sure we can survive even on minimal income for the first couple of years.'

'We?'

'I'm planning to do this with a partner. Aiyana.'

If Johnny had a view on this he was careful not to show it.

'Anyway, my idea—our idea—is that if we can persuade granddad to let us have the use of that side room in the hotel, the one at the back with its own door onto the street, then we would have minimal financial exposure and risk. It costs him nothing because he doesn't use it and actually it can only bring him more business for his bar, because our café would attract a different kind of customer than he gets at the moment. Probably not that many, but at least some people would come in to eat and end up going for a drink afterwards—particularly if he stocked a few decent wines and not just beer.'

'So you're expecting him to give you that room for free?'

'Yes, I am,' replied Julie confidently. 'Think of what he gets out of it. He gets more and different customers, most probably younger ones, and on top he gets his room refurbished for free. You can't tell me he wouldn't benefit from that, most of his existing ones are as old as he is—and assuming you inherit the hotel one of these days then that should be something you'd like to see too. So what I'm proposing is that he gives it to us rent-free for a year, and at the end of that time we start paying rent.'

'So when you say you want my support, what do you want me to do?'

'We both know how stubborn granddad is. In order to convince him I think I'm going to need you to tell him that it's a good idea and that you support me.'

'Okay.' Johnny picked up the business plan and casually flipped through it. 'You say you're not asking for money, but presumably you'll need to buy catering equipment and to refurbish the room?'

'We've saved up three thousand between us. We think that will be enough to do some minimal redecoration and buy enough kitchen stuff to get started—maybe starting with a menu that doesn't need us to cook hot food on the premises.'

Johnny nodded, agreeing that sounded sensible.

'Why Aiyana? Does she have any experience of running a café?'

'No, neither of us do. But she's a good cook especially with traditional recipes, and one of the things we want to do is to have a strong local flavour and revive local dishes that people have forgotten about. We don't want to be just another bland café serving bacon and eggs for breakfast.'

Johnny wrinkled his nose disapprovingly. 'I'm not sure she's the best partner you could choose to be honest, she's too dreamy. I know she's your friend but this is business and you want someone with a sound business head. It sounds to me like she's the one with a passion for cooking and she's just using you to achieve her dreams. Are you sure she's not taking advantage of your good nature?'

Knowing of his disapproval of her best friend Julie avoided rising to the bait. 'We complement one another. She's more creative, I'm more practical. I don't think either of us could do this without the other.'

'Okay. What about the room? There's a good reason your granddad stopped using it. It's a real mess, it's got a nasty patch of rot in one corner and it smells. It's going to need a lot of work.'

Julie winced. 'No, we haven't seen inside, but this is just a first estimate. If he agrees then the first thing I'd do is a more accurate costing before we start doing anything. Maybe as you say the room is unusable or he doesn't agree, in which case we'll have to find somewhere else—but the general plan still holds.'

Johnny dropped the document back on the table. 'I guess I have a couple of concerns if we're being honest. The biggest would be whether there's really a demand for a café in Edenshaw at all. This isn't some trendy city, people eat at home—they don't go out for breakfast. If they really want something they go to your granddad's place, but even that doesn't do much food service. Second would be how much business you'd need to make money. Your granddad survives because he has almost no costs—the hotel was paid for decades ago, and most of the time he's the only person working there. He only needs to sell a few beers an hour to cover his costs, and what food he does do is mostly just microwaved from frozen. For you and Aiyana it's going to be quite different—even without paying rent you have capital expense and ongoing costs for food, and you'll need to pay yourselves properly. My gut feeling is you'd have to be a lot busier than he is and I just can't see it happening, not here in Edenshaw.'

'But the reason he has so few food customers is the place is so bad! It's a bar where only older people feel welcome—nobody below the age of thirty would be seen dead there. The food is almost non-existent, like you say just frozen pizza that he reheats in a microwave, and the coffee is undrinkable. He puts on a pot in the morning and lets it stew all day. Are you really surprised no one goes there apart from his cronies?'

Johnny scowled, knowing she had a fair point. 'Okay, I've seen better places I admit, but it still serves as the social hub for the village, especially since he's the Mayor.'

Julie shrugged. 'I guess whether there's a demand for a better eating place in Edenshaw is a personal judgment. I think there's a lot of people who want something to eat but don't want to go to a hotel bar. Right now they have nowhere, and I just think that if they had an option like this they'd come. There's also quite a few mothers who wouldn't mind meeting somewhere for a decent cup of coffee.'

'Fair point.'

'But even if you're right and there isn't the demand, the beauty of this plan is that it costs nothing except our time to try. What's the worst case? He gives us the room for the year, we clean it up and run it, we're careful not to spend money we don't have, and at the end of the year we realize the demand's not there and we give up, he's lost nothing and we've learned something about running a business.'

'And wasted a year you could have been getting a qualification in.'

Julie didn't say anything.

'Consider my alternative. You go to Vancouver and study for a qualification for a year, maybe two. We're not talking a full university degree, we're just talking a practical qualification in something like accountancy, perhaps business administration. You're really good at organization, it's one of your strengths you get from your mother, you should find it really straightforward. Then you've got something of real value you can always use. You would be in a much better position to actually run a business, much more likely that it would succeed. You'll have more options. You could stay in Vancouver and get a job, a well-paid job, or you could come back and try your own business like this café, or maybe you could even come back and work as an accountant here.'

'What is it with you and accountancy? I hate accountancy! I was useless at maths, I would fail the course and even if by some miracle I passed I would hate every day in that kind of job.'

'You don't know until you try,' replied Johnny defensively. 'Anyway, look at the bigger picture; a year in Vancouver or somewhere else wouldn't just get you a qualification, you'd meet people too.'

'Meaning?'

'Life isn't just about getting a job. Eventually you'll want kids and a family, and let's face it your options in Esh are pretty limited. You don't seem to have met any boys here after all, you'd have more choice in Vancouver—more choice and a better chance of happiness.'

Julie laughed bitterly. 'Oh that's just perfect! So really you just want to see me married off and making babies?!'

'No,' he replied patiently 'I'm just saying there's more to life than just earning a living. Are you really likely to meet the right person stuck in your granddad's back room?'

'Believe me, that's not your concern,' she replied tersely.

Johnny held up his hands defensively. 'Okay, okay,

not my business, I get it. I'm just saying you should look at the whole picture, but let's stay talking about your business plan; you want to remain here and have a business here, that's fine. So how do you best equip yourself to do that?'

Julie threw her hands in the air in frustration. 'I know where you're heading with this, you're going to say that I need to get a degree in business before I can run a business. Dad, we're not talking running some big corporation here we're talking about running a café! I doubt if more than one small business owner in twenty has any kind of relevant qualification—that's not what makes them successful or not, it's usually passion for what they're doing and a reasonable amount of common sense. Do you have any qualification to run your boats? Does granddad to run his hotel? No!'

'But would it hurt? Tell me that?'

'Yes, it *would* hurt! Spending a year doing that would just waste my time and your money and delay everything. I need to do this while the opportunity is here, while I have the enthusiasm, while Aiyana does, while we have some money to start it.'

Johnny sighed in frustration. 'You should learn some lessons from your brother. He has a clear plan to get his engineering degree, knows what kind of work experience he needs to get accepted on the course next year.'

Julie laughed. 'Him? He's earning minimum wage installing solar panels! It's one step up from washing cars!'

'The solar industry is the future of energy, he's being smart and positioning himself ahead of the pack. Learning how those panels work is the best experience he can get, it'll help him understand that business.'

'Jeez Dad, he's just screwing things to a roof! The guys he works with are roofers, there's no difference between putting up shingles or panels—it doesn't make them tech geniuses. Their only skills are to be able to use a nail gun without shooting themselves in the foot or falling off.'

For a moment they glared at one another, nothing constructive to say.

'Okay,' she sighed, 'you say I should look at the big picture and not just the job. That's exactly what I'm doing. My whole passion is for rejuvenating Esh. This is my culture and heritage—and I don't understand why you and granddad, who lived through the residential schools and all the suppression of our culture and language for decades, want me to disappear into Vancouver and forget it all. I truly believe Esh can be a wonderful place again and my career plan is about helping me to do that.'

She paused. 'What are the most successful businesses in the island right now?'

Johnny shrugged. 'I dunno, the logging companies I guess…'

'I was thinking about those sport fishing lodges tucked away up the coast. You know how much people pay to stay there? Five thousand dollars a week! They're staffed by chefs and fishing guides from the mainland, the customers fly in direct to the lodge, they rent high-end boats—and never visit Edenshaw. We get absolutely no benefit from them at all. We don't own the businesses, our people don't get to work there, we don't supply the food or the fishing tackle or the boats. If we could do something as simple as convincing the provincial government to only license local companies to run those operations then Esh would have full employment immediately. I want to see an Esh where us locals own those businesses and then we could arrange it so the customers come through Edenshaw on their way there, buy their bait and tackle here, buy their souvenirs at Gaia's shop, eat in our restaurants—we could make much more out of it.'

Johnny stared at her for a moment, wondering where she'd got these ideas from. 'I agree with you but it's all politics. You can bet that those companies who got the licenses to run the lodges did a deal in Vancouver—it's easy for Vancouver to insist that companies must have prior experience of that kind of business to easily exclude us. I'm pretty sure your granddad tried to get a license when they first started coming here and it was some kind of excuse like that.'

Julie nodded, trying to be conciliatory. 'Okay, but you get where I'm coming from, right? I *do* have a big picture in my head that is not just getting my first job but to build a better community, but to get there we need some sort of social hub. I need a small business and the café is where both those things come together. It's low risk and doesn't need investment I don't have, it just needs a place to get started, and for that I need granddad's help and your help persuading him.'

'You don't think we've all felt that way at some time? Of course everyone would love to see full employment on Esh and of course we know that means replacing the salmon with new industries, but it's just not realistic. We've tried everything you've mentioned and more, honest we have. As for you personally, of course you can run a café or small business without any qualifications, but as you said yourself that's just the first step in your plan. When it grows or you want to do something more ambitious you're going to need some kind of qualification, and if that means spending a few years to get it then that's what you're going to have to do.'

Julie looked at him impatiently. 'So are you going to support me or not?'

'I'm not going to ask your granddad to help you lock yourself into a dead-end career, no. You're doing this the wrong way round. If you got your qualifications first then it wouldn't matter if your café failed because you would have a fall-back option. But if you spend even a couple of years trying the café and it doesn't work out then it may be too late for you to get accepted for a course.'

'You're my father! You're supposed to support me achieving my dreams, not block them!'

'Yes I'm your father and that means I have a responsibility to stop you doing something that five years from now you'll realize was a big mistake. Right now you might believe with all your heart that it's the right thing to do, but I just think there's a big chance you'll regret it. It's my job to stop you doing things like that, or at least to not facilitate them.'

Julie rolled her eyes. 'You really have no way of knowing that. Besides, I could put it the other way round: how can I go to college if I don't know what to study? I need to get some work experience first to find out what I'm good at and want to do. Only then would I know what qualifications I'd need to get further in that line of work.'

Johnny was getting visibly exasperated. 'I don't think we're going to agree on this, but you don't need my blessing to make your decisions, and I can't force you to do anything either. You're perfectly capable of going to talk to granddad about it yourself; you're still his granddaughter and he's always going to be to help you if he can, you know that. Like you said, he doesn't use the space and I'm sure he'll see the benefit for him. And he'll probably enjoy having you around the place. I promise I won't stand in your way, I'm just not going to be actively encouraging you down that path. But if he asks for my opinion I'll be honest.'

CHAPTER 8

Smoke and Mirrors

As the floatplane carrying Michael Malik dropped below the cloud base he got his first view of the grey waters of Edenshaw Sound and reminded himself once again that he was just here for the votes.

Initially he wasn't even going to bother replying to the local Mayor's request for a visit to discuss the impact of climate change, he was more than happy to deep six it into his waste bin. But then his assistant reminded him that this was a part of his constituency.

Worse, this particular electoral district had been pretty marginal at the previous election, and despite only winning by a few hundred votes he had not visited it once in his four years of representing them. She respectfully suggested that with the next election only six months' away it would behove him to show some interest in their problems and to pay them some attention.

Then he had remembered that he only needed three more flights on the Air West air taxi service before the end of the year to retain his gold status, and that had pretty much clinched it.

Even so he was reluctant because he knew almost nothing about the impact of climate change, a topic which he had no interest in whatever, but that excuse had gone away when his assistant tracked down Adam Winter, Senior Research Officer at the Ministry for Climate Change. Initially he just wanted to ask for some briefing notes but was pleasantly surprised when Winter had offered to come with him. In fact he'd seemed remarkably keen to get out of the office for a few days, something about Echelon being preferable to the North Pole if he'd heard him correctly, and Malik was happy to oblige.

Personally he didn't have much sympathy with the inhabitants of Edenshaw though. As he was saying to Winter as they came in to land, he couldn't understand why anyone in the twenty-first century would want to live here in the first place. It was practically off the edge of the known world, and with their livelihood gone and sea levels rising it was a no-brainer to him that they should quit whining about the inevitable and move someplace else. Plenty of new condos in Vancouver. Then they could designate the whole island a national park and get some extra brownie points from the federal government for taking an environmental initiative. He checked his briefing notes again and saw that it *was* a national park. Oh dear, that didn't help matters at all.

As a second-generation immigrant born and brought up in Toronto to Asian parents he readily admitted that he didn't like the rain-soaked west coast one bit, but it was considered a plum job by most, besides which beginners can't be too picky. Hopefully after the election he would be moving on to a Ministry job and he could start positioning himself for a seat closer to civilization. Michael was an ambitious man and had already been tipped in the media as 'one to watch' in the next government, and he planned to seize any political opportunity presented to him firmly and with both hands.

The plane skimmed the calm waters of the sound and then decelerated rapidly as the floats dragged on the water. Within a couple of minutes they were tying up at the floatplane pier. He peered out of the window at the small reception committee and wished again that he was somewhere other than this gloomy and miserable place. Why was the Pacific northwest so bloody wet all the time? Even the moss growing on the trees and the older houses gave him the feeling of decay. He worried that if he stayed still for too long his feet would start to rot.

'Mr Mayor! Just fantastic to be here!' he exclaimed enthusiastically and insincerely as soon as the door was open, pumping Saul's outstretched hand. 'It's such a privilege to be able to visit this beautiful corner of our land, I really appreciate your extending the invitation to us.'

Saul smiled but said little, motioning the two men towards his truck. If Malik thought Echelon was so wonderful, how come he'd never visited before? He kept his thoughts to himself and explained the arrangements for the meeting as they drove the three minutes to the community hall, where a crowd of about a hundred had gathered, some interested in what he would have to say about climate change, most merely curious to see what their elusive MP looked like.

As they entered the room Malik smiled and waved to everyone, and then walked along the front row shaking hands and waving and pointing to those at the back as though he knew them. After a few minutes Saul called the meeting to order and introduced him properly.

'Friends,' began Saul, 'a few weeks ago we had a discussion about the impact of climate change and the economic problems we have in Esh due to the decline in the salmon catch, and we heard one possible proposal for tackling it. We decided then that we should first hear what the government's position on these topics is, as a result of which I asked our MP, Mr Michael Malik, to visit and talk with us. I am pleased to say he accepted and is here today.' With that he pointed to Malik and motioned him to take the floor.

'I'd like to thank you for giving me the opportunity to visit Edenshaw and the Echelon Islands,' he started, humbly. 'This really is a truly wonderful part of our country, and one which surely deserves more of our attention. Now, I've brought with me today Dr Adam Winter who is an expert in climate change and the government's plans and policies in this area, and who is going to support me in the presentation and help answer your questions.' He paused and Winter nodded and smiled.

'I think the first thing I'd like to say is that preventing climate change and the problems it brings, including global warming and sea level rise, is a top priority for this government. Top priority.' Malik paused again to emphasize how serious he was and looked around the room.

'That is why we are committed to reducing carbon emissions and are encouraging the provinces to introduce carbon taxes which will bring down the levels of CO2 in our air, which will in turn result in lower temperatures. This is very important for all of us, and something which we are committed to doing for the future of our country and of our children. Our government has therefore agreed targets for safe CO2 levels and put a timetable in place for their implementation.' He smiled broadly, as if he had now solved the problem. 'And now to give us more details I'd like to invite Adam to explain more how all this is going to work, and then we'll open it up for discussion and answer your questions.'

Winter stood up, looking a little surprised to be up so early. The organization seemed a bit chaotic, but better than getting dragged into a trip up north at the beginning of winter. He'd been glad to leave Hawthorne to sort that one out. He was the one who'd wanted to give Eddington 'more rope' after all.

'Er, thank you Michael, and thank you all for the invitation to come here.' He smiled at the faces in front of him for a second. 'As Michael mentioned, the fundamental problem here is carbon dioxide, which builds up in the atmosphere and acts as an insulator, resulting in the gradual warming of our planet—the so-called greenhouse effect you've probably all heard about.'

Looking again at the blank faces he wasn't so sure they had heard of it but he continued anyway. 'The concentration of CO2 in the air is measured in parts per million and has recently passed four hundred parts per million, which is the highest level we have seen on this planet in about sixty million years, since the age of the dinosaurs. If CO2 levels continue to rise then the planet will warm up by three to four degrees centigrade by the end of this century, and that will have a big impact on every aspect of our lives—from food production to the spread of disease and insects, loss of low-lying cities due to rising seas and so on. So obviously it's something we take very seriously and want to prevent.'

'Now in a way the solution is obvious—find a way of slowing the increasing level of CO2 in the air and ultimately reduce it. It's also obvious that we need to do this in collaboration with other countries—if we only reduced our own CO2 emissions we would still receive CO2 from other countries since the air doesn't respect national boundaries. The way our government has chosen to do this is firstly to sign up to international treaties on carbon reduction, and secondly to introduce incentives for industry to reduce the amount of CO2 it produces.' Winter could sense he was losing a few people, he usually did at this point, but continued anyway.

'So for example if a paper factory on the mainland is producing a hundred thousand tons a year of CO2, the carbon tax we are talking about will charge that factory a tax based on those hundred thousand tons. It's treated as a pollutant. That's a big incentive for them to improve their processes and find ways to emit less carbon. Of course it's not just big factories that produce carbon dioxide—cars and airplanes produce it too, as well as power stations that generate the energy we consume to heat our houses and light our offices. That is why we also took initiatives to work with car manufacturers to find ways to improve engine efficiencies, and brought in regulations to promote low energy lighting by outlawing the old incandescent bulbs.'

He looked around, by now convinced that not a single person in the room, Malik included, had any idea what he was talking about. 'Any questions so far?'

Gaia put her hand up, and Winter nodded to her.

'Dr Winter, so you've explained you have these

policies in place. What has the actual impact been so far?'

He hated these kind of questions. His answer would have been very different if it had been asked in London, but here he had to wear his Canadian hat and give the official Ministry line.

'We're making progress. Our target is that by 2030 we will reduce emissions by thirty percent compared to 2005 levels.'

'So that's your target, but what has the actual progress been?'

'We're confident of meeting our targets.'

Gaia held up a government report. 'With respect that sounds like it's going to be a stretch given our country's track record of reducing CO2 emissions so far. According to the government's own statistics greenhouse gas emissions in Canada have only dropped by two percent since 2005, so we're halfway to 2030 and we've only achieved two percent of the thirty percent needed. It doesn't sound very likely that we'll achieve it, does it? And this same report also gives an updated forecast and says that emissions by 2030 will actually be exactly what they were in 2005—not even close to the thirty percent reduction target.'

Winter felt uncomfortable. Malik had given him to understand that the audience were going to be pretty basic, certainly not quoting reports at him. This was more like the kind of well-informed hostility that he would have expected from big cities like Toronto. 'We have a way to go, that's for sure.'

Malik jumped up to steer the conversation to safer ground. 'How about some other questions more specific to the local issues', he suggested cheerfully.

Now it was Aurora's turn. 'Your comments on

climate change are very interesting, but our problem here is actually a bit different—we're mainly concerned about the impact on our salmon and their reduced numbers. So could you explain the link between climate change and our decreased salmon run?'

'Well…' began Winter, hesitantly. 'There is most likely a connection for sure, but it's not well understood. We don't know, for example, whether the salmon have stayed away because the sea temperature here is now higher, or whether it's more due to a change in ocean currents caused by shifting weather patterns. Since the ocean temperatures have not actually risen much yet, it's more likely to be the latter.' He hesitated as if trying to remember his notes.

'Hmm, so if you don't understand the connection between climate change and the salmon run, do you actually have a strategy for bringing the salmon back?'

Winter looked startled. 'Bring them back? No, I'm afraid that's impossible.' He looked around him. 'I mean, we are fairly sure the changing climate is a factor in their behaviour but even if we could magically cool the planet a couple of degrees it's unlikely the weather and ocean patterns or salmon migration would go back to exactly how they were before.'

Winter's comment caused an audible murmur in the hall as Aurora continued. 'That's unfortunate because the loss of salmon in this part of the world is devastating our community. So just to be clear, you don't believe that the government's climate change strategy will reverse our loss of salmon.'

Winter looked guiltily at Malik before answering. 'Not in the near term, no. In the longer term well, maybe…perhaps.' He shrugged.

Having put the knife in, Aurora now twisted it.

'"Near term" being…?'

'Fifty years, perhaps', mumbled Winter unhappily, knowing it wasn't the answer Malik wanted him to give or that anyone in the hall wanted to hear.

Malik stepped forward to take back control. 'Let's not get too stuck on the details here. The important thing is that the government is totally committed to lowering our carbon dioxide emissions long term and to reversing global warming,' he interjected, managing to miss the point about the salmon yet again and thereby inadvertently steering the discussion back to carbon dioxide emissions. 'We believe the scientific evidence is clear: climate change is one of the greatest threats of our time and we are committed to taking firm action. We will provide national leadership on this issue and partner with both provinces and the international community to put a price on carbon and combat climate change.'

'So how long do you think it would take for global warming to be reversed once your carbon pricing scheme is up and running?' interrupted Wolf, smiling at Gaia. 'Are we talking weeks, years, what?'

'Somewhere in the middle,' replied Michael, nodding thoughtfully. 'Obviously not weeks, but I would also hope not many years. Maybe a few summers.'

Winter made a strange choking noise. 'Ahhh, actually that's not how it works.'

Malik gave him a forced smile. 'Let's hear from the technical expert then.' Why had he brought him with him? This was not going well.

'Well…it would be more like a hundred years I'm afraid. Probably several hundred.'

'No, no, no! That can't be right!' laughed Malik. 'I think you've got yourself a bit confused there Adam because the government policy is to bring down CO2 levels within decades not centuries—we have our targets for 2030 and 2050 so we should be noticing an effect well before that, right Adam?'

Wolf smiled. 'I've been doing quite a bit of study on this and I believe Adam is absolutely right, it would take not decades but centuries for a reduction in CO2 concentrations to feed through to reduced temperatures. There's a long time lag in these atmospheric processes.'

There was an awkward pause as Malik opened his mouth to speak, thought better of it and turned to Winter, who in turn was staring intently at his shoes. When Gaia raised her hand again Malik limply nodded for her to continue, realizing that he could hardly ignore her.

'The Center for Global Development in Washington recently ranked Canada's record on the environment as twenty-seventh out of the world's twenty-seven most developed countries. A European report has also ranked us fifty-first out of fifty-seven countries in terms of progress in tackling greenhouse gas emissions, ahead of only Australia, Iran, Saudi Arabia and the US. That does not fill me with confidence in the government's ability to tackle the problem. You could be doing considerably more, as most developed countries are.'

Ever the politician, Malik managed to see the positive in even this stark statistic. 'Which is exactly why tackling climate change is a top priority for this government! Obviously what we and previous administrations have done so far as a country has not been enough, and we need to step it up a notch.'

'But you would agree that your government's

record so far has been, let's face it, pretty dismal?' persisted Gaia.

Malik grimaced. 'Well obviously it's not been the best, but in our defence I'd like to point out that most of that was under the previous government. Other questions?'

'Perhaps I could ask you about something else,' said Saul, trying not to embarrass their guests too badly. 'Not so much on climate change but I think of interest to everyone here. Since the collapse of our salmon fishery we have a big problem with employment. Our young people have no jobs and many are leaving. The only support we've seen from the government so far has been social benefits which we appreciate, but which are only a temporary solution. What can you do to help us for the long term?'

Finally there was something Michael could be positive about, even though he knew that realistically the chances of it actually helping Edenshaw were slim given the competition from larger communities with more votes.

'We have all kinds of programs to help communities such as Edenshaw develop new industries. I think there's great potential here for tourism for example. You can't fight Mother Nature and if the salmon have decided to go elsewhere for whatever reason, then we should be looking at helping establish some alternative sources of employment here, and I would be proud to champion your cause if you were to apply to those programs.'

Saul nodded in agreement, sensing some easy money and a refurbished hotel down the line. 'How about research funding? Suppose we wanted to do some experiments on attracting those salmon back. Are there government schemes that would help with that too?'

Michael Malik found himself agreeing that there certainly could be, perhaps positioned more as scoping studies for a new salmon cannery or something related to employment initiatives than pure research, but he would see what he could do.

Winter fumbled in his briefcase and pulled out some brochures. 'You might also be interested in these,' he said, placing them on the table in front of him. 'We have a range of programs to encourage low-carbon lifestyles, whether its switching to an electric vehicle or something as simple as LED bulbs or better loft insulation. The average family can save hundreds of dollars a year in heating bills, as well as reduce their carbon footprint.'

'That's good news,' replied Saul cautiously. He looked around the room and judged that people were about ready to leave. 'So unless there are other questions I think we should thank Mr Malik for coming here today and let him get on his way,' and he raised his hands to initiate the applause.

As they drove without speaking back past the decrepit houses on the way to the floatplane jerry, Michael Malik gloomily thought how utterly unrealistic the people of Edenshaw were. Who the hell knew what went on in the mind of a fish? Or how to persuade them to change their migratory patterns? And why did they think the government could influence them anyway? He wished they would just get real, give up on this decaying backwater and relocate to Vancouver. Nobody there bitched about climate change destroying their jobs.

- - -

Apart from giving him an excuse to sidestep Eddington's visit to Iqaluit, there was another reason why Adam Winter had been interested to accompany Michael Malik to Echelon, something Hawthorne had raised a few weeks after he'd arrived. It had all started with an ill-advised after-work drink, during the course of which Hawthorne had been surprisingly candid about his frustrations with his job.

'These emissions targets are a joke! I've spent years trying to meet them, people just aren't interested, they won't make the necessary sacrifices. It's never going to happen, I guarantee it.' Hawthorne leaned closer conspiratorially. 'It's time to plan for a warmer world.'

Winter was confused.

'Ten or twenty years from now the permafrost will be cornfields, south-facing slopes will be vineyards, and Baffin Island will be a *Frozen* theme park,' continued Hawthorne. 'There's already cruise ships doing the northwest passage, right? That's why I've invested most of my pension in projects that will benefit from all that!' He sat back in a self-satisfied way and took another deep gulp of his beer.

'Isn't that a bit of a gamble?'

Hawthorne shrugged. 'Hey, I've just been cleaned out by my ex-wife, I have to take a few risks to make good again. I'm getting in on the ground floor of some amazing opportunities.' He grinned at Adam. 'And of course this job is ideal for spotting some of those.'

'You know we're not allowed to financially benefit from our inside knowledge,' said Winter with genuine indignation.

Hawthorne raised an eyebrow as he drained his

third pint. 'Seriously? Come on, who's to ever know, man?'

And there it rested for a while, a mildly concerning conversation which seemed to be more talk than substance, until a few weeks later when out of the blue Hawthorne had proposed his 'Western Islands Development Project'. He had established an inter-departmental study group to look at the future of some small islands off the west coast, the Echelon Islands. True, they had suffered more than most from climate change, but there was no indication that Echelon's future was under real threat.

Other departments had been reluctant to get involved, not seeing it as a priority, but Hawthorne had persisted and in the end the group had met a few times and endorsed Hawthorne's recommendation that all government departments should not 'artificially prolong' the life of communities on the islands in the event of continued impacts from climate change. They would discourage new investment and had suggested that the best long-term use for the islands would be to house industries where a local population was not desirable, such as an oil terminal or processing facility.

The more he thought about it, the less comfortable Winter felt with it. He even wondered if this was the sort of pension investment he'd alluded to. So he'd eventually confronted Hawthorne, who did not deny that it was part of his 'agenda'.

'Sure, like I said before, we have a duty to plan for the future. It would be irresponsible not to.'

'But building an oil terminal there? That would only increase carbon emissions, not reduce them.'

Hawthorne pulled a face. 'We have to face reality, Adam. These things have to go *somewhere*. Better out there where they bother no one than on a populated part of the coast. You try getting it built in lower mainland BC!'

'Please tell me this isn't where some of your pension fund is invested!'

Hawthorne just smiled.

'But is Echelon really such a basket case?' pressed Winter. 'From what I've heard they're doing okay—high unemployment admittedly—but a stable population of several thousand nonetheless.'

He'd never got a straight answer.

The more he thought about it this was mad: his boss was actively working against the system by investing in schemes that depended on climate change getting worse not better. He had to do something about it, to speak out, but he knew how whistleblowers were treated. Not for the first time in his career he felt a conflict between his conscience and his duties as a government employee. But this time it wasn't really his government, was it?

If he did anything, he had to make sure it could never be traced back to him. So after stewing on it for a few sleepless nights Winter had done something he'd never done before and sent a copy of Hawthorne's Western Islands Project recommendations anonymously to a journalist, an act which he'd immediately regretted.

But that was nothing like the regret he'd felt a few weeks later when he'd discovered that she'd been killed, presumably while following up his email. Which was why he'd jumped at the opportunity to see Echelon for himself. He'd read later that the death had been ruled an accident, but nonetheless he felt he owed it to her to visit, to find out more.

Unknown to him though, it was his own actions and not Hawthorne's that had already set in motion a chain of events whose consequences were to change life on Echelon forever.

CHAPTER 9

Nothing Ventured

Dr Langara Renouf walked into her office, slammed the door, and swore loudly and repeatedly. She had been a senior researcher in oceanography at the University of Upper Montreal for longer than she liked to admit and the university council had just refused to support her funding application for research on the impact of global warming on Canadian arctic sea ice, something she was a recognized expert on. And to make it worse this was the second time she'd been turned down and she had no Plan B.

The first rejection had been down to overall budget constraints the previous year, so understandable; she had to take the lean times with the good like everyone else and she knew many others who'd been turned down or delayed that year. But this time, with her existing funding about to run out the excuse was different and completely perverse; they'd argued that since she had already shown that the sea ice was melting more rapidly than was previously believed and that it would be completely gone within just a few years—decades sooner than most scientists thought—there was little point in continuing to monitor it when the outcome was inevitable. Not quite Catch-22 but close.

It wasn't just the money though, what really bugged her was their lack of appreciation for her work. They claimed they understood how important it was, but didn't show any interest in doing anything about it. It was as though she'd just given them a warning that a hurricane was imminent, and all they wanted to do was make sure the memo got filed correctly under 'H'. They totally failed to make the connection between her results and the real-life consequences, or the urgency.

According to her analysis the consequences for the world's climate and human life over the next couple of decades would likely be severe, especially in the northern hemisphere. Weather patterns, rainfall, the position of the jet stream, the number and severity of extreme wind events, everything could change…yet no one seemed to care. It was as though they were just hoping it might never happen, that somehow something would come along to change the situation.

Apart from the sheer frustration of people not listening to her, the lack of funding was a major roadblock for her career, and quite possibly a terminal one. No-one could justify a researcher who didn't do research for long. The chances were that her teaching post would be the next thing that they didn't feel able to continue funding, and at fifty-four years old she was unable and unwilling to retire—and there were not many job vacancies elsewhere for oceanographers.

Her temperamental personality didn't help of course, she knew she was sometimes seen as someone with 'issues'. Within the university she had a reputation as a risk-taker both professionally and in her personal life. Her reply starting with the abbreviation 'WTF' to a group email from the vice-chancellor justifying the appointment of a well-known right-wing politician to the university senate was still talked about, as was the cogency of her subsequent arguments. Likewise the rumour that she had once shared her cabin on a research cruise with a Senegalese deck-hand for a month added to her unconventional reputation, something that hadn't actually happened but which she had been slow to deny, rather enjoying the unconventional twist it gave her already wild image.

Now in her early fifties she was tall and slim with long black hair that she had always worn straight to her waist, and strong cheekbones and a straight nose that she put down to her part-Native genes. Envious female friends complained that she looked a decade younger than her age.

Deep down she suspected another reason for her funding rejection though: Professor Bill Bradley, head of the Faculty of Geoscience and her immediate superior. They had never really gotten along, mostly because of his ridiculously macho attitude towards her subject. Bradley was a hard rock geologist and never tired of joking that the best thing about sea ice was that it was fun to skidoo across to get to his rock outcrops. The oil-bearing rocks his research focused on brought in millions of funding from the oil companies, which over the years had unfortunately led to his developing a rather patronizing attitude towards his colleagues whose subjects were of less commercial interest. Success had gone to his head.

Above all it had been her unambiguous rejection of his suggestion one evening three years ago at a conference in the US that they share a bottle of champagne in his room and 'see what happens' that had soured their working relationship. Not so much her rejection of the offer of sex, which was something she could easily have laughed off, but her failure to hide her revulsion at the very idea of intimacy with him—perhaps hard for a man ten years her junior to take. He had pretended it was just a misunderstanding, but his attitude had become unmistakably cooler since that day.

Without Bradley's support as her head of department no funding application was going to get anywhere. As in so many organizations, the pages of supporting documents and references that she had painstaking compiled counted for nothing when the man presenting them to council grimaced when asked for his view: 'Solid researcher unquestionably, leader in her field…but I have to ask myself whether we really need to spend millions more to confirm what we already know?' had been his unenthusiastic response, before the committee chair had reminded them that this was the *second* attempt by *Miss* Renouf to flog this particular horse. It wasn't as though she could just go someplace else. At this late stage there was nowhere to go other than a US institution, where climate change research was even less likely to get funded than in Canada. She was screwed, and not in the way Bradley had offered.

Lan stared out of the window of her office on the tenth floor of the Earth Sciences Tower. Most of her non-academic friends seemed to think that life in a university was genteel and polite compared to the commercial world, but in her experience it was just as bad. At least in commercial companies everyone was ultimately on the same page, motivated to maximize and profits. In universities it was the politicians who ultimately decided who got the money, which departments thrived and which closed. And oceanography, being closely tied with climate science, was particularly susceptible to political whim. All you needed was some politician with a pro-job, pro-oil agenda to be put in charge and actual work and scientific progress could be stifled for years. Despite the helpful efforts of photogenic polar bears posing on shrinking ice floes they were once again in such a phase; such was reality and she knew she had better face it.

\- - -

In this mood of frustration and cynicism it was therefore later than usual that morning before she looked at her mail. There was only one that looked interesting, unusual because it appeared to be typed on an actual typewriter, something she hadn't seen in quite a while:

> *Dear Dr Renouf,*
>
> *I am writing to you from the Edenshaw Village Council, Echelon Quartet Islands, of which I am the Council Secretary.*
>
> *As you are doubtless aware, the salmon run on the Pacific northwest coast has been in decline for many years, something which is frequently blamed on global warming. This has had a very damaging impact on our economy and way of life, and accordingly the Council has decided to investigate any options we may have for reversing this trend. Without action our existence on these islands may become untenable within a few years.*
>
> *The Council recently came across your work on iron fertilization and is most interested in testing it here with*

the objective of creating an artificial phytoplankton bloom in the hope of attracting salmon.

Would you be interested in a collaboration? It seems to us that this could be a win-win situation—it would allow you to test your idea and if it works it would enable us to restore our salmon fishery.

I look forward to hearing from you,
Sincerely,
Aurora Jones

Lan stared at the letter and then re-read it. Maybe she had a Plan B after all. The iron fertilization idea was not really hers, it had been around for a while, but she had used some spare time on a research vessel a couple of years previously to try and create an artificial plankton, and had then floated the idea of trying it on a bigger scale a few times for research grants but hadn't had any bites. Actually it had probably done her more harm than good as a couple of the referees for her grant proposal had rather ridiculed the whole idea. Maybe this was her chance to get her career out of its current impasse. She wondered if the Echelon Islands Council had any money.

The scientific community debated engineering solutions to global warming *ad nauseam*—carbon capture, reforestation, cloud brightening, space-based sunshades, ocean fertilization, precipitating carbonates in the ocean, injecting carbon dioxide into abandoned oilfields, the list was endless. A couple of years previously she'd even been asked to evaluate spraying white paint onto sea ice so that it would reflect more sunlight and stop it melting so fast. Yet these ideas were rarely tested on a scale large enough to have a proven benefit.

Any scientist who successfully demonstrated one *and* reversed any of the impacts of climate change, such as by increasing salmon yields, would get noticed for sure.

She looked at her watch. Almost lunchtime, time for her weekly lunch date with Rick…her, what was he? Lover? Partner? That would be putting it a bit strong, given that he had consistently declined to commit to her, still bruised from a divorce five years earlier. He had called it an 'improbable alliance'. He was a professor in the arts faculty whom she had met running in the park one lunchtime, improbable in itself since neither of them ran often. They'd stopped at the same kiosk for a juice last summer and it had kind of progressed from there. A mutual curiosity about their very different subjects had led to joint runs, progressing in the winter months to weekly lunches before eventually also becoming physical, but it was still based principally on their animated and wide-ranging discussions, and most of the times they met they just talked. She found his different perspective refreshing and often intriguing. Today she would ask him his opinion of the letter from Aurora Jones.

He was already at the sports bar they'd agreed to meet, a few blocks from her building but not somewhere that was popular with academics. After the usual catch-up and telling him the bad news about her funding she took out the letter and passed it to him.

'What do you think? Crank letter or genuine opportunity?'

He read it quickly and raised his eyebrows.

'Sounds genuine. I guess my first question would be whether they're deluding themselves. Do you think it's doable? They're referring to your own work?'

'I think she's talking about an article I was interviewed for a month or two back. The fertilization is definitely possible, I actually did some experiments a few years back and we produced a plankton bloom fairly easily, and I put the idea in a research proposal a while back but it didn't go anywhere. The big unknown is whether it boosts the salmon population and if so where they go. That's in the lap of the Gods. If there are no salmon there to start with you could do everything right and it still not affect the salmon run one iota.'

'I do like the practical angle though,' said Rick. 'Or should I say the human angle, the fact it's not purely academic, that it could positively impact real lives.' He folded the letter and passed it back to her. 'Sounds like you would be advised to find a new area of research anyway though. Actually if you can't get funding to continue what you've been doing then you really have no choice. Either that or just give up research altogether and focus on teaching. Nothing wrong with that, it's the primary function of universities after all.'

Lan wrinkled her nose. 'I know, but it's never been my forte. I don't have the patience for all the preparation, or for all the dumb questions during and afterwards.'

'Frankly I would look at the funding issue as an opportunity. Instead of continuing along in a linear fashion you can jump ahead to a new hot topic. Have you told many people you were turned down? I would be inclined to turn it on its head—let it be known you consider you've answered all the big questions in your current area and are looking for a bigger challenge. What you definitely don't want is for people to get the idea you're washed up and have nowhere to go.'

As usual he made some very good points, annoying

as some of them were the same that Bradley had made.

'And if you're looking for a big challenge what could be bigger than climate change?'

'It's a crowded subject.'

'But you have better credentials than most. You're not some young kid coming in with nothing more than good intentions and no real knowledge to contribute, you have a lot of relevant experience, you just want to apply it in a new way.'

'It does give me a chance to continue that experiment I did a few years back,' she agreed. 'But this 'Village Council' just looks so…flaky. It's not an academic institution, it's just a community with a problem. I don't even know if they have any money.'

Rick shrugged. 'Ask them. Maybe it all falls apart, but maybe it turns out they have some solid ideas and a bit of money. It's not Bradley's million dollar corporate grants, but the PR from a successful engagement with a real community could be huge. I think it's worth a discussion with them, that's all I'm saying. Nothing ventured and all that.'

'You're right, I should keep an open mind. I'll reply.' She put the letter back in her pocket. 'How about you? Anything new?'

'I'm off to that conference in Barcelona next week. You sure you don't want to come with me? It might give you a change of scene to think about new things.'

'No, thanks! Nothing more unromantic than being the woman in your hotel room when your colleagues are around. Do I sit in the room while you go off to the conference dinner, or do you introduce me as your 'colleague' and everyone smirks? Either way I would hate it.'

'I know, I know, it was just a thought. Anyway,

there's that for a week and then a couple more weeks visiting institutions in Europe, so overall I won't see you for a month.'

Lan shrugged. 'Never mind, it'll be nice when I do eventually see you again. Maybe I'll have some conclusions by then.'

She mulled over Aurora Jones's letter for two more days without seeing any major downside. Taken at face value it was an interesting and challenging project, the risks were manageable as long as they kept her involvement confidential until she was sure it was going to work. She suspected the folks on Echelon probably felt the same way.

When she eventually sent Aurora her cautiously positive response she therefore wasn't expecting much to come out of it, probably a couple of phone calls to establish further details followed by a polite withdrawal. She didn't suspect for a minute that she had just taken a life-changing action.

CHAPTER 10

Carbon Credit

By the time Lan stepped off the ferry and into the ramshackle terminal building at Edenshaw two weeks later she had had three lengthy phone conversations with Aurora. On each occasion she had started the call with the firm intention of politely declining the project, and each time she found herself drawn in further by the challenge of seeing whether there could be a simple human fix to this biggest of human problems.

Another factor was that she was increasingly intrigued by Aurora's passion for this small outpost of civilization—the more Aurora talked about these wild tree-cloaked islands, their ancient history and the eagles slowly soaring amongst their mist-shrouded peaks, the more engaged she felt and the more curious to see them and to help them. She'd even become curious about Aurora herself, unsure whether she was white or First Nation; her guess was the latter, but then the smiling white-haired Caucasian woman holding a piece of paper with her name on it put her right.

'Dr Renouf, I presume?'

Aurora welcomed her with a hug, perhaps a little over-enthusiastically given that they were meeting for the first time, and offered to help her with her bag, which Lan politely declined.

'My house is just up the street, so I thought we could walk while I tell you a bit about Edenshaw,' Aurora continued. 'Plus I don't actually have a car.'

'Good for you. I'm guessing folks around here don't exactly have a long commute!' she smiled.

Although Lan had not been to the Echelon Islands before she had sailed past them some years before and had stopped at quite a few similar northwest fishing harbours in her thirty years of fieldwork. It was late October and gloomy weather but she immediately felt at ease with the familiar slightly run-down houses and potholed roads. Nothing ostentatious here, none of the chain stores or restaurants she was used to in Montreal, just practical things. One supermarket, one garage, the post office, a Dollarama, a launderette and a paint store (the last two both closed), and a few houses that seemed to have small businesses in them, a hairdresser and a clothes repair place. It was all very quiet—once the handful of trucks and cars that had come off the ferry had driven off the only noise was the dull vibration of the ferry's engine. For a city-dweller the most noticeable thing about Edenshaw was the quietness and the absence of activity.

As they walked down the street Aurora cheerfully explained the village history as they went. 'That house with the green roof is probably the oldest building here, no one really knows, but we think it dates from the early twentieth century. Of course the roof has been replaced numerous times and the walls have been repaired too, but there are some original beams in it with nice traditional carvings.'

She waved to a woman on the other side of the road. 'That's Elsie, you might meet her tonight. Poor woman, her son killed himself last year. They say it was a drug overdose, but he knew what he was doing if you ask me. Strange boy. Should have seen it coming; he used to torment cats.' She pointed to an area further down the street. 'All these buildings were built after the second world war, but there's been a community here for at least five hundred years. People living on these islands for probably over ten thousand.'

They had stopped in front of a house set a few metres back from the street, one of the few two-storey houses in Edenshaw and with a large greenhouse attached to the front which on closer inspection contained the withered remains of a few tomato plants. 'This is my place,' said Aurora. 'You'll be staying here the next three days.'

Inside, the rooms were clean and tidy in an old-fashioned sort of way, floral wallpaper and a few too many knick-knacks and paintings for Lan's taste, rather like an antiquated B&B. The furniture was solid, comfortably predating the modern flat-pack stuff she was used to. A red setter was asleep on an old but comfortable-looking sofa. Hearing Aurora enter he opened one eye and idly wagged his tale. There were a surprising number of books, not just novels but a lot of biographies and non-fiction. Evidently she had a thirst for knowledge—then Lan remembered that Aurora had mentioned that she was a schoolteacher before she had retired.

'You have a nice place,' said Lan, sincerely. She realized she was tired from the long journey—a five hour flight, then fifteen hours on an overnight ferry. 'I like the view, must be nice in the mornings. You get the sunrise in this room?'

Aurora seemed appreciative and invited her to take

a seat. 'When it's not overcast,' she smiled, 'but on good days yes, you get the sunrise and then the sun a lot of the day. I like sitting out there, I use it as a sort of conservatory, it's bright and warm. Good for aged joints.'

Lan nodded, looking around the room, which was fairly basic in terms of furniture but nicely decorated with a few paintings, presumably reproductions, mostly abstracts by the likes of Kandinsky, and some Lawren Harris, the Canadian landscape painter. 'What are the winters like? No snow, I assume? Just lots of rain?'

'Dark by four-thirty, short gloomy days. Won't be long now.'

'And you've been here how long?'

'Seventy-two winters, apart from three spent in Montreal back in the sixties.' Aurora smiled. 'Winter is a bad time for depression, not for me particularly but for the local kids. The village has a fifty percent unemployment rate…' She didn't bother to complete her sentence, the social problems of indigenous communities were well known, even to city folk.

'Anyway, this evening around six we'll go over to the community centre for the public meeting where the Mayor, Saul Davidson, will introduce you and chair the meeting. The idea is for you to explain how an ocean fertilization project might work, what's involved and how likely it is to be successful, and then take questions.' She hesitated. 'I should warn you that people are a bit divided on the topic; one or two are nervous about the legality of it, and others probably have unrealistic expectations.'

Lan smiled. 'That sounds fine. Obviously I will be honest and realistic with people, but it's a bit of a balancing act. I definitely want to avoid giving people the impression that this is a sure-fire thing, but if I were to be coldly scientific and say the chances it will work perfectly are no more than ten percent then that might be overly pessimistic and kill the whole project. So I'll aim for 'optimistic realism' if that's okay with you—play it by ear.'

Aurora nodded. 'That sounds perfect.'

'It'll be just the villagers there tonight, right?'

'Yes.'

'Good, because I would suggest we avoid unnecessary outside publicity at least for the first phase until the fertilization is actually done. Don't want to make a big splash about it and then have some embarrassing failure. There are also potential legal issues as you mentioned and while I am fairly sure we can do this in a way that is all above board, the Council could face some difficult questions if the wrong people got to hear about it too soon.'

'Perfect,' replied Aurora. 'I don't know if any of this is going to work, either the project itself or even persuading the rest of the Council—and I appreciate from our conversations that it's more likely to fail than succeed—but we have to try it. This community is falling apart because of the lack of salmon; our whole economy was based on it. No salmon means no fishing fleet, no cannery, no tourists, no jobs.'

She leaned forward. 'I'm just asking you to help me convince the others to try it, and then afterwards to help us avoid dumb mistakes—do things at the right time of year and in the right place, that sort of thing.'

Lan nodded in agreement. 'Absolutely, and I wouldn't be here if I didn't think there was a reasonable chance it could work. I'm glad we're on the same page.'

She wandered over to the fireplace to look more closely at one of the abstract landscapes, tree-covered mountains across a stretch of water glistening in the sun. 'I love Lawren Harris, there's something really special about them, isn't there?'

She stepped forward to take a closer look. 'Oh! I thought this was a reproduction but it's an oil. So who's it by?'

'Lawren Harris.'

Lan looked confused, and peered again at the painting. 'But…this is an original oil.'

'That's right,' replied Aurora hesitantly. 'He painted in oils. It's of the view across the bay from a little way down the beach.'

Lan spun around, open-eyed. 'This is an *original* Lawren Harris?!'

'Yes.'

'But it must be worth a fortune!'

Aurora sighed. 'You're probably right. I've not had it valued, but I'm guessing one or two million. It's smaller than most of his works so wouldn't fetch top dollar, but too much for me to afford the insurance, that's for sure.'

'It's not insured?!' Lan looked flabbergasted.

'Well no, that would probably cost a fortune in itself, especially since I have no security on the house—we don't lock our front doors around here.' She looked bemused as Lan continued to stare at her. 'You're actually the first person in thirty or forty years to have realized what it is. I don't think anyone else on the island even knows *who* he was.' Lan continued to look astonished. 'There are two more upstairs in my bedroom if you're interested.'

'*What?!!* But…how?'

'How are they here?' Aurora laughed, amused by Lan's incredulity. 'Well, Mr Harris stayed here one summer in the early fifties. He came to Esh to paint with another of the Group of Seven, Mr…Jackson. I was only eight at the time, but the two of them rented a room from my parents for a couple of months and they would go off painting every morning, and I would tag along sometimes.'

By now Lan was more fascinated than incredulous. 'You actually met him?'

'Oh yes, I remember him well. He was very nice to me, he used to explain what he was doing sometimes. Anyway, when they left he gave each of us a painting. That one is mine, and the two upstairs were my mom and dad's.'

Lan was smiling and shaking her head in disbelief. 'But you know they're worth millions, you could, I don't know, sell them and buy a mansion in Vancouver or somewhere.'

'Vancouver? I'd only get a small condo for them there,' laughed Aurora. 'I take your point, but first of all I don't want to live anywhere else, and secondly I really do like all three of them, so selling them would be counter-productive.'

'Do the—I don't know—the art world, the people that catalogue Harris works, know about them?'

Aurora frowned. 'I doubt it.' She looked at Lan. 'And I'd prefer to keep it that way, I don't want people asking questions. Or stealing them. So now you have to swear to keep this to yourself.'

'Sure…yes, I guess so.'

'Seriously. I don't want to get burgled. It has to stay a secret.'

Lan looked her in the eye. 'Don't worry. Hard

though it will be I won't tell a soul, promise.' She shook her head in amazement.

Aurora got up to put some coffee on and for a minute there was silence.

'Do you have children?' asked Lan, changing the subject.

There was a pause while Aurora put water in the coffee-maker. 'Once, a long time ago. But I lost her.'

'Oh?'

'I'm sorry, I don't want to talk about it. How about you?'

Lan felt embarrassed that she'd inadvertently touched on what was obviously a delicate subject, although she was curious what Aurora meant by 'lost'. Not really her business though.

'No, no children.'

'Husband?'

'Not one of those either. I'm not very good at compromises, if you know what I mean.'

Aurora murmured sympathetically. They were turning out to have more in common than she'd expected.

- - -

In the afternoon they went for a longer walk around Edenshaw for a couple of hours and talked about Lan's work, the surprising viciousness of university politics, and places in Montreal that Aurora had known that were now mostly redeveloped. Finally after another round of coffee they set off on the fifteen minute walk to the community centre just as the sun was beginning to set.

Several dozen people were already there, including Gaia and Wolf who embraced Aurora and introduced themselves to Lan, and Saul and Johnny who welcomed her and thanked her for coming such a long way. To Aurora's relief she couldn't see Charles Abbott or his wife.

The audience seemed to be a good-natured bunch so once the meeting was called to order and she had been introduced, Lan relaxed and got into the mechanics of how the project would work right away.

'The idea of the project is to increase the salmon population by seeding the ocean in one of the areas where the migrating salmon pass through. What we actually do is spray iron sulphate into a large ocean circulation called an eddy, a sort of slow-moving whirlpool a couple of hundred kilometres across. That keeps it in one place so that it can be effective instead of just getting dispersed, and we try and pick an eddy that is drifting towards Esh.'

She looked at a sea of concentrating faces. 'The iron sulphate boosts the plankton which in turn boosts the number of smaller fish, which provide food for the salmon. The idea is that this will result in larger numbers of healthier salmon, which should will mean there are more available to return to their breeding grounds, and hence more salmon in Esh's rivers.'

There was a polite round of applause, as though she had performed a small magic trick.

'You'll notice I said 'should' several times,' she smiled. 'I want to emphasize that we only have control over one part of this process—the iron seeding. The rest is up to Mother Nature. There are a lot of things which are out of our control, so for example we could successfully make a plankton bloom but the salmon who pass through it are returning somewhere further up the coast, or for a dozen other reasons it doesn't work. We could go to all this effort and merely end up fattening American salmon on their way home to Alaska instead.'

There were a few sniggers at the last comment as Lan continued. 'However, I do believe that the strategy the Council is considering has a fair chance of success. I just want you to be aware that it's not a sure-fire thing.' She looked around the room, some faces optimistic and others blank. 'We may do this three or four times and nothing happens. Or maybe it works the first time. But if I were you, given the lack of other options and the severity of the impact of the lack of salmon, I do think it's worth doing given the large potential upside and modest cost.'

One of the First Nation Council members raised his hand. 'There's something I don't get here. Why doesn't the government do it? They say they have a climate change policy and that it's a big priority for them. Surely it's something they should be doing?'

Lan smiled. 'The government? They focus on the bigger picture, which is to say reducing carbon dioxide emissions, not dealing with the consequences such as reduced salmon numbers. So their climate change initiatives are targeted at national issues like retiring coal-powered power stations, promoting renewables, getting cities to switch to LED streetlights, that sort of thing. All worthwhile things but much longer-term and not of any help to you or your salmon I'm afraid.'

Johnny stood up. 'I own the two boats that we would most likely be using. Obviously I want to see the revitalization of the village too, but I'm also a businessman so I can only afford to do this if it pays. Can you give us a better idea of what's the ROI going to be?'

Lan frowned. 'ROI?'

'Return on investment. You're supposed to be the consultant, shouldn't you know that?' he mocked.

'Not my department,' fired back Lan. 'The Council will need to cost up the project as well as its potential benefits in terms of additional salmon, and then decide whether it's worth it. If this goes ahead my main role will be to tell you how many tons of iron sulphate you'll need to deliver where and when, and then to monitor formation of the bloom. I will do the science and you folks do the implementation. As for the 'return' in terms of increased salmon catch, that's hard to quantify. If I were you I would assume a best-case scenario of a return to the type of catch you used to have, but also consider a couple of less-good cases.'

Johnny made an impatient gesture. 'What I am asking is how much extra fish we're going to get, so we can decide whether it's worth doing.'

Lan shrugged, irritated. 'I could make up a number but it would only be a guess. Best case scenario you get back to where you used to be no more, after all you're limited to fish that were born in Esh rivers in the first place. Worst case nothing extra. Most likely scenario, somewhere in between. But, I would suggest you don't get too hung up over exact numbers because that's not really a helpful way to look at something like this. Given how serious the consequences of not having salmon have been on the way of life for the village, and the lack of any alternatives, I think you should consider whether you want the assurance of knowing you did everything you could, and not get too hung up on exactly what percentage improvement in salmon numbers you might see.'

Aurora stood up quickly before Johnny could

respond. 'Let's get this in perspective folks. As Lan says this whole project is a last resort. We heard our MP tell us a few weeks ago that nothing they are doing will help bring our salmon back. So we're already a hundred percent sure that as things stand the situation won't improve, in fact it will most likely just get steadily worse as each year there are fewer salmon laying eggs. As a result our village is dying and our kids have to move away to find work, and eventually there will just be old folks left here, a dying village. But if we try this project with Dr Renouf then there is at least a chance that we can attract the salmon back and our kids will have a life. So we shouldn't be trying to approach this like a conventional business decision—it's a last resort, literally the last chance that our kids can have a future of good employment staying in Esh.'

Johnny looked as though he was about to respond, but then thought better of it and sat down and crossed his arms instead.

There was a murmuring amongst the group, so Saul took the chance to raise the concern about legality.

'A very good point,' smiled Lan, 'I was meaning to mention that. Obviously there are laws about what you can dump in the ocean, mostly aimed at preventing pollution by washing out oil tanks at sea or dumping toxic rubbish and that sort of thing. It's debatable whether iron sulphate would be considered a pollutant in that sense because not only is it a nutrient but it quickly breaks down in the food chain, so I am confident this project would not damage the environment—but having said that iron fertilization of the oceans was banned by the International Maritime Organization in 2008 *except* where it is done as part of a scientific research program. So either you could just do it and rely on a lawyer to argue that it isn't a pollutant, or if you want to be totally safe then we should frame this project as a research program. It's like the Japanese claiming that their whaling is always 'research'. Longer term, if you were to be repeating this every year there might be some other issues, but that's really getting ahead of ourselves.'

Saul still looked concerned. 'What about funding? Do you think we can we get the government to pay for it?'

Lan grimaced. 'Honestly, I think that would be a push. Historically the government has been reluctant to fund any kind of climate change related research, and although there's now funds from the Carbon Tax they seem to be spending that mainly on public transport, things that will reduce the number of cars on the road.'

'Oh,' said Saul looking surprised. 'That's a big problem. We can't afford to pay for this ourselves.' He sat back, as though he was washing his hands of the matter.

'You mean you'd prefer someone else did,' commented Aurora. Saul scowled.

Lan looked hesitant. 'Actually I've been thinking about that too and there might be a financial solution. In fact if the project is successful you could even make money out of it.' She paused. 'Boosting the salmon population is not the only outcome of this project, the plankton bloom created will also absorb a significant amount of carbon dioxide gas from the atmosphere as it grows. The reason that's relevant is that some people will pay good money for carbon dioxide taken out of the atmosphere. Simply put, companies which produce CO2—big polluting factories and the like—buy what they call 'carbon credits' from projects which remove

CO_2 from the atmosphere. Usually that means forestry projects and the like where they grow trees specifically to absorb carbon dioxide, but in principle this is exactly the same—although for reasons I won't bore you with this technique would be hopelessly inefficient as a way of permanently removing CO_2 from the atmosphere, but technically it would still qualify as a carbon capture scheme.'

Lan looked at the blank faces in front of her. 'Essentially you could sell carbon credits for the project based on how much extra carbon dioxide is absorbed by the ocean. You probably wouldn't be able to do that until after the project is completed and we have worked out how much was actually absorbed, but at a wild guess it should be possible to get your costs covered and with luck you might even make a profit.'

A broad smile developed across Saul's face. Aurora knew that this was exactly the kind of financial angle that Saul loved. He nodded his agreement, and others watched approvingly.

'So we might actually *make* money from it?' he grinned.

'Sure. You'd need to do some extra work in terms of measuring the impact and it would probably take a couple of years to get it properly accredited and so on, but if you could get to a stage where you did this on a regular basis and were able to show CO_2 absorption as a result then there's no reason why not. And that would apply even if it had failed to boost salmon numbers, so there's much less risk to it.'

'And you could show us how to get accredited and all that?' pressed Saul.

'Absolutely, I can show you how to apply. That bit's easy, it's just paperwork.'

There was a pause as Saul absorbed the idea and looked towards Zeb who indicated his support with a faint nod.

'So are we going to do this?' asked Gaia after a few seconds, catching the mood of the room. 'Seems to me that we have nothing to lose, and just doing nothing now we know there's a possible solution is no longer an option, right?'

Saul stood up to take control of the meeting again. 'I agree it sounds very encouraging. Let's have a show of hands. All in favour?' Most of the room put their hands up. 'Against?' No one.

'In that case I think the Council has the village's approval to take it to the next stage. Tomorrow morning we will look at our boats with Dr Renouf and see if they are suitable for this.'

As the meeting broke up and people pushed back their chairs Lan could feel the obligations on her tightening. It would be hard to back out now.

CHAPTER 11

Skin in The Game

Johnny sat alone in the dark on the aft deck of *Raven*, the older of his two fishing boats. It was the first one he'd owned outright and the one he'd spent most time on and had the best memories of. He crumpled an empty can of Canadian and reached for another from one of the lockers.

He was annoyed with himself for having been so negative during the meeting. He knew he had come across as being rude when most people clearly supported the project, but the truth was he didn't want it to succeed. He didn't want to go back to the days when the entire village smelled of fish. He hated fish. He resented the fact that despite his best efforts, fishing was all he'd achieved in life. Above all, he dreaded the idea that his children would have only one career choice, fishing.

It was a mild night for so late in the year and he leaned back on a pile of tarpaulins and looked up at the stars. It was a clear moonless night full of stars. Time was when his own ambitions had been up there in the heavens but marriage and kids had brought him down to earth, helping his dad on the boats and his other businesses. Despite a couple of years working on an oil rig in Alberta there had never been any real prospect of his leaving Esh and doing something else, and while Angie had been alive he'd never wanted to. Everything he wanted in life had been right here on Esh.

Then that day fifteen years ago when she had been taken from him, and taken so needlessly, killed by a falling crate of frozen fish when visiting the fish processing plant. The irony was she wasn't even working there anymore, she'd quit a couple of weeks before and was only there to pick up her last pay. He'd been angry about it for a long time, the injustice of it all. He'd looked at suing them, not for the money but to close them down—he'd just wanted revenge, pure and simple. But then the American owners had closed it anyway due to lack of business and half the village had lost their jobs, and his anger and energy for the matter had faded.

With two small children to care for life had changed immediately, not that he would have had it any other way. With Angie gone they were the only people he cared for or wanted to be with. In retrospect it hadn't hurt him financially, in fact on the contrary it had forced him to stop going away on the boats so much himself and be the boss instead, to order others around and to be ruthless and business-like about it, no time to be 'nice'. That was when he'd bought the second boat, unusual in Esh. Back then the fishing was still good though, not like now.

His son had been in Vancouver now for a while getting some life experience, but Julie was only nineteen and he worried about how best to set her up in life, to have a better life than could traditionally be had in Esh. She was intelligent and he desperately wanted her to go to college, to see more of the world than this backwater, but it was clear from their recent discussion that she didn't want to. He couldn't help thinking that if her mother were still around she would have found a way to persuade her, that he was letting her down. In a way he was pleased that she'd shown interest in her own business, but did it have to be in Esh? She didn't seem to be doing anything about it though, just swanning about the place, sneaking smokes around the back of the house with that dopey girl Aiyana when she thought he wasn't watching.

Mind you, he wasn't doing much better really. Nothing like as successful as his father with his hotel and three shops, as well as a boat. It bothered him that he kept making comparisons, although of course things were different when Saul had been his age. As far as he could figure he'd paid almost nothing for the hotel, just taken it over from the receivers, so it probably hadn't been that much of a financial risk for him. He knew for a fact that it had lain empty for five years before Saul had gotten involved. Which reminded him, he should talk with Saul about it again; most likely he was going to inherit it eventually as Julie had said, in which case he should get more involved in its running.

Above him two shooting stars streaked across the heavens a split second apart, as though one were chasing the other. Johnny smiled. It reminded him of the old legend about two sisters who liked to watch the stars and one night were carried up by an eagle and a raven and became shooting stars themselves. He liked the old legends and wished he knew more of them.

Of course what he really wanted was for Julie to grow up like Dr Renouf, a well-paid professional with a proper job. Lan was obviously méti, a mix of white and Native, and he wondered where from. With a French name like that she was probably born out east so one of the Quebec nations, Algonquin or Huron maybe. He shuffled to find a more comfortable spot and sipped his beer.

Maybe he was looking at this wrong. If he helped Dr Renouf then maybe she could inspire Julie by showing her what she might achieve, what sort of options she might have in the wider world. She seemed a decent person and if she was going to be here for a while he had a chance to get to know her. Who knows, it might go further, she was a pretty good looking woman after all. Bit of a temper on her though. Must get that from the French side.

- - -

Two hundred metres away, as unaware of Johnny's presence as he was of hers, Lan sheltered against a large log washed up against the high-tide mark and watched the same pair of shooting stars. 'What's the chance of two meteors so close together?' she thought, before realizing that they must have been one rock that had split into two, circling the sun together as a pair for thousands of years before burning up in Earth's atmosphere a split second apart. So nothing really special but romantic in their own way.

She wished she had had a partner so faithful. Any partner actually. Rick didn't really count, there was no mutual commitment there, just a lustful friendship. What did they used to call it? Friends with benefits. She was past fifty now and despite her bravado she increasingly wanted someone to look after her who didn't insist on keeping his own apartment. It wasn't as though she hadn't had offers, and she knew exactly why none of them had worked out—her impatience. She had a low boredom threshold and easily lost patience with people, a character flaw which in the classroom merely got her low ratings from her students but in her personal relationships tended to be rather more terminal. A psychologist had once told her—as he broke up with her—that it was probably an inherited trait, one of only a handful of occasions she wished she knew more about her biological parents. Perhaps he was right and one of them had had a short fuse, but as he had also pointed out, that should be no excuse for not trying to work on her shortcomings herself.

No chance of confronting her bad tempered mother or father though, finding them had proved to be impossible. She had been born in a hospital in Montreal and immediately given up for adoption, all records sealed. Lan knew that she was mixed blood—that much was obvious simply from her appearance and something she had easily confirmed with a DNA test, but that's as far as she'd been able to get. The only tantalizing clue was that her adoptive mother had told her that it was her biological mother who had named her Langara and requested that it not be changed. It was a Spanish surname, so she presumed she was the product of a Spanish mother and First Nation father. Or maybe the other way around and Langara was her father's name? Just to confuse matters, in addition to being a surname it was also Spanish slang for someone who is vague or unreliable, a slippery character, so perhaps it was a comment by the mother on the father; there was no longer any way of knowing. Eventually, getting nowhere, she'd made a conscious effort to not let her past dominate her future and stopped searching.

Oddly enough the thing she missed most about not

knowing her real parents was their not knowing of her professional success. Somewhere out there were two people who would surely have been proud of her. Mind you that might be about to change if she didn't sort out some alternative funding for her research soon. When Aurora had first approached her she had hoped that the unusual nature of the project might take her career in a refreshingly new and unpredictable direction, but the more involved she got the less likely she thought it was going to work out. It was human nature to be optimistic, but logic told her it was a long-shot.

She also now regretted suggesting that the project be framed as a research project. Although her reasons made sense it meant she would have to be a public part of it at some point. Now all she could think of was the damage it would cause her if it got out that she had been helping with what was, in truth, an unscientific and largely unmonitored experiment. The more she thought about it she'd much rather her involvement remained secret, at least until they knew whether it was a success or not.

On the other hand Esh itself had had a surprising impact on her, it was a place she immediately felt comfortable and related to. Its isolation had the unexpected effect of making her feel relieved of all responsibility—although it had mobile phone coverage it wasn't great and she had decided to leave her phone off since she arrived, and would tell anyone who asked later that she hadn't been able to get a signal. She hadn't actually told anyone specifically where she was going, only that she was away for a few days and probably couldn't read emails. Above all she enjoyed Esh's deep silence, the slow pace of life and the way the mountains across the bay appeared and disappeared in the clouds. The whole appearance of the place could change quite dramatically in a few minutes, from sparkling blue water with mountains beyond, to a melancholy grey sky where you couldn't see them at all. Sometimes the pines would rustle and seem alive with animal spirits, and sometimes they provided an enigmatic *Twin Peaks* aura to the village. The village itself had its moods too, busy when the ferry came in, but a cosy hamlet with warm lights on and smoke curling from the chimneys in the early evening.

As for the people, she still hadn't figured Aurora out yet. Obviously she was passionate about the future of her community and was the driving force behind this project, but sometimes in an oddly detached way. Whilst she was warm and friendly with almost everyone, at the meeting she'd also noticed she seemed to keep many of them at arm's length too. Almost as if she didn't want to get involved in their problems too much.

Her commitment and sincerity were not in doubt though, something she wasn't sure she could say about all of the others. Saul and Zeb were unknown quantities and she didn't know where their allegiances really lay, whether genuinely for the greater good of the community or just to enrich themselves. Her gut feeling was the latter, that they had found some way of profiting from it or thought that they would. Johnny was a loose cannon; shame because he was quite engaging in some ways, but she felt uncomfortable about entrusting the success of the project to such a prima donna, assuming he was going to be the one to run the boat operations and actual fertilization as he'd claimed. All in all she just wasn't sure how much she could rely on them if this really went all the way and became a high-profile project that her future career depended upon.

What had she been thinking? Was it too late to back out?

- - -

Further along the coast from Johnny and in the opposite direction from Lan, Zeb and five friends were engrossed in their weekly poker game. It was an unashamedly macho affair run in the workshop at the back of the garage, lit by a couple of industrial strip lights and surrounded by vehicle engines in various stages of disassembly. Zeb was drinking rye from a dirty glass and telling two of them who had missed it about the village meeting with Lan.

'She's a university professor from Montreal that Aurora found. She seems quite practical, actually had what sounds like a smart idea about how to pay for it all.' He tried to explain what carbon credits were but stopped abruptly when he realized he didn't understand it himself. 'Anyway, the general idea is that if we measure the impact of the project we can sell some kind of tax credits to polluting companies on the mainland and get our costs covered.'

'So a legalized con, basically,' commented one. Zeb grinned and nodded.

'But that would all go to the village council, right? Not get shared out?'

'They'd use it to cover the costs of the iron and the boats, yes.'

'So to Saul and his son then? And you maybe?'

Zeb shrugged non-committally. 'My guess is that the iron powder is going to be the main cost and Saul and Johnny will just get their fuel covered. Not sure any of the boats are going to be good enough anyway, they're going to have a look tomorrow. No one's making money on this my friend—the only benefit, if it works, would be for the whole village by bringing the salmon back.'

He played another card and for a moment there was silence as the others focused on their response.

'Sounds like Saul's got this one sewn up, as usual,' complained another.

'You got a boat they can use?' replied Zeb. 'You're welcome to offer it and get paid for it. But there's not much that's needed. Buy some iron sulphate, put it on a boat, throw it over the side. How many people do you need for that?'

'You reckon this is going to work then?' asked the first questioner, leaning in to place a card. 'Or is it just a make-work project?'

'The professor says there's no guarantees. Well, she was a bit more negative than that I guess to be honest. Said she wouldn't put money on it. Just too many unknowns—where the salmon are, which way they're headed, that sort of thing. But she did say that if she were us she'd do the project, given that we haven't much to lose and the present situation being what it is.'

'Hmm, I wouldn't mind putting some money on it myself. Just to have some skin in the game, if we can't participate any other way.' He hesitated. 'You going to run a book on it, Zeb?'

Zeb leaned back and sipped his whisky. 'Hadn't thought. Which way would you want to bet?'

'On it working of course! Play the long shot. Put down fifty or maybe a C-note.' A couple of the others nodded their interest.

'I ain't running a book if you're all betting the same way, I could lose my shirt on that.'

The first man put his cards down on the table and looked Zeb in the eye. 'But you could do if you talked to one of the big bookmakers in Gastown, couldn't you? They take bets on anything. People bet on what the grain harvest is going to be like, we could bet on the salmon harvest. Don't need to tell them Saul and Johnny might be helping it along.'

Now everyone had paused and were resting their cards, the topic of betting being more interesting than the game.

'Yeah,' replied Zeb slowly, thinking. 'I could do that.'

'That way there would be something in this for everyone,' justified one of the others. 'It would be more fair, wouldn't it?'

Zeb nodded. 'Let's keep this quiet for a bit. I'll make some calls tomorrow, see what I can do.'

After a couple of iterations the terms of the bet were agreed a few days later. To avoid the very real prospect of the wager being invalidated by news of the experiment getting out Zeb had made the bookkeeper aware of it, but describing it more as a wild experiment that was unlikely to succeed. The bookmaker's condition was that the salmon migration, as certified by Fisheries and Oceans Canada's published monthly numbers, would have to be at least ten times the previous year. For that and a minimum bet of twenty thousand dollars he was willing to offer odds of fifty to one. They'd done their research and there had never been a year where the official salmon migration had increased by ten times in a single year anywhere on the west coast, the best had been three times, and that only following one particularly bad year.

By the end of the month half the men of the village had wagered an average of a hundred dollars on a positive outcome, a few had put in even more. Zeb was surprised by the demand, it was almost as if the high minimum insisted on by the bookie had motivated people with the larger potential gains. He couldn't remember so many betting on anything before since he'd run a sweepstake on a race between two porcupines they had found under Saul's house one spring.

Almost the entire village had skin in the game now. Collectively they had a million dollars at stake.

CHAPTER 12

Old Ways

The morning after the village meeting found Johnny, Saul, Aurora and Lan peering into the black emptiness of the hold of the *Raven*. It was an overcast day and everyone seemed slightly on edge, as though none of them really wanted to be there. Lan wondered if, like her, Johnny hadn't expected the project to get this far.

Like the other two boats, *Raven* was a fifteen-metre trawler designed to haul a purse seine net up to three hundred metres long to encircle shoals of fish, traditionally salmon although these days they mainly went after the more plentiful lingcod and herring. All they could see of the hold was a ladder extending down into the gloom to a glistening wet floor five or six metres below. There was an overpowering smell of fish and Aurora wondered how anyone could work in such an enclosed space without gagging.

'She can hold twenty tons of fish down there, so we should be able to transport the same weight of iron sulphate,' said Johnny.

Lan was shielding her eyes, trying to make out details of the dark interior. 'Is this hold watertight? We'll need to mix the iron sulphate powder and get it into solution before you pump it overboard.'

Johnny and Saul looked at one another. 'Of course it's bloody watertight! But if you think I'm filling it with water you can think again!' replied Johnny irritably.

'It might get rid of the smell,' muttered Lan. 'No, I'm thinking you could just fill the bottom metre or so with water, then tip sacks of sulphate in, let the motion of the boat mix it up, and use a pump to pump it out and over the side. Pump in more seawater and make it a continuous process.'

Saul looked at her incredulously. 'That's never going to work. Have you ever actually been on a boat woman, or just read about them in books?'

If she was upset by Saul's sarcasm Lan serenely ignored it. 'Believe me it would work. You fill this thing with fish, they're just as heavy as water. It won't sink. Think of it as ballast.'

'Oh for Christ's sake! You'll be suggesting the boy cuts a hole in the bottom of the boat to let the bloody stuff out next!'

'Calm down,' urged Aurora, putting a hand on his arm. She'd known Saul all her life and she could never be quite sure what would set him off. 'We're all trying to achieve the same thing here. Trust me, Lan's spent years on research vessels in her career, she just has a different approach to things than we do. We're simply brainstorming ideas for how best to get this stuff into the sea and we'll decide together.'

Saul shrugged and walked away, looking out over the water.

Lan looked annoyed. 'I guess you could install some kind of tank inside the hold, but you'll never get the volume and it'll take a lot longer.'

'Just tell me what amount you need and where you need it, and leave me to think about how to mix it and get it into the sea. Okay?' replied Johnny. What was it about this woman that wound him up?

Aurora looked at Johnny and Lan. She felt like she was back in the classroom. The two of them were bickering like a pair of siblings.

Lan raised her hands in mock defence. 'Perfect! This shouldn't be that difficult, it's not rocket science. Anyway, if each boat can hold twenty tons and we need about a hundred in total, so we'll need five boats. Do you have five boats?'

'I have two, Zeb has another, Saul has one but that one's a bit old. Not sure we'd want to risk taking her that far out with her engine, or that we could find enough crew for all four,' grunted Johnny. 'We could make two trips. It takes about a day to get three hundred kilometres out, so we could make two drops two or three days apart. Or if we send the boats out one at a time twenty-four hours apart I guess you could make a continuous operation—depends how quickly it takes to dissolve and pump out twenty tons of this stuff I guess.'

Lan shook her head firmly. 'No, it all has to go in at once. You'll need to find two more boats.'

Johnny remembered his resolution of the night before and resisted his instinct to argue. He couldn't see what possible difference a couple of days would make on something like this. Didn't she know how big the Pacific Ocean was? Whatever they did was a drop in the bucket, in fact less than a drop in many, many buckets. Out of sight of land and the Pacific was limitless. It would be like pissing into the Niagara Falls.

'Sure,' he conceded, 'I can bring in a couple more boats. Just increases the external cost that's all.' And I'll make sure I get a cut on hiring them too, he thought to himself.

They progressed through the rest of the vessel, Lan inspecting his bridge, aft deck and engine and pronouncing them fit for purpose, although not before highlighting scope for improved maintenance and a number of legal requirements. Johnny bit his lip and nodded sullenly while ignoring all of it.

While Lan found fault with Johnny's boat Aurora wandered over to make peace with Saul. He wasn't a bad guy really, just had a tendency to flare up. The good thing was that he cooled down quickly too. He smiled sheepishly as she came over to lean on the guardrail next to him.

'I heard about you finding that girl on the beach,' he said sympathetically. 'She was in my bar the afternoon before, seemed nice enough. They say it was an accident? Fell through the landing dock over at the old cannery?'

'Yeah, that's pretty much it. George Harrison found the spot apparently.' She looked out across the water. 'So why was she in your bar? Asking questions?'

Saul shrugged. 'Oh nothing special. She was in after lunch, wanted something to eat, ordered a pizza and a coffee. She was telling me why she thought her grandmother might have been from Esh. She was asking if I knew anyone called Judith living here in the thirties or forties who left the island. We had a bit of a chat and he left.'

Saul glanced at her. 'Anyway, I told her I didn't remember anyone of that name back then, so I gave her your name actually, I thought you might know more than me about that sort of thing.'

Aurora looked at him strangely. 'You gave her my name?'

‘Yeah,’ he looked a bit bashful. ‘I didn’t think you’d mind. I wrote it on the back of a beer mat for her.’

Aurora shook her head and laughed. ‘That explains it!’

‘What?’

‘When we found the body Alan was looking through her wallet for ID and found that beer mat. We couldn’t for the life of us think how she had my name on her. It was just uncanny that she would have the name of the person who found her body in her wallet, that’s all. Like she could foretell her own destiny or something.’

Saul chuckled. ‘Yeah, I can imagine! Sorry if it gave you a fright.’

Aurora shook her head in disbelief. She had never been much of one for the supernatural, but this had stretched her beliefs a bit. There was a logical explanation for everything after all.

\- - -

As they walked back to Aurora’s place afterwards, Lan sulking and looking at the ground thoughtfully, they ran into Edwin Reid and his son Edward. Edwin was walking slowly and using a stick, Edward was carrying his shopping.

‘You been looking at Johnny’s boat,’ the old man stated, smiling but vaguely accusingly. ‘You going to use it for this bring-back-the-salmon project?’

‘Yes Edwin, that’s right,’ Aurora replied, and introduced Lan and her potential role in the project.

‘I don’t pretend to understand all this science,’ said Edwin after listening carefully, ‘but you must do it with respect for the salmon. Our people have lived in harmony with the salmon for generations, but some folk don't treat them with enough respect anymore and they've gone elsewhere. People need to respect the old ways more.'

Aurora half-expected Lan to ridicule his non-scientific beliefs, but to her surprise she was sympathetic. 'The world is out of balance these days Edwin, that's for sure. Too much carbon dioxide, too much warm weather. You've noticed that, haven't you?'

'Oh yes, the seasons get earlier. Bears don't have long enough to sleep in the winter anymore so they wake up grumpy. The sea is warmer and that confuses the fish too—probably they're going further north where its colder. Then the seals and the eagles don't get enough fish.' He shook his white head slowly. 'It's a goddamn mess.'

Lan smiled at Edward, patiently standing there with two bags of vegetables. He looked different than most of the villagers, more like a city dweller, his skin not darkened by working outdoors, a thinner frame. He had a kind face, smiling eyes.

'But this ain't the first time they've left us,' continued the old man. 'When I was a boy we had a cold spell when the summers were always cool and no salmon came here then either. And when our people first came here there were no salmon at all—we had to go and ask the salmon people to send them here.' He said it as though he knew the people who'd paddled to the horizon to meet the chief of the Salmon People personally.

'I can tell you the legend later,' commented Aurora, not wanting to burden Lan with another of Edwin's long-winded legend-telling sessions.

'Actually I'd like to hear it from Edwin, if he has

time,' replied Lan, putting her hand on his arm in encouragement. 'Why don't we sit on the harbour wall and you can tell me? Would you mind if I borrowed your dad for a few minutes, Edward?'

'Not at all. There's a lot of interesting stuff in the legends, and quite a bit has been borne out by the archaeologists now too. Dad, I'm going to take these things home and see you there, okay? Some of its frozen, I need to get it into the freezer.'

Edwin shrugged reluctantly as though he had no choice and allowed Lan to take him by the arm, and then spent twenty minutes explaining some of the island's myths as pertaining to salmon, to which Lan listened avidly, much to Aurora's surprise.

When they eventually left Lan still seemed fascinated by Edwin's tales. 'When you think about it, it's astonishing that any kind of oral history could have lasted this long. Humans have been living on Esh for around ten thousand years, so those stories probably have their origins tens of centuries ago as people attempted to rationalize what they saw around them. Stories like the one about the sea being lower and the islands being joined to the mainland have their basis in fact for sure, so you have to wonder whether the ones about the origins of the salmon are too. The numbers have obviously varied in the past, I expect stories like that are an attempt to explain to themselves why the salmon were not always there.'

'Please tell me you're not going to drop the project and suggest we scatter fish bones instead,' Aurora smirked.

'Of course not, ' laughed Lan. 'But I do wonder whether we shouldn't ask Edwin to bless the boats when they go out,' she added, perfectly seriously. 'I mean, it couldn't hurt, could it?'

- - -

Back at the house Lan wandered around the comfortably cluttered living room while Aurora made tea. She was admiring the Lawren Harris painting again when she noticed that behind the sofa there were three more oils on canvases, this time unframed. She pulled them out and held the first one up—it was a similar style, a snow-covered landscape with bright coloured vegetation. At that moment Aurora walked back into the room.

'Ah, you've found my stash,' she smiled.

'Please don't tell me these are more priceless Harrises.'

Aurora pulled a face. 'Er, no, not really. Those are more like Jacksons. He has a somewhat different style, not so abstract.'

Lan's eyes widened. 'But even so, just stuffed down the back of the sofa?'

'They're not worth so much.'

'Genuine Group of Seven paintings? Are you kidding me!'

Aurora put down a tray of tea and biscuits and hesitated before replying. 'Those are just in Jackson's style, they aren't genuine. I did those myself.'

Seeing Lan look confused she continued. 'When Harris and Jackson spent the summer here I would watch quite closely how they painted things, and sometimes in the evenings they'd even give me little lessons. So I got interested in it and after they'd left that summer my father continued to encourage me. Anyway, a few years ago I picked it up again and I found myself naturally painting in that same slightly abstract style they had.' She handed Lan a mug of tea. 'I did a few seascapes that I was pleased with, and for a while that was it. But then one year I had a lot of expenses repairing this place, it needed a new roof, and I was kind of desperate for cash.'

She turned away and looked out of the window and shrugged. 'So…I did one on an old piece of canvas I found and signed it A.Y.Jackson, all in capitals the same way he did, took it to Seattle with some of the photos I had of Harris and Jackson staying at the house, and told them it was a family heirloom. They put it in an auction and three months later I had a cheque for four hundred thousand for it. Americans are so gullible. Paid for the roof though. Paid for a lot of people's roofs actually.'

Lan laughed. 'Serious? Good for you!'

Aurora looked a little relieved that she didn't disapprove. 'I've done it twice since, once when I wanted to spend a year travelling and once when there was a child here who was ill with leukaemia and they were raising money for his treatment. But I think any more and someone would get wise to me, so I've reluctantly 'retired'.'

Lan shook her head slowly in disbelief, smiling. 'Well as long as the buyers were happy with their paintings. Sounds like the money went to a good cause.'

'Teachers out here aren't well paid. Besides, I never actually lied, believe it or not. I just told them the story about those gentlemen staying with us all those years ago, presented the painting, said I'd found it in the attic, and let them draw their own conclusions.'

They moved through to the greenhouse and sat on a couple of camping chairs that had been left there.

Despite it being an overcast afternoon it was relatively warm under the glass and Duncan padded through and lay down in front of Aurora. After laughing about Aurora's questionable past Lan looked more serious as though something was bothering her.

'You seemed a bit out of sorts today. Getting cold feet?'

'I'm not exactly thrilled by Johnny's attitude, that's for sure. The man's a dinosaur. This project needs careful planning and preparation, all the more because we're having to make the best of the boats we've got available rather than properly equipped research vessels, but he won't listen to me or try anything new. He's a bit of a cowboy and we risk having a failure on our hands if he tries to take short cuts. I can just see that on the day he'll make some random decision out there that none of us will know about until afterwards and which will put everything in jeopardy.'

Aurora nodded. 'He's a bit pig-headed I grant you that, but he is the captain of his ship. He has the right to take decisions out at sea, and it's hard for you or me to advise when we're not there.'

'It's weird, there's just something about him that makes me want to slap him!' sighed Lan. 'I can see he's a decent man and he's trying to be helpful, but…he just winds me up. As I said this morning, this really isn't rocket science. The difficult part will be deciding the best place and time to inject the iron, but I need to know I can rely on him to do exactly what I tell him, not to come back later saying he decided to drop it somewhere else that was more expedient.' She looked out to sea. 'But maybe I'm being too much of a perfectionist about it. It's not like we have a high probability of success anyway. This is more like a trial run really. If we manage to make a decent plankton bloom and it drifts towards Esh that would be a good start.'

For a minute they drank their tea and were lost in their own separate thoughts. It was an overcast day but the sun room was beautifully warm.

'Talking of low probabilities, how do you feel about mankind's ability to tackle global warming overall? Will these international agreements save the day? Or are we just kidding ourselves?' asked Aurora.

'Oh we're screwed, no question about it!' replied Lan cheerfully and without hesitation. 'I mean you—and probably even I—won't personally suffer the worst of the consequences, but there's no question that the planet is going to end up four or even six degrees warmer by the end of the century. This two degrees limit that they're all talking about staying below is just a delusion. Carbon dioxide takes over a hundred years to be removed naturally from the atmosphere so even if we were able to magically stop all CO2 emissions tomorrow what's already up there will keep heating up the planet for the best part of a century, taking the world's climate well beyond two degrees.'

Aurora was a bit startled. 'That's a bit pessimistic, isn't it?'

'I'm a realist.'

'But I thought world governments had all committed to keeping it below two?'

Lan sighed. 'They have, but our track record on actually *meeting* the emissions targets is terrible. Almost all countries have consistently failed to achieve their targets. The models show that to actually prevent global warming from passing the two degree limit—above which life starts to get really unpleasant—we would all have to cut carbon dioxide emissions by ninety percent *and* remove a good chunk of what's already in the atmosphere, all within a few decades. The Paris Agreement calls for a hundred percent reduction but it allows countries *eighty years* to get there, and with no plan at all for removing the existing carbon dioxide. Frankly it's just well-meant hot air—they're steps in the right direction alright, but not nearly enough and far too slowly. The only ones who really get the urgency are some of the younger generation, people like that Swedish schoolgirl. She's absolutely right, it's an emergency, but Governments just treat it like it's another trade issue, to be negotiated with everyone's national interests front and centre. They're not seeing the big picture.'

'But at least they're agreed on where they have to get to. Maybe they'll speed up as they get into it?'

'Maybe, but those are just targets, numbers on a piece of paper. There are also projections for each country based on emissions to date and the policies they've actually implemented, and those are generally showing they'll miss the targets by miles. Canada committed to a thirty percent reduction by 2030 but is actually projecting more than a ten percent increase, and we're not the only ones going in the wrong direction. You can't help thinking that most governments are not really trying, either that or they're just really bad at actually achieving them. Personally I think it shows they're still not taking the threat seriously. If they were they'd be trying a lot harder. There's simply no sense of urgency.'

'Surely they understand the urgency though? They're not idiots, they're going to suffer too.'

Lan laughed cynically. 'Ah but you're forgetting the

human factor. It's one thing for scientists to say 'we need to cut emissions to zero by mid-century and remove what we've already put up there', but to actually do that would kill half the planet, literally.'

Aurora looked puzzled.

'Think about it. To achieve what's needed in the timeframe required would mean shutting down many things that are essential to human welfare, such as coal-fired power stations, desalination plants which are mostly gas-fired, lots of polluting factories and industrial processes which people rely on for jobs—there's a long list. In the developed world you'd be looking at things like banning gasoline-powered vehicles altogether, severely limiting air travel, forcing people to live in compact communities where heating can be optimized, even restricting the type of food people ate—it would be a vegetarian diet for all because beef production is a major contributor to CO2 and methane production—major, major things which would have a huge impact on people's lifestyle and personal freedom.'

'Hmm, they're not going to buy that are they?'

'Nope, not at all. It would mean mass migration and starvation in developing countries, and in the developed ones it would lead to civil unrest or worse. You just can't do it, literally. Any government which tried to implement such severe measures would be thrown out long before they actually managed to do so. Only authoritarian cultures where the population is already accustomed to limited personal freedom and putting the common good above that of the individual are likely to make any progress, which is one reason why China is now leading the world on actually implementing climate change initiatives.'

'I didn't even realize they were,' sighed Aurora. She sighed heavily. 'Well, this is becoming a bit of a heavy conversation.'

'Hey, you started it!'

'True. But I see your point. People assume that governments can control the outcome but lack the will to do so, but in reality they actually have very little power to do anything drastic without risking social meltdown. So that puts the burden on individuals, or at least those who are able to take action to modify their lifestyles to use less energy—whether it's taking the bus to work, going on fewer foreign holidays, or eating less beef, but how many people will do that? Not many, which means not much impact on CO2 levels.'

'But that's what you're trying to do here with the salmon experiment—doing something that will directly offset the impact of climate change without waiting on the government or asking them to pay for it. If it works it will more than pay for itself through the increased salmon catch for the whole community.'

Aurora nodded. 'You make it sound very altruistic.'

'Well, it is. You're unusual in doing something which is not purely short-term and reactive, something that requires some investment of time and money to get a better result later. That's one of the things that attracts me to this whole venture.'

'What child psychologists call delayed gratification,' smiled Aurora.

'Of course the stuff that governments do is still worthwhile—I don't personally think it will be enough but at least the problem won't be as bad as it might have been. Perhaps we'll end up three degrees warmer instead of six, and only a few hundred million people displaced by droughts and rising seas instead of a billion, but what they really ought to be doing is accepting that a +2C world is a likely scenario and planning for it. They should be thinking about relocating food production to areas which will have the right climate in the future, building new cities away from coastal zones that are going to disappear beneath the waves, that sort of thing. Any rational US government would ban all further development in coastal cities like Miami for example, because we already know without any doubt that in twenty or thirty years it will either be underwater or require vast amounts of public money fighting a losing battle with sea defences.'

'You try telling that to the voters in Florida!'

'Yeah, they're all in denial, we all are. Most people are too busy just trying to get by in life to really think about it, they have more immediate problems. I mean, I totally get it—I don't think I'd be willing to voluntarily have a massive reduction in my quality of life just in the hope that it would allow more people to have a better existence in fifty or a hundred years' time.'

She sighed. 'There's too many people on the planet anyway, maybe we'd all be better off if the food and water shortages of a +2C world resulted in a smaller but less hungry population. Honestly, if humans don't manage to fix the problem then that will most likely be Mother Earth's solution; high CO2 levels will lead to crop failure, mass starvation and disease, which will cull the population and reduce CO2 production—the hard way.'

CHAPTER 13

Misdirection

By the time Lan returned to Montreal the following evening they had agreed on a plan. Aurora would find a supplier for the iron sulphate and look into how they could recover their costs by selling carbon credits. Johnny would figure out a way of dissolving and pumping it. Lan would identify a suitable location to spray it when the north Pacific eddies began forming in June or July the following summer. To support the pretence that it was a research project Gaia would monitor numbers of salmon on a daily basis once the project started. They had seven months to make it all happen.

To avoid tempting fate they agreed to try and keep the project out of the public eye. Aurora would order the iron sulphate in small quantities from different suppliers and if anyone asked where the boats were headed Johnny would say he was 'just fishing'. The village council and the majority of villagers were united behind them, mostly out of frustration after Michael Malik's visit. Ironically the government had made the biggest contribution after all—his inability to give them any assurance that the government was tackling the issue of dwindling salmon numbers had united them and energized the villagers into action.

Charles Abbott was the only vocal opponent, and although he was aware the project was on the cards the others were careful to keep him in the dark on the details, or even to confirm that it was definitely going ahead. Whenever he cornered Aurora in the supermarket and asked how it was going she just said sadly that the more they looked into it, the more challenges they faced. Which was true, they just weren't insuperable challenges.

Back in Montreal Lan immersed herself in the more immediate problem of securing funding for her research. Her staff teaching position at the university was in no immediate danger and if it came to the worst then she could spend the last ten years of her career doing that, but that wasn't something she found particularly satisfying. She would much rather be discovering new things than regurgitating existing knowledge through lectures. So she wrote funding proposals about everything and anything that interested her to every domestic and international body she could find. After a decade of working in the same specialised field she found it exhilarating to come up with new ideas to investigate. Maybe Bradley had been right all along, damn him.

The salmon project was a different kettle of fish however. As the weeks went by she found herself questioning it more and more—not so much the people, she liked Aurora and admired her dedication to finding a solution for the long term future of her community—but the risk to her career. She'd looked into it more and unfortunately there was no question that dumping a hundred tons of chemicals into the sea would be unlawful unless it was done within the context of a bone fide research program, however that would require a lot more than just sticking a label on it which said 'in the name of science'. It would mean peer-reviewed proposals, approvals by scientific bodies, properly calibrated measurements, writing reports, and the group in Esh simply didn't have the money or equipment. She would have to take a visible role to ensure it could be classified as research and avoid any legal issues.

The more she thought about it, the more she became convinced that she could not be part of the project. Even the normally risk-taking Rick had to agree that it was starting to look foolhardy given the inevitability of her role eventually becoming known. Yet she also understood why those in Esh felt they had to do it, slim though the chances were—there was no other option for trying to bring their salmon back. It was a dilemma. Eventually in December she called Aurora.

'Hi there. It's Lan.'

Aurora could tell right away that something was wrong.

'Hi. You sound like you've had a bad day. What's up?'

Lan laughed. 'Oh dear, you're getting to know me too well. You're right, it's not been a very good week.' She went on to explain about what she termed her crisis of faith about the project and her inescapable conclusion. 'I just don't think I can continue to be a part of this Aurora, but at the same time if I were you there's no question I would go ahead.'

Aurora paused before answering. She'd got so far with this, didn't want it to fall apart now. 'I'm sorry you feel that way, but I see your point and of course we wouldn't want to do anything to endanger your career. We really appreciate what you've done for us so far.' She hesitated again. 'Look, we're going to do this anyway, *I'm* going to do this anyway. How about…how about if you were to just let us know when and where to dump the iron? You could just phone me and let me know where and when, no record, no one will ever be able to connect you to the project. Would you be able to do that for us?'

Lan didn't see why not. She had daily access to the necessary satellite imagery of the northwest Pacific anyway, all that was required was for her to discretely give Aurora a call when she saw the right pattern emerging. And not undermining the project eased her guilt.

'Sure, I can do that for you. I'd be glad to, Aurora.'

They chatted a bit longer before hanging up. Both wanted to stay on good terms and didn't want any awkwardness over the project to ruin their friendship.

\- - -

For Aurora it was a significant setback but not a terminal one. She would keep Lan's departure from the project secret from the others, obviously. Keeping Johnny and Saul onboard still required her constant encouragement, but the prospect of making money out of it remained a strong motivating factor for them. So without Lan's involvement there was no research angle and the whole concept of selling carbon credits was a non-starter, hence if they knew that Lan was no longer involved then she was sure they would back out. She just needed a way to keep Lan in the background, to channel any contact through herself so they didn't get to speak with her directly, at least until the fertilization itself and their involvement in the project was done. That was half a year away though, a long time to keep up a pretence... She was still mulling over how that might be possible when she saw Johnny in the supermarket later that afternoon.

'Hey Aurora, just the person I was coming to see,' he said, as he joined her in the fresh vegetable section.

Perishable goods only arrived in Esh every Thursday afternoon on the ferry, so after the weekend they were starting to get down to the bruised and misshapen ones. Aurora was trying to find two apples that didn't look like they'd been found at the side of the road.

'I've been trying a few ways of dissolving sacks of salt in the hold without a whole lot of success and wanted to talk to Lan about it. Have you got a phone number for her?'

'Hmm, I do,' replied Aurora smoothly, 'but it's not going to help you much I'm afraid. I just had an email from her to say she's on a survey vessel for the next couple of months. In…the Antarctic of all places, can you imagine?'

'She's on a boat?'

'Yes, that's what oceanographers do Johnny. They go on boats. On the ocean.'

Johnny looked surprised. 'Yes, I guess so. Funny, when she was checking out the *Raven* I just assumed she hadn't been on one before. I mean, not a working one.'

'Oh, she's been on lots. I know you were a bit sceptical about her being too academic but she was telling me that last year was the first year in ages that she'd not spent her entire summer working on a survey vessel. And they're long trips, over a month at a time.

She probably has more days on boats than you do!'

Johnny raised his eyebrows. 'Oh…the Antarctic eh? No mobile phone coverage then?'

'I'm afraid not, that's what she emailed me to say. But you can always email her.'

He looked disappointed. 'It's going to be difficult to do this project if we can't talk to her.'

'I thought you didn't really appreciate her suggestions?' smiled Aurora.

'Yeah, well, not all of them that's for sure. But we still have to work together.'

'She's really very good at what she does Johnny. We wouldn't know where to put this stuff without her. Even if she is a bit…inaccessible.'

'I guess email will have to do then,' replied Johnny and pulled out his phone to write down the address.

'Ah, I don't have it with me. But I can text it to you as soon as I get home if that's okay?'

As soon as Johnny had left she finished up her shopping and hurried home. It had been a while since she'd created an email account from scratch, but within an hour she had made one in Lan's name, created a suitable signature and an out-of-office message saying that she was currently doing fieldwork and would reply to the email as soon as she could. Then she texted the address to Johnny and waited.

It was a few hours until she heard a 'bing' from her laptop and sat down to read Johnny's email.

```
Hi Lan
As agreed I have done some tests on using the forward hold as a mixing tank for the iron powder (I used salt since we don't have any iron sulphate yet). The extra ballast of having water at the bottom of the hold is OK, but two
```

problems. 1) My cargo hold is not as water-tight as I thought, and some water is leaking into the hull. That could be fixed with a bit of work. 2) A bigger problem is that getting the salt to dissolve takes too long. Even with the movement of the boat in choppy seas the salt just piles up at the bottom. Probably can't get more than a couple of 25 kilo sacks dissolved per hour. So not looking good. Any ideas?
Johnny Davidson
PS: What's the Antarctic like?'

At least he'd kept his word and tried Lan's suggestion, that was a start. As she reflected on his email she realized that not having Lan involved in the day-to-day operation was going to have its advantages. Lan had more or less admitted to Aurora that she'd been too fussy in her demands on how to do the experiment itself, so it wouldn't hurt to remove a few unnecessary hurdles for Johnny.

Aurora resisted the urge to reply right away and waited three days before responding.

Hello Johnny,
Thanks for trying, it looks like pre-dissolving the iron sulphate is not going to work on your boat. On the research vessels I'm used to working with we have 5000 litre tanks with motorized mixers, so much easier. For this experiment to work we will need to spray 100T of iron within a few days, that's 4000 x 25 kg sacks, so we will have to give up that idea. My concern on dumping the powder straight into the sea was that it would sink too fast and not dissolve properly, but probably it would be OK. So my apologies – I think if you just slit the sacks and pour overboard (downwind) it will be

fine. Probably best to wear breathing masks to avoid inhaling though.
Cheers, Lan.
PS: Antarctic is warm! It's summer here. We are monitoring some icebergs
PPS: I won't say anything about your leaky hold! ☺

Aurora hoped that the light-hearted postscripts would help improve the fractious relationship between the two of them, although the chances of them ever meeting again looked remote at this point. Johnny replied almost immediately. He was evidently in a good mood.

LOL!! Don't tell my Dad about the hold! Maybe that's why our catch is not what it was—the fish are escaping ☺ Whole boat leaks to tell the truth.

She restrained herself from replying. The secret to maintaining a good lie was not to overdo it.

- - -

When Aurora saw Johnny in the street a couple of days later she couldn't resist asking him if he had managed to contact Lan, but when she got closer saw that he was annoyed about something.

'You okay?'

He grimaced. 'It's that daughter of mine, giving me ulcers over her future…'

'Julie? I remember her, she could have gone to uni that one. Not many of them could.'

'And she doesn't want to! Can you believe it? We had another argument about it last week, I was trying to convince her to enrol for classes in Vancouver and get some qualifications before it's too late, but she just wants to stay in Esh and try and run her own business. It makes me so mad, I don't want her to be stuck here all her life, and I don't want her to pass up the chance and then find out later she hasn't got any other options. But she's adamant about it… What can I do, eh?'

Aurora remembered Julie as intelligent but shy, in tenth grade the year she'd retired. At the time she had encouraged her to think about university but she'd obviously not gone since she saw her working at the Co-op sometimes. She was exactly the sort of girl who should be able to make something of her life outside of Esh if she wanted to though, rather than being stuck behind a checkout.

'For what it's worth I think you're doing the right thing to encourage her, don't give up,' she reassured him. 'Kids can get very set in their ways though, the more you push her the more she's likely to resist. Maybe give it a rest for a few weeks? By the way, did you manage to contact Lan?'

'Yeah, I had a couple of emails with her.' He looked a bit distant. 'We have a problem. I tried her idea of using the forward hold as a mixing tank and it just doesn't work, it leaks too much and anyway doesn't dissolve quick enough. But she's insistent it has to be dissolved before its sprayed into the ocean, so to be honest I can't see a way forward at the moment.'

Aurora looked at him. She knew he was lying, which meant he had some other reason for not wanting to go ahead. Laziness perhaps. Or resentment. He had been upset when it became clear that without any government grants there was no up-front money for paying commercial rates for the boat leases, but she thought he was past that. It wasn't as though he was likely to have a better offer for the boat—he'd told her that last summer he had only used it for fishing about one week a month.

'I see,' she replied slowly. 'It would be a real shame to give up on the whole project just for that. Maybe she can be convinced to agree to just emptying the sacks over the side? I mean, can it really make that much difference? There's not really any other option is there?'

Johnny shrugged. 'Not that I can see, but she's pretty adamant about it.'

'Maybe I should email her myself, see if she can't be persuaded,' smiled Aurora, watching Johnny's face. From the fleeting look of alarm she could see he hadn't quite thought this through.

'Well, she didn't entirely close the door on it. Actually she said some things I didn't fully understand. Let me have another couple of emails with her first,' he replied quickly.

It was clear though that he still wanted to try and find a good reason why the project couldn't work, or at least with his participation.

They were about to part when Aurora put her hand on his arm.

'Johnny, I have a proposition for you. This project is important to me, and you are crucial to making it happen—without your boats we can't do it. Your daughter is important to you. If you promise to make this work one way or another then I promise to do my best to convince Julie to go to university. She might have left school but she's still a teenager so she's at the stage of doing the exact opposite of what her dad tells her, but she might just listen to me.'

He looked surprised. 'You think you can talk some

sense into her? I can't even talk with her anymore about it. She just gets angry every time I raise it.'

Aurora shrugged. 'I can't give you any guarantees, but she will listen to me in a different way than you. I'm not her father and I won't get emotional or angry with her, I will just tell her what her career options will be with and without a university education, and obviously there are a lot more doors open if she gets a degree. Just promise me you will try and make this project work. I think you'll find Lan is more accommodating than you expect.'

Johnny looked relieved and for a moment Aurora thought was going to hug her. 'We've missed the window for this year, but if you can get her to at least think seriously about enrolling next year that would be fantastic. Like you say, right now she's just closed her mind to it. Even if she realized she'd made a mistake she's probably unable to admit it.'

'Have you discussed what she would study?'

'We never got that far, and to be fair she has said that one of the reasons she doesn't want to go is that she doesn't know what to study. I've been pushing her toward accountancy, but she says she's not got a head for maths.'

Aurora nodded. 'If she doesn't even know what to do that's likely to be a big part of the problem. I can talk to her about what kind of jobs might be open to her and what subjects she'd need.'

He shook her hand with a big grin. 'And I'll work something out with Lan, I promise. We'll make it work one way or another.'

CHAPTER 14

Side Benefits

'I'm not going!' Julie looked both upset and very determined when Aurora opened her door late the following afternoon. 'So there's no point me coming in, right?'

Aurora frowned at her. 'Despite what your dad might have told you, I have no intention of persuading you to do anything you don't want to,' she said firmly. 'So come inside and have some coffee.' She hadn't been a schoolteacher for fifty years without being firm when she needed to be.

After hesitating a moment, Julie reluctantly stepped inside.

'You were one of my smarter students,' continued Aurora, moving towards the kitchen, 'so I am pretty sure that if you don't want to go to university you have a good reason, I'm just interested to hear it. You want a cookie with your coffee?'

Julie nodded and sat down at the kitchen table, looking completely miserable. Aurora had a lot of sympathy for her. She'd been a nice kid, a bit shy but genuine—reluctant to join in group activities or sports, more of a bookworm, someone Aurora related to. If she'd had a daughter she would have been proud if she'd turned out like Julie, and quite apart from her deal with her dad she wanted to help her.

They were standing in the kitchen while Aurora put on the kettle and found the cookies. Julie had not been in her house before and was looking around inquisitively, picking up an international newspaper she found on the table.

'I haven't seen anything other than the local news for ages. Did you get this in Vancouver?'

'That? It's my little luxury, I get it by post once a week. The internet here's so slow it drives me nuts trying to read it online. You can take that one if you want, I've read it. Cream?'

'No thanks.'

'Okay, forget about your dad and university. If you could do anything you wanted what would be your dream job? Or not even job; if you could do anything and be anywhere in the world, what would it be?'

To her surprise Julie didn't hesitate in her reply. 'I want to stay in Esh and run a café right here in Edenshaw. My friend Aiyana wants to do it with me and she's a great cook, we know exactly what we want to do—we just need a place to do it. We really think our community needs somewhere like that, a social hub. Right now there's my granddad's hotel but only older men go there. For anyone in their twenties or thirties there's nothing. We think we can create something really good.'

Aurora handed her her coffee. 'That's actually very impressive. Most people can never decide what they want to do and so never achieve anything. What's your dad got against that?'

Julie hesitated. 'Huh! We had a huge row about it a while back, and then again a few nights ago. He insists there's no future for me in Esh and that I need to go to college and get a degree so I can get a decent job somewhere else—and also that there's no demand for a café here. All I was asking was for him to support me by asking my granddad to use a back room in his hotel but in the end he refused.'

Aurora looked surprised so Julie continued.

'Where do you go for a cup of coffee here? There's nowhere. There's that area at the back of the Co-op selling bad coffee and stale muffins, that's it. Or you can go to the hotel bar and wait for my granddad to finish chatting with his buddies long enough to make you a cup of instant. Imagine if there was a nice place you could sit and have really good coffee and cake, or a small meal or a soup, you'd go there every day, right?'

Aurora nodded. She had a point. Somehow people in Edenshaw just didn't congregate anywhere. Even the hotel bar was not exactly buzzing in the evenings, people tended to socialise at home. None of the big brands like Starbucks or McDonald's had ever set up in Esh because there simply weren't enough people to make it worth their while. There wasn't even a Timmy's. It had been a gastronomic backwater for so long nobody expected anything else.

'Sounds a good idea to me, at least worth trying. You might not make that much money at it but you'd be doing a big public service for sure. Did you talk to Saul?'

'Of course, but he was dead against it too, his ears were blocked the moment I opened my mouth. I'm sure my dad already talked to him although he swears he didn't. They both insist I could achieve much more in Vancouver and there's no future here for me, but that's like abandoning the community and losing my culture completely. I can't imagine anything more horrible. Besides, I'm just not good at that sort of bookwork—I'm good at organizing things but I only just scraped through maths and there's no way I could get through a three year degree course in something like that.'

'At least he wants you to be able to be independent in the world. Most of the dads on Esh just want their daughters to get married and make babies.' They both laughed. 'Okay, so imagine a couple of years down the road and you and Aiyana are running this café. You're doing well and making money, maybe moving to bigger premises, hiring a couple of staff. You'd have to get your food hygiene certification, run a payroll, pay employment benefits, file tax returns. Do you know how to do all that?'

Julie shrugged. 'Not right now, but I'd pick it up. That's just figuring stuff out, I can do that.'

'You don't think you're being a bit limited in your ambitions? Running a café might be enough for now but will it be in ten years?'

'No, of course not. The café is just a first step. What we actually want to do is revive Esh and bring new businesses here. Those luxury fishing lodges for example, we want to see those locally owned and operated—that in itself would make a huge difference to our economy. What we want is for the café to become a catalyst for new local businesses, a place where young people can meet and kick around ideas, not just a place to eat.'

'So if you're going to be trying to start a range of businesses wouldn't they be even more successful if you had some training first?' Seeing Julie frown she quickly added 'Just kicking ideas around here!'

'Well, maybe...but if I was to leave for three years and do all that training, apart from just about killing me with boredom and stress, I'd lose the momentum Aiyana and I have for this right now. I guess the point I was trying to make to my dad was that at some point you just have to jump in and start swimming. Spending three years studying for something when you're not even sure what that something is is not going to work.'

Aurora wandered over to the big window facing the water, sipping her coffee. She could see her point. More than likely she would chuck it in halfway, or city life would eat her up and spit her out. It wasn't easy. Many First Nations girls who moved there ended up on drugs or abused. What her father thought he wanted for her might destroy her instead. And her longer-term plan was hard to fault—who wouldn't want to see a better Esh, one that had a healthy range of businesses and not be dependent on only salmon and logging? She should be encouraging her to broaden her options, not narrow them.

She was still standing by the window that faced into the greenhouse, with its peeling paint and collection of dead plants. She looked at the cracked concrete floor and stained windows—dirty but all intact and water-tight. It had survived the seventy years she'd lived there pretty well and already had power and water…

She turned to Julie. 'I've got a proposition for you. Hear me out before you interrupt.'

Julie nodded.

'How about I help you get your café off the ground? You use this greenhouse on the front of the house as your premises, you're responsible for renovating and painting it, and if you need it I will even loan you some money for equipment and start-up. You and

Aiyana run it for a year and see if its viable and what you really want to do.'

Julie stared at her wide-eyed. 'Are you sure? If you are then I can tell you right now—yes!'

'…but before you get too excited there's one big condition,' Aurora continued. 'Actually two. The first is that you also make a fall-back plan and enrol for some course starting October next year. I don't actually care if you ever attend, the important thing is that you have your name down for something. Then we can tell your dad that you're signed up for the next academic year but in the meantime you'll spend the next twelve months running the café to get business experience, and that you will then get your qualifications while Aiyana continues to run it. But in reality you can decide at the time whether it makes sense—if the café is going well you can decide you don't need it. However if the café doesn't work out then at least you will have a Plan B.'

Julie looked thoughtful. 'But wouldn't I have to commit to it now? I mean choose the subject and everything?'

'Enrolment usually starts around February, so you have a couple of months to think about it. You might want to do Food Science or Hospitality or something instead of Accountancy if that makes more sense for a food business, but it doesn't really matter, you can always cancel. I'm honestly not expecting you to ever go, just to have it as an option.'

Julie grimaced. 'Okay, I guess I can live with that. But I can tell you right now I can't really see a scenario where I'd go through with it.'

'That's just fine, we just need to get your dad off your back by telling him there's a plan, it doesn't really matter what it is.'

'You said two conditions?'

'Yes. The second is much simpler. I need you to make sure your dad doesn't give up on the salmon project. You're right that Esh's future shouldn't have to depend on fish, but boosting their numbers can't hurt, and if we're successful in bringing them back it would pull along a lot of other things like tourism. Anyway, it's important to me—so I need you to do whatever you can to convince him to stick with it.'

'As far as I know he's still planning on doing it, but no problem for me to keep telling him how important it is. I've been telling him the revival of Esh is really important to me so it would make sense.'

'Good! Do you want to take a closer look at the greenhouse now?'

Aurora led her through. It was a large structure about five metres by twenty, originally built by her father, but still in good condition.

'There's water and electricity at that end so I would think if you had a counter you could make a kind of food preparation area there. You'd need tables and chairs and a sign outside, but nothing major. It never gets too cold in here, in fact in the autumn and spring it's very pleasant when it's still cold outside.'

'I think it's a brilliant space,' enthused Julie. 'The location is a lot better than the back room of the hotel actually—much more visible from the road, and to be honest I was worried we'd just be seen as the food part of the bar. This would solve those problems and give us a much better space.' She moved around some of the empty plant pots. 'We could use the fact it's a place designed to grow food to our advantage, maybe decorate it with crates of vegetables, or even have some things actually growing here. I could imagine growing tomatoes up the windows in the summer for shade for example, and then using them as they ripened.'

'It would be good to have it used more. All I do is sit in it some afternoons, it's wasted really. My father mainly used it for tomatoes, but that was a long time ago.'

'But there's one thing I don't understand,' continued Julie. 'Why are you doing this? Why are you helping me? It'll be quite an inconvenience for you.'

Aurora shrugged. 'Believe it or not I want to see Esh flourish again as much as you do, probably more. I can remember it being much more lively than it is now and I have to say I think the idea of a café as a social hub is a brilliant one. Just because we've never had one before and people tend to eat at home doesn't mean that people wouldn't congregate somewhere if there was a nice place. Worth a try anyway.'

She paused. 'Besides, and don't take this the wrong way, but if I'd had a daughter I would have wanted her to be like you. And I will expect endless free coffee.'

'That sounds like a third condition,' grinned Julie. 'But no problem.'

Aurora looked a bit embarrassed. 'Now, all I have to do is sell this whole crazy scheme to your dad. This is the exact opposite of what I promised him but you've convinced me so now I'll just have to convince him.'

- - -

At the same moment his granddaughter was inspecting her new premises Saul was conspiring once again with Zeb.

'So we get reimbursed for use of the boats, that's fine but it's not going to do much more than cover our costs, especially if the real money from this credit scheme doesn't roll in for a year or two. We need to make sure there's a bit more fat on the pig for us here my friend. Leverage, that's the key—how can we leverage this project to our advantage?'

Zeb looked at him blankly. 'What do you mean, leverage?'

'How else can we make money out of this?'

'Get a cut on the iron sulphate?'

'I guess we should have thought of that earlier, but Aurora's already taking care of that. Besides I don't think they'll be much margin to play with on something like that. No, we need something else.'

Zeb took a swig from his beer. 'Not much else that the project needs supplying with, the way it stands today. Stuff to dump and boats to dump from, there's nothing else. Our time, maybe a bit of carrying and ferrying the iron sacks.'

'What about the salmon harvest itself?'

'We should have a head start on everyone else with the nets, but only by a day or two. As soon as they reach the shore everyone will be in there.'

They sat in silence for a while.

'Wagering?'

'Done. Half the village is in at fifty to one. We get ten percent of the bets but that's still only two grand.'

There was further silence until eventually Saul tapped his forefinger on the bar thoughtfully.

'Maybe we're looking at this wrong. We've got blinkers on man!' He paced up and down behind the bar. 'Lan always said that the biggest risk was that no one knew where those salmon would end up right? She said she was confident the iron would make a plankton thing, but it was down to luck where the salmon which fed off it ended up. How about we charge the other communities around here for the salmon that end up with them? There's bound to be a few, and they won't know we didn't send them their way, right?'

'Okay,' said Zeb slowly, 'but that's the point, we don't know where they'll go.'

'How about this. We go—you go—to some of the communities up the coast and tell them what we're doing, but make it sound like we have more control over where the fish end up. They all have the same problem, no fish. Tell them that we're investing all this money to bring the salmon back to Esh next summer, but we're offering them the opportunity to buy into the project by sponsoring some extra iron to get sprayed in the places that will benefit them. Charge five grand each, they'll all be able to afford that.'

Zeb's craggy face broke into a grin. 'There's about a dozen communities up there, that could be fifty grand!'

'Tell them that the key to this is the satellite images and Lan's science stuff, just in case they get ideas about doing it themselves. Tell them we're paying big money to the university for the information on exactly where and when to fertilize the ocean which is why we're looking for partners. Make it sound really high tech. And make sure it's all verbal so they can't sue us; best efforts and all that.'

Saul celebrated his scheme by pouring them both a shot of whisky, and sat down to flesh out the details.

'As I see it there's three ways this could go. Most likely scenario, the whole thing is a bust anyway and nobody gets any extra salmon. In that case we say we did our best, remind them that we never guaranteed anything, and that's the end of it. Second scenario, it works but the salmon end up all over the place and it looks like we knew what we were doing and we have happy investors ready to try again next year. Third scenario, Lan's a lot smarter than we give credit for and it works and the salmon do come mainly to Esh. That's the only bad one for us cos it will look like we swindled them.'

'But how likely is that, eh? I mean it would be a miracle if it actually worked, right?'

Saul shrugged. 'As long as you're careful not to promise too much we should be alright. They'll know it's all a big gamble, and we're not asking so much they can't afford to lose it. Even the smallest villages up there can afford to spend five grand out of their funds without worrying about it.'

'Of course, there's another thing we could do,' added Zeb. 'It's going to take five or six trips so all of us are going to be involved, not just Johnny. On one of those trips I could divert fifty clicks up north and drop a load nearer to the other villages. That should guarantee not everything came back to Esh, in the unlikely event it actually works.'

'Not bad. Yeah, we can do that. Let's just keep it between us though, no need for Johnny to know. I don't want him corrupted,' Saul smirked.

Zeb looked pleased with himself for providing a piece of the puzzle. 'One load here or there isn't going to make any goddamn difference. I mean, 'it's not like this is rocket science', eh?' he laughed, imitating Lan's Montreal accent.

Saul chuckled and downed his whisky in a single gulp.

CHAPTER 15

Haze

As Julie herself was to say later, 'We didn't quite think this through, did we?'

The disruption of having her front room turned into a café was considerably more intrusive than Aurora had expected, not so much the renovation of the greenhouse itself but the use of her kitchen for cleaning and washing up at all hours meant Julie and Aiyana were constantly coming and going through her living room. Duncan hated it. Sometimes Aurora ended up simply going upstairs and reading in her bedroom. She worried whether it had been wise to lend them so much money, but the fact that most of it was being spent on improving her own property was reassuring—worst case, she'd get a renovated greenhouse out of it.

Julie's partner Aiyana turned out to be an intriguing character, markedly different than the other local girls. Aurora remembered her because she'd transferred to the school mid-year and had been a bit of a handful, rebellious. Her mother sounded as though she had been some kind of latter-day hippy. Originally from New Mexico she had found her way to Esh in the early nineties, fallen in with a local boy, and the two of them had then gone to live off-the-grid up the Alaskan coast for a few years, during which time they had had two children. It wasn't clear to Aurora if they had been ostracised by her father's family and forced out, or simply taken themselves off, probably a bit of both—white girls marrying into First Nation families was still fairly rare, even now. Aurora shuddered at the thought of being pregnant and giving birth in a log cabin with no medical support (or epidural) but that's what they'd done. As a result of her 'wildhood' Aiyana spoke several First Nation languages, was impressively efficient with a knife and axe, and most importantly had picked up her parent's love and knowledge of First Nation folklore and cooking. She and Julie appeared to be very compatible as business partners, with Julie's organizational and planning skills complementing Aiyana's artistic ones.

They started on the outside, cleaning all the windows, replacing the cracked panes and sealing the leaks in the roof that Aurora didn't even know she had, then hanging drapes inside the upper part to provide shade and insulation. After some debate it was decided that they could not do any baking in the greenhouse itself, but would use a combination of Julie's house and Aurora's kitchen. Instead they installed a large work area for food preparation plus refrigerators and a coffee machine that they had shipped from Vancouver, the most expensive single item of the entire project. A bonus was that Aurora rarely needed to cook anymore because in between reno work the two of them worked on the menu, inviting her to give her opinion on a range of dishes as they refined their ideas on what Haze was going to be.

Outside, Aiyana repaired the pathway, tidied up the flowerbed and the grass, and put up a large sign two metres wide to announce the name, which had become simply 'Haze'. Inside, to avoid customers feeling too exposed they'd decorated it in a style inspired by the Pacific rim rainforests, with creepers hanging from the roof partially covering the windows and some large strangely shaped bits of driftwood from the beach placed artistically around the room.

On a shelf at the back Aiyana had placed some items from her past that had special meaning for her—a stuffed ocarina tern that she'd inherited from her father, three large round white stones of oriental origin which she termed her 'imaginary skulls', and an anodized mug with a flower painted on it. Aurora was so impressed with the overall look and style of the place that she half-seriously suggested they open a B&B too, just to see what they could do with the rest of the house.

The opening itself was a quiet affair, but business in the coming days was brisk, fuelled by people's curiosity, and Julie and Aiyana were acutely aware of the importance of making a good impression with their food so that they came back a second and third time. They had decided to focus on daytime trade and forget about opening for dinner for the time being, mainly because people in Esh simply weren't in the habit of going out to eat in the evening. Most of their effort went into the breakfasts, which to Julie and Aiyana's delight quickly became the talk of the village. Their poached eggs on sourdough toast with smoked salmon and avocado, cinnamon sugar waffles, and breakfast wraps with bacon, egg and potato proved extremely popular, washed down with excellent fresh coffee.

Julie was aiming to repay Aurora's loan within one year and to thereafter be in a position to pay her rent.

Within a few weeks Haze was covering its costs including a monthly loan repayment to Aurora. Much of its daily business was done before ten in the morning which left Aiyana time to work on new recipes for the lunchtime customers, always including at least one traditional island dish. Although they had targeted locals, after about a month they noticed that some of the crew from the morning ferry had started coming in too. Word was spreading.

- - -

Meanwhile Aurora got down to the business of figuring out a way to pay for the salmon project. The biggest external cost was the iron sulphate itself, which she estimated to be about ten thousand dollars. Otherwise it was the cost of Johnny's and Zeb's boats—they had asked for a commercial day-rate for hire of the boats, but with research funding ruled out the funds to pay them would effectively have to come from their neighbours, half of whom were unemployed, which seemed unfair. Nobody argued about reimbursing them a few hundred bucks for the fuel, but expecting them and their crews to both donate a couple of weeks of their time and potentially lose earnings didn't seem fair either.

Other options such as commercial sponsorship looked even less likely. Asking the Co-op to effectively support increasing the amount of salmon available for free was going to be a tall order, for example. Thanks to Saul's spendthrift nature the Council actually had plenty of money saved up for discretionary spending on facilities to benefit the community, but Saul had been adamant it not be spent on such a speculative project. He was right of course, it was easy to get caught up in the enthusiasm, but the likelihood was that this time next year they would have little to show for it.

On paper the carbon credit route was still the most viable financing option, but the problem was that it was too long term and too risky—they couldn't actually sell any credits until the project was complete and the results certified, which could easily be a year later, probably two. In the meantime they would need to pay for the iron sulphate up front with money they didn't have. Aurora was therefore particularly pleased with the creative solution she came up with, and even more proud of persuading Saul and Johnny to agree to it. There was no question in her mind that without it the entire project would have withered and died.

The deal was that Council would own the rights to the carbon credits that would be created by the project, and in return would invest working capital into the business. The village council would be the majority shareholder and put up twenty thousand dollars, in return for which it would get seventy percent of the shares in the company that they would create to trade the carbon credits. Johnny would get ten percent as payment for his time and usage of his boats, and Saul, Zeb, Lan and Aurora would each get five percent for their participation and work on the project, but without an obligation to put up working capital.

So despite Saul's original insistence that the village not pay for the project, effectively that was exactly what they were doing, but now he could save face by telling people that their money was being invested in a commercial venture and it stayed on the Council's books as an asset, not an expense. Johnny still grumbled that he wasn't getting paid cash, that it all came down to asking him to take a gamble; his shares might be worth nothing, or they might be worth something, but no one could tell him how much. But largely thanks to pressure from Julie he was going along with it anyway. In his mind he had already written it off as a week of his life that he would never get back.

What Aurora could perhaps have made clearer than she did was how tradeable the carbon credits might be. There was a well-established market for carbon credits but they were mostly forestry or biomass projects, where plants were grown specifically to absorb carbon dioxide and turn it into vegetable matter or wood. Without a way of scientifically measuring how much carbon dioxide their project was absorbing the credits were simply not sellable.

The fact that the Echelon Quartet Carbon Offset Company was therefore unlikely to be able to carry out its stated purpose did not bother Aurora one bit however. In her mind the important thing was that they would have the funds to try what everyone agreed was the only possible hope, however remote, of bringing salmon back to Esh, and it seemed quite reasonable to her that the community as a whole, as the main potential beneficiary, should be the one paying for it. It was just better she didn't say so too loudly. They would all thank her in the end…

The day after she had persuaded Saul and the rest of Council of the arrangement and to pass and sign a formal resolution creating the company, she took the day ferry to Vancouver to go to a registry to create a company, and with that to open a bank account. The whole process was beguilingly simple. She could just as easily have registered a charity, opened a bank account, passed a resolution to build homes for displaced polar bears, and asked well-meaning nature-lovers to give her money. Or any other wild scheme really, like companies to exploit Esh's forests, set up tourism ventures, search for gold, maybe a company to bottle pure Esh rainwater… All she needed to start the process was a printed company resolution that she had typed herself.

After a full day's work she caught the overnight ferry back, went to the bar and bought a whisky as a nightcap, and slept the sleep of the just, confident that so far everything had been done completely legally and honestly. Just not particularly transparently.

- - -

That same evening Gaia and Wolf were engaged in an ethics conversation of their own in the cramped living room above the shop.

'It's almost spring and we haven't yet had a single booking for Esh Escapes. We need to think about better ways of attracting people here,' began Wolf.

Gaia made a face. 'But do we actually *want* to? The best way to preserve Esh as it is would be to *not* promote it as a tourist destination.'

Wolf stared at her in bemusement. 'Hon, that's going to be a bit of a problem for a business that's dependent on tourists. The locals don't have much interest in buying wood carvings or souvenirs, and as things stand we're losing money every month. Our whole business strategy was that Escapes would attract the people to Esh, and the shop would then capitalize on that. If we can't persuade people to come here in the first place it all falls apart. We would be better going somewhere else.'

'We can't leave! We're the only ones looking after the wildlife and caring for the environment!'

Wolf raised an eyebrow. 'Really? The flora and fauna have survived here for thousands of years without us. There's virtually no development and most of it's a protected area anyway, so where's the threat?'

'That's not the point,' replied Gaia crossly. 'My heart is here and it's the only lifestyle I can exist in now. Leaving is out of the question.'

There was silence for a few moments as Wolf paced the room.

'In that case we still need to find a better way of attracting people here. Either that or we find some other form of livelihood. Your inheritance isn't going to last much longer.'

Gaia glared at him. She hated to be reminded that their existence on Esh was not, to use one of her favourite words, sustainable.

'Well as long as they're the right kind of people,' she said slowly. 'We want to attract eco-tourists, people who will take care of the place and not pollute or poison the environment. And of course strictly limited numbers...'

'Perhaps we should include a questionnaire about their environmental credentials with the booking form? Check how many species they've saved from extinct-ion, or ask them what their carbon footprint is before we accept their business?' suggested Wolf sarcastically.

'Good idea! We could at least ask them if they've ever done any hunting, if they say yes then we say we're fully booked.'

Wolf rolled his eyes. Sometimes…

'Okay, let's try a different approach. How can we leverage the salmon project to attract more tourists? It's the big event for this coming year that we know is pretty much guaranteed to get TV coverage. We need to have two plans to raise tourist interest on the back of it—one if the project is successful and there's lots of salmon, and one if it fails and there aren't.'

'Okay. So if it works then the message has to be that a small community can accomplish something that the IPCC and the international organizations couldn't,' enthused Gaia. 'Practical steps on a local scale, and encourage other communities to take action everywhere. Local action, global scale.'

'Perhaps a slogan like 'come and help fight climate change for your vacation'?'

'It needs to emphasise that, yes.'

'Not something to do with salmon, perhaps, possibly?'

'Okay, but it needs to tell people *why* there are so many salmon.'

Wolf sighed. 'How about simply publicizing the fact that there's a bumper salmon run? Nice and simple and aimed at the sport salmon fishing crowd?'

'Just as long as they're environmentally conscious fishermen,' added Gaia. 'Strict limits and all that.'

Wolf made some notes, which bore little resemblance to Gaia's comments. 'I can get the TV crews here once the salmon arrive, and also put out the news on Twitter and Facebook or wherever I can. So what about the more likely scenario where the experiment fails and nothing happens? We won't actually have anything to show so it'll be difficult to get media interest.'

Gaia shrugged. 'Then we forget about the salmon aspect and say that the experiment was mainly about removing CO2 from the atmosphere. Say that even though Esh already has just about the lowest carbon footprint on the planet we're still going above and beyond to do our bit.'

'How's that going to attract people?'

'Real environmentalists will be interested to see where it happened, talk to us and learn lessons.'

'Encouraging people who are keen to have a low carbon footprint to fly all the way to Esh just to look at a fishing boat might be a bit…hypocritical.'

'True, and there wouldn't be much to see,' admitted Gaia. 'Perhaps we should just have some publicity to emphasize the unspoiled purity of the place, while also mentioning that it's the site of the first community-based CO2 absorption project?'

Wolf stared at her and eventually wrote the single word 'Purity' on his notepad. Then he crossed it out and wrote 'Talk to Johnny about sport fishing venture'.

- - -

Johnny was emailing Lan again.

Hey Lan
Not sure if you've been talking with Aurora recently so thought I'd give you an update. The council approved creating a company to trade carbon credits to fund the project, so I think she's in the process of ordering the iron sulphate now—then just waiting for your go-ahead. June or July wasn't it?

How's your research trip going? Over here my daughter has agreed to sign up for university next year but in the meantime is setting up a café in Aurora's greenhouse! Still not sure how I feel about it—it's supposed to be temporary for the business experience, but I have a nasty

```
feeling it might become permanent. Maybe when we see you next you could talk to her and tell her about all the doors a university education would open for her?
Cheers, Johnny
```

Aurora didn't see it until she got back from her trip to the mainland, and was unsure how to respond. At some point Johnny and Lan were going to meet again and when they did they would figure out pretty quickly about Johnny's one-sided conversation and who was to blame. That could cause all kinds of problems, which is why Aurora had tried to keep 'Lan's' responses short and factual. She wasn't too pleased with his comment on the café either, given that he'd been quite supportive when she'd explained her agreement with Julie to him. She left it a few days before replying.

```
Johnny, Good to hear you're ready your end. When I get back I will start reviewing satellite images and let you know when a suitable eddy develops, and as you say that's normally in the summer months. Not sure what to advise about your daughter. Lan
```

Aurora hoped to God that the two of them never got to have a social chat. She kicked herself for saying that she was on a trip to the Antarctic, even though it had seemed a smart way of avoiding phone contact. She could just imagine the first conversation they were going to have when they met again. 'How was your trip to Antarctica?' 'What trip?' 'The one you emailed me about' 'What the hell are you talking about?!'

If and when Lan returned, and she hoped she would, she would either need to fess up to Lan or spin her some other yarn. Life was getting complicated.

- - -

Everything was in place now for the salmon experiment. One hundred tons of iron sulphate in twenty-five kilo plastic sacks was now safely in the warehouse attached to Zeb's garage, having been brought over in numerous small truckloads on the ferry. Ever frugal, she'd bought end-lots from various suppliers on the mainland and then had the Manyshots boys hire a truck and go around collecting them, paying cash as they went. None even knew that Esh was the end customer.

Johnny and Zeb were now more wholeheartedly on board and expecting to devote a solid couple of weeks of their time to the actual fertilization sometime in June or July. There was an air of quiet optimism amongst the villagers about the outcome, and even the generally grumpy Saul was upbeat about it.

Aurora would have liked it if Lan had called her more often as she'd enjoyed their discussions, but she reminded herself she couldn't have everything. They would hopefully be starting the experiment itself in a couple of months. Generally speaking life was pretty good.

Then one morning in late spring she received a phone call that changed everything.

CHAPTER 16

Miss Jones Misleads

'Aurora Jones? This is Adam Winter, we met last year when I visited Edenshaw with Michael Malik?'

Aurora recognized the English accent and the unusual name, but struggled for a moment to recall when they'd met. Then she remembered the poor sod who Malik had dropped in it to make the presentation on climate change, and then publicly contradicted him when he had told the truth.

'Mr Winter! This is a surprise.'

'Yes, well, good to talk to you again. Actually the reason I'm calling is that we've had a report that Echelon Village Council are planning some kind of geoengineering experiment to try and boost salmon numbers. I understand you're the Secretary of the Council?'

He didn't sound critical or hostile, and for a moment Aurora wondered whether he was calling to offer support, or even funding. She hesitated before replying. It was documented in the Council's minutes and the local newspaper that the plan had been voted for, so best not lie.

'After your visit we did discuss the possibility of some kind of research project, but nothing has been done about it. Why do you ask?'

Winter suddenly sounded a lot more serious. 'So you can confirm that the Council does not intend to undertake a geoengineering experiment?'

Aurora paused. She needed to be careful what she said. 'No final decision has been taken. We discussed it and took a vote to investigate further, but have not done anything yet.'

'In that case I need to advise you that any form of ocean fertilization or seeding, or disposal of materials of any kind at sea, whether inside or outside the territorial limit, is illegal and we would prosecute if we were to learn that you had done so.'

'Oh, I see. Well thanks for the warning.' She tried to sound casual, even though she was mildly terrified.

The voice on the line sounded exasperated. 'This is a big deal, Miss Jones. It would be a violation of several international maritime treaties if the village council were to go ahead with any form of ocean seeding experiment, and since you've confirmed the Council are considering it we will now be conducting a visit to ensure you comply with the law.'

'Okay, but as I just said, we have no firm plans to do anything, we've merely discussed it. Frankly from what we've learnt so far it would be prohibitively expensive with a low probability of success, so I doubt we ever will, especially since you're telling me it's illegal.' She hesitated. 'But look, Adam, I don't want us to get into trouble here. On behalf of the village council I'd like to say we would be happy to voluntarily submit to an inspection if that would put your mind at rest.'

Winter seemed a bit taken aback. 'The idea is that they're surprise inspections. We don't normally inform the other party when we're coming.'

'Fine,' replied Aurora cheerfully. 'I'm not sure what you'd be wanting to look at since as I said we've not actually done anything, but you're welcome to visit whenever you like.'

Winter hesitated, disarmed by Aurora's cooperative manner. 'Well thank you for the offer and I'll bear it in mind, but as I say we do have a protocol we have to conform to.'

After he'd hung up she wondered who he'd got his information from. It was hard to imagine he was a regular reader of the *Echelon Echo*, and it certainly hadn't been reported anywhere else. The musings of the village council barely counted as newsworthy even inside Edenshaw, let alone further afield. Perhaps Gaia had put something on her blog? It was the sort of thing she might do.

Or maybe it was Charles Abbott? He was the sole person who was strongly against the project, but would he go to the bother of tracking down Winter and telling him? Unlikely. She couldn't even remember if Charles had been at the meeting with Malik and met Winter. For sure he hadn't bothered to attend Lan's talk, she'd expected him to come and had noticed when he didn't show up. Since then Aurora had done her best to give him the impression the project was going nowhere, but she'd better be more careful what she said around him. It was a bit of a mystery.

- - -

One of the benefits of having been the island's principal teacher for such a long period of time was that she knew everyone and all their children, including the ones who had left the island to work on the mainland, who were generally the more motivated ones. After thinking for a few minutes she smiled to herself and relaxed a bit. It was a Tuesday. Winter was based in Ottawa and would therefore need to spend at least a full day travelling to visit Esh, longer if he didn't have the extravagance of hiring a floatplane and had to take the ferry. But either way he'd need to fly into Vancouver. He wouldn't want to use up his weekend flying home, so he would come mid-week. Aurora set out for the post office.

'Hello Maggie,' she said to the lady behind the counter. Maggie Oldman had been working there for years.

'Nice to see you, Aurora. What can I get for you today?'

'Actually, I'm hoping you can save my bacon. I've got the son of an old friend visiting me next week and I've managed to totally lose his details, and I'm too embarrassed to call him to ask again because this is the second time I've done this. Would you believe I had to call him last week, and I wrote it down again somewhere, and then lost it!' She played up the flustered old lady act a bit, looking around her with an air of despair. 'Anyway, I'm pretty sure he said he was coming next week and I need to try and figure out which day he's coming on. I was wondering if your daughter was still working for the airlines and could possibly check for me?'

Maggie beamed, always happy to help. 'Of course. Lizzie is still there and she remembers you well. Often says if it wasn't for you pushing her to take those exams she'd never have got that job. Let me give her a call.'

Aurora waited while Maggie phoned her daughter and explained the situation.

'Well yes, I know you're not supposed to give out passenger names honey,' she whispered. 'But this is for Miss Jones, and she already knows the name. What harm can that do?'

Lizzie evidently relented because Maggie asked for the name, which Aurora had already printed on a scrap of paper.

'Winter, as in the season. Adam. She thinks he's coming next Tuesday or Wednesday into Vancouver and then the ferry from there.' There was a pause while Lizzie checked. 'Oh. Not on those days? Maybe it's the *next* Tuesday or Wednesday?' More waiting. 'A week on Thursday? You're sure? You're a doll, thanks so much! When are you coming over again?' 'Oh, well hopefully the month after then. Anyway must go, talk soon.'

'So not next week but the week after?' asked Aurora, feigning surprise.

'Yes, he's booked a week on Thursday,' smiled Maggie, handing back her piece of paper.

'That's a relief, I was in a bit of a panic trying to get ready for next week. This gives me some extra time. I can't tell you how grateful I am! You thank your daughter properly for me when you see her next!' And with that she was gone, hurrying back down the street. Almost two weeks, that should be no problem at all.

\- - -

On the Sunday Johnny received another email.

```
Hi Johnny. I've got a big favour to ask you. I've managed to get some time on one of our
```

satellites on Thursday, a special high-resolution satellite which can detect our iron sulphate seeding and calibrate both the amount and the response in terms of plankton production. But I only have access to the instruments on that one day! It would however be extremely useful in terms of supporting a claim that the project is 'research'. Would you be able to go out very early that day with a small load, say one ton, to a location about 100 km offshore and deposit the iron? As I say, it would be extremely helpful if you could. Thx, Lan.

PS: How's your daughter doing? I found a course that might be of interest, must share it with you next time I see you.

To Aurora's relief Johnny confirmed his availability and willingness within a few hours, prompting a follow-up email from 'Lan'.

That's great news! Thanks so much. Don't want to tell you how to you crew your boat, but could I suggest your dad and Zeb go along with you on this first attempt, just to get some experience of the seeding process?

Johnny actually found one week's notice a bit tight as far as the loading went, but with the two Manyshots boys and a flatbed truck from Zeb they got forty iron sulphate sacks stowed in *Raven*'s hold by the Tuesday evening. Then he went to see Aurora to let her know what was going on. It was a good opportunity to see how Julie was getting along too, and although he wouldn't encourage Julie by admitting it he was secretly impressed by the professionalism of the café. He bought a coffee and pastry and sat down with Aurora.

'So, I've been talking with Lan and we've decided to do a test run next Thursday. She says it will help her calibrate her satellite response.'

Aurora seemed surprised. 'Oh, I thought she said she wouldn't be ready until June or July?'

'This is just a test,' explained Johnny. 'We'll be dropping one ton a hundred clicks offshore, so probably leaving on the first tide about five in the morning, then back by nightfall.'

'So just yourself and the Manyshots?'

'And dad as well. I thought we'd best have a trial run together. For the main project we'll be using all our boats so a good idea for all of us to give it a go, see how it goes pouring the stuff over the side and any problems.'

'What about Zeb?'

'He's away for the week. Taken his boat north to visit some friends up the coast apparently.'

'Wasn't he away last week too?'

'Yeah. Said he was visiting some relatives I think. Unusual now you mention it. Maybe he doesn't have much work on at the garage.'

Aurora nodded. 'Oh well, fingers crossed then, eh?'

\- - -

On Thursday the morning ferry got in about seven, which just gave Aurora time for breakfast and to then sit in the café to wait Winter's arrival. She was almost tempted to go and loiter by the harbour, but decided not to do anything to arouse his suspicions.

It took Winter an hour to find the café after getting off the ferry. She was just beginning to wonder whether he'd decided to stay the night in Vancouver and then fly up instead of taking the ferry when she saw him standing in the street outside staring at the new Haze sign.

'Miss Jones, someone told me I might find you here!' He was beaming, evidently pleased that he had been able to keep his inspection a surprise.

'Mr Winter! Oh, I didn't really expect you would come.' She tried to be flustered. 'What do you want to inspect? Or have you done it already? Perhaps you'd like a coffee first?'

He smiled. 'Mostly done actually. I've already looked at the two boats in the harbour. Now I want to see where you've stored all that iron sulphate!'

Although he was putting a brave face on it, the truth was that Winter was more than a little pissed-off at even being there. He was a strategy guy, not a bloody site inspector! But MinCC didn't have anyone else, not like London where they'd had a small army of factory inspectors and guys measuring CO2 levels to call on. But he hadn't complained too loudly—it gave him the chance to spend the weekend with a friend in Vancouver afterwards and saved him an expensive airfare.

'Iron what?' She stared at him blankly.

'We know that you've recently purchased a hundred tons of the stuff.'

Aurora laughed. 'A hundred *tons*? Oh come on, you're being ridiculous!'

'We have it on good authority that you did.' She knew he was bluffing, she'd been rigorous in keeping the Council's name out of it as the end buyer, and anyway there was no way he'd been checking sales receipts for the mainland suppliers, far too much work.

'Iron sulphate? The stuff you treat wood with? I do

have some now you mention it, not quite that much though,' she chuckled and led him to the garage at the back of the house and opened the freshly painted wooden doors. It was a wooden double garage, probably originally built back in the fifties, repaired many times. It had not housed a vehicle in decades, but was an Aladdin's cave of junk containing numerous half-used cans of paint, abandoned projects and other things she'd forgotten about laid out on tables and in cupboards. Aurora went to one of the tables and picked up a tin.

'Iron sulphate, bought last month to treat the wood to stop it rotting. I bought twenty tins because it was on special offer, used about ten on this garage and sold the rest to friends.' She picked up a faded invoice lying on the table. 'Here you are—special offer from Canadian Tire on the mainland, nine ninety-five a tin.'

Winter held the invoice and looked at the tin. 'This doesn't prove much, you could have more somewhere else.'

Aurora rolled her eyes and pointed around them. 'Where? If you want to go through all these old paint tins and clean up my garage while you're at it you'd be doing me a favour, go ahead!'

Winter looked at his watch. Aurora knew that the only return ferry today was in two hours' time, and she suspected a city slicker like Winter would not want to be staying overnight. 'Okay, I also wanted to take samples from the boats in the harbour, but the owners were not around. Can you see if you can find them for me?'

They walked together down to the harbour and peered down at Saul and Zeb's boats.

'Let me see if they're around,' said Aurora, and

walked across the street to the hotel. She went inside and asked for a glass of water, drank it slowly and came out again. Out of the corner of her eye she noticed Charles Abbott lurking a hundred metres down the street, watching proceedings. So it *was* him.

'Apparently they're all out fishing today,' she told Winter, shrugging apologetically. 'But I'm sure they won't mind if you look around. I can be your witness if you like.'

With that Winter climbed aboard the *Spirit Bear* and walked around the deck looking at the equipment, and then lifted one of the hatches. Pulling out a torch he gingerly descended the hold ladder, emerging about a minute later.

'Doesn't seem to have been used for anything recently,' he commented.

'I know the fishing has been pretty bad this last year. I've not seen this particular boat go out for months, probably longer.'

Winter climbed back onto the harbour and walked down to Saul's boat, the *Sea Eagle* and repeated his descent into the hold before eventually emerging with a plastic bottle and declaring himself satisfied. There was still an hour and a half until the ferry left but no point risking things by letting him spend time with Abbott, who surely knew about Zeb's warehouse and might guess that the sacks were stored there.

'Anything else you'd like to look at?'

Winter looked defeated, although still suspicious. He must have guessed how easily things could be hidden away on the island.

'No, I guess that's it. For now.' The truth was he felt this just vindicated why it shouldn't have been him that was sent out to check in the first place. He had no idea of where they might have stashed the stuff. For all he knew it could be in some cabin in the woods. They started walking back towards the main street.

'I told you this is a quiet place. Nothing happens here, certainly not grand schemes of the sort you're imagining. Although we did have a death a month or two back. Quite mysterious at the time though, an environmentalist.'

Winter's interest seemed to perk up at the news. 'Yes, I read about that. Judith Altmann wasn't it?'

Aurora nodded. 'I didn't realize she was so well--known.'

'Did they ever figure out how she died?'

'She had an accident while she was wandering around the old cannery a few kilometres down the coast. It looks like she fell through some rotten planking and knocked herself out, then fell into the sea. She washed up along the coast there.' She pointed west.

For a moment Winter seemed lost in thought.

'So just an accident then?'

'Yes, it looks like it.'

'Any idea why she was here?'

Aurora shrugged. She remembered the mysterious document. 'According to her blog she was looking into the decline in our salmon, I guess that's why she was at the cannery. The place is a death trap, falling to bits.'

Winter grunted and looked towards the ferry terminal and then his watch.

'Are you going back on the afternoon ferry?'

He nodded sombrely.

'In that case come back to the café and have that coffee and something to eat then. The food's very good. And there's nowhere else to go really,' and with that she led the way back to Haze, chatting about how good the eggs benedict were and what nice weather it was.

Winter seemed quite despondent when they sat down. He seemed a decent enough guy, she sensed that he wasn't particularly happy in his role as climate cop.

'So what's it like working at the Ministry?'

He shrugged. 'One step forward, two steps back. Sometimes hard to feel we're making much progress to be honest.'

'Sounds frustrating.'

'Yes.'

Aurora smiled. 'But there's plenty of things people can do, recycling their bottles, insulating their lofts, that sort of thing.'

Winter laughed. 'Yeah, I suppose so.'

'You don't think will help?'

He pulled a face. 'Let's just say I think those things have more of a psychological impact than they do on actual emissions.' He looked at her for a moment. 'The big reductions can only come from widespread changes in attitudes to things like eating meat, travelling less, driving electric vehicles… It won't be quick.'

'Human nature. People don't really change, do they?'

Winter sighed. 'Eventually they'll have to. In the meantime, we'll just keep promoting the loft insulation, eh?'

'Sounds like your job is more PR than actually fixing the problem.'

Winter hesitated and then looked at his watch. 'That's just my personal opinion anyway. I think I should be going now after all. I need to write up my report while my memory is fresh.'

Aurora was left with the feeling that he was more

going through the motions than acting out of true conviction. It must be rather like being a priest; even if you had doubts, you can never admit them. Was the Ministry's whole climate battle just for show?

- - -

By the time she deposited him at the ferry terminal an hour later, making sure he got on board without being button-holed by the lurking Charles Abbott, Aurora felt that she had expended more small talk and charm on Mr Winter than she normally needed to in a year. It had been exhausting but worth it—she was pretty sure she'd convinced him that although the village had bullishly talked about the idea, further investigation had convinced them of the practical difficulties of doing it and the hopelessly low chances of success. She deserved a reward and decided to drop by the bottle store to get some wine and ran into a stern Charles Abbott coming out.

'Was that Mr Winter from the Ministry that I saw you with earlier?' he asked brusquely.

Aurora smiled. 'Yes Charles, it was. Why do you ask?'

'I was hoping to have a few words with him,' he shrugged. 'We've had some…communications,' he added pretentiously.

'Ah, I thought you might have,' she smiled sweetly.

Abbott stared at her, realizing he'd been caught out. 'This ridiculous project of yours had to be stopped by someone, don't blame me if your activities fall foul of the authorities.'

Looking at him, Aurora realized he was still furious, but she was genuinely puzzled by why. What was it to him? But climate change was one of those emotive subjects that, even if it was not affecting people directly, seemed to inflame passions one way or the other—like the conspiracy theories about whether man really landed on the moon or who really shot JFK.

'You know, I really don't understand why you think it's so ridiculous, Charles. I agree it might or might not work, but where's the harm in trying?'

'It's the principle! There is no such thing as man-made climate change! It's well known that it's a hoax created by the Chinese to make US manufacturing uncompetitive. Don't you see? The world's not getting warmer, they've just faked the data and created a panic so that western countries put restrictions on our industries to stop them being so productive.' He waved his arms around in agitation. 'Do you honestly see it getting warmer? Where are the goddamn palm trees?!'

For a moment Aurora thought about just walking away, but she was in no hurry and wanted to see whether he could actually defend his nutty views.

'But we're not talking about tens of degrees, just one or two degrees by the end of the century. Even that has been shown to have a big impact on the environment, especially the weather. You must have seen on the news all the extreme weather they've had down in the States, more hurricanes, more flooding…'

Charles was becoming even more agitated. 'Well exactly! Hurricanes! It's the hurricanes that bring the warm weather off the Pacific and cause flooding in Florida. How could it be the other way round?'

'Actually its warmer ocean water that causes hurricanes. And ultimately it's the higher concentration of carbon dioxide in the atmosphere that warms the air and in turn the oceans. That's a fact, you can't dispute it surely? Steadily increasing CO2 concentrations have been measured all over the world for many years.'

Abbott laughed. 'You believe that nonsense? And who gives us the measurements?'

'Scientists.'

'Exactly!' He waved a finger at her. 'Scientists! The most corrupt, money grabbing, self-serving people you'll ever meet! First they fake data showing the carbon dioxide is going up, and then they demand more money to keep taking the measurements. It's just a protection racket! Can you even *see* carbon dioxide? No! They tell us it's there, but is it really?'

The thought of meek scientists in white lab coats demanding money with menaces under threat of revealing to the world that there was no carbon dioxide and that temperatures were just fine was indeed a bizarre one.

'I think we're just going to have to agree to disagree on that Charles. But in any case, if it sets your mind at rest I don't think this experiment is likely to ever happen anyway—the more we looked into it the more difficulties we found.'

Abbott seemed surprised. 'So why was Mr Winter here?'

'He came to satisfy himself that there was no project. He looked very thoroughly at Saul and Johnny's boats, took samples, snooped around my garage and asked a bunch of questions, and quite rightly decided there's nothing to investigate.'

'Oh.'

'Anyway looks like fishing season has started, I see the boys are out today and I would think they'll be busy with that in the coming weeks. No time to go off doing iron experiments even if they wanted to,' she added, hoping to pre-empt any curiosity Abbott might have if he saw sacks being loaded onto the boats in coming weeks.

As she walked home Aurora tried to convince herself that she had been truthful to Charles. As she saw it she hadn't actually lied, and the way things were going it might turn out to be true anyway. She hadn't heard from Lan for months and if she continued to have cold feet and decided she wasn't comfortable even telling them where to spray the stuff the project could never happen, period. She was glad she had not participated in the village betting scheme; much as she wanted it to happen and wanted it to be a success, she was not optimistic at this point.

But it wouldn't be long now until they'd know for sure. Assuming Lan kept her word they needed to do the real fertilization in June or July, which could be as soon as a few weeks away.

CHAPTER 17

The Echelon Experiment

It was a gorgeous afternoon in June and Lan had climbed the winding path behind the university up Mont Royal to reach the ornamental tea shop at its summit. She normally found its breath-taking views across Montreal and the St Lawrence River inspiring, but not today.

Her research funding had ended a month earlier, meaning that she'd had to formally cancel plans for research work the following year and was unable to continue paying her two research students, although fortunately she'd found positions for both in other groups. Despite working almost full-time on grant applications for the past six months she still had no firm money. Bradley wanted to talk with her about moving into a full-time teaching position when the academic year started in September, only three months away. She felt the walls closing in on her.

In her more paranoid moments she even wondered whether Bradley had anything to do with the brick walls that she kept hitting. Since he had been appointed to a position as advisor to a consortium of oil companies looking to develop production in the arctic eighteen months ago, his attitude towards climate change had softened considerably. Before, he was pretty much like anyone else, which is to say he sympathized with the problem while finding excuses for his own high-carbon lifestyle. His wife needed the SUV because of the kids, he couldn't really take public transport to work because he lived too far out and would have to change twice, and he needed to do a dozen international flights a year because it was important he be at conferences to promote the university.

But recently he had pointed out that with the summer sea ice gone it should be possible to start doing exploratory drilling soon, and that a warmer climate might result in higher crop yields in the Canadian prairies and more productive Atlantic fisheries. On one occasion he'd even enthused to Lan about how if the sea ice were completely gone in the summer and much thinner in the winter it would enable a complete shift in North American energy policy—if the fields in the Arctic Ocean were as large as some people suspected then Canada and the US could become the dominant world suppliers once again, undercutting the Middle Eastern countries. Yes, and as an authority on the sedimentary geology of the region he would hopefully have some much better-paid career options than mere university professor, she thought to herself.

The one positive thing to come out of this career-changing experience was that she now appreciated the importance of communicating the seriousness of the changes that were taking place in the arctic. She saw how arrogant she had been in assuming that it was the journalists' job to find and communicate her results to the general public. If even fellow scientists evaluating her grant applications did not understand its importance, how could politicians making decisions, or the general public? Previously she had been reluctant to seek interviews or appear on TV, but she saw now that that had been a mistake. Apart from anything else she would have found it easier to get funding if people had heard more of her, were more aware of her track record. There was a job being advertised as Executive Director of a climate change organization in Ottawa which to her surprise she found herself excited about applying for, even though it would mean leaving university life altogether.

First she had a phone call to make though, something she felt quite awkward about, but had given her word she would. She pulled out her mobile phone and fidgeted with it before finding the number and calling it.

'Aurora? It's Lan.'

'Lan! Lovely to hear from you!' Aurora sounded both surprised and genuinely pleased. 'What have you been up to? More exciting voyages?' before remembering that the trip to the Antarctic had existed purely in her imagination.

'No, I'm afraid not. I've been writing grant applications pretty much continually the last few months but nothing to show for it. I hope you didn't depend on grants for your project?'

Aurora had forgotten that government grants had once been their big hope for funding, back at the beginning. 'No, we didn't try that in the end, you convinced us to not even bother. The village council paid for the iron sulphate but to save face for Saul we set up a company that will own the carbon credits, so in theory they'll get their money back eventually. Or not. I'm not sure if Saul really thinks they will but it wasn't that much in the end, about fifteen bucks per Edenshaw resident, but of course they're the ones who will benefit if the project delivers.'

Lan laughed. 'Yeah, without measuring the CO2 absorbed that's going to be a challenge, but whatever it takes, eh?' She paused. 'It sounds like you're in a restaurant or something, is now a good time to talk?'

'Ah, that's Edenshaw's new café! Remember my greenhouse? Johnny's daughter has taken it over to have a go running a café. Does pretty good breakfasts actually.'

Lan tried to imagine what it might look like, it had been pretty messy as she recalled. It sounded typical of Aurora to sacrifice her comfort to help someone else though, she admired her for that. 'I see…anyway, have you actually got the iron sulphate yet?'

'Yep, it's all here and ready to go. Johnny fixed some of the stuff on his boat you pointed out, and we're just waiting on your call. I'm hoping that that's what this is?'

It had been six months since Lan had been personally involved in the project, and she'd forgotten how much Aurora was banking on it working. She felt bad for them—bad because she still did not have much confidence it would work, but they'd come this far…

'Er, yes, it is,' she cleared her throat, 'although I hope you appreciate that I really shouldn't be using government satellite data in this way. Strictly speaking it's an abuse of university resources.' If she was hoping for some kind of appreciation from Aurora she got only a murmured 'Mmm...'

'Anyway…I've been watching one of those Pacific eddies we talked about. It started to form a few weeks back and has now reached a good size and is moving steadily towards Esh so I think this would be a good candidate.' She explained that she'd done some calculations of where it would be in two weeks' time in order to allow enough time for Johnny and the other boats to reach the area, and gave Aurora the coordinates.

'Anywhere within about a thirty kilometre radius of that location should be okay, within a window of one to two weeks from now. But try and get Johnny to put it all in one spot, don't spread it out too much or it will dilute the impact.'

Aurora felt like a weight had been lifted from her shoulders. When June had arrived without any contact from Lan she'd started to become increasingly nervous about waiting for her call, without which she faced the prospect of having to explain to Saul and Johnny how she'd wasted ten thousand dollars of the village's money. 'I can't thank you enough, Lan. It should be alright, I'll go and talk to him right away. So any chance we'll see you here again?'

'I need to stay here and watch the satellite imagery to see if you manage to create a plankton bloom, apart from which I'm still chasing up a few long shots for getting my research funded. But we should keep in close contact from now on—you tell me when Johnny drops the stuff and I'll let you know what I see on the satellite images. Any impact on the salmon will be several months off though, and you'll see that first not me. I can't see fish on the satellite.'

'Well you're always welcome here, you know that.'

Given the complete uncertainly of her future, Lan found the idea of a bolt-hole on Esh surprisingly comforting. 'You never know…at this rate I might not have much of a job by the end of the year. I'm actually thinking of applying for some non-academic positions with environmental organizations if I really can't continue with research work, and some of those are in Vancouver and Seattle, quite close.'

- - -

Ten days later *Raven* slipped out of Edenshaw harbour on the evening tide, loaded with a crew of six and twenty tons of iron sulphate. The Manyshots boys managed to keep the loading operation secret, moving a van-load of sacks at a time in the evenings; to passers-by they looked no different than the sacks of ice they loaded when they were going fishing, and Johnny had put the word out that he was going out for lingcod. Not even the crew knew what their real objective was until they were out of the harbour, but they were really only concerned how long they might be out for, which was going to be several days less than they were expecting. It would take them about a day's sailing to get to the drop zone, so as soon as they had gone Saul started loading the *Sea Eagle* and planned to sail twenty-four hours later, then Zeb would make a run in the *Spirit Bear* before Saul did his second trip and then Johnny would finish up. Johnny was nervous about Saul using the Sea Eagle and suggested he take his second boat instead, but his dad had insisted, stubborn as usual. Five trips should do it. The plan was that they would always have a vessel on location dumping the iron, working in rotation.

The journey out was uneventful, monotonous even, with most of the crew trying to get some sleep during the night, although being so far north and summer the sky never got truly dark. The sea was a bit rough for the time of year and the first indication that they had reached the eddy, a gently rotating body of water a hundred kilometres across, was that it became smoother. The weather forecast was good for the next few days, although there was a low pressure area moving in that would reach them eventually. Johnny just hoped they could get all the trips done before then.

Once they got to the coordinates Lan had given they started sailing slowly back and forth along a twenty kilometre track, dumping the iron sulphate powder off the leeward side of the boat. Pretty soon the crew had a good rhythm going, two men bringing the heavy sacks out of the hold on the winch, two slashing them and pouring them into the sea. They found they could empty about two or three sacks a minute and switched around every hour. The whole load took ten hours to dump including breaks. Of course the stuff got everywhere, so when they were done they hosed down the deck and sluiced that into the sea, then headed home.

As they sailed back south Johnny regretted that Lan was not there to witness the process—he smiled at her earlier insistence that the powder be dissolved first. The contents of a twenty-five kilo bag dissolved instantly in the water, and gazing at the huge expanse of the horizon brought it home what a tiny amount they were depositing. Not for the first time he wondered whether the whole project was just pissing in the wind—it was really hard to imagine that this tiny amount would have any impact at all in the vastness of the Pacific, or even much effect on the plankton.

About a third of the way back they saw the *Sea Eagle* coming towards them, and Johnny chatted with

Saul on the radio for a bit about how it had gone, and warned him to make sure they all kept their face masks on—the stuff blew everywhere and tasted bitter if you got any in your mouth. Then he went to get some rest for a few hours while his first mate took over; he could see that this whole thing was going to be a bit of a marathon, they all needed to pace themselves. Back in harbour the crew all went to get some rest while the Manyshots boys and four of their mates loaded Zeb's boat and then waited for the evening tide again.

By the time he set out Johnny had gone to bed and Saul was on his way back, but in the morning Johnny chatted to Zeb on the radio for a bit. In typical Zeb fashion he sounded very laid back about it.

'So you reached the drop zone yet?'

'Just got here.'

'Only now? That took a while.'

'This old boat don't go as fast as yours. Don't want to push her too hard.'

Johnny knew how long it should take him to get there, but he had a point. No sense in risking engine trouble so far out. Sounded like he had it all in hand though so he went down to help get *Spirit Bear* reloaded.

The weather held until Johnny's last trip when the low pressure area that they'd been watching finally reached them in the form of a squall line. Lan had only been looking for a suitable ocean eddy and not considered whether it would be good weather or not, he couldn't really blame her for that, but he probably wouldn't have come out if it hadn't been necessary to finish everything. For a while it was alright, but after a couple of hours the boat was pitching and yawing so much it was getting dangerous to be on deck. Johnny wasn't about to lose any crew for the sake of this.

'Eddie!' he yelled at the elder Manyshots brother, 'This is getting too rough! We need to just dump this stuff and get out of here!'

On the satellite weather display he could see the front was coming from the north-west so decided to start sailing south to stay ahead of the worst of it. They rigged up the hold winch to pull up ten sacks at a time, ran a knife down the side of each and simply threw the sacks overboard. No time to do it neatly, but the way the weather was headed it would all be well mixed up anyway. The new technique proved considerably faster and they were done within three hours and a third of the way home.

Aurora had been down to see each of the boats off, but it was only on that last one that she caught sight of Charles Abbott lurking across the street again, camera phone in hand. She walked across to talk with him.

'Hello, Charles. Good to see the boats going out fishing again, isn't it?'

'Fishing? Is that what you call it? I know what you people are up to. Don't think I don't know!'

Aurora smiled. 'I told you Charles, we gave up on the idea. This looks like regular fishing to me.' She leaning towards him conspiratorially. 'But who knows what they really get up to out there? Maybe they're doing some illegal activity, like whaling! We will never know, will we?'

Charles indignantly took a photo of her in front of the *Raven* and stomped off.

\- - -

'Well I'll be…!' Lan said to herself under her breath.

It was three weeks later and Lan was looking at the daily infrared satellite image of the Pacific northwest from NASA's Aqua satellite. She thought she'd seen a faint smudge on the image a few days before that might have indicated something, or might just have been a cloud, but this morning it was unmistakable: a milky yellow-green circular spot growing in the middle of a swirling eddy in the oceanic circulation, its characteristic colour caused by the chlorophyll in the plankton. Johnny must have done a good job, it was almost dead-centre in the eddy, apart from one wispy trail to the south. She must compliment Johnny on a job well done when, if, she saw him again. Mind you, it looked as though there was some natural plankton bloom formation going on as well—about a hundred and fifty kilometres further north and nearer to the coast there was another smaller smudge forming too.

She called Aurora and passed on the good news. 'Don't get too carried away though, this is just the first stage. The salmon have to find it yet!'

'Funny to think that the success of this thing is now in the hands of a bunch of fish!' she laughed.

Lan also emailed a copy of the image to Aurora so she printed off a copy and took it to show Johnny, who was in the hotel bar in a discussion with his father.

'Hi guys! I just got this from Lan and thought you might like to see the results of your work.' She put the image on the bar top between them.

'So what are we looking at?' asked Saul, reaching for his reading glasses.

'It's a satellite image which shows the plankton—I think it's actually in the infrared but changed to use real colours, if you see what I mean. This is the BC coast here,' she traced the outline, 'we're here, and the place you did the fertilization is about here. You can see the shape of the eddy that Lan was aiming for, going around here.'

'Cool!' said Johnny. 'So this big blob is the plankton that's eating the iron sulphate?'

'Yep. The eddy's actually moved a bit since you were out there, its drifting slowly towards Esh but you can see the blob where you put the iron is pretty well dead centre in the eddy, which apparently was what you were supposed to do.'

Johnny gave his father and Aurora a high five. 'I love it when a plan comes together!' he joked, mimicking holding a cigar. He made some rough measurements on the image with his fingers.

'Looks like it will reach Esh in a couple of months.'

'Lan says she'll send me a few more of these so we can track progress.'

Johnny was looking at the image more closely. 'There's a weird tail to it, this line coming back towards Esh.'

'Yeah, Lan says she doesn't know what that is.'

'Ah, I bet I know. That's my last trip, where the weather started to close in and we had to make a run for it.'

Aurora looked questioningly.

'I know, it's not what we were supposed to do so maybe you shouldn't tell Lan, but the swell was getting real bad. The guys couldn't stand on the deck pouring the stuff over the side or they would have gone with it, so I decided we'd have to keep moving south to stay ahead of the weather front. So that last, I dunno, half a load, we dropped as we were moving south at seven or eight knots which is why it shows up as a line.'

'Makes sense. She says she thinks this smaller blob

up here might just be some natural plankton.'

Saul peered at the image. 'Quite close to the coast that one,' he commented. 'Hey let me give Zeb a call, he might be interested too,' and reached for the phone.

Zeb ambled across a few minutes later, oily rag still in hand, and the image was explained to him.

'Very beautiful,' he smiled.

'This second small blob is about a hundred and fifty kilometres north of our dump site and Lan thinks it's probably natural,' said Saul. 'It's quite a bit closer to the coast so it'll probably miss Esh and hit the coast some place further north.'

Zeb looked at the image more closely and smiled. 'Looks like someone is going to be getting some extra salmon,' he replied, and winked at Saul.

'So is this satellite photo going to get us in trouble?' asked Johnny. 'I mean we went to a lot of trouble to keep the actual operation secret, but this shows that someone has artificially created a plankton bloom out there. Does that mean our secret is out?'

Aurora shrugged. 'I guess an expert would know its artificial, although Lan didn't seem to be able to tell between say the main blob which you guys made and the smaller one that's natural. But there's nothing to tie it back to us specifically.' She remembered that the others didn't know about Adam Winter's accusation or inspection visit.

'But for the carbon credits thing we need to be able to prove we did it anyway, right?' added Saul.

'True.' She picked up the satellite image. 'I think the prudent thing for now is that we keep all this stuff and then decide later whether we make it public to support the carbon credits.'

The others nodded.

'Actually we should also keep the navigation data from your boats so that we can prove you were actually there. Otherwise there's only your word.'

'Sure,' replied Johnny. 'Mine is still on the boat's nav system but I'll make a copy for you. I'll do that for *Raven* and *Sea Eagle* too.'

Zeb pulled a face. 'I think I already deleted mine. I usually do that every few weeks when I clean up the boat. Sorry.'

'No big deal,' replied Aurora. 'If you can all just give me the nav records you have and anything else you think might be useful, any photos or phone video anyone took out there. I'll keep it all locked up until we decide what to do with it, in case we ever need it.'

Lan continued to send images over the next few weeks, showing the movement of the eddy itself as it drifted slowly towards the coast, and the growing bloom within it. Over time other eddies formed, and from time to time one would bump into another, spawning yet more. The bloom itself also developed and spread inside the eddy, and sometimes when the eddy bumped into one of its neighbours bits of the bloom would spill into the neighbour. To Aurora the images reminded her of Van Gogh's *Starry Night*, all swirls and yellow-green blobs. She had no idea satellite images could be so artistic.

As she looked at them she wondered where the salmon were, whether also concealed in these vast slowly rotating patches of water were the millions of fish they needed. Only time would tell, and it would be at least another month until they would find out.

CHAPTER 18

Starstruck

The leisurely progress of the yellow-green blob across the northwest corner of the Pacific through July and August was surprisingly stressful for everyone involved in its creation. The anticipation of whether it would bring a bonanza of spawning salmon, or nothing at all, was palpable.

As far as the project went Gaia was the only person with something active to do, monitoring salmon numbers to be sure they had reliable data before and after the effects of the fertilization reached them. To do this she had marked out a three-metre square on the riverbed with small piles of pebbles at a point near where the river entered the bay and she could observe it from a high section of the river bank. The idea was that she would count the number of salmon she saw in a fifteen minute period within her 'box'. Not fancy but practical and hopefully consistent. It had become her routine each morning and evening to walk down to the river mouth and do her count, often using the morning walk to decide what she had to do for the day. So she was lost in thought when she looked up to see two oddly familiar figures standing beside the quay watching her.

For a moment her mind was confused. She knew them, yet she didn't know them. This was because Craig Cuomo and Yaz Garcia were two of the best-known faces in Hollywood—Cuomo in his sixties with distinguished white hair and kindly face, famous for his 'quiet tough-guy' roles, his Buddhist faith, and for speaking out against man's polluting the planet with carbon dioxide, and Garcia in his thirties and full of energy, the action man. But they shouldn't be here.

'Jesus! You're Craig Cuomo!' she burst out involuntarily, startled and wide-eyed.

Cuomo grinned. 'I know. And this is Yaz. And you are?'

'Gaia. Wow! I mean…*wow*! What are *you* doing here?'

Garcia held out his hands as if to say 'why not'. 'We're on our way up to Craig's place and thought we'd stop for coffee. Know anywhere decent round here?' he grinned.

Gaia laughed. 'You've come to Esh for *coffee*? Most people come for the eagles and the wildlife. But I can show you where you can get a great cup of coffee, for sure!'

'That would be fantastic,' smiled Craig, hesitating for a moment. 'Perhaps you'd like to join us?' She was a nice looking girl after all. Very natural. Great hair.

'Are you sure? I'd love to!'

She turned around and started to lead them back towards Haze. 'But what are you doing here?' she persisted, looking baffled.

'Oh, I have a summer home on one of the islands. I thought all the locals knew about it?' replied Cuomo breezily. 'It's about thirty kilometres up the coast, west of here. On an island off the main island, actually.'

'I never knew! How long have you had it?'

'Twenty years. But I'm not here much.'

He explained to her how he'd originally bought the place on a whim, fifty acres of lush tree-covered paradise that he had renamed 'Utopia' with a direct view west to the setting sun. It had taken him five years to get permission to build his dream home on it, overlooking a private bay and accessible only by boat or floatplane, an elegant piece of steel and glass engineering designed by a firm of New York architects who'd won an award for it. In keeping with his well-known environmental beliefs it represented the ultimate in eco-friendly, sustainable living, something that its owner found to be both important and satisfying, taking pride in everything from its solar panels to its biogenic sewage disposal system, and from its reverse osmosis water purification plant to its zero thermal emission roof. Indeed Cuomo regarded his construction of the house on Utopia as one of the most important things he'd ever done, right up there with his four Oscars.

Five years ago he had decided that he would spend every June and July on Utopia in uninterrupted meditation and self-purification. No mobile phone coverage, off the grid, catching his own fish, drinking his own rainwater. Directors and producers wanting to discuss projects with him had got used to working around his schedule. Truth be told, now that he was in his early sixties he needed the time to regenerate from ten months of Hollywood parties and politics.

Usually he came alone, using an air taxi floatplane to take him directly to his jetty, but this year was different—he'd hitched a ride on a thirty-metre sloop sailing up from San Francisco to Kodiak Island with

Yaz and his crew, six rowdy thirtysomethings. They'd just finished filming together and as soon as he'd heard about his island Yaz had insisted he join him, and in a moment of weakness Craig had allowed himself to be caught up in his enthusiasm. As it turned out it hadn't been too bad, apart from the three day stopover for further partying in Vancouver…that had been a bit much.

His new-found best buddy's crew of extras and Hollywood hopefuls hauled the ropes and did the real sailing while Craig and his friend steered the boat, drank beer, and speculated on who ought to date who to create the perfect power couple. As they'd passed the end of Edenshaw Sound they'd decided on impulse that they needed to make land and check out the local culture. Despite living only a few kilometres up the coast Cuomo had never actually stepped foot in Edenshaw since the year he'd come to meet with the village elders to assure them he wasn't going to dig up any burials he might find on his property, and he was curious to see it again.

The three of them walked down the high street towards Haze, Gaia trying hard to stop herself from gushing her admiration for Craig's environmental work. 'That thing you did last year when the pod of dolphins got beached near San Francisco was just so crazy, especially that bit where you were in a wetsuit helping to lead them back into the deeper water. Did you just happen to be passing, or what happened?'

Cuomo grinned with the boyish charm he had built his reputation on. 'Oh that? Well I was filming nearby and we heard about it, so a group of us just went down to the beach to see if we could help. People were already helping to keep them cool and hydrated until the tide came back in, I just took the credit,' he grinned.

'You think he's kidding, he's not,' interjected Garcia. 'This guy's always taking credit for things he didn't actually do. That's actors for you.'

Cuomo pretended to look hurt and touched her arm. 'No, honestly, that's kind of what happened—I didn't get there until near the end when they were preparing to re-float them, and I just happened to have my wetsuit in the back of the Jeep so I got in the water and tried to guide one of them out and the rest kind of followed. Probably they would have got them back in anyway, it was the guys who kept them sprayed with water for six hours until the tide came in who really saved them.'

They had stopped in front of Haze. 'This is the place. Best coffee on the island. Only coffee on the island. Good breakfasts too.'

Julie looked up from sorting cutlery and did a double take.

'Jools, I brought you a couple of customers. A couple of guys I found hanging around the harbour who are looking for breakfast,' explained Gaia deadpan.

Julie continued to stare at the two of them, forks still in her hand. 'But, they're…you know who they are, right?'

Gaia looked at them and back at her. 'Well I thought they were just a couple of resting actors I found hanging around the quay. But you think they might be famous or something? They do look a bit familiar now that you mention it.'

Garcia laughed. 'She's just kidding you, nice to meet you Jools. Gaia here's been telling us what great coffee you have. Any chance of some? I'm parched.'

'Wow! Yaz Garcia and Craig Cuomo in my café! Take a seat and two coffees coming right up. How do you want it?'

'Black.'

'Cappuccino?'

'Of course. You want some breakfast too? We make the pastries ourselves and can make you pretty much anything you like—I've got eggs, bacon, avocado, salmon—any combination.'

'How about a traditional First Nation breakfast?' asked Yaz. 'What would that be?'

'Salmon.'

'And?'

'More salmon. I could make you some smoked salmon with some maple grilled salmon and maybe some eggs and sea samphire? That's about as trad as you can get.'

Craig laughed. 'That sounds like Monty Python and the spam sketch. Anything you want as long as its spam. Spam and eggs. Spam, spam and eggs. Spam, spam, spam and eggs…' He chuckled to himself.

'That's what traditional cooking here is like I'm afraid,' grinned Julie. 'Our whole culture revolves about salmon.'

'Sounds great, two trad salmon breakfasts and coffee!'

While Julie got to work on their orders Cuomo asked Gaia what she was doing on Esh, surprising her with his interest. She explained her passion for the wildlife on Echelon and her and Wolf's plans for building an eco-tourism business, and Cuomo nodded. 'It's a double-edge sword of course. Attract more people here and you risk destroying the very thing they've come to see.' They chatted about the birds and marine life that Cuomo had seen around his home over the years and Gaia's expeditions into the back country to watch bears.

When their breakfasts came Cuomo handed Julie his phone. 'Here, take a photo of Yaz and me. This is going on Facebook.'

'Sure!'

She took the photo and Cuomo played with his phone for a minute. 'There you go. 'First class First Nation salmon breakfast at @HazeCafeEsh in Echelon Islands. Awesome!"

'Thanks! That should do something for my ratings!'

Sensing an opportunity Gaia remembered why she'd been out that morning in the first place. 'This place used to have a lot more salmon than it does today, but changes in the climate have brought their numbers way down. It's actually affected the village here quite dramatically, almost everyone was employed in salmon before, they even used to have a cannery here. Now its fifty percent unemployment.' Cuomo shrugged sympathetically but Garcia didn't look up from his plate. 'But we think we've got a way to reverse all that. This summer we're doing one of the largest ocean fertilization projects that's ever been attempted—in fact the seeding was done a few weeks ago, we're just waiting to see how it impacts the salmon population.'

'Serious?' Craig looked up from his breakfast.

'Yup. The village council just sprayed a hundred tons of iron sulphate three hundred kilometres off the coast.'

'That's pretty amazing. So you're involved in that?'

'Oh absolutely! That's why I was out this morning, I'm monitoring their numbers ahead of the annual salmon run in September and October. Assuming it works I'm also going to be doing some publicity—we want to make people aware that real action against climate change can happen at a community level.'

Cuomo smiled and looked at her attentively, mildly flirting with her. 'That's really interesting, Gaia, I'm so glad we ran into you. So how are you going to publicize it?'

'Social media and local TV probably. I'm hoping the local station would do it just for the community interest and pretty pictures, but we're not sure whether we could get national attention—these things are always a bit hit-and-miss. Depends on what else is happening that week.'

'Well I might be able to help with that. I might not have been to Edenshaw much but Esh has been an important part of my life for years and I'd like to see it flourish.'

'Wow! Are you serious? That would be great!'

They'd both finished their food and Garcia was looking at his watch. 'I hate to break this up, but we're going to have to leave soon. The tide…'

Gaia looked a bit alarmed. 'How can I keep in touch with you to talk about this some more?'

'Hey, why don't you just come with us? Come and check out Utopia and later on I can run you back in the motorboat. Then we can discuss everything properly.'

Gaia didn't need asking twice. As they walked back to the quay she phoned Wolf to quickly explain the unusual situation, promising to be back by the evening but not to worry if she wasn't, and was relieved that he understood—and that he didn't ask to come.

On Garcia's boat the crew were ready to leave as soon as they returned, quickly raising anchor and sailing back out the easterly channel before turning north-west to follow the coast around towards the Pacific side of the island. It had been years since Gaia had been on a sailboat and she was loving the experience, the brilliance of the sky and vigour as the boat cut through the waves. Cuomo was in his element playing the part of the captain, inviting her to take the wheel and then standing close behind her, his hands on hers to help control it. She knew he was playing with her but didn't mind—hey, how often do you have Craig Cuomo trying to seduce you? Well, probably quite often if you lived in Hollywood she admitted to herself, but out here it was a once-in-a-lifetime opportunity. She was doing it for the salmon she told herself, rather lamely.

It took about three hours to reach Utopia, mostly because Garcia didn't want to arrive at Utopia at low tide so took the opportunity to go further out around a couple of the larger islands before coming back down. By the time they edged their way into its floating jetty Gaia was exhausted from the incessant motion of the boat and her eyes were itching from the sea spray.

The house was as remarkable as Craig had made it out to be, a beautifully elegant structure poised on the clifftop with the trees wrapping around behind it. It was a spectacular house designed to be viewed from the sea, not that there were many other options of course. At first glance Gaia thought it was reminiscent of a tepee, a huge A-frame with large sloping windows looking out over the ocean.

'It's supposed to be an eagle,' replied Craig. 'Won an award for it actually. You see the two wings on either side? One is the living area and the other is where the bedrooms are.'

'Oh yeah, I hadn't noticed those. The tepee is more

like a head, with that front part making a beak.'

As they came in to dock she could see more of it, the two wings were actually covered in solar panels. Craig pointed out a small stone building on the beach a few hundred metres from the house. 'That's where the water purification system is, there's a couple of pipes going out under the sea a few hundred metres, it brings in water through one pipe and slightly saltier water goes back out through the other. Otherwise the place is self-sustaining—all the electricity comes from the panels and the waste goes into a septic tank back in the woods. But the squirrels probably produce more poop than we do even when the place is full.'

They dropped anchor some distance offshore and took the dinghy to the jetty. Inside, the three of them relaxed in the main room, and when the rest of the crew arrived the couple who looked after the place while Cuomo was away showed people to their rooms and served drinks. Craig seemed in no hurry to discuss details of what he might do to help publicize the salmon project, preferring to show Garcia around the house and then play pool with him. 'Something you'll never be able to do on that beautiful boat of yours,' he smirked.

Eventually they came back and Craig announced that they were going to have a barbeque on the terrace overlooking the ocean. 'It's going to get dark soon so I thought we'd do that and then I can take you back in the morning,' he said to Gaia. 'Are you okay with that? I know I said I'd take you back this evening but time's sort of run away with us.'

The truth was that she was a bit annoyed with him for leading her to believe that he would help her with the salmon project and then apparently losing interest, but it seemed churlish to insist on being taken back to Edenshaw and giving up any prospect of his endorsement on the way. She assumed he was going to try and see if his mature charm would get him anywhere with her that evening, but he didn't seem the type to push things too far. Her virtue was probably safe.

So she smiled sweetly. 'Sure, no problem. Time practically stands still in Edenshaw anyway, there's nothing I need to rush back for.' Even so, she made a point of focusing more of her attention on Yaz Garcia from then on, asking him about movies she could remember him from, just to make sure Craig got the message that she wasn't there just for him.

It was a magical evening of course and she had to remind herself that half the women on the planet would have killed to be in her shoes. They had two big barbeques going with steak and fish, a fire pit stacked with pine logs that burned brightly in the darkness, and wind chimes tinkled in the breeze. Eventually everyone went to bed, and in the morning she reminded him about why he'd invited her to come along and his offer to help raise awareness of the project—when and if it was successful of course.

'So when will this be?' asked Cuomo vaguely.

'September or October, not sure exactly when.'

'Hmm. I'm only here until late July. I'll be filming in Tanzania and LA in September and October. But I might be able to fly up for a day or two if there was a specific event you wanted me at.'

'That's a lot to ask, are you sure? Maybe we can do something like offer them an interview in LA instead?'

Cuomo shrugged. 'Whatever works. Maybe we just play it by ear—it depends a lot on exactly when it happens, and my schedule is likely to move around a bit anyway.' He leaned back in his chair. 'I can 'like' and retweet things you put out too, that's easy and should get a wider audience.'

'That sounds good. I really appreciate your interest.'

'Well, it's important. Like you said yesterday, there's a lot of talk about climate change but very little actually gets done. Or, I suppose very little that has this sort of immediate impact gets done. The stuff that governments work on like shutting down coal-fired power stations is important, but it takes decades to have a real impact.'

They were interrupted by Garcia announcing they were about to leave, and offering to drop Gaia at Edenshaw on their way. Craig got up and gave her a hug and promised to keep in touch for the salmon run and do his best to be available to help publicize it, and made her promise to come back for a few days and check out his whales.

'They come right past the point here, you can just sit and watch them from the terrace, it's really something. You could come back for a week and just chill out and we could talk more.'

As the sloop got out of the harbour and began to pick up some wind she looked back and could see him watching them from the terrace, a white haired figure looking older than he had seemed close up, alone on his Utopia. How old must he be? Mid-sixties? Occupational hazard, he was no longer the action man of screen and surf like Yaz here, and botox didn't help much from four hundred metres away. She wondered whether he was really there for the wildlife and the meditation as he claimed, or just to get some rest. He was certainly active in championing a variety of environmental and human rights causes, but his knowledge of them had seemed fairly shallow when they'd been talking last night. Maybe he just found them convenient causes to endorse his image as the more mature, thoughtful man that his public image had moved towards in recent years.

As the house grew more distant Gaia remembered Yaz's comment about the dolphin episode and wondered if she had been wise to ask for Craig Cuomo's help.

CHAPTER 19

Busted

After her surreal encounter with Hollywood royalty, Gaia's life reverted to its routine, up early and out to check for salmon. It was beautiful at that time of day and she loved the tranquillity of the river and the trees.

Throughout July and August she'd not seen any at all, but in early September she started to see one or two every day. This morning there were twenty. She'd been so focused on her stopwatch and the small square of river bottom in front of her that she hadn't looked out at the channel itself, so when she eventually finished her counting and looked up and out across the river it was with a jolt that she realized that what she had thought were ripples on the water surface caused by wind were actually red and pink salmon, thousands of them. The whole river was teeming with fish, so many that they made the water appear to boil. It was the fifteenth of September, a date they would all remember.

She ran the kilometre back to the village to Haze which had just opened. Julie was busy slicing bread.

'Where's Aurora?' she demanded breathlessly.

'Upstairs, I guess. She's not usually down before eight.'

Gaia ran into the house and shouted her name, and a worried Aurora came down in her pyjamas.

'What's going on? Are you okay?'

Gaia grinned and grabbed her by the shoulders. 'They're here Aurora! They're here! Salmon, millions of salmon! Come and look, I've never seen so many.'

Aurora quickly got dressed, phoning Zeb as she did so and telling him to meet them at the harbour as quick as he could.

Ten minutes later the three of them were walking down to the jetty and even as they approached could see what Gaia was talking about. They could see shoals of the pink fish here and there, patches with masses of pink bodies churning in the water. As they walked along the beach road to where the river entered the sea they became more and more frequent, and when they got to the river-mouth itself it seemed as though thousands of salmon were jostling to swim upstream.

'That's more than I recall ever seeing,' said Aurora. 'What do you think Zeb? Is this more than last year?'

'It's a *lot* more. I haven't seen this many since I was a kid.' He gazed at the water in awe and then turned to Aurora and Gaia and high-fived them both. 'I think we did it folks, we brought the salmon back!'

For a while they just watched the spectacle in front of them, calling friends to come and look. By eight there were almost a hundred people standing along the harbour excitedly looking out at the water.

'We need to make sure this is properly documented,' said Zeb after a while, muttering something about scientific procedure but privately thinking about his punters. 'I'm going to call Fisheries Canada,' and went back home to make the call.

The numbers seemed to be increase as the day

progressed, and before long the attention of the villagers shifted from simply marvelling at them to organizing nets across the river mouth to catch them. They caught hundreds that day, but it didn't make a dent in the numbers. Later it was officially estimated that there were forty million salmon in the annual migration, compared to one to three million in previous years. The celebrations continued into the evening with bonfires on the shore to cook the fish, and singing and dancing.

Aurora called Lan as soon as she could to tell her the news, and sent her a couple of photos of the shoals.

'That's crazy, Aurora! It looks like you could almost walk on the water there's so many!'

'Yeah, it's absolutely extraordinary. No one here has seen so many in years, it's more than we used to get even in the old days.'

'I'm coming over to see this for myself. I'll text you when I know what ferry I'm going to be on, hopefully tomorrow some time. Can I stay at your place?'

'No problem, I'll get the spare room ready for you. I think they're planning another big celebration down on the beach tomorrow night too.'

\- - -

Lan managed to get there just in time for the party, arriving on the late afternoon ferry the day after and walking up to Aurora's house.

'This café is just fantastic! What a cool idea!'

They hugged. 'I'm very happy you could make it, it's so great you could come and see what you've helped achieve.'

Lan shrugged. 'It was really you and Johnny that

made it happen. I'm the one that bailed!'

'Yeah we must talk about that…let me buy you a coffee first.' They sat down by the window. It was still quite bright and Lan had already had a good look at the shoals from the ferry. 'They're going to have a big bonfire on the beach tonight and some traditional dancing to thank the spirits for the salmon harvest, so we can go down and join in that later.'

Aurora introduced Lan to Julie who explained more about how Haze had come into existence and enthused about becoming a focal point for the community and the level of interest in their food. Lan thought the idea of running one's own business and not being vulnerable to the whim of others sounded very appealing.

Julie left them to serve another customer and Lan asked how Johnny was. 'I must congratulate him on how well he did the fertilization. As far as I could see from the satellite images he got that stuff exactly where it needed to be.'

Aurora looked thoughtful. 'He's fine, I think they all found it a bit exhausting going so far out twice each during that week, but it all got done right in the end.' She hesitated. 'By the way, I didn't tell the others that you had withdrawn from the project back in May because I was concerned they would use it as an excuse to throw in the towel. So I'm afraid I misled Johnny about your continued involvement, so if he makes a few odd comments about you being inaccessible or being away on a trip, just go with it, okay?'

Lan laughed. 'Er, okay! I guess I deserved that. What did you tell him?' But at that moment Julie came back with a sample of quiche that she wanted Lan to try, and then Johnny himself showed up.

'Hey Lan! We did it!' He stepped forward and

embraced her. 'I'm so glad you were able to make it. You've brought our village back to life again.'

He sat down and the three of them talked about what a miracle it had been, and Johnny and Lan both admitted that they had not actually thought that it would work. It seemed that only Aurora had had blind faith in its success. 'You should always have faith,' she said firmly. 'Otherwise you never achieve anything in life. Look around you—without faith even this place would never have happened.'

Haze did not have an alcohol license, but she went to her kitchen and brought back a bottle of wine. 'Let's start the celebration early,' she said, handing out the glasses, 'then we can go down to the beach and join the party.'

An hour later and they were standing on the beach with hundreds of others beside a huge bonfire that the children had been building all day out of driftwood. Aurora had gone off to chat with Zeb and Saul and a group led by Edwin Reid were beating drums and chanting, which Johnny explained to Lan was a traditional salmon thanksgiving ritual. He went to get her a beer and together they toasted Esh's unexpected harvest. Although she recognized a few faces from the Council meeting she didn't really know anyone there other than him and Aurora, so appreciated that he seemed to have taken it upon himself to look after her for the evening. Maybe he was more chivalrous than she had thought.

'So how was the trip?' he asked after the noise of the drums had abated a bit. 'Sounds like it was quite an adventure, long way to go.'

'Er, yes,' she stammered. 'Long way.'

'Where exactly did you go?'

Go with it was what Aurora had told her. 'Er, what do you mean?'

'Oh, just wondering how you got down there. Did you sail down from South America or over to New Zealand first?'

'*Down* from South America to…*the Antarctic?*'

'Yes, that's where you were wasn't it?'

'Oh absolutely, yes, the Antarctic. Big white continent, that's where I was!' What the hell had Aurora been thinking?!

Johnny seemed happy just to keep talking so Lan let him, fearful that she would put her foot in it if she led the conversation.

'I think you said in your email that you were looking at icebergs? They must be tricky to get close to.'

'Hmm, yes. Icebergs, sea ice as well. Most of my work has been on sea ice. But anyway, I thought you did a really good job of dropping that iron sulphate in the right place. You saw that screenshot of the bloom after you dropped it? It was exactly in the middle of the eddy, couldn't have been better.'

Johnny shrugged and pretended to be embarrassed. 'Well, you know, I just used your coordinates. It was nothing really. Took us a week though, five trips in all.'

'And you managed to get the stuff dissolved alright?'

She was still asking about that? Johnny thought she was alright with it. 'No, we just poured the powder into the sea, like you agreed in your email. As long as we did it downwind it worked just fine, and kept our mouths shut of course. Blew all over the place actually.'

'Oh? I thought we'd agreed you'd dissolve it first?'

Now she was getting really weird. 'But in our emails

you agreed it wasn't going to make any difference. Don't you remember that?'

'Emails?'

'The emails you sent when you were down in the Antarctic?'

Lan stared at him for a few seconds. 'Excuse me for a minute Johnny. Don't go away. Lots more to discuss!'

She saw Aurora talking with Zeb a few metres away and quickly walked over to her and tapped her on the shoulder. 'Aurora, can I have a quick word?'

'Er, sure. Excuse me Zeb.'

'What the hell's all this about me telling Johnny it was okay to just toss those sacks of sulphate over the side?' Lan hissed.

Aurora looked like a guilty child who had been caught doing something she'd been told not to. 'Ah…well Johnny just couldn't get the stuff dissolved whatever he tried, so he wanted to discuss with you what to do,' she said quietly. 'So when you decided not to be involved anymore I had to have some way of answering his questions so I set up a fake email account in your name. You've had quite a few conversations with him. He got quite chatty with you actually.'

'Marvellous! You might have warned me!'

'I was trying to in the café when he showed up, if you remember,' replied Aurora indignantly.

Lan turned to leave, then turned back. 'What else am I supposed to have done? Quickly!'

'Er, you've been on a boat in the Antarctic, out of phone contact for several months. You asked him to go and do a trial run a few weeks before the main event—that was to get him out of the way when that government inspector came here—and I think you might have promised to help his daughter go to university.'

'Government inspector? When the hell did they show up?' her eyes were wide with alarm.

'Oh, months back. Don't worry I took care of him. He didn't come back.'

'Oh dear God! We're all going to jail. This isn't the end of this. We'll talk later,' and with that she strode back to Johnny, who had made himself useful finding a couple more beers.

'Just remembered something I had to tell Aurora,' explained Lan, grabbing the beer and taking a couple of large gulps. 'Yes, we were lucky to have email on that boat. No phones or anything and the internet was really crappy, but at least we could send and receive emails sometimes.' She took another mouthful of beer. 'I'm sorry I'd forgotten about them, but good that it all worked out in the end.'

Someone had started playing country music on a boom-box.

'You like a dance, professor?' asked Johnny, crumpling his beer can and tossing it into the bonfire.

'I'm not a professor, and I might not be anything soon, but yes, that would be nice,' replied Lan. As they went over to a section of beach where people we starting to dance she filled him in on how her funding had run out and she was looking at other options.

Johnny took her hand. 'Been a while since I've done this, just yelp if I tread on your toes.'

Lan was surprised how comfortable she felt with him, how unpretentious he was. Straightforward, that was probably a better description. They didn't dance for long, agreeing that neither of them were particularly good at it, and went to sit on some rocks from where they could watch the proceedings instead. He was curious about her background.

'You're métis, right? Which people are you from?'

Lan looked at his face, illuminated by the bonfire. Without warning she felt very melancholic. 'I don't know. I tried to find out once but I couldn't… I was adopted at birth and never knew my real parents.' A tear rolled down her cheek.

Johnny looked embarrassed. 'I'm sorry, I didn't mean to pry. We can talk about something else.'

Lan sniffed and wiped her face. 'God! Where did that come from?! Sorry, I didn't mean that to happen.' She blew her nose. 'I was brought up in Montreal so I'm guessing maybe Algonquin or Cree, but I really have no idea.' She laughed. 'I'm a fake métis, I was brought up by an older French-Canadian couple, so I guess culturally that's what I am, but they died a few years back.'

'That must be tough, not having roots. All of us here on Esh have been here forever. 'Since time immemorial' is the phrase we use. Of course that has its drawbacks too, all your relatives are living on your doorstep and in a small community like this everyone knows everything about you. No secrets. Sometimes it's nice, but it can be very annoying at times.'

Lan shrugged. 'Not much I can do about my situation. My adoptive parents were pretty good, I had a happy childhood, good education, I've been successful, nothing to complain about… But it would be good to know where I came from, it would make me more complete.'

The two of them talked for quite a while, about his hopes for Julie, her career issues, his problems with his own father and his fiery temper, his sadness when his wife had been killed and his feelings of guilt about it. Eventually the bonfire started to collapse and people drifted away. Then he walked her back to Aurora's where they stood like teenagers on the doorstep for a minute. They hugged and she gave him a kiss on the cheek before he left.

Observing them from her unlit bedroom window Aurora watched them embrace and then part. 'Oh crap. I did not see that coming,' she muttered to herself.

CHAPTER 20

Bad Publicity

Despite the best efforts by the entire village to catch as many salmon as possible using gill nets across the river mouth, forty million are an awful lot of fish and there was little danger of their numbers being depleted. It was after all a labour-intensive process, with twenty or thirty people needed to deploy and haul in each net and others busy gutting and filleting the fish and extracting the roe. For a few weeks unemployment on the islands was a thing of the past. Haze served non-stop hot meals and coffee to all involved, with pan-fried salmon for breakfast, lunch and dinner. The good times were back.

Notably absent from this frenzy of activity were Gaia and Wolf, who were embarked on a frenetic fishing effort of their own. In keeping with their agreed marketing plan for Echelon Escapes they were busy getting out the news of the bumper salmon run on social media, posting photos of the river teeming with salmon on Facebook and Instagram and asking everyone to forward the news. Busy but not product-ive, because after a few days they realized that although a lot of people looked at the pictures and 'liked' them, it was not resulting in any bookings. An annual salmon migration way up north did not make much of a dent in the viewing figures for the latest cute cat videos, and they failed completely to make any of the trending topics lists that they had hoped.

Early on Gaia had emailed Craig Cuomo asking what his availability was, only getting a response a week later to say he was in Tanzania and wouldn't be back until November—filming was running weeks late and he was plagued by bush flies. Disappointing, but in a way she was secretly glad he wasn't there to provide a magic solution. This would force her to prove that she could do it herself, and she was more comfortable on social media than TV anyway. She would just send him a few Facebook posts and ask him to like them instead.

Wolf's pragmatic view had prevailed and they had decided to keep the message simple and not talk about *how* the fish had got there, just the fact that there were millions more than most years. Most of Wolf's posts were aimed at potential tourists and fishermen, and the ease of catching them—'Wow! Look at how many salmon there are up here this year! Check out #EchelonEscapes' was his main tag line for his dozens of salmon photos.

'You know what the problem is?' said Gaia one morning. 'People are seeing this as advertising—but worse than that, advertising at the wrong time of the year. Its October, everyone has gone back to work and no one is interested in fishing holidays. We need to change the message.'

She was right of course—it might be big news to them, but to the average Canadian or American it was noise-level news from a place they'd most probably never heard of and there were more interesting things going on; the football season was now well underway, an event simply more important in most people's minds.

'I hate to go back on what we agreed but the real story here is not the fish but how they got here—that this is the first time a community got together to successfully combat the impacts of climate change. If we focus on that we can raise public awareness of Esh. And then next spring we can do the advertising and it will have more chance of working because people will remember it as the place that had so many salmon.'

Wolf went along with it, not that he really agreed but because they could do both, so the following day Gaia phoned up the news desk of one of the national broadcasters. She finally got through to someone called Duane who said he handled news tips, so she explained the miracle of Esh's plentiful salmon migration and the fact that it was man-made. Duane sounded unconvinced.

'Yeah…but you don't really know for sure your dumping this stuff caused the increased numbers, do you? And to be honest, even if it was, I think this would be more for our science guy than national news.'

'But this is a huge story!' gasped Gaia. 'It's the first time anything like this has been done!'

'Like I said, science guy,' replied Duane. 'Sorry!' And with that he hung up.

The science guy turned out to be a girl called Fran. After listening to Gaia for a few seconds she interrupted. 'Are you calling from a university?'

'Er, no, I'm a concerned environmentalist from the Esh community.'

'We really only take news stories from regular science organizations. And to be honest I'm not convinced that a bigger-than-usual salmon migration really counts as news anyway. Thanks all the same!'

Swallowing her pride she emailed a few posts to Cuomo, who duly retweeted them the following day, but that didn't generate any extra interest or web traffic for Echelon Escapes either. Curious, she looked at his Twitter page and immediately saw the problem.

Gaia returned glumly to Wolf. 'This is insane! Do you know how many followers Craig Cuomo has on Twitter?'

Wolf shrugged. 'No idea. A million? Two?'

'Two thousand. Two bloody thousand! He said he had lots!'

'Sooo…not quite as media savvy as you thought,' he smiled sweetly. He was still quietly sore about the speed with which she'd accepted his invitation to jump on Garcia's boat and go off to Utopia without him. He would have enjoyed telling people he'd played pool with Yaz Garcia.

The following day was better—she phoned the local TV station in Vancouver, getting through to one of the assistant producers and pitching the salmon run as a community event they might like to cover, and to her relief he agreed that it could be something worth sending a crew out for. 'We haven't done anything on Esh for ages, so I guess this could be timely,' he said unenthusiastically. Gaia agreed to meet their presenter and his crew off the ferry in a few days' time and to take them to the river where they could get good shots of the salmon shoals and the gill netting.

The 'crew' turned out to consist of a sullen girl called Alex who behaved and dressed like a teen gang member—trainers, bomber jacket, a baseball cap on backwards and a camera bag on her shoulder—and a young man in a suit called Gordon who was the reporter. They didn't seem to be talking to one another, like a couple who'd just had an argument. Perhaps he'd tried to chat her up on the ferry. Both were clearly way out of their comfort zones on the muddy main street of Edenshaw, but Gordon at least seemed determined to do what they'd come for.

They started off by heading up to the river mouth to film the villagers pulling in the nets, with Alex wading into the shallows to film them close up and getting some nice low-level shots of the river teeming with fish, glistening in the sunlight. Next, Gordon said he wanted to interview some people about the harvesting process so he talked to four of the folks hauling the nets about their traditions, whether they did this every year, and how important the salmon had been to their community in the past. He seemed particularly pleased with his interview with a young girl of about eight who said that she'd never done this before but it was a lot of fun, and she especially liked cutting their heads off after they'd caught them. Finally they went back into town and did some shots of Edenshaw village and the harbour, and then Gordon recorded his introductory piece to camera.

'Here in the Echelon Quartet Islands it's time for the annual salmon run when millions of salmon return to the river they were born in after years at sea. It's a big communal event and everyone gets involved in the catch, even the little 'uns! We talked to some of the villagers.' He stayed still while Alex played it back and checked there wasn't anything distracting in the background and then nodded that it was okay.

'That should do. What time's the ferry back?' he asked Alex, checking his watch.

'Hang on a minute,' interrupted Gaia. 'You haven't

even mentioned the real news story here, the fact that this year's run is much larger than usual because we seeded the ocean with iron sulphate.'

Gordon looked startled. 'You did what?'

'Seeded the ocean. We sent out the village fishing trawlers and dumped a hundred tons of iron sulphate dust which caused a bloom of plankton which boosted the salmon population.

'I'm not sure our viewers are going to be interested in that,' replied Gordon cautiously. 'It's really just a piece about the salmon as an annual event for the village…'

'But that's just the point!' exclaimed Gaia in frustration. 'It's not been an annual event in recent years because there were no salmon. We brought the salmon back!'

Gordon looked at his shoes, appearing to think about what Gaia had said. 'Ferry's in an hour,' commented Alex, with a gesture indicating that she for one planned to be on it. After mentally weighing up the relative merits of being harassed by Gaia for a full hour until the ferry left, versus humouring her and being sure they made the ferry, Gordon relented.

'Okay, let me interview you about that and you can explain it. I can't promise we'll use it though, that's really down to our production editor.'

They set up again facing the harbour and Gordon did the intro again. 'Local environmentalist Gaia Thompson explains why this year's salmon run is so much larger than in previous years.'

Gaia explained as enthusiastically as she could about how global warming had changed the salmon's migratory habits and the devastating effect it had had on the village, and how after talking with their MP and realizing that they were not addressing the issue the village had taken matters into their own hands and decided to experiment with ocean fertilization. 'It's really just a research project at the moment,' she concluded, remembering Lan's warnings, 'but obviously it's an experiment that looks like it's working.'

'That's fascinating Gaia!' replied Gordon into his microphone. 'So this iron sulphate is sort of like fish food then?'

Groaning inside at how he kept dumbing things down she gritted her teeth and smiled as she replied. 'Yes Gordon, it's like we laid a giant trail of breadcrumbs from the ocean back to the river to attract them back.'

'Brilliant!' enthused Gordon. 'That's a really good visual statement to end on, I like that. Right Alex, I think that's a wrap, let's grab a cup of coffee and then make sure we don't miss that ferry!' He thanked Gaia for setting everything up and for showing them around, and then the two of them headed off towards Haze. Gaia shook her head in despair as she watched them depart and hoped that her 'visual statement' as Gordon had called it would be enough to get her comments included.

- - -

Despite Gordon's promise that he would let her know when the piece would air, Gaia was as surprised as the rest of Edenshaw to recognize their village in the last item on the evening news a couple of days later. Quite a few of the villagers had seen Gaia showing Gordon and Alex around of course, but nobody had bothered to ask who they were, and the general assumption was that they were just a couple of her friends with a fancy camera.

Zeb was drinking in Saul's bar when they saw it.

'That's your hotel!' exclaimed Zeb, turning around to look out of the window as though he expected to see the film crew still there. The camera cut to the river and groups of people straining on nets to haul in the salmon.

They watched in silence until Saul winced at the bit where Gordon mentioned that the village had given nature a helping hand by spraying the ocean with iron sulphate.

'Cat's out of the bag now,' growled Saul. 'Thought we'd all agreed to keep this quiet?'

'We did.'

'She shouldn't have said that last part. No problem with them coming here to film the salmon, that's all good publicity, but that last bit is going to be trouble.'

Zeb shrugged. 'Maybe, maybe not. Chances of someone in some government department seeing it don't worry me, it's only the local news. And it helps us with our friends up north—we never gave them any proof that we'd done the project and had sprayed off their coast too. Most of them have seen more salmon than usual but not as much as here and I've had a couple of calls about it—a bit sceptical how much we really helped. If they see this and know that we got a really good result and hear her saying why then they're going to believe us a bit more. Don't want them all getting together and coming down here and making problems for us.'

Saul nodded. The last thing he wanted was people knowing that he had profited from what was supposed to be a project for the common good, paid for with community money.

'You're probably right. No reward without risk, and we did make fifty G's from them. Best thing we've done all year my friend.'

'Made me a believer in global warming alright! Finally got something out of it. Makes up for all these years of funny weather and rising tides.'

- - -

Two others who had benefited from the TV coverage were Julie and Aiyana, who were delighted with the five seconds of screen time that Haze got.

'It looks great, Jools!' exclaimed Aiyana. 'They got some nice interior camera angles, you can hardly tell it's just a converted greenhouse.'

'And so full of people, looks so busy.'

'It *was* busy! Being towards the river end of town was a real stroke of luck these last few weeks. I've seen so many people walking home from the netting who just stopped and came inside. Do you realize people were actually queuing outside yesterday lunchtime?'

Julie shook her head in amazement. 'Just crazy! I hope we manage to keep some of them as regulars after all this has finished.'

'I hate to say it, but your Dad's climate project was the best thing that's happened for us in terms of publicity. Before it happened we had a pretty stable clientele but now virtually everyone in the village has eaten here or at least walked past us going back and forth to the river. Thanks to the salmon everyone knows who we are and where we are—they won't be back every day but they will now and then, even if it's just for coffee.'

Aiyana gave Julie a hug. 'We should start to think about what we do next. I mean not right away, but we've proved that we can create and run a profitable sustained business. We should think about how we follow it up. It was always supposed to be a first step towards creating a better Esh,' she added thoughtfully.

'Yeah, I was thinking about that. If this fertilization project is going to be a regular event then we should take advantage of it. I was thinking that next year we could start bottling and selling the roe. Right now people are just harvesting it for their own use, but if we could package and distribute it properly we could sell it to the shops on the mainland. I bet those delis in Vancouver would love it.'

Aiyana smiled. 'That could be a really good add-on business. And it would give us a chance to get the Haze name to a wider audience. Right now we're unknown outside of the village.'

'And it would bring some outside money into Esh...'

'We could become the distributor for the whole village,' continued Aiyana, thinking out loud. 'If we spent some time this next year to make contact with some of those shops then we'd be ready for next season.'

'And once we have the contacts we could supply them with other local food...not just seafood but there's local market garden produce too. It could end up bigger than Haze, and we'd need to hire people for it—I don't think we could do both. We need to think this through.'

'I'll ask Aurora what the plans are for doing this again. If it's definitely going to be repeated then it could be worth us buying bottling equipment and stuff to do this, but it will need quite a bit of organization.'

Julie looked thoughtful. 'There's increased tourism too. I know Gaia and Wolf are trying to attract more of them here, especially sports fishermen after the salmon. That would give us another outlet for the food side. But it really only works if we can get a clearer idea of what the plans are to repeat the project on a regular basis.'

Less than enthusiastic about the TV coverage of the salmon run was Aurora herself, who had not seen Gaia showing the TV crew around and was surprised to see the scenes of Edenshaw on the evening news. At first she didn't associate it with Gaia at all, it just seemed to be one of those light community pieces they pad out the end of the news with when nothing much is happening. As the scenic shots of the river glinting in the afternoon sunshine continued with Gordon's cheerfully inane voiceover she started to relax, and then froze as Gaia's smiling face appeared.

Gordon's commentary continued to explain why this year's salmon run was much greater than in previous years, thanks to some help the salmon had gotten from the villagers, before he cut to Gaia's final comment: '…we laid a giant trail of breadcrumbs from the ocean back to the river to attract them back.'

'Oh shit,' she muttered. The cat was out of the bag now. But what would be the consequences?

CHAPTER 21

Supping with The Devil

Gaia might have been frustrated by the absence of any strong climate change message in the TV interview, but it was certainly effective in producing results. The following morning Wolf got a phone call from a man in Calgary keen to arrange some group salmon fishing for that weekend.

'There's four of us and we'd be looking to hire a boat for the weekend and do some salmon fishing out in the sound, and of course we'd need accommodation for the Friday and Saturday nights, and meals etcetera.'

'No problem, that's exactly what we cater for,' replied Wolf smoothly, not mentioning that this would actually be the very first time they'd catered for anyone. He made a note of the growing list of requirements and promised to call the guy back within an hour with some firm pricing. The good news was that they were bringing their own fishing gear which was one less thing Wolf needed to source and also showed that at least they knew what they were doing. Boat, booze, rooms, meals, evening entertainment. How hard could it be?

As soon as he was off the phone he was across the street to Saul's.

'I've got some guys want to hire a boat and book four rooms for this weekend. Can you help me out?'

Saul looked up from reading his newspaper. Afternoons were a quiet time in the bar.

'Boat no problem. Rooms big problem. We haven't had the top floor guest rooms open in five years.'

'Well they ain't going to come at all unless they've got a place to stay! Can't you open them up?'

Saul shook his head gravely. 'They're a mess, Wolf. You can take a look but they really need repainting and new furniture. People used to complain about the beds and I don't even have sheets anymore—that's why I gave it up, so much work needs doing.'

'Let me at least take a look,' pleaded Wolf. 'This is the first group we've had, I have to do something. And you'll get some good bar business out of them too, they're coming to enjoy themselves.'

Saul shrugged and led the way upstairs. It was dusty and the wallpaper was peeling in some of the corners, but it wasn't quite as bad as he made out. It wasn't as though the floorboards were collapsing or anything. The two of them went through the rooms one by one and Saul begrudgingly agreed that if they swapped some of the furniture around they could salvage four usable rooms, but on condition that Wolf and Gaia did the moving and they vacuumed the hallways and gave the top floor a general clean. And they'd need to provide their own bedlinen.

'Okay, we can do that. So how much for the rooms?'

'Fifty bucks a night. Each.'

Wolf reflected that there was after all some benefit to the fact that Saul hadn't rented the rooms in years. They were still only two-star accommodation, not even

TVs in the rooms, but he knew that you couldn't get a motel room on the mainland for much under a hundred. Saul obviously felt he was getting a good rate, but he didn't need to know that.

'Fifty? You just said yourself they were barely rentable. Even after we've cleaned them up—*I've* cleaned them up—they're going to be very basic. You're going to get plenty of bar business and a boat rental out of it, see the big picture. And its eight nights in all, you have to give me a discount for that alone.'

'Jeez, man, you were just begging me for them! Where else are you going to put them? I don't see any other hotels in Edenshaw.'

'You've got me by the short and curlies this time, but this is just the first group. It's only one day after we got that free publicity on TV and I'm expecting quite a few more. I might have to invest in some log cabins or something if you're going to gouge me every time.'

Saul fidgeted with the mats on the bar.

'Okay, tell you what—I'll give you a fifteen percent discount on the rooms, but I want five hundred a day for the boat and they buy all their beer from me.'

'You're not leaving me much margin for mark-up, but I guess I can live with that. Payment when I get paid, okay?'

Having dropped by Haze and made Julie's day by agreeing prices and arrangements for the weekend, Wolf did some quick sums and phoned back his client.

'Okay, so I've checked availability for the boat and accommodation and we're looking good. In total it'll be two thousand five hundred for the weekend all-in, which includes all transportation and a campfire barbeque on the Friday evening, and plus your meals and drinks at cost.' He held his breath and waited for the response, hoping he'd not overplayed it.

There was a short silence. 'Sounds very reasonable, we'll take it. We're planning on hiring a floatplane from Victoria and flying up probably Friday early afternoon, so could we look at maybe a quick late lunch when we arrive, and then head out for a few hours to get the feel of the water?'

Wolf wasn't a fisherman himself but had a nasty feeling that their schedule would be governed by the tides, but the salesman in him said yes anyway and he promised he'd pick the group up personally from the floatplane jetty as soon as Ron gave him a firm arrival time.

'And as soon as you can confirm a hundred percent we'll need fifty percent payment by credit card.'

'Sure, no problem. By the way do you think we'll be able to see any whales? A couple of the group are into that.'

'Whales? It's late in the season, but they do come through the channel so I would say you have a fighting chance. No guarantees though.'

This was working out better than he'd hoped. As soon as he disconnected he found Gaia and gave her the good news.

'Echelon Escapes is in business, hon! I'm just waiting for the guy to make sure the group can get their flights sorted and then we should get the deposit.'

Gaia beamed and gave him a congratulatory high-five.

'Makes everything worthwhile! Any idea who they are, exactly?'

'They're coming from Calgary and didn't seem too concerned with the price, so I'm guessing something to do with the oil industry, maybe.'

'Let's hope they appreciate the nature then.'

'He did ask about the whales—I'm assuming they wanted to watch them and not hunt them, although maybe I should have checked…' He grinned. 'There is however one small catch with all this though.'

'Uh oh.'

'We have to clean up Saul's hotel rooms ourselves. And shift a couple of the beds. And provide sheets and pillows.'

'I can live with that. Do you want to wait for the guy to confirm, or just get on with it?'

As it turned out Ron called back thirty minutes later with flight times and a credit card number, so the two of them spent the afternoon cleaning the upstairs corridors and rooms at the hotel. By the time they'd finished Wolf was feeling that his mere one hundred percent mark-up on the price of the rooms and fifty percent on the boat wasn't nearly enough, but even so they should make almost a thousand dollars profit from two days effort, more than they made in two months from the shop. And as he kept telling Saul and Gaia, this was just the tip of the iceberg; as soon as word of the salmon spread they could expect plenty more groups to follow.

- - -

Wolf borrowed Zeb's big truck to pick up his guests and their fishing gear from the plane, which landed two days later a little after two o'clock as promised. The four all looked to be in their early forties and had that easy demeanour of successful professionals who were senior enough to take Friday off and wealthy enough to spend a thousand each on a fun weekend. Although it was less than a minute's walk to the hotel he made a show of carrying their luggage and checking them in to a smiling Saul, who for all his initial grumbles played the part of the hotel-keeper immaculately. Once they'd dropped their stuff in their rooms he got them back in the truck and took them down the street to Haze, where Julie had laid out a late lunch table buffet for them. Soon she was getting compliments on their cooking.

'This quiche thing is amazing,' commented Ron, a man who obviously enjoyed his food. 'We weren't expecting anything so good for somewhere so isolated.'

Julie beamed as she refilled their coffees. 'Thank you! Appreciate it.' She pointed to the large photo of her two Hollywood celebrities which now occupied a prominent position on the wall. 'Craig Cuomo said exactly the same thing when he and Yaz Garcia were in here a couple of months back, so you're in good company.'

'Craig Cuomo? Seriously?' remarked one of the others, looking impressed.

'Yes, he has a place here on the island, comes every summer,' replied Julie nonchalantly, omitting the fact that he hadn't actually bothered to set foot in Edenshaw for a decade until June. Several of the group nodded, impressed, hopefully thinking how fortunate they were to have found this west coast gem.

At the hotel the group had changed into what they evidently regarded as suitable fishing trip attire, long shorts, colourful polo shirts and baseball caps. All were slightly overweight and Wolf was not surprised that they favoured sports where you could sit down, like fishing. So not really the hiking outdoor types that Gaia had been hoping for, but bums on seats nonetheless.

'So what do you guys do when you're not fishing?' he ventured curiously.

'Oh, we're commodity brokers,' replied Ron cheerfully. 'We buy and sell stuff, mostly wheat and metals, but out here we'll deal with whatever people want.'

'Out here?'

'In Calgary. It's not a major community hub so we don't specialise like they do in Toronto, out there you get guys who just deal with one thing all day long. I know plenty of guys who only trade a single commodity, like just palladium for example. We trade whatever comes along, except oil and gas. There are separate firms which deal with that.'

Wolf nodded, not even sure what commodities were really, let alone why they needed people to negotiate their buying and selling.

'So, what? Lumber, corn, coal…?'

'Sure! You'd be surprised what people need. We had some European brokers wanting a forest the other day. Not the lumber, just to keep the forest as forest, for the carbon credits.' He looked out of the window across the bay at the hillside beyond. 'Steep hillside like that is likely worth more for carbon credits than lumber.'

Wolf looked puzzled.

'Steep slopes are labour-intensive and expensive to fell. And most likely problems with erosion afterwards if the trees are removed, which means remediation costs.'

'Ah, I hadn't thought of that, interesting. Sounds a bit like the project we did here that caused the exceptional salmon run this year. You heard about the Echelon ocean fertilization project?'

Ron nodded as he munched on his third Cajun

chicken wrap. 'Saw it on TV, yes. Didn't really understand it.'

Wolf was about to try to explain but thought better of it. 'It was an experiment the community here did to boost the ocean's uptake of CO2, a sort of marine version of forestry. But it had the side-benefit of bringing in the salmon as well, which is what you folks are here for. Talking of which we need to get you to your boat before three so you can get in some decent fishing before the tide turns.'

They piled back into Zeb's truck and headed down to the harbour where Johnny was waiting with the *Sea Eagle*. Saul might be making the profit from the rental but that hadn't stopped him from calling on his son to do the actual work. Plus *Sea Eagle* was a slightly smaller vessel better suited to line fishing.

'There's a crate of beers in the cooler,' said Wolf cheerfully, 'and sunset is at six-thirty so it's a short day today. Johnny's just going to take you near the river mouth where the salmon are, near where the TV crew were last week, but tomorrow you'll have the full day and we can try a few other spots further out.'

After waving them off he picked up Gaia and they drove a couple of kilometres along the coast to a spot on the beach where people often had campfires. After dark it was an atmospheric place with a great view across the water, with the mountains silhouetted against the sky and the lapping of the water on the shore. By some fluke of the current it also got a lot of driftwood washing up there so you didn't have to go far to make a fire, so they took advantage of the daylight to set up a fireplace with rocks and gather a couple of piles of wood for later on.

- - -

'They seem to have enjoyed themselves, drank all the beers anyway,' commented Johnny, when Wolf asked him that evenings in the hotel foyer if the afternoon had gone alright. 'Actually they're not a bad bunch, at least they know how to handle a rod. But they're city folk nonetheless...'

They were interrupted by the group coming down from their rooms, so Wolf bid Johnny goodnight and the rest piled into the truck for the drive to the camp site.

'Not much nightlife in Edenshaw so we've laid on a barbeque down on the beach for you,' explained Wolf. 'Julie and Aiyana from the café are going to be roasting a couple of the salmon you caught this afternoon, and my partner Gaia who you saw on the TV will be there too.

'Sounds great!' replied Ron, whose bouncy demeanour and cheery face had started to remind Wolf of an overgrown puppy. 'Just as long as you're not planning on any campfire songs or karaoke, we could do without those! But some good food and a few more beers would be just what we need.'

The campsite was in a cove where the trees came down to the beach and as they approached they could see the flare of the fire in the darkness. Julie and Aiyana had a gas barbeque set up for the fish and a table for the rest of the food, and Gaia was busy breaking up sticks and feeding the fire. As soon as she saw them arrive she went and opened a cooler and started setting out the beers.

'Here you go guys, help yourselves!'

She introduced herself and Ron, James, Dave and

Kev did likewise.

'I'm useless with names, but great to meet you. Looks like the food will be about twenty minutes, so just chill out and feel free to chuck more wood on the fire if it needs it.'

Most of the group wandered down to the water's edge, gossiping about their catch that afternoon. Kev stayed next to the fire and gave Gaia a hand snapping some of the longer pieces of wood.

'This is cool,' he said. 'It's so dark out here! We don't get this in Calgary, too much light pollution. And I love the way you can hear the waves.'

'Cheers!' Gaia clinked beer bottles with him. 'So Wolf said you are commodity brokers?'

Kev scowled. 'We're here to get away from work! Just boring stuff, nothing special. I'm more interested in what you do actually, I saw you on TV talking about some experiment you'd done to bring the salmon back?'

Gaia and Wolf had agreed that as far as this evening went they wouldn't push any political agenda on the clients, since they were paying handsomely for everything, but since Kev had specifically asked and he knew from the TV that that was her interest it would be rude not to tell him a bit about it. She explained how the whole community used to be based on a plentiful annual salmon run, but that it had dwindled dramatically over the last few years, and that climate change was most likely to blame.

'Hard to know for sure though, isn't it? It's like all that stuff about there being more hurricanes in the US—there might be a vague general connection with increased temperatures, but…' He shrugged, not completing his sentence.

'True, it's not like anyone will ever be able to say that a specific factory belching out CO2 in Texas caused a specific hurricane in Kansas or anything like that,' agreed Gaia. 'It's not like that, it's a more general correlation—more CO2 equals warmer air in the atmosphere, which leads to more variability in circulation patterns and more frequent extreme events in the weather short-term.'

The others were walking back up the pebbled beach towards them.

'I guess so. I mean I'm not a climate change denier, don't get me wrong, I'm not questioning the science. I know that ninety-five percent of the world's scientists agree on it and all that, I'm just saying that so far the impact has not been that noticeable so I don't think anyone can be absolutely sure—either that there will be more severe effects down the road, or that cutting emissions will actually change the future and make things go back to how they were.'

'Climate change, eh?' grinned Ron, who had joined them. 'All bullshit if you ask me.'

Gaia opened her mouth and then closed it. The client is paying she told herself, the client is paying. And he is entitled to his opinion.

'You're just saying that to wind me up,' she smiled serenely.

'Yeah, a bit,' he laughed. 'Jury's still out if you ask me.'

Gaia shrugged. 'But don't you worry about it just a little bit?'

'Seriously? No, I don't. I reckon I have more of a chance of being hit by a bus than I do of dying from global warming.' He grimaced. 'It's just…it's kinda out of my timescale. They say we might start getting some serious impact here in like fifty years, but I'll be dead by then. Maybe it'll be a big deal for my kids, maybe, but honestly I think there will always be other things that will have a much greater impact on their lives—their health, whether they have a job, marriage—all the usual stuff.'

The other three nodded their agreement.

'It's easy for you to be green out here,' added James, defensively. 'For us living in the city, not so much. You've got your commute, business trips, all that stuff, you can't not do them. It's not like we get to choose whether our electricity comes from a wind turbine or anything like that.'

Gaia was almost going to point out that you could do exactly that, even in oil-rich Alberta, but didn't.

'Me, I reckon it's the government's responsibility,' said Dave, swigging his beer. 'Let's face it, it's a very complex issue, more complex than Joe Public can really understand. We're all relatively well-educated guys and we don't understand it—only those UN bodies and the government have the resources to really make a judgment on it, and only they have the ability to pass legislation to do something about it. And they are—they've changed the rules to ban new coal-fired power stations, to phase out old-style electric light bulbs, make electric cars more competitive—they're doing all the things that need doing. We just have to trust them.'

'Hey! Looks like the food's ready!' shouted Ron, pointing behind the others to where Julie and Aiyana were unwrapping two large salmon from silver foil. 'Time to eat, guys!'

Wolf and Gaia hung back as their guests went to get their food.

'They're not idiots,' said Gaia after a moment.

'They're well-educated successful people. So why is climate change such a blind spot for them? Why don't they get it?'

'They just don't see it as a priority, or urgent. I guess deep down we are all adapted to react to short-term threats, we don't know how to react to something a long time in the future. It's like if someone was driving a car towards you and you can see from a kilometre away they're headed straight at you. Your best strategy is to wait until it's a few seconds away and then jump out of the way. If you move too early you know the car can still easily hit you by simply adjusting its direction slightly, but that's not so easy when its closer.'

'Hmm…so you're saying man will ultimately be incapable of responding to climate change in a logical way because our decision-making processes developed in the stone age, in response to a need to outwit a sabre-toothed tiger?'

'Exactly. If these guys are typical—and you know they are—society will wait until the effects are really hurting, and then react to the consequences and not to the root cause.' Wolf shrugged. 'And who's to say they're not right? Maybe the fastest way of reducing the world's carbon dioxide levels to safe levels is not to reduce slowly over thirty years, but a sharp-shock reduction caused by a catastrophe which decimates the human population? Maybe there is no nice orderly solution.'

'Pass me another beer,' replied Gaia. 'It's my stone-age coping-mechanism.'

CHAPTER 22

Channel Change

'Ah Lan, you're in. Could you do me a favour and talk to this guy from Channel 5 about some ocean experiment that's been done in the Pacific northwest?'

Before she had a chance to say no Bradley had transferred the call and hung up.

'Hello? This is Dr Renouf, how can I help you?' Lan spoke into the void, with no idea what to expect but not connecting it to Esh. There were plenty of academic oceanographic studies done every year and she assumed it would be one of those that they were interested in getting a comment on.

'Hi, this is Colin Neal from Channel 5. We're covering a story about a small village in the Echelon Quartet Islands which has apparently done some kind of ocean seeding experiment offshore BC to boost salmon stocks? We're looking for a university oceanographer who could give us some comment on it for a news segment.'

Lan felt the hairs on her neck raise in alarm—she was totally blindsided by this, but she needed to know what was about to come out. 'Okay…in principle yes I'd be happy to,' she replied cautiously. 'But I don't actually know anything about it. Can you tell me more?'

Colin explained how they'd picked up on something an environmentalist called Guy Thompson had said on a local news piece in Vancouver about the annual salmon migration on Esh, that the numbers were up this year because the villagers had taken upon themselves to dump tons of iron dust in the ocean to boost growth of plankton and hence salmon. What they wanted was to have Lan as an oceanographer comment on the science, and were going to ask someone from the Ministry for Climate Change to talk about the climate aspects. They hoped to record the piece in the next couple of days for an evening news segment. Colin said he could email her the link for the original piece so she could get up to speed on it.

After Lan agreed she immediately phoned Aurora.

'Aurora! What the hell's this about Gaia giving a TV interview? I've just had Channel 5 news on wanting me to join a discussion about it!'

'Do they know you were advising us?'

'No, but I thought we'd all agreed not to publicize it at all? So why's Gaia talking to the local news about it?'

Aurora sighed. 'Yeah, we all found out about that yesterday when it aired. Zeb and I went to talk to her about it today. Apparently she and Wolf see the main benefit of the project as being an example of how communities can take matters into their own hands, and felt strongly that the whole benefit of the project would be lost if they didn't tell the world the story of how a small community did this when the government failed them. It seems that for them it wasn't about so much bringing the salmon back and reviving Esh's fortunes, it was more a political message.'

'Silly bitch! How selfish.'

'My sentiments exactly. But what's done is done, now we have to handle it and minimize the damage.'

'So has she mentioned I was involved? Or is she going to? If Channel 5 are picking this up others are going to too. It won't be the last interview she's asked to give.'

Aurora reassured her that Gaia had promised that she had not mentioned Lan's involvement, and didn't plan to.

'Okay, well hope she understands she could well be costing me my job here. It's all very well her saying she won't name me but I can easily imagine her being questioned about how they knew where to drop the iron sulphate and whether the village had any expert help, and her admitting there was someone and then the media will be digging into who that could be and why they aren't talking…'

'Of course, I see your point entirely. I'm really sorry about this—I'll go back and emphasize that she needs to keep her mouth shut,' replied Aurora. 'Can I tell her you've been asked to talk about it on Channel 5?'

'Sure. And ask her to let you and me know if she's going to do any more interviews, so we're not in the dark about it.'

Aurora updated Lan about how busy everyone was with the salmon harvest and how much it had changed life in Esh, for now at least. Aurora tried to reassure her that she had done a good thing and reminded her that it was probably the village council rather than Lan who were more likely to get prosecuted if this thing went any further.

'After all the villagers are the only ones who actually did something concrete—we bought the iron sulphate and went out and dumped it in the ocean—all you did was talk about it, and there's nothing that ties back to you. I don't honestly think anyone could come after you for that and we could always say you tried to dissuade us—which in a way you did, you always stressed that the chances of it working were low.'

'Yes, I guess when you put it that way I shouldn't worry too much. Just that my whole future at the university is pretty fragile at the moment, for reasons nothing to do with this, and I suspect it would suit some of them to have an excuse to get rid of me.'

- - -

The following afternoon Lan made her way to the Channel 5 studio in downtown Montreal for the interview. She knew Gaia in the Vancouver studio but she'd not met the government spokesman, a Paul Hawthorne from the Ministry for Climate Change in Ottawa.

Once everyone was ready, Colin Neal explained the format—he would introduce the piece, then talk to Gaia first to ask her about the project, then ask Lan to comment on the science behind it, before going to Hawthorne for a response. Then they would open up the discussion for a few minutes and see where it led. The broadcast piece would only be three or four minutes long, but they expected to talk for about fifteen minutes and then edit it down. It seemed straightforward enough.

After the initial intro Gaia gave an impassioned explanation of why the village had felt it necessary to do the project, emphasizing that it was both experimental and a last resort after their MP had told them that nothing the Government was doing to combat climate change was likely to have any impact on salmon numbers in the foreseeable future. 'Our community is entirely dependent on the salmon harvest. Without it most of our people are unemployed. People have been leaving and our only hope of remaining as a viable community is to find a way of bringing the salmon back and this was an act of last resort.'

Colin then came to Lan. 'So, Dr Renouf, before we get onto those policy issues, can you describe the science behind this ocean fertilization approach?' He sounded quite neutral about the matter, careful not to be judgmental.

Lan explained how ocean fertilization had been proposed before as a possible geoengineering method, using iron sulphate to feed the plankton which in turn consumed carbon dioxide as they grew—but in this case the focus was not on absorption of carbon dioxide but the plankton themselves which ended up being additional nutrition for the smaller fish and migrating salmon who fed upon them.

'So the science is sound, but as a way of boosting the salmon numbers it's a high-risk strategy and specifically where they end up to is anyone's guess, it could easily have been Alaska, for example.'

'So there's a scientific basis to it, albeit experimental, but shouldn't it be something the government should be promoting as part of the fight against the impacts of global warming?' asked Neal, turning to Hawthorne.

Hawthorne smiled patronizingly. 'Our policy for tackling climate change is aimed at the big picture, not at trying to fix individual consequences such as a temporary shortage of salmon. You need to address the root cause so we aim to reduce carbon emissions across

Canada and in developing countries too, not just one small island in BC. We are promoting a collaborative approach to climate action, keeping emissions in check, while at the same time promoting transparency and accountability.'

'But surely there's a place for a local response to specific problems too?' pressed Colin.

Hawthorne sighed. 'Not really, this is one small community in a remote part of the country. Their carbon emissions are minimal anyway, not much industry or vehicles, so this sort of activity is simply unnecessary. It's an inefficient use of resources. Seventy percent of global carbon emissions come from big cities so that's where we should focus our effort, not in places like the Echelon Islands. So not only is it unnecessary it actually distracts from the more important national and global efforts that the government is engaged in.'

'You're missing the point, it's not emissions from Echelon that are the issue at all,' interrupted Gaia, visibly frustrated. 'We're just one location suffering the consequences of the whole planet warming, in the same way the Maldives are suffering from rising sea levels caused by warming elsewhere. Of course the government should be focused on the big picture of reducing carbon dioxide emissions nationally and globally, but our nation's response to climate change is the worst in the industrialized world—in a recent survey Canada was ranked twenty-seventh out of twenty-seven developed countries in terms of our effectiveness in tackling greenhouse gases.'

'Harsh words, Mr Hawthorne! What do you say to that?' countered the host, sensing good television in the making.

'I'm afraid that's simply not true. I'm not aware of this report you're referring to, but I can assure you that the government strongly supports the long-term goals laid out in the Paris Agreement, and we will continue to advocate for climate action internationally and to engage with sub-national governments and non-state actors to develop ambitious climate solutions,' replied Hawthorne smoothly, as though it was a line that he had trotted out many times before, which indeed he had.

'But is our track record really as bad as Ms Thompson claims?'

Hawthorne looked offended. 'I can assure you we are far from the bottom of the pack when it comes to tackling climate change. By 2030 we will have delivered a *thirty percent* reduction in CO2 emissions. Of course I can't predict how that will affect individual fisheries but I can assure you that under the government's policies the climate is under control.'

Colin turned to Lan for another comment. She was genuinely shocked at how blatantly Hawthorne was lying, either that or he was extremely poorly informed considering he was the government's chief spokesman on the subject. Either way, pretending that there was nothing to worry about was very misleading. There was no sense of urgency or even a recognition of the seriousness of the situation. She felt she had to put the record straight.

'I am familiar with the report Gaia's referring to, it's from a reputable European institute, and as she says it puts Canada at the absolute bottom of the league,' she said carefully. 'One of the reasons they rank Canada so poorly is that they don't believe we will meet our 2030 emissions targets that the Deputy Minister is referring to. In their opinion—which I have to say I share—there seems to be a complete lack of appreciation of the urgency of the situation by the government: we no longer have decades in which to gradually reduce our carbon dioxide emissions, and if he thinks otherwise he's highly optimistic.'

'As just one example, a research project that I have been part of shows that the arctic summer sea ice is disappearing much faster than was forecast. We used to think that it would be there until the end of the century, but the latest data show that it will be gone within five years. Once that has happened and we have dark sunlight-absorbing water at the top of the world instead of reflective white sea ice it will change atmospheric circulation patterns across the whole northern hemisphere, which will in turn accelerate the warming further. But instead of tackling this urgent issue the government is actually cutting back on research that will help us understand the problem and find solutions. They seem to be just hoping that the problem will go away, but it won't—it will bite us all in the ass.' She paused. 'So quite frankly I think it's both understandable and commendable that a community like the Echelon Quartet Islands, which has by all accounts been particularly hard-hit by climate change, are now taking matters into their own hands. Kudos to them!'

On the monitor Lan could see that Hawthorne was upset, taking the criticism almost personally. 'I'm sorry but Dr Renouf is being unnecessarily alarmist and quite irresponsible here. On the issue of sea ice the IPCC and world scientists are completely agreed that it will be at least 2050 before any significant melting occurs, and our policies to cut emissions are entirely adequate to meet those dates. For her to claim she has some different and special knowledge that the world's scientists don't have is just ridiculous. And as for this one community taking matters into their own hands, it's more than irresponsible, it's illegal. There are international conventions to protect our oceans and dumping large quantities of chemicals into the sea contravenes those conventions too. It's clear to me that this was a completely unscientific project, almost an act of marine vandalism, and that there's no real evidence that the larger than usual salmon run was nothing more than coincidence and definitely not caused by this 'experiment'.'

Lan jumped back in as soon as he finished speaking. 'Mr Hawthorne, the reason I am claiming special knowledge of the state of our sea ice is that it is my research group which has been measuring it and providing the data to the rest of the scientific community for over ten years, so I can tell you categorically that it is melting far more quickly than previously thought,' she replied indignantly. 'The IPCC only updates its forecasts every seven years and their forecast is simply out of date, precisely because the situation is changing so rapidly.'

She hesitated, aware that she should probably leave it at that, but couldn't. 'As for the Echelon fertilization experiment, I was actually involved in its early stages in an advisory capacity and I can assure you that the location for fertilization was carefully chosen to maximize the chance of boosting salmon stocks returning specifically to the Echelon Islands. It was not random chance as Mr Hawthorne claims—it was a geoengineering experiment which has actually achieved more concrete and positive results than the government's policies have delivered in decades.'

Realizing he had a minor scoop on his hands, Colin quickly followed up. 'So a bit of a first then?'

'I would say it's both a first and an initiative this country should be proud of,' replied Lan tersely, knowing she'd said too much already. Diplomacy was never her strong suit.

'Final comment, Mr Hawthorne?'

There was an awkward pause for a few seconds in which Hawthorne seemed to struggle to know what to say before recovering his composure and smiling calmly. 'I'd just reiterate that our policies are long term and solid—based on the recommendations of the many hundred climate scientists who put their names to the IPCC report, not on last year's measurements of sea ice which might be just a blip in the long-term picture. We will continue to implement long-term control measures, not engage in one-off projects that might increase CO2 uptake over a few hundred square kilometres of ocean for a few weeks. People should be confident that we will reach our targets and that we will protect this country from the threat of climate change.'

'Lots of interesting developments and different opinions there,' summarized Neal. 'The way of the future or marine vandalism, only time will tell. Remember you heard it first here on Channel 5 news!'

On the monitor Lan could see Hawthorne rip off his mic and walk away. He looked pissed. Had she been a bit harsh? She didn't think so, but the consequences were to be considerably further-reaching than she could imagine.

CHAPTER 23

Crazy Talk

'I'm sorry, but we simply can't allow a situation where ordinary citizens are taking control of the weather! That's the government's business.'

The meeting was getting tense and Winter didn't like how the Minister was becoming agitated. Since the Government had been returned in the election and his own position reconfirmed Winter had noticed that he had become more confident, more dogmatic in his views.

In addition to the Minister, Hawthorne and Winter there was also Michael Malik and a couple of government lawyers in the room. Winter was about to point out that the Echelon people had not actually been modifying the weather but simply responding to existing changes by spraying chemicals in the sea, but thought better of it.

Hawthorne frowned. 'In principle I sympathize with any community that wants to do something about climate change,' he replied. 'But I agree entirely with you that it has to be done in coordination with the Ministry. They can't just try whatever crazy geoengineering scheme they find on the internet. We need to be firm about this.'

Eddington turned to the lawyers. 'Okay guys, how do we put a stop to this?'

The more senior of the legal team leaned forward and opened the file in front of him. 'Well, Minister, the main legal instruments applicable to this case are the United Nations Convention on the Law of the Sea, the 1972 Convention on the Prevention of Marine Pollution by Dumping of Wastes and Other Matter, also known as the 'London Convention', and the 1996 Protocol to the London Convention which is known as the 'London *Protocol*'. Assuming the account given in interviews is correct, there's no question that these people have violated UNCLOS and…'

Eddington interrupted. 'Un-what?'

The lawyer was caught off guard. 'What?'

'You said they had violated un-something?'

'Oh, UNCLOS. The UN Convention on the Law of the Sea. UNCLOS for short.' He smiled.

Eddington nodded and the lawyer continued. 'So there's no doubt they've violated these conventions, but there are a number of obstacles to actually prosecuting them for it. First, we have no proof that they've actually done anything at all.'

'But the Thompson woman admitted it on national TV!' exclaimed Hawthorne. 'Twice!'

'And all we have is her word for it,' continued the lawyer. 'People take credit for things they haven't done all the time, but more importantly she has never admitted any personal involvement—she merely implied it was other unnamed people from the village, but it could equally have been a third-party who they paid to do the work—we simply don't know. So who do we prosecute? We would need to identify the individuals involved. Second, they could say in their defence that they were not polluting the ocean but *nurturing* it—that the iron sulphate they put in had the effect not of poisoning marine life but of feeding it. The ocean-dumping clause was really designed to prevent people dumping scrap metal and the like, not relatively small amounts of chemicals whose effect is ambiguous. So, in a nutshell they haven't committed a specific crime and even if they had we wouldn't know who to prosecute.'

Eddington rolled his eyes. 'Look you see my problem don't you? We can't have communities up and down the west coast taking climate change into their own hands and dumping stuff into the sea in the misguided hope it will fix their problems. We have to do something to discourage it.'

'Couldn't we send out the Fisheries guys to find some problem with their boats and get them impounded?' growled Hawthorne.

Malik winced. 'We have enough unemployment out there without putting more of them out of work. Before you know it they would have a crowd of fishermen in front of a TV crew saying the government is preventing them from earning their livelihood. Anyway, as you point out we really don't know who was involved in this and there are too many fishing trawlers up there on the coast, even assuming it was one of theirs which was used.'

There was silence for a few moments while everyone tried to look as though they were thinking hard for a solution.

'How about…' began Malik, still thinking through what he was trying to say, 'we treat it like that time they were blockading those sport fishing lodges? As I recall we arrested the ringleaders on the grounds of causing public mischief, held them in jail for a few days and let them off with a warning—and they didn't do it again.'

The senior lawyer shook his head. 'Not the same at all, I'm afraid. That was close to shore, this happened well outside the territorial limit. And we have no evidence they were disturbing other people, no 'mischief' involved.'

'Perhaps we're looking at this wrong, Minister,' smiled Hawthorne. 'Perhaps we shouldn't focus on the act itself, which as they say is tricky because we have no actual evidence of it, but concentrate on the consequences for public order, which after all is what we are really worried about.'

'I don't follow you,' replied Eddington blankly.

'I'm thinking *incitement* to cause illegal acts, rather than the act itself. Couldn't we prosecute Gaia Thompson—on the basis of the two TV interviews she's already given—for inciting others to break the law?'

Eddington shrugged. 'You might have something there. I don't really care about what this one group have done—they're welcome to their free fish—it's the prospect of dozens of villages up and down the coast all following suit that's the real issue. That would really make it look like we couldn't enforce our international treaties. Bad news.' He looked at the two lawyers.

'Yeah, but they haven't actually encouraged others to do the same, have they? They made some comment about doing it because the government's climate change policies hadn't done anything to solve their salmon problem, but they didn't suggest others do the same.' The younger lawyer was flipping through a transcript of the Channel 5 piece. 'Nope, can't see any incitement here.'

'But surely you don't need to specifically look into

the camera and say 'we encourage you to try this yourselves'? Can't you just incite by example, as it were?'

The older lawyer shook his head. 'No, you need to issue some kind of instruction to a third-party in order to commit incitement. Otherwise just about anyone who committed any kind of offence could also be charged for incitement. If you parked your car on a double-yellow line—civil offence—you would end up being prosecuted for inciting others to do the same—criminal offence. It would be unworkable.'

'Seriously?' asked Hawthorne. 'So if I get into a bar fight I could be arrested for assault, but if I shout 'come on lads' while I do so then it would be assault *and* incitement to violence?'

'In theory, yes. But in practice it would need to be a bit more forceful than that, ordering someone to attack a specific individual, for example.'

'Useful to know,' replied Hawthorne thoughtfully.

'Okay, let's be logical about this,' said Eddington. 'The law they've broken is this UNCLOS thing. First, we need to investigate and see if we can gather any actual evidence. There's a good chance we can come up with something, maybe we can figure out who was involved and which vessels, maybe seize navigation records or something. For all we know these people videoed themselves or kept records of how much they dumped. We should check their Facebook pages.'

'I'm not sure even that will get us very far,' interrupted the lawyer. 'Let's think this through. Suppose you gather evidence that specific individuals went out on such-and-such a day to a specific location and dumped X tons of iron sulphate. There are three major loopholes they could use to avoid prosecution. First they could claim that iron sulphate is not a pollutant but a source of nutrition, which as far as I can see is a very defensible claim. Or, if they made any kind of measurements they could claim that this was done as legitimate scientific research, which is exempt from the convention. Or thirdly, they could claim that they were not disposing of the iron sulphate but merely *placing* it in the ocean.'

Eddington looked up wearily. 'Excuse me?'

'The London Convention does not cover the placement of material for a purpose other than the mere disposal thereof, provided that it is not contrary to the aims of the Convention. In other words, you would have to prove that they were dumping the stuff with the specific objective of getting rid of it in order to prosecute them.'

'But they were deliberately putting it in the ocean to feed the plankton,' objected Winter.

'Precisely. They were placing it there to nourish the plankton, not trying to dispose of the iron sulphate itself.'

The group was silent again. 'That oceanography professor did claim to have advised them,' observed Hawthorne after a while. 'She could also easily say this whole thing was her university research project, whether or not it really was.'

The more senior lawyer nodded. 'And not to depress you further, but there's another potential legal showstopper. These are all international marine conventions that we are signed up to. We are also signed up to several climate change treaties, notably the United Nations Framework Convention on Climate Change, that actually *require* us to take steps to reduce the amount of carbon dioxide in the atmosphere and the oceans—which is precisely what these folks claim they were doing. The judge would first have to decide whether their actions should be viewed as illegal under a fifty year-old marine pollution convention, or legal under a five year-old climate change one. You really would be at the mercy of the individual judge on that one. It's entirely possible you bring a case and the judgment finds not only that the older conventions no longer apply to iron sulphate fertilization, but the judge commends them as good citizens for helping meet our climate change obligations.'

'That would be your basic nightmare scenario,' chipped in the younger lawyer cheerfully. 'Not only do you lose this case but the Court specifically says it's okay for others to follow suit.'

'We're not risking that!' replied Hawthorne tersely. 'But we can't do nothing either!'

There was silence while they all tried to think. One of the lawyers was thinking about when he could move on to another portfolio. Malik was thinking about how he could get Hawthorne's job, and Winter was thinking about how ridiculous this all was.

Winter was the first to break the silence. 'Why not?'

'What?' retorted Eddington.

'Do nothing,' smiled Winter. 'Or to be exact, open an investigation and say we're going to prosecute them—and then do nothing. The world will see we're doing something and know that if they try it we'll take action against them too. The folks in Edenshaw will probably all be too scared to try it again.'

Eddington looked at him, raised a finger as if to make a point, but then turned to the lawyers.

'How long could we keep a case like that active without actually going through with it?'

The older lawyer sighed. 'Four, five years maybe…'

Hawthorne beamed with pleasure. '…which is well into the next parliament.'

'And therefore most likely someone else's problem!' replied Eddington euphorically. 'Nice pragmatic solution, completely defensible, no one can blame us for this whichever way it goes! Paul, instruct the agency to open an investigation. Make sure you speak to the Director yourself so he understands what we want: thoroughness, but don't let it interfere with more important matters. Tell him to take his time, leave no stone unturned. Smart thinking, Adam!'

He stood up to leave. 'And see if you can't do something about that professor. She shouldn't be going on TV shooting her mouth off like that. At the end of the day she's a public servant. She shouldn't be telling people they can actually do something effective about climate change without waiting for the government to tell them what to do. I mean, that's just crazy talk, right?'

'Yes, Minister.'

CHAPTER 24

The Great Climate Change Debate

It did not take long for several consequences of Lan's spirited attack on Paul Hawthorne to emerge. Two weeks after the Channel 5 piece aired she was invited to appear as a guest on another TV channel. The producer introduced himself as Steve Evans and explained that they were based in Toronto.

'We're putting together a one-hour discussion program about the impacts of climate change on communities and potential conflicts between individual and government actions, and we'd really like you to be on our panel.'

Lan hesitated. 'Last time I did that it didn't go too well.'

Steve chuckled. 'Actually we absolutely loved the way you walked all over Hawthorne. It was so obvious you know your stuff as well as have passion for your subject, that's the main reason we'd like to have you on our program.'

Lan could see his point, but she'd found even the short news discussion quite stressful. She didn't really see herself as an environmental activist and said so.

'Okay, but this will be a great opportunity to showcase your research and communicate its importance to a mass audience too. That must surely have value to you, not to mention your university.'

She hesitated. It wasn't that she didn't want to do it, but it wasn't a great time. She really needed to focus on her funding and any negative publicity might well hurt her chances. The last thing she needed at the moment was to attract the wrong kind of attention.

'We can pay you an appearance fee,' he added hopefully.

Lan hesitated. 'Look, why don't you let me think it over for a couple of days? To do this properly will take me several days for prep as well as coming over to Toronto and I'm not sure I have that much time.'

Reluctantly Evans said he could call her back tomorrow, but stressed that he would need a commitment from her then. It was a hot topic and they wanted to get it in the schedules and start advertising it which meant they needed to know who they would have on—and trying to get four people together in a studio at the same time was, as he put it, like herding cats.

The second boot fell two hours later. At four o'clock she got a call from the department secretary saying Bradley would like to see her. When she got to his office he motioned her to take a seat. He looked miserable, as though he was about to go to the dentist. He didn't beat about the bush.

'Lan, I'm sorry to tell you that the university is terminating your contract of employment with immediate effect.'

She had never been fired before and it hit her like a two-by-four across the forehead.

'What?'

'You'll be given six months' pay in compensation for early termination, of course.'

Having got the bad news out of the way it seemed that Bradley just wanted to keep talking and avoid any awkward silences, or was perhaps he was afraid of an angry response. 'Your criticism of government environmental policy on Channel 5, made in your capacity as an employee of this university and as a public servant, was both unauthorized and in clear violation of our communications policy, and we've been instructed to let you go. I'm sorry.'

Lan was stunned. 'But you asked me to talk to them! You passed the call to me, remember?'

'I asked you to take the call. I didn't ask you to appear on their program. And I certainly didn't authorize you to state opinions which contradicted government policy.'

'I'm stunned,' she said. She looked at Bradley incredulously. 'I've been here twenty years. Academics appear on television and talk about their work all the time. I can hardly be the first one to correct an MP or a government minister about a matter of fact. He had everything wrong. Wasn't it my job to correct him?'

Bradley looked embarrassed. 'It all depends on who they are and how you correct them. This one did not take it well. You could have been a lot more diplomatic and I think you know that. Basically you chose to pick a fight with a senior government official on climate change and you lost.'

Lan said nothing, it was still sinking in. Deep down she was relieved in an odd way. One of her conclusions from her unsuccessful funding search was that she'd been concentrating so much on the research that she'd failed to communicate the conclusions of her work adequately to other scientists and the public. She had been thinking that perhaps it was time to do something else, but stepping out of academia completely was scary. Having this door closed, or perhaps more accurately slammed in her face, made it a lot easier to take the decision. Now she could devote herself one hundred percent to exploring those other options.

Her instinct was to defend herself and to argue but she realized it was pointless, at least at that moment. Bradley was clearly just the messenger, better not to say anything now, maybe file for wrongful dismissal later when she was thinking straight. From her limited knowledge of employment law she suspected that you had to give someone at least one verbal warning before firing them, but right now she wasn't even sure she wanted to stay.

When she got back to her office Lan the first thing she did was call Evans back and ask how much the appearance fee would be. She was pleasantly surprised by the answer. Maybe life outside academia wouldn't be so bad after all.

- - -

A few days later Lan was sitting on a stage in a television studio in Toronto wondering what she had gotten herself into. The program was a much more elaborate production than the ten minute interview she'd given for Channel 5.

There, she had been sitting in a booth with an earpiece and a photograph of the Montreal skyline behind her, talking at a TV monitor and safely separated from both the interviewer and the other participants, and without an audience. Now, there were four of them sitting uneasily side by side in armchairs, facing an audience of two or three hundred people, and it was live. She had naively assumed that any rash comments could be edited away, but no chance of that now. She needed to remain in control of what she said and not allow herself to get carried away like last time.

Her other panellists were a well-known and suitably bearded environmentalist, Bob Cowan, the MP for the Echelon Islands and most of the west coast, an enthusiastic and surprisingly young Asian man named Michael Malik, and Alan Goodman—an odd man who she understood to be a professional climate change sceptic. He was the retired CEO of a small oil company and now ran some kind of lobbying organization. When Lan innocently asked who his organization represented he became defensive and said 'the people of our country', before adding acidly that who supported him financially was none of her business.

The program was called 'The Great Climate Change Debate' and loosely followed the classic debating format with each of them being asked to outline their position in five minutes, then opening the floor for counter arguments and ending with closing statements. Evans opened the program by making introductions and explaining that the subject was topical because the world had just witnessed the first successful attempt by a community to counter a consequence of global warming, raising questions of legitimacy as well as whose moral responsibility it was to take action against climate change—individuals or governments—and what should be done when they were in conflict.

Michael Malik went first, his speech filled with buzzwords and catch phrases, reassuring the audience in soothing tones about how the government was 'fully engaged', that their emissions targets would ensure that they would meet the goals they had committed to in various international agreements, notably the Paris Agreement, the Doha Amendment, COP21 and COP22 and that through a combination of carbon taxes and investment in renewables the country was on track to have a near zero-carbon power generation grid by the middle of the century.

Lan found herself fascinated by the contrast between his confident body language—smiling, relaxed and assured—and the meaningless verbiage actually coming out of his mouth. But if the audience had had to vote at that moment she would have guaranteed he would have won the debate hands down.

If viewers were wondering at this point why they were even bothering to have a debate since all the challenges had obviously been overcome already, the earnest and bearded Bob Cowan quickly put them right—painting a picture of dire catastrophe, factories belching pollution and carbon dioxide, a world in which acid rain fell from the skies onto parched fields, chaotically changing weather turned wheat fields to dust, and profit-hungry oil companies pumped out ever-increasing amounts of black poison into a world in which governments were too feeble to stop them. Offshore, ocean acidification was killing the fish and on land the extinction of species after species through loss of habitat threatened a collapse of the global eco-system. In five minutes the audience was flipped from cheerful exuberation to wanting to slit their wrists, the easy way out of the Armageddon awaiting them.

But Alan Goodman swiftly comforted them, re-assuring viewers that Cowan's world view was simply wrong, a fabricated nightmare put about by the Chinese to sucker feeble western minds into the foolishness of renewables and wind turbines, an industry that the Chinese dominated and benefitted from. He even claimed that American solar panel manufacturers were in on the con, encouraging such paranoia and callously twisting public opinion away from the more efficient gas-fired power stations. Wasting resources on tackling climate change was paramount to throwing money away and signing up to 'bad, bad, ridiculous' international protocols such as the Paris Agreement was merely eroding the country's ability to remain competitive. The audience's desperation was quickly replaced by anger at how gullible their naïve government had been to fall for such a blatant ruse as the Paris Agreement and it's foolish emissions targets.

Lan was up last. Introduced as 'a climate researcher from the University of Upper Montreal' the first thing she had to do was emphasize that today she was not speaking on behalf of the university but as one of the world's leading authorities on arctic sea ice who had recently shown that the arctic was warming considerably faster than had previously been believed, and secondly that she was also involved with the Echelon experiment which had aimed to try and reverse one of the consequences of climate change at a local level, namely declining salmon stocks—but that tonight she would be talking mainly about the wider issue of global climate change and CO2 emissions.

'Tackling climate change is a psychological problem' she began, to chuckles from the audience, and a loud 'hear, hear' from Goodman. She glanced at him before continuing. 'I didn't say climate change *is* a psychological problem, *tackling* it is. We just can't bring ourselves to do it, and if we carry on as we are we will fail and the consequences are going to be very painful.'

She had people's attention.

'Let's face it, not just this country—which by the way ranked last in a recent study of national effectiveness at responding to it—but humanity as a whole has been completely hopeless about doing anything about it. We've known about the problem and how to tackle it, namely to stop pouring carbon dioxide into the air, literally for decades. It's been over twenty years since world governments agreed the first international agreements to respond to it, the Rio and Kyoto Protocols. But decades have passed and almost no countries have honoured their commitments. Instead, we fool ourselves into thinking we're doing something by coming up with schemes to justify not reducing emissions—schemes such as carbon credits and offsets. It's as though you had cancer, but instead of going to the doctor you put a few coins in the tin for a cancer charity, hoping that your own cancer will somehow be cured. It won't be because you're just ignoring the real problem.'

Years of giving lectures meant she was pretty relaxed about presenting, and she was getting into her stride now.

'So why don't governments meet those targets? Is it really so hard? No, it's because they know it would be the last thing they do. Electoral suicide. For a developed country like Canada or the US to actually achieve their emissions targets would mean extreme restrictions on people's liberties and way of life—it would require actions such as making it unlawful to use your car when there's a public transport alternative, the complete phasing out of gasoline-driven vehicles, and making air travel so expensive that nobody could go abroad for vacation. Coal and gas-fired power stations would have to be replaced by nuclear or renewables right away without waiting for them to reach the end of their economic lives. Those sort of measures would be so unpopular that no government would get even a tenth of the way through a true emissions-reduction program without being voted out. So they just can't do it, and to be honest I don't really blame them—it's human nature. Who of us would accept being forced to put up with a much worse quality of life today in the hope that it could mean a better life for some future population fifty years from now?'

'Governments are basically powerless to tackle climate change effectively, they're constrained by the voters. They can do some useful things of course, like passing legislation to ban those old inefficient light-bulbs, or adjusting taxes to make it more favourable for power companies to use gas to generate electricity instead of coal, but it's not enough to meet those emissions targets. Not even close.'

She looked around at the audience and pleased to see many were leaning forwards, obviously interested in what she had to say.

'Now part of the reason that they are held back by the voters is that there is a perceived lack of urgency. As I say, we've known about this problem for decades but for most people there's been very little visible evidence of global warming affecting their lives. People who live off the land might have noticed spring coming a bit earlier or the weather becoming less predictable, but most of the world's population haven't seen anything drastic. So it's natural to assume that if we've got through thirty or forty years without seeing much change we'll probably get through another thirty or forty.'

She smiled. 'Psychologists even have a name for it: it's called the 'boiled frog syndrome': if change happens slowly then we don't perceive it as urgent to react to that change. The theory is—and please don't try this at home—that if you put a frog in a saucepan of cold water and heat it slowly until it boils then the frog will die, because it doesn't sense the change and it stays in the pot—but if you drop the frog directly into hot water it instinctively jumps out. It's the same with climate change—because we don't see any visible change around us we don't perceive any danger and we therefore don't do anything to respond to it.'

'Of course it doesn't help that we keep being assured that things are not so bad or that they're being taken care of,' she continued. 'Mr Malik and Mr Goodman just told you that there wasn't a problem and we are constantly being bombarded with similar reassurances that things are okay. Think of all those oil company ads that show you how clean they are, how they've rehabilitated some bit of wetland, or that their cleaner fuels means less smog. There is a PR policy by many of the polluting industries to portray themselves as good citizens, to downplay the damage that burning fossil fuels is causing. Why do they do that? Because they don't want public opinion to force the government into measures that would damage their businesses, such as discouraging gasoline-powered cars.'

'And that brings us to the only people who can truly fix the problem: you and me, individuals. The solution is most likely going to come not from government initiatives but from individuals, from a younger generation with a sense of urgency, because this is a real crisis now, even though it might not feel like it. And a part of that will be groups of individuals working together on a specific issue, as happened in the Echelon Islands. While the government focuses on the larger national and international issues, they should also be encouraging the general public to take their own individual or collective action on reducing CO2 emissions within their control, whether it's insulating their homes to reduce energy consumption, or something bigger like getting together to build a village wind turbine.'

'Finally, let's not forget that climate change presents a huge opportunity for entrepreneurs and industry to provide commercial solutions. Companies that are early in the game of developing solutions to problems we know are coming should have a big market advantage—whether its developing crops better adapted to warmer conditions, or more energy-efficient desalination methods, or even something as simple as buying up property inland from cities under threat from rising sea levels and developing new communities. Why do you think the Chinese have been so keen to become the leader in wind turbines? Not just responsibility but commercial advantage too. There must be many opportunities to both help society adapt to the warmer planet we know is coming while also creating jobs and profits along the way, nothing wrong with that at all.'

Steve nodded to her to indicate that her time was almost up.

'So, my message to you is simple. Don't rely on your government to clean up the planet for you because they can't do it alone—it has to be an individual effort by millions of individuals like you and me. It has to be done urgently now, and it will mean significant lifestyle changes. There are things individuals can do in their own homes or lives—such as giving up foreign holidays, taking the bus instead of the car, switching to a meat-light diet—but also communal actions, such as group schemes for installing domestic solar panels. And finally, industry should look for opportunities from the warmer world we know is coming and take the initiative to develop commercial solutions which will benefit them as well as society.'

Applause followed and Steve invited Goodman to respond. He proceeded to disagree with everything she had said but didn't give any evidence or arguments, merely stressing that supporting jobs and industry was going to have a far greater positive impact on people than 'killing jobs by trying to restrict a necessary gas that we need. Biologists will tell you that plant life couldn't exist without it—that's why it's called a necessary gas.' Lan rolled her eyes.

Although Malik and Goodman were supposed to be on broadly the same side as the debate progressed Malik quickly distanced himself from him as someone who was clearly fairly radical in his views, and Goodman lambasted him back for promoting policies which pandered to the 'ridiculous and totally unproven lie of climate change'. Likewise, Lan found she really had little in common with Cowan—she didn't share his deep pessimism that nothing could be done or his doomsday attitude; he didn't put forward any solutions, only problems. She was a realist but an optimistic one; he had already given up.

By the end of the debate the final audience vote was almost evenly split, and none of the speakers had changed or moderated their views. From Lan's persp-ective the one that she felt she had most in common with was Michael Malik, after all they wanted the same thing, just disagreed on how to get there. Even so, she had the strong suspicion that he was merely spouting the party message and saying what he thought voters wanted to hear.

'You were a bit harsh about governments not being effective,' he commented to her afterwards. 'Us politicians are not always driven by public opinion you know, and we have achieved a lot by bringing in a carbon tax. It will drive a lot of clean behaviour both by industry and the public.'

Lan winced. 'Yes, but that's only because public opinion is pushing you to take action. You're following opinion, not leading it.'

They were joined by a colleague of Michael Malik's, who he introduced as Dr Adam Winter with the Ministry for Climate Change.

'I hear you're no longer at the university,' grinned Winter. 'So where do you see yourself going now?'

'Right now? I'm headed to Vancouver for a job interview.' She decided it was best not to elaborate.

He looked at her in an oddly detached way. 'I see, good luck with that.' And with that he asked if Malik was ready to go and the two of them left together, leaving her alone on the stage with Cowan who had been loitering, obviously wanting to ask her something.

He congratulated her on a good debate and then asked if she'd care to join him for dinner. No longer in his adjustable armchair she was startled to see how short he was. His beard made him rather ape-like. 'I feel like we have a lot in common, we're both…nature lovers. We should…compare notes,' he said with a simpering emphasis and a lecherous grin, presumptuously holding his arm out to escort her.

'Seriously?' She laughed and walked away.

CHAPTER 25

No Evidence

Lan's first face-to-face job interview in two decades was with an environmental organization headquartered in Vancouver. After getting over the initial shock of being cast out of her familiar university, the only work environment she had ever known, she was starting to find herself intrigued by the possibilities outside, and she'd always liked the city. However in hindsight she should probably have followed the advice she gave her own students and prepared for it properly.

Relying on instinct when asked what she thought the organization's policy should be towards alleviating water stress in the third world was not a good idea, for example. She did not know how constrained they were by the politics of the countries in which they operated, not to mention Canadian foreign aid policy and rules. It turned out that although her gut response of 'just drill as many water wells as funds permit' might have been pragmatic, it was not politically correct. She expressed astonishment and exasperation that an organization should allow itself to be so limited by other people's regulations. By early afternoon she was disillusioned about the position on offer, and the position itself was no longer on offer.

Disillusioned and depressed, she sat down in a café on West Pender Street and considered her options. She already knew how hard it would be for her to find another job in a university, her field was just too narrow, but the realization that it would be equally hard to find work in the private sector came as an unpleasant shock. Nobody had mentioned it yet, but the fact that she was mid-fifties had to be a factor. For the first time she felt mild panic and wasn't sure what to do next.

What she wanted to do was step off the elevator for a bit, just remove herself from the pressure of trying to find a job and think, but that would have been irresponsible. Or would it? Nobody depended on her. Her apartment was paid for and locked up. There was no cat to feed or child to take to school, and she had enough saved to survive for a while. For the first time in twenty years she had no deadlines, no meetings to get back to. Why couldn't she just take time off? The thought brought a smile to her face.

She looked at her watch, then checked a few things on her phone. The decision was made. Finishing the coffee she hurried back to her hotel, checked out, and jumped in a cab to the bus terminal for the ferry. She hadn't felt this exhilarated for months.

\- - -

Eighteen hours later Lan walked down the foot passenger gangway onto Edenshaw dockside. It was still early but she thought she sensed a livelier air since last month's salmon bonanza, more people about and vehicles on the road even at this hour, and the people had more of an air of purpose. She walked down the main street. It was too early to wake Aurora but maybe the café would be open, which indeed it was. Lan went inside and a waitress she'd not seen before smiled and invited her to take a seat.

She asked for a coffee and a croissant and read a newspaper she'd picked up on the ferry, killing an hour before seeing Julie arrive.

'Lan! You can't stay away, can you?' she smiled. 'What brings you back so soon?'

Lan laughed. 'Long story, but I was in Vancouver and had some spare time. Actually I need to talk to Aurora, do you know what time she usually comes down?'

'About now. She's probably in the living room. Do you want me to go and look?'

'No, I can go and find her, thanks.'

Lan got up and pushed open the door to the living room, carrying her bag with her. Aurora was hunched over her computer with her back to her.

'Hi Aurora. Surprise!'

'Lan!' She turned round, 'What are you doing here? I mean, lovely to see you, but I had no idea you were coming.'

'Neither did I until yesterday afternoon,' she replied, going over to give her a hug. 'I realize this is going to sound very reckless, but I decided to take a few months off and hoped I could spend it in Esh. Staying with you. I know it's an imposition…'

'No problem! Be delighted to have you…but what happened to your job? Or are you taking one of those, what do academics call them? Sabbaticals?'

Lan grinned sheepishly. 'Ah, yes, I guess I need to catch you up a bit. Maybe we should have a coffee first?'

Aurora moved towards the kitchen and then stopped. 'What am I doing? Julie makes a better cappuccino than I can. Have you had breakfast?'

'Yes, but I'll watch you have yours.'

Aurora waved to Julie as they sat down by the window. 'Two cappuccinos, and a croissant for me thanks.'

'I saw you on that TV debate the other night, very good performance I thought. But what was that about not speaking for the university?'

Lan realized that Aurora was unaware that she'd lost her job, so explained what had happened.

Aurora was shaking her head. 'It's all my fault, I should never have asked you to help us on this. And now it's cost you your job, that's terrible.'

'No, it's really not much to do with that. I mean that was the immediate reason I was on the TV interview, but the bigger reason was my difficulty getting funding. If I'd had a year or two of money lined up for my research I can guarantee you my boss would have fought to keep me on staff and I'd just have had a warning. It was unfortunate timing, this just gave him the excuse he was looking for to trim costs.'

Aurora shrugged. 'So what now? Another university?'

Lan explained the difficulties in finding another post and her decision to simply drop off the grid for a while.

'I need to step back and get some perspective, and I can still keep an eye on any positions that come up, not that I expect there to be any. It's the wrong time of year for university posts to be advertised, and there's precious few other ones that I'd be suitable for. No, I just need to completely disengage and try and think of something different.'

Julie brought their coffees.

'Maybe Julie would give me a job now the local economy's picked up,' Lan joked.

'Actually that might not be such a bad idea,' commented Julie. 'We already had to take on another waitress, things get so busy around here.'

- - -

In addition to learning how to make a decent cappuccino at Haze, Lan gained an enthusiastic student in Julie who turned out to be captivated by her research. During quiet periods in the café the two would often talk, Lan finding it stimulating to explain the challenges of climate change to someone without preconceptions.

She also realized that Julie often asked basic but thought-provoking questions that she'd not asked herself in years, such as: 'I don't understand why countries are not falling over themselves to develop renewable technology first. Surely if they're first, then they can corner the market and sell it to everyone else?' Good question. Or 'So the problem isn't caused by just a few individual dirty factories, its caused by billions of us individuals all driving cars, eating beef and leaving the lights on?' Correct. 'So doesn't the solution have to come from persuading all those individuals to change their lifestyles, rather than carbon-taxing factories which are not actually causing the problem?' Also a good point…

Helping out at the café was also a great way for Lan to meet more of the villagers and although most didn't show much interest in her professional background, one who did was Edwin Reid's son, Edward, on his monthly visits to Esh. As he guiltily explained to Lan one day, he had become quite dependent on Haze.

'I don't want to run down Edenshaw, really I don't, but after you've lived in a place like Victoria for a few years you really miss a decent cappuccino in the morning. Before this place opened there just wasn't anything. My Dad doesn't even own a coffee machine and the stuff in Saul's place is undrinkable. Plus the food here is great, makes the trips back home a lot less daunting. And there seems to be more and more going on here, it's become quite a social hub.'

Edward was also one of the few from Esh to have gone to university, something he credited largely to Aurora's teaching and encouragement. Apparently he was one of her first students to graduate, back in the early eighties, studying engineering at Victoria.

'Without her I don't know what I'd be doing, probably some unskilled job in Vancouver or maybe working on one of the logging camps. Either way I wouldn't have been very fulfilled, and I certainly wouldn't have as good a quality life.'

He was interested in the types of jobs she was thinking about and encouraged her to think outside the box. Their discussions reminded her a bit of those she use to have with Rick, who had quietly faded from her life since she'd announced she would be staying in Esh for the foreseeable future.

'If you're too narrow-minded about it then you would only apply for academic positions in oceanography, for which you say there's only two or three posts advertised each year. So you really need to broaden your outlook. But you've been studying sea-ice for years, wouldn't it be more interesting to do something else? Heck, I've been an engineer for thirty years and if I got made redundant I'd want to try something new! Maybe you should try something where you could use your oceanographic and arctic knowledge but whose focus is more environmental? Climate change is a hot topic these days, must be a few interesting opportunities there.' Lan found it reassuring that he'd come to the same conclusion as she had, and largely from a different direction.

Being disconnected so abruptly from her city life and university routine was odd though. She often found herself lost in thought, mentally exploring possibilities that had not occurred to her before and which would have been impossible to pursue previously even if she had. It was in one of these day-dreams that she came down one morning two weeks after she arrived and saw a man sitting in the café having his breakfast whom she knew that she knew—had just recently met—but it still took her several seconds to place him. He also seemed surprised to see her.

'Ah, Dr Renouf!' he smiled hesitantly, lifting his coffee cup in greeting.

Lan walked closer, recognizing the face but still not remembering the name. 'You're the colleague of Michael Malik, right? From the TV debate?'

'Yes, that's right. Adam Winter, Ministry for Climate Change. I was involved in some discussions with the Esh village council when they were first thinking about their project.'

'Ah, I see,' she replied non-committally.

'And now I'm back to investigate further on behalf of the Minister.'

She looked at him quizzically.

'The Minister wants a report on what exactly

happened. How much iron was injected, where and by whom. Actually I was trying to contact you in Montreal but couldn't find you, I wasn't aware that you were here. Since you claimed to have been involved in the project…'

Lan realized that she needed to be careful what she said. She looked at her watch. 'Sure. We can meet later today if you like. Maybe lunch, here? Right now I'm late for something though.'

Once out of the house she phoned Aurora. 'Don't go downstairs. There's a man called Adam Winter having breakfast in your front room who's asking questions about the salmon project.'

'Again?' Aurora quickly explained that it had been Winter who had come for the inspection six months earlier, before they even did the seeding.

'It's important none of us incriminates one another,' said Lan. 'How about we meet with Saul and Johnny right away to get our stories straight? And better call Gaia too, especially Gaia.'

Fifteen minutes later they were all standing in Saul's bar and Aurora was apologetically explaining how their trial run of five tons of iron sulphate had actually been a decoy to get their boats out of the harbour during Winter's previous visit.

'You might have told us,' grumbled Johnny. 'We could have just gone up the coast for the afternoon, done a bit of fishing.'

'Sorry,' shrugged Aurora. 'I was trying to protect you. Or to be exact Lan and I were,' she winked at Lan, remembering the email saga. 'If I'd told you then you would have been part of the conspiracy. At that point we didn't have any coordinates and for all we knew there might not have been suitable conditions this year and the whole thing might never have happened this year anyway.'

Lan updated them in on her brief conversation with Winter that morning as well as his earlier comments after the TV debate. It only took them a few minutes to agree what each of them should say. Gaia looked uncomfortable.

'You're sure that's what you want me to do?' she asked timidly.

'Just stick to the script this time,' replied Aurora firmly. 'No more improvisation please.'

Saul turned to his son. 'You'd better talk to your crew too.'

Johnny nodded.

'And we should all be careful around Charles Abbott,' added Aurora. 'It was him who tipped off Malik or Winter about the project in the first place, and I caught him taking pictures of the sacks being loaded on Johnny's last trip.'

'Hmm,' replied Johnny thoughtfully. 'Then maybe we could use that to our advantage…'

\- - -

Two hours later Lan re-entered the café and joined Winter at his table, where he was busy on his laptop, having not moved. 'This place might be wild and beautiful and all that but everything takes forever, especially if it involves Canada Post.' She smiled and put her phone on the table and picked up a menu.

'Anyway, tell me about this investigation. It sounds intriguing.'

Winter folded his laptop. 'Sure. As I mentioned in Toronto the Ministry has the responsibility to uphold the UN Convention on the Law of the Sea which outlaws dumping of chemicals at sea and ocean fertilization specifically, both laws which you appear to have broken.'

'*I* have broken?'

'According to what you said on Channel 5.'

Lan looked attentive. 'No, I don't think so. What I said was that I had been involved in the early stages of planning it. I didn't claim any involvement with the experiment itself. My involvement was limited to giving them some basic oceanographic knowledge about plankton bloom formation that they could have read in a textbook. I am—or was at the time—a lecturer in oceanography and part of my job was to educate people about oceanography. And as far as I'm aware UNCLOS only bans the act of ocean fertilization, not thinking about it.

'I suspect a lawyer might see it differently,' replied Winter dryly. 'They would argue that individuals involved in the planning and purchase of materials would be just as guilty as those who actually dropped the stuff in the water.'

Lan put her menu down. She was starting to think that the conversation might not go on long enough to make it worth ordering a soup, even if the government was paying for it.

'Why don't you just tell me what your involvement was and our lawyers can worry about whether it was legal or not,' continued Winter.

Lan thought for a moment.

'That sounds fair enough. Let's think. I was approached by someone claiming to be acting on behalf of the village asking if I would advise them on whether ocean fertilization would be an effective way of restoring the salmon run. I told them it would not be, and that although it might create a phytoplankton bloom there would be considerable uncertainty whether it would boost the salmon population, and that even if it did then the chances of those salmon returning specifically to Esh were low. They would have to be salmon who were born here basically.'

Winter nodded as if in agreement.

'Despite my discouragement I was phoned some time later and asked if I could use the satellite imagery that I have access to in order to tell them where to deposit the iron.'

Winter looked interested and made some notes on his phone.

'I told them that it would not be ethical to use university resources in that way.'

'And then?'

'They didn't phone me again. Quite a lot of time went by, many months I think, and I was contacted by Channel 5 asking if I would give a comment on the scientific background as part of a short piece they were doing with Gaia Thompson and one of your colleagues, Paul Hawthorne. During that discussion Gaia claimed that the village had gone ahead with the project, and I was surprised that it had produced the result they were claiming, and said so.'

'Yet you defended what they had done.'

Lan smiled. 'Yes, but that's not the same as participating in it, is it? I spoke up for it in that interview because in my opinion the government's efforts on combating climate change have been inadequate—even my own research has been cut—and in the absence of any firm government action in this area I believe communities should have the right to take action themselves, within the law of course.'

Winter made more notes.

'Do you know who purchased the iron sulphate?'

She shook her head.

'Do you know who sprayed it in the sea?'

'No.'

'Do you know the names of *any* individuals who were involved in the project?'

'Apart from Gaia? But I don't think she claimed to be personally involved either, did she? I'm quite curious to know how it was done actually. I've done a lot of ocean experiments over the years and I know how much logistical effort is required.' Lan leaned forward. 'Look, to be honest I'm sceptical they did anything at all. I suspect the salmon run was just natural variation, just a good year, and Gaia simply took the opportunity to get some publicity out of it. She and her partner run some kind of tourist operation here and it's in their interest to encourage people to come here for the fishing.'

Winter raised an eyebrow, as though he had not thought of that possibility. 'What about the person you talked to? Who was that?'

Lan frowned as though trying to remember. 'Hmm. Their name was sort of religious as I recall.'

'Religious?'

'Yes…Monk? Abbott? Something like that?'

'Charles Abbott?' Winter seemed surprised.

'That name is definitely familiar, yes...'

CHAPTER 26

Doubling Down

Next on Winter's visit list was Gaia. With its window full of flowers, soaps and hand-carved decorations her shop by the harbour was easy to find. She seemed surprised to see Winter, which pleased him—it was after all a surprise visit.

'How's business since the salmon came back to town?' he asked cautiously, still remembering the grilling she had given him at the village meeting with Michael Malik the year before.

She shrugged. 'Not much impact on tourism yet, which is what my shop mainly depends on, although we did get one group for the fishing. That's where the real money is: thousand dollar a day boat rentals and lots of booze. Soap and souvenirs, not so much.'

Winter smiled. 'Does that mean you're planning to make this iron fertilization an annual event?'

Gaia shrugged. 'Honestly, your guess is as good as mine. You know the reason why I called that TV station in the first place? Because nobody in this village can agree on anything, it's a wonder they got as far as they did. Don't get me wrong, I think the whole idea of taking direct action to combat climate change is great, but I'm probably the only person here who understands what that actually means. If there hadn't been the possibility of increasing the salmon harvest, almost as a by-product, then no one would have supported it. But hey, I've only lived here a couple of years so I'm still an outsider and they don't confide much in me yet. Maybe in a couple more generations.'

Slightly surprised by her lack of community-oriented response, Winter pressed on. 'So who was the actual instigator of the project?'

Gaia smiled innocently. 'The Edenshaw Village Council took a collective decision a few weeks after your presentation with Mr Malik. Somehow the general topic of doing something proactive to tackle the demise of the community came up, and the next thing I heard the whole plan seemed to be decided—but who exactly thought of it and who did what I couldn't say. Then there was a long time when nothing happened—months—until last month when the salmon arrived and people started saying what a large run it was and how it must be down to the iron fertilization.'

Winter looked at her sceptically. 'Really? Who exactly said that?'

'You could ask Saul. I only got involved because I felt we should publicize it as a grassroots climate change project, but I've come in for so much criticism from some of the villagers I wish I hadn't bothered now.'

'But who actually went out and did the fertilization? I only see a couple of boats over there,' nodding at the harbour, 'so it must have been one of them, right?'

'There's only four fishing boats in Edenshaw and I've not noticed anything unusual with them. They don't often go out and I didn't see anyone loading them with chemicals, but for all I know they contracted some big boat from Vancouver to do it for them. I'm guessing you couldn't just use a fishing trawler without some kind of special gear.' She shrugged as if it was all a mystery to her.

'So you're saying you have no knowledge of who did it, just that you were aware such a project had been discussed and then you saw the end result?'

'Pretty much. I mean the two had to be related, right? Those salmon didn't just swim here by themselves, did they?'

Winter looked at her in bemusement.

'What I don't understand is that a few weeks ago you seemed to know enough about it to act as the village spokesperson on TV, twice. Yet now you're claiming ignorance of everything. That doesn't add up.'

Gaia looked embarrassed. 'Well I had to do something! After the salmon arrived the villagers were all busy catching them—harvesting the roe is a big deal around here—but no one outside was even aware of it. We weren't seeing any tourists coming at all. So my partner and I decided we should at least publicize the fact that there was a record salmon run this year, so we called the TV station. When they were here we were looking for angles to emphasize how unusual it was and my comment about helping matters along and laying a trail of breadcrumbs just came out. It was like the last five seconds of a ten minute piece they did, that was all.'

'I see…'

It seemed that Gaia was more naïve than he'd thought, she certainly seemed embarrassed about it. For the first time Winter wondered if the whole thing really was natural after all; the fact that some other communities further up the coast had seen higher-than-usual salmons runs would certainly support that.

Realizing that he wasn't going to get anything else from her he thanked Gaia and went on his way. If this really had happened there must be other people who must know something, like the ones who'd actually done the dumping, the boat owners. He was starting to get quite intrigued by the whole business—it was like a detective story trying to figure out who did what and whether it had even happened at all.

But his afternoon proved fruitless.

Saul Davidson was friendly enough, welcoming him back to Edenshaw and even thanked him again for his first presentation, but would confirm only that the project had been discussed at a village meeting and claimed that he was unaware of the 'logistical details'. He denied that his boat had been involved and invited Winter to check his ship's log for any period he suspected the experiment had taken place, but warned him that his satnav had malfunctioned a few weeks earlier and he'd had to reset the whole thing, losing his digital logs in the process.

'We don't know exactly when this happened,' replied Winter. 'I was hoping you'd tell us.'

Saul raised his eyebrows. 'That's unfortunate. I can't recall dates of trips I made months ago but I'm sure I'd remember if I'd been doing something other than trawling for lingcod or herring.' And with that he retreated behind his bar and started loading glasses into his dishwasher.

Johnny Davidson laughed at the idea that a fishing boat could be used to spray iron sulphate into the ocean at all. 'Have you ever been on a trawler at sea in rough weather, Mr Winter? You can't just sprinkle things over the side, you'd be swept away. You'd need some kind of tank and pump arrangement just to get the stuff into the sea. You're welcome to look at my boat but I can assure you I don't have anything like that.' Winter peered cautiously into the hold and had to admit he couldn't see any tanks or pumps, and knew that there was no way of proving anything after all this time.

The one person he hoped might have more information was Charles Abbott since he'd made him aware of the plan for the project in the first place, although after Lan's claim that he had called her he was thoroughly confused about his true role. After tracking him down to his house behind the Co-op he quickly started to have his doubts about his reliability too. Unlike the others Abbott was keen to talk, too keen—clutching Winter's arm as though he might try and leave.

'I saw them with my own eyes, big trucks loading them boats up with sacks in the middle of the night. Coming and going, they made lots of trips out there.'

'Can you give me the dates?'

Abbott laughed. 'Dates? Last summer some time, I didn't keep a record. It went on for several nights.'

'Okay, but how can you be sure they were loading iron sulphate and not ice?'

'Ice? Why the hell would anyone be loading ice onto a fishing boat?' asked Abbott incredulously.

'That's what trawlers use to preserve their catch. They pack the holds with ice and keep the fish in it until they get back to port.'

Abbott looked at him suspiciously. 'Really? Are you sure about that?'

Winter had a nasty sinking feeling in his stomach. Not only had he failed to find any evidence of illegal activity, he was now starting seriously to question if it had ever happened at all.

'Let's just go over this again. You were at a village meeting when the idea of a project was first discussed, before Michael Malik and I visited. And you say that a few weeks after our presentation there was another discussion at which it was agreed to investigate iron fertilization as a strategy?'

'Yes sir, apparently so.'

'Apparently? You weren't there?'

'No, that was just the village council people. I heard afterwards that they'd discussed it and were planning to go ahead.'

'Alright, and what happened after that?'

'Well I don't know!' Abbott looked flustered. 'At the very first public meeting, the one before you came, I had argued strongly against it—strongly I tell you—but when other folks voted to look into this climate change rubbish I told them to go to hell and left. I didn't bother to go to any meetings after that because it was obvious they were going to be a waste of time.'

Winter looked at him wearily. 'You left? So you weren't actually there?'

'Damn right I wasn't!'

'So you *assumed* that they made plans to go ahead, and later you saw some trucks loading something onto the fishing boats which you *assumed* was iron sulphate?'

Abbott nodded vigorously. 'Saw that truck on and off for weeks. And then that environmentalist woman announced on TV that they'd done it.'

'But you don't know which individuals were involved?'

'They all were! You should lock up the whole damn village council, they're all a bunch of First Nation liberals!'

Winter took a deep breath. 'Nothing wrong with being liberals, Mr Abbott, or First Nation, you know that. Most of the population around here are First Nation, and they have a long cultural history of preserving the environment. It's their right, whether or not you agree with it.'

'Huh!'

'One last thing. We were told by Dr Renouf that you had called her on behalf of the Council to ask whether the fertilization technique would actually work. Can you confirm that?'

Abbott looked thoughtful. '*Doctor* Renouf? Look, I talk with a lot of important people, I can't keep track of them all. I don't remember calling her but I certainly wouldn't deny it. Maybe she called me, I can't remember.'

'You weren't representing the village council?'

'Of course not! They probably just claimed that because I'm a respected member of the community. If they said that I'm going to sue them!'

Winter started to explain that it was Lan who had made the claim not the Council, but Abbott didn't appear to be listening. This whole thing was more and more contradictory and confusing.

Depressed, he thanked him and retreated again to Edenshaw's only café, where he found Aurora reading a newspaper in a corner.

'Ah, the inquisitive Dr Winter,' she commented dryly. 'I'd heard you were around again. Did you find our secret stash of chemicals? Or our fleet of ocean-going tankers?' she grinned mischievously.

'This is a serious matter Miss Jones. We don't really need to find physical evidence since your spokeswoman has already admitted that the project took place.'

Aurora laughed. 'Our spokeswoman? You mean Gaia? She certainly wasn't representing the community here when she did that silly bit of self-promotion. She was just taking advantage of the annual salmon run to encourage a few tourists to her tour business.'

'But she clearly stated that it was a deliberate act by this community to try and reverse the decline of the salmon.'

Aurora rolled her eyes. 'Look, she's no fool when it comes to marketing, she knows she has to say something outrageous to get attention. That local station has barely any news but even they wouldn't have put her on if all she'd had to say was that the annual salmon migration had started. Where would have been the news value in that?'

'You're saying she invented the whole project?'

Aurora sighed. 'Let's just say that the first most people in Edenshaw heard of this 'fertilization' project was when she appeared on TV and claimed that's what had happened. Sure, there had been some discussion about it at a village meeting last year, over a year ago probably, in fact I think it was probably me who might have first mentioned it, but as I recall it never got beyond just talk. Besides no one here had the first clue on how to make it a reality.'

She suddenly remembered about the existence of the Echelon Quartet Carbon Offset Company and hoped that he wouldn't look into recently registered companies on Esh and discover it, but there was no reason why he should.

'So you're saying there never was a fertilization project, it was all just talk? I seem to be hearing that a lot today.'

Aurora leaned towards him. 'That's what I've been trying to tell you all along! Do you really think this community has the resources or the knowledge to do some major ocean engineering experiment? Seriously?'

Winter admitted it stretched credibility.

'Isn't it a lot more likely that the increase in the salmon run was just natural variability?' Aurora sat back and sighed. 'The honest truth is that it was discussed and we did some preliminary research, from which we discovered that we would need hundreds of tons of iron sulphate which we couldn't afford, a large vessel we didn't have, fitted with tanks and pumps we didn't have, and above all knowledge that we didn't possess of where to drop the stuff—not forgetting a huge amount of luck. Overall it looked like the chances of it working were virtually non-existent. In the end we decided that the whole thing had so little chance of working that nobody in their right mind would try it.'

'So why did Gaia think it had actually happened?' he pressed.

'She wasn't involved! She'd been at the public meeting and that was about it. But by some fluke she was the one who first saw the salmon, months later—she goes out for early morning walks—so she put two and two together and made five. I guess she felt some kind of personal involvement simply because she was the first to see them, in fact she came running down the street telling people! Before we'd even had a chance to discuss it she'd gone off and invited that TV crew round. Now half the village believes her.'

\- - -

Winter presented his findings a few days later at a

meeting in Ottawa. He was about five minutes into it when Eddington impatiently put his hand up for him to stop.

'Let's cut to the chase. You couldn't find any concrete evidence that this experiment actually took place, and most of those you believed to be involved are now saying that it never even happened, that it was just bravado and talk.'

'Er, yes, Minister.'

'Do you have any evidence they actually dumped chemicals at sea?'

Winter frowned. 'No. Honestly, I don't think it ever happened. I couldn't find any evidence at all, no bulk purchases of iron sulphate, no evidence of the boats used, or of any individuals involved. No one admitted to doing it and no one saw anything. I think they were put off by the cost and difficulty, but then when they happened to have a good salmon run anyway Gaia Thompson decided to try and use it to her advantage. Her business depends on tourism.'

'In a way it's irrelevant though isn't it?' chipped in Hawthorne. 'The important thing is that everyone from Alaska to Chile *thinks* there was a successful experiment and are wondering if it would work for them too.'

Eddington nodded. 'Precisely. Since our last discussion I've even had the Americans complaining about it. Apparently there's some salmon fishery body up in Alaska openly talking about sponsoring a similar project. The last thing we want is a bunch of cowboys dumping more toxic chemicals off our coast.'

'Or their cowboys trying to out-gun our Indians,' quipped Hawthorne.

'Could we get Miss Thompson to retract?' asked one of the lawyers.

'Hard to see why she would publically, despite the fact that she as much admitted it to me,' replied Winter. 'Her whole 'thing' is encouraging ordinary people to take action against climate change. Even if she knows it wasn't true she can see how popular it's become. For her to come out and admit it was a con would destroy her credibility. She'd never do it.'

'So we need a way to convince people that the technique doesn't work and that this first one—regardless of whether it actually happened—was just beginners luck,' summarized the Minister. 'We basically want to stop people thinking this is a viable way of influencing the climate or fish stocks.'

The more senior of the lawyers took a sharp intake of breath. 'Oh you're skating on thin ice there, Minister! You have a duty to find ways to reduce carbon emissions, and that sounds very much like you're prejudging the issue.'

'But we know it can't actually work!' protested Eddington. 'Winter says there's very little scientific basis for it, and he's found no real evidence it even happened. He's just said it was probably a fluke.'

'Yet the phenomenon was clearly observed and people have claimed they caused it. If I were acting for an environmental group, let's say, then I would argue a clear case of dereliction of duty here by the Ministry. You are not doing all you can to investigate ways to reduce emissions, you're doing the opposite—obstructing the investigation of what one could argue might be a viable technique. You could be accused of ignoring climate change instead of fixing it.'

Eddington scowled.

Slowly a smile spread across Hawthorne's face. 'Then we're going to have to *prove* that it doesn't work,

Minister. We should do it again!' he said confidently.

'Do it again? Are you nuts?'

'Do it again. Repeat the experiment. Lots of publicity, go out there with a boatload of scientists, drop a hundred tons of iron sulphate and show that nothing happens.' He smiled broadly, pleased that he'd taken Eddington by surprise. Good to show his younger and more imaginative boss that he still had a few radical ideas. Eddington was starting at him.

Winter looked uncomfortable. 'Assuming that nothing does happen…'

'You're not confident?' frowned Eddington. 'A moment ago you were arguing that the chance of it actually working and producing a good salmon run was miniscule.'

'It *shouldn't* work, but you can never say never.'

Eddington nodded slowly and then stood up and paced around the room.

'Actually…I think I like it. This way we become the good guys. We say that the scientific evidence is against it but obviously we're as keen as the next man for it to work so we'll spare no effort in trying to make it work. We invite everyone along, TV crews, scientists, environmentalists, and we hire a boat and go out and dump the stuff and then—unless we're *really* unlucky—absolutely nothing will happen.' He smiled at his audience. 'Then we say 'Sorry folks, looks like that technique's just a load of hogwash and it was a fluke the first time', and everyone will forget about it.'

Hawthorne nodded and smiled broadly, secretly surprised that Eddington had accepted his suggestion so readily. 'Of course if you're worried about the outcome there are ways of guaranteeing it fails…' Seeing his colleagues look blank he continued. 'Are we really *certain* they used iron sulphate? Adam didn't find any trace of the stuff, so perhaps they used cement powder, or sand—in which case perhaps we should too?'

Eddington pulled a face. 'That's getting a bit underhand Paul. Remember there will be lots of scientists on the boat, they would find out. Best to be honest.'

Hawthorne shrugged. 'What about budget?'

Eddington shrugged with the ease of a man used to spending other people's money. 'I would guess it would only be a few mil, right? It would actually be helpful to be seen to fund another research project with the Carbon Tax revenues, we have hardly any right now and it gets embarrassing when the tax all goes on electric buses and the like. Or…perhaps we invite that Alaskan salmon fishery that wants to sponsor a project to pay for it.' He looked around the room seeking agreement.

Winter looked at Hawthorne. From a scientific point of view he was curious to see if it worked, and it was after all what the department was supposed to do, investigate new techniques to absorb carbon dioxide. Why not?

'Absolutely, Minister,' he smiled.

CHAPTER 27

Post Mortem

'I told him exactly what we agreed!' said Gaia, defensively.

It was the day after Winter's visit and the five of them plus Wolf were comparing notes over beers and wings at Saul's bar.

Aurora smiled. 'I'm sure you did dear, but did he ask anything we didn't foresee?'

'Nope, mainly just kept asking who was the brains behind it and who did the dumping. I managed to convince him that I was neither the brains nor a dumper,' she giggled. 'I think I came across as bitter and twisted because that the rest of the village were more interested in salmon than saving the planet. I should have won an Oscar. Then I casually admitted that I hadn't *actually* witnessed anything.'

Saul looked cheerful. 'I told him I didn't recall the idea ever getting off the drawing board, but that my boat certainly wasn't involved.'

Johnny chuckled. 'I told him he was nuts if he thought you could stand on the deck of a trawler in rough weather sprinkling sacks of chemicals over the side. Invited him to check out the hold but he wasn't much interested.'

'And I told him that someone called me about the oceanographic aspects of the project because I'm like, an oceanographer. He also asked me if I'd heard of the name Charles Abbott and I said yes. Somehow he then made a connection between those two statements. I don't think I got a chance to correct his misunderstanding,' beamed Lan.

'I told him outright that I thought the whole thing was just a figment of Gaia's imagination,' laughed Aurora. 'Sniffing too many exotic herbs in her shop. No, seriously, I said the council had discussed it and had concluded it was expensive and there was little chance of success. Then I challenged him and asked if he really thought a tiny community like Esh had the resources or the expertise to do what was obviously a major engineering project and he agreed it was a stretch. Finally I told him that the last discussion I'd been a part of had concluded that the project would be costly and have little chance of success, which of course is correct. He seems to have concluded that we then decided not to proceed, and that the good salmon run was just a coincidence.'

'So he really believes that it was all just talk, that no project actually took place?' asked Saul, surprised.

'Actually, I think he might. He clearly came here hoping to get a list of names they could threaten with prosecution, but with no physical evidence and everyone questioning it even happened he has nothing. I even think he might find it easier with his bosses in Ottawa to go along with questioning if it happened. Ridiculing our ability to do the project would be his easy way out.'

'Must be very difficult for them to really prove anything, if you think about it,' commented Johnny.

'The only thing they can really look at is the iron sulphate, if we bought any and how we dumped it. There's no records of us buying any, no trace on the boats to show they were used to deliver it, and no nav data to show we were there.'

'Good job you never followed my suggestion of installing tanks and pumps, wasn't it?' joked Lan. Johnny grinned.

'How about the satellite images?' asked Aurora. 'They show that someone created an artificial plankton bloom, don't they?'

Lan frowned. 'I wouldn't say its conclusive, certainly not something you could use in a court of law. It's clear that the bloom formed rapidly, but that's what happens naturally sometimes. Fortunately because it was done over the course of a few days the shape of the bloom was fairly irregular, it doesn't look like a nice square pattern or anything. And there's that weird tail and the other smaller formation further north which both look genuinely natural, so I think any expert looking at it would have their doubts.'

Saul spread his hands on the bar top and looked thoughtful. 'I reckon we shouldn't worry too much then folks. Just as long as no one admits anything it's going to be impossible for them to prove anything. We just need to watch what we say.'

Wolf looked up from a pile of chicken bones. 'I wouldn't get too optimistic. This is the government we're talking about, I think they'll start a court case against the village council anyway. They're kind of legally obliged to do something. Do you think they will drop it merely because they don't have a watertight case? No. They'll start a case anyway and talk a lot about the enormous environmental damage we're supposed to have caused, try and convince a court on the balance of probabilities and using Gaia's public statements, and debate how many millions the village should pay to fix the Pacific Ocean. They have unlimited legal resources so they don't need to win, just drag things out until our legal costs force us to give up.' For someone so sure the sky would fall in, he seemed to have a remarkable appetite for chicken, which he now continued to indulge. The others looked at one another despondently.

'Good job you and Gaia have so few possessions to be sued for then, isn't it?' replied Lan mockingly. 'But I'm afraid you may be right, although I agree they have no hard evidence so I don't think they could win but as you say that might not be their strategy. It would be more for show, to show that they've done something.'

Free beer and wings didn't do much to alleviate the worries that Wolf had voiced, and although in the end they agreed that the chances of anything truly terrible happening were slim. Nobody was keen to discuss plans for an annual repeat of the experiment, which as it turned out was probably just as well.

- - -

It was a couple of weeks later and Aurora and Lan were watching the evening news and drinking wine.

'The government announced today that it plans to repeat the controversial ocean fertilization experiment originally conducted this summer by the community of the Echelon Islands in what has been seen both as a bold attempt at reviving salmon stocks as well as a prohibited geoengineering project. Mr Nigel Eddington, Minister for Climate Change, spoke to reporters earlier today about the reasons behind the surprise announcement.'

Aurora sat up quickly and looked at Lan. 'Good God, are you seeing this!'

'Last year's self-proclaimed ocean fertilization experiment by the Echelon Islands Council has rightly been condemned both for violating international maritime laws on the dumping of chemicals at sea, as well as potentially damaged our valuable marine ecosystem,' continued Eddington. 'Most scientists doubt that such a technique could ever have achieved the intended result of boosting salmon stocks, and due to the lack of proper scientific monitoring on that project we can't know whether the increased salmon run that was observed was the result of the dumping, or just a natural annual variation—and in fact several communities further north also had a relatively good year, which suggests the latter.'

He paused and took his reading glasses off to show how seriously he took the matter.

'The government finds itself in a difficult situation. On the one hand we of course recognize the devastating impact climate change has on arctic and our coastal communities and the need to try and mitigate that impact including on fisheries. On the other hand the best scientific advice we have received is that this particular technique is unlikely to work. But if there's any chance it does then of course we would want to make use of it—and the Canadian people deserve to know.'

'Therefore I am announcing today that we are going to conduct a proper scientifically monitored study next summer to determine once and for all whether the technique has any merit—essentially we will repeat the Echelon experiment. In the meantime we will uphold the law and will take a firm line against any further unauthorized experiments. Thank you folks.'

The camera cut away from Eddington taking questions and the presenter moved onto the next news item.

'Well, I wasn't expecting *that*,' said Lan. 'Not at all. I honestly thought they'd either prosecute or tie us up with some endless enquiry.'

'So is this good or bad?'

Lan reached for the bottle of wine on the table between them.

'That depends very much whether you think we got lucky the first time. If the success of our project was just a lucky break then the odds are that repeating it will fail, in which case they will feel much more confident about making an example of us and prosecuting. But if you truly believe it's a reliable technique then we're fine—the second attempt will also work and the government will have to eat humble pie.'

'And you're still a sceptic?'

Lan looked apologetic. 'I'm afraid so. I'm quite sure that our efforts were responsible for the plankton bloom, and obviously I got the location right so that it moved towards Esh, but I still think it was mostly luck that it drifted across enough salmon that were headed home to Echelon rivers.'

She took a sip of wine. 'And there's a worse scenario—it would be very easy to ensure it doesn't work. All it would take—whether by accident or deliberately—would be for the stuff to be dropped outside the eddy so that it doesn't even make a bloom but just disperses, or for them to do it too far out and the eddy goes someplace else, or too close to shore and the salmon don't have time to grow. If they really want to ensure this fails they could do any one of those things and it's unlikely anyone would notice or be able to prove it. This could all be an elaborate ruse to improve their chances in court.'

'You really think they're that devious?'

'Probably not…look, I'm more confident about this technique than I was when we started but it's still high risk. There must be at least a twenty, thirty percent chance it doesn't work, and if we get unlucky then I'm pretty sure after my last discussions with Winter—and seeing how single-minded the Deputy Minister was at the TV debate in Toronto—that the government will use it to their advantage and prosecute us.'

Aurora tried to put on a bold face. 'Well they can't fire you, they already did that, and it's not a criminal offence so they can't put you in jail. How bad could it be?'

'Pretty bad, financial ruin basically. We could each end up spending all our savings on legal fees. I'd probably never work again in a senior level job, so it would be pretty bloody bad. And not just me—you, Saul, Zeb, Johnny, the rest of the village council.'

Aurora could see that the prospect was weighing on Lan's mind, she'd obviously been more worried about this than she'd let on. In a way she blamed herself for persuading her to join the project in the first place, although not too much. After all, Lan had removed herself from the project early enough to avoid any association and it was purely her own admission on Channel 5 that had made it public and ultimately gotten her fired. No, she didn't blame herself, but she still felt sorry for her.

'Honestly, I don't think it's as bad as you think. Redoing the experiment is a huge deal for them and will be very costly, so I think that means their lawyers must have told them that they don't have enough evidence as things stand. They must know that they would lose a court case. They're only doing this as a last resort and are taking a gamble that it will fail to bring any salmon. It's their last hope, and ours.'

'Worries about your pending destitution and financial ruin aside, there's no doubt in my mind that the project has been worthwhile and had a positive impact for Esh. You did the right thing Lan. We all did.'

'And that will be a great comfort to me as I live out my impoverished retirement,' smiled Lan ruefully.

Despite her reassurances to Lan, Aurora worried that she might be right. There wasn't much they could do about it though, unless…perhaps there *was* a way of taking back control of the agenda. Perhaps it was time to make the government's true intentions clear, and publish the secret memo that had indirectly led to Judith Altmann's death. It might embarrass them enough to drop any ideas of punishing the village council and Lan.

The two of them sat in the darkening room, lost to their own thoughts.

\- - -

Someone else with a keen interest in the Minister's announcement was Zeb.

'I reckon we should all double down,' he was telling his poker group. 'Everyone expects this second one is not going to work cos that's what the government's saying, but I think it will.'

'I already spent my winnings,' replied the man on

his left, jerking his head to indicate the new truck parked outside.

'Okay, but for those who haven't, this is a once in a lifetime opportunity. You got fifty-to-one the first time, just imagine if you got the same again. On a hundred bucks that's a quarter million!'

Johnny shook his head. 'We won't get such good odds the second time. Bookies aren't stupid.'

'Not right now we wouldn't, but give it few months with the government telling everyone how unlikely it is to succeed and that the first time was just luck and they'll think they're safe. I reckon we'd still get good odds, not fifty, maybe ten. Still worth having.'

'Not sure I trust the government not to fix the result this time though,' added another. 'I mean they've not exactly been supportive, have they?'

'Yeah, and they don't have Dr Lan either.'

'You think the location was that critical?' asked Zeb idly.

Johnny shrugged. 'I reckon the timing and general area was, to make sure that it formed inside one of those big eddies. Probably didn't matter within twenty or thirty kilometres though. Mind you I heard quite a few places up the coast had a better year than usual too, so maybe it was all just random like the government guys claim. Who knows? But a helluva coincidence if it is, eh?'

'I heard that,' replied Zeb slowly. 'Might still have been the same salmon we fertilized though, just swam in a different direction. You can't expect every last one of them to come back to Esh.'

He gathered the cards and dealt again.

'Maybe we need some inside info. Johnny, what does Lan think, you talk with her quite a bit? She say anything to you about whether it'll work a second time?'

'Dunno. I know she was surprised it worked the first time.'

'We got lucky the first time,' said another. 'Doubling down is pushing it. A hundred bucks is a flutter, but I ain't putting my five grand all back in.'

'Ask her what she thinks,' persisted Zeb. 'I'm want to put my money back in but I don't plan to leave it to chance. See if she can't figure a way of getting those Esh salmon to bring along some of their Alaskan buddies this time, eh?'

Sometimes Johnny wondered what went on inside Zeb's head.

CHAPTER 28

The Island of the Past

'I'm planning to take the boat and go and visit a couple of the old abandoned town sites tomorrow. Would you be interested in coming along?' asked Edward slightly hesitantly one morning. 'We could stop by your island on the way.'

Lan was serving him his morning cappuccino and croissant that he often came in to Haze for when he was visiting his father over a weekend.

'*My* island?'

'Langara Island. It's just up the coast, about two hours from here by boat.'

Lan stared at him. 'Are you serious? There's a Langara Island? I had no idea.'

'Oh, I thought you knew. It's quite large, five or six kilometres across, there's a sport fishing lodge there. The town site I want to check out is just opposite it on the main island and used to be the largest settlement on Esh, before the population was decimated by smallpox in the nineteenth century. You can still see the footings of the old buildings and maybe some of the mortuary poles, if they haven't all fallen down by now. It's quite a special place. Very different from here and worth seeing if you've not been to the more remote parts of the islands yet.'

So far she hadn't seen anything of Esh outside of Edenshaw and this sounded like a great opportunity so she didn't hesitate in accepting. They agreed to meet at the harbour the following day, Sunday, at seven, so that evening Lan asked Aurora about Langara Island.

'Oh yes, I hadn't thought about the name—I'm so used to calling you Lan I'd forgotten it was short for Langara,' she replied rather distractedly. 'I believe the island is named after a Spanish explorer, so maybe you're both named after the same person? Not much there though, it's covered in forest and no one lives there, apart from a fishing lodge for tourists during the summer, but they come and go by floatplane so we never actually see them. I've only been there once, years and years ago—some nice sandy bays as I recall, but I believe there are rocks offshore so it can be tricky to land.'

'Well it will be fun to see,' replied Lan. 'I was wondering for a moment if that's where my biological mother came from, but if you say its uninhabited I guess it couldn't be.'

Aurora shrugged. 'I don't think there's ever been anyone living there, not in living memory at least. Maybe before white men came, but Edward would know about that, he's into that historical stuff.'

The following morning was bright and calm despite the lateness in the season and they made steady progress. Once out of Edenshaw Sound they followed the coast westwards and Lan was surprised to see just how unspoiled the island was. Within a couple of kilometres after leaving Edenshaw there were no signs of human habitation at all, not a single house or beach hut, just trees extending right down to the high water mark for the most part. During the first half hour they passed the occasional lobster pot marker, but after that nothing.

'The fishing boats go further out,' explained Edward above the chug of the engine, 'and this part of the island is protected against logging so no one goes there now, I don't think there are even any tracks you could get a vehicle down. It must be one of the most untouched parts of the country, but years ago it was well populated.'

'You mean in the eighteenth and nineteenth centuries, before the smallpox epidemics that wiped out the original population?'

'Yeah, and even before that. Esh was on the migration route that humans took at the end of the last ice age when they populated the Americas from Asia, running across the Bering Strait when it was still dry land, then down the coast by boat until they got to Oregon and California and further inland. They've found evidence of human habitation on these islands as far back as thirteen thousand years ago—the oldest in North America, pretty much. Of course they were bigger back then.'

Lan looked at him puzzled. 'Bigger?'

Edward smiled. 'When the ice sheets covered BC and the Rockies the sea level was lower because so much water was locked up in them. So the sea level was about a hundred and twenty metres lower down, Esh was still connected to the BC mainland and wasn't fully an island, and the coast on this west side was a few kilometres further out.'

'And people in Miami worry about a few feet of sea rise!' laughed Lan. 'Puts it into perspective, doesn't it?'

They chugged along parallel to the coast for

another hour until they seemed to be headed into a corner with a headland out on their right.

'That's Langara on our right. You can't see it yet but it's actually separated from the main island by this channel we're going into now. The place I want to show you is on the main island a couple of kilometres ahead of us, so I thought we could land over there and explore for a few hours, and then head over to Langara afterwards.'

'Sounds good!' It was a glorious day and Lan felt invigorated by being out on the water. She hadn't left Edenshaw for a month and could happily have spent the entire day on the boat or sitting on a beach, as long as the sun and sea spray were in her hair.

Edward slowed the boat and looked at his map, checking the location of the town site before eventually nosing his way through the shallower water towards a wide sandy beach where they beached the boat before jumping out and hauling it up as far as they could.

'We need to make really sure it's above high water,' said Edward. 'You don't want to be stranded out here. Let's just drag it as far up as we can and then I'll weigh the anchor down with a rock.'

Once the boat was secure they grabbed their rucksacks and walked halfway up the beach before Edward paused.

'So, do you see it yet?'

Lan scanned the trees in front of them.

'See what?'

'The village. It's about a thirty metres in front of us.'

Apart from a dead tree and a couple of stumps Lan couldn't see anything.

Edward laughed. 'I guess this is what they call not

being able to see the wood for the trees, eh? Let me show you.'

They walked up to the nearest dead tree, which was about a metre in diameter, its cracked and lichen-covered wood leaning at an angle.

'See the eagle's face? This is an old mortuary pole, carved with an eagle because this village was the home of the Eagle clan. Here's the beak…'

'Wow! Yes of course! How could I not see that?' She started to trace the eagle's eyes and beak with her finger.

'The village consisted of a dozen large communal houses built parallel to the shore,' explained Edward, indicating the slight rise in the ground above where the houses had once been. 'But you can't see much now, they've been gone for over a hundred years. Many of them had totem poles in front of them but they were nearly all taken away to museums back in the sixties. Probably just as well, they rot pretty quickly in this wet climate.'

They scrambled through the scrub where the houses had once been, but apart from almost stumbling on a few boulders that might or might not have once been footing stones, there was nothing to see. Edward explained how the village had been there when European explorers first came to the area in the late seventeen-hundreds, and drawings from that time showed the communal houses with their long canoes lined up on the beach in front of them.

'After their first contact with Europeans the villagers did well for quite a while trading sea otter pelts, which they didn't consider to be anything particularly special but which were highly prized by the Russians in particular. Then later on white men brought smallpox and syphilis, diseases to which the natives had no immunity, and after a series of devastating epidemics which killed ninety-five percent of the population the survivors abandoned the village entirely in the eighteen-fifties, never to return. Later European visitors reported finding only a ghost town with personal belongings, boxes, cooking utensils and stone mortars left lying on the ground. Perhaps it was karma that they had suffered the same fate as the sea otters which they had helped to hunt to near-extinction.'

They stood trying to spot other carvings on the trees around them and piecing together a mental image of how a community might once have lived on this spot, with its natural harbour and the beach wrapping around two sides, and protected from larger waves both by Langara and a reef offshore. Suddenly the tranquillity was broken by the roar of outboard engines and after a few seconds three large power boats rounded the headland and sped through the channel in front of them before heading out to the open sea.

'That's how you can spend your time on Esh if you have money,' commented Edward, not disguising his annoyance. 'They stay at the luxury fishing lodges around here and will be heading out for their day's fishing.'

'I haven't seen any of them in Edenshaw. They hardly ever seem to get tourists there actually, I don't know how Gaia and Wolf keep that shop going.'

'You're not going to see them either. The guys that fish here never come to Edenshaw, never bring any economic benefit to the island at all in fact—the lodges don't even employ locals. They're completely self-sufficient, their guests and their food are flown in from

Vancouver. Most of these places are owned by American companies and they hire kids for the season to run them, like a ski resort. But they don't pollute the environment, they're based in temporary structures and have their own generators and sewage disposal, so they have no trouble getting their licenses to operate.'

'Can't the village just not give them permission?'

'If it was up to the islanders they'd be shut down tomorrow, but the licenses are issued by the provincial government and they sit down in Victoria and just think it's part of the tourist industry, which they want to promote. What they don't consider is the impact on our fishing stocks, which is becoming quite significant, especially as these sports fishermen only go for the bigger chinook salmon. There have been protests of course—one year we organized dozens of small boats in a blockade and managed to stop them landing their customers for a whole week, but at the end of the day it was our guys who got arrested for breach of the peace and the lodge just carried on as before. It's not so bad today because it's very late in the season, but in July and August this channel would be full of boats.'

As the noise of the craft faded they made their way further into the forest, which was a different world. A primeval rainforest with old trees a hundred metres or more high and over a metre in diameter towered above them and enclosed a vast space like a natural cathedral. At ground level absolutely everything was covered in moss—the forest floor was swathed in it, fallen trees and boulders were draped in a thick spongy blanket of it up to six inches deep and tendrils of it even hung from the trees themselves. Everything was a rich green.

'I feel like I'm hallucinating,' laughed Lan. 'All I can see is green, a really vibrant green! And it's so quiet.

The moss must absorb the sound.'

They wandered through the forest a while longer, taking photos and trying to decide whether a rounded square shape could be the remains of a house, or just a natural feature where trees had fallen. Eventually they went back to the beach and sat beside the boat and ate their lunch. In front of them, five hundred metres away across the water, lay the equally lush and primeval Langara Island.

'After you mentioned it yesterday I checked again on the internet,' said Lan, eating a packet of crisps. 'As far as I can discover that is the only place in Canada called Langara, which means that somehow I must have a connection with the place.' She explained how she had got her name, and that it was her only tangible link with her birth parents or clue to who they were.

'It's hard to see how you're connected. Nobody lives there, or have done for at least two centuries. Surely it's more likely that it's simply your mother's surname, or your father's,' suggested Edward.

'It's true that it's a Spanish surname but a very unusual one. According to a genealogy website I found there are less than two hundred people in the world with it. Apart from the guy that the island in front of us is named after the only other Langara I could find was a Spanish footballer playing in the thirties and forties, but he never came to Canada.'

She drank one of the beers Edward had brought. 'I dunno, maybe I should follow that angle up more. He did manage a team in South America in the fifties so I guess it's not inconceivable that I'm the love-child of a Canadian woman and a fading Spanish football star.'

'If it's a rare name that would actually make it more likely that it's a family name connection. Look at it this way, if your dad had been called Jones your mother wouldn't have seen any point in naming you after him, would she?'

'Good point. I could only find one living person in Canada with that surname—a man in Toronto who arrived from Spain less than five years ago. I actually called him and he couldn't think of any connection, no family members who had come to Canada before him. He said he'd never heard of anyone with Langara as a first name either.'

Edward looked thoughtful. 'If I were you I'd see if I could find out more about the footballer then.'

'It won't be easy, he died twenty-five years ago. And if it was him and he never came to Canada, and I was given away at birth, then most likely my mother never told him about me either. Hard to imagine his children having any knowledge of a holiday romance fifty years ago that he would most likely have kept quiet about anyway. But as far as that island goes I think I have to agree with you, if no one has ever lived there then I just can't see how there could be a connection.

She paused to take a photo of a fern. 'I mean, if I had been totally logical and come to Langara Island specifically searching for my mother then the nearest place I would have to come to would be Edenshaw …but it's not like anyone there has jumped out and embraced me as a long-lost daughter, is it?'

CHAPTER 29

Retribution

If any of the inhabitants of Edenshaw had dreams of getting rich on the back of the Government's repeat of the experiment then their hopes were quickly dashed. It was announced that the project was to be run out of a marine research establishment in Vancouver using a large government vessel called the *RV Northern Lights* which was almost ten times the size of the *Spirit Bear*—the sort of vessel that Lan had been familiar with in her previous career. The project was to be led by Dr Kevin Kim, one of Lan's old PhD students, an irony not lost on Lan. Onboard laboratories, satellite links, accommodation for fifty scientists and crew, a canteen, the works. Completely self-sufficient so no chance of Saul getting rich on government business.

Thanks to Eddington's eagerness to show that the Government was being open and doing all they could to give the experiment every chance of success the project was regularly on the news, usually with Kim being interviewed in an orange safety jacket on the deck of the *RV Northern Lights.* His quiet character didn't really make him the best spokesman for the project, especially since he didn't seem sure whether his success was going to be measured in terms of numbers of salmon, or their absence. He alternated between a scientist's natural enthusiasm for a positive outcome and a sober reflection that demonstrating that salmon were not tempted by iron sulphate would still be a good result, they merely wanted to prove one way or the other whether the technique worked.

Had Johnny or Zeb been involved they would have been shocked by how differently the same project was run when Government resources were behind something. The budget was not ten thousand dollars but a couple of million, hundreds of times more. If something needed fixing it wasn't Johnny and a wrench but a team of technicians and a large workshop bound by health and safety regulations. Satellite time was booked and paid for. Contracts were put out to tender, evaluated and awarded for the construction of onboard tanks, supply of fuel, even waterproof jackets for the visiting scientists with 'Northwest Pacific Geoengineering Project' emblazoned on the back. A couple of cabins were converted into mini-studios for the use of the TV crews who would be joining the journey to report and explain the science.

Apart from the crew of twelve, a further thirty scientists and journalists would be on board the following summer for what was expected to be a three-week journey once they got the go-ahead that a suitable eddy was forming. In addition to the main research vessel itself six smaller vessels would be redirected in the weeks ahead of the fertilization itself in order to search for salmon and try and identify where they were. In an idle moment Lan calculated that the project would generate more carbon dioxide than the inhabitants of Esh would create in five hundred years, not just all that fuel oil but in the hundreds of air flights to bring people in from all over the country. And all for the sake of proving a point.

Nigel Eddington or Paul Hawthorne would periodically give a press conference and remind the public that they were open-minded whether the technique would work and that 'no news will still be good news', but that after analysing salmon runs further up the coast scientists on the project increasingly felt that iron fertilization had not caused last year's record salmon run, that it had been a natural event. 'Unlike the original project which had little scientific value, we aim to measure everything and to answer the question of the value of ocean fertilization once and for all. Even though there's little evidence spraying iron sulphate in the sea resulted in a higher salmon catch, we owe it to the Canadian people to prove or disprove it once and for all,' said Eddington defiantly.

- - -

Life on Esh quickly returned to normal as autumn gave way to winter, the benefits of the salmon run fading, although quite a few houses had been repainted and trucks fixed up on the proceeds. Gaia and Wolf shut up shop and went south to Arizona for a month to commune with nature. Julie and Aiyana changed their menu from summer salads to winter soups and turned on the heating in the greenhouse.

Lan made several trips for job interviews, picked up a few weeks' work in the US reviewing research on how climate was impacting sea ice extent, and then got a nice contract with a shipping company to study options for commercial shipping routes through the arctic. At the rate the sea ice was disappearing the fabled northwest passage would soon become a reality and the shipping company wanted to know the optimal routes and dates for using it.

When she wasn't doing contract work she was Julie's assistant in the café and as a result saw Johnny fairly regularly, who after seeing the success she and Aiyana were making out of Haze had largely come around to his daughter's way of thinking regarding the issue of leaving Esh for a better job. Sometimes the three of them plus Aiyana would have dinner together. One evening he revealed that he himself had left Esh in his early twenties.

'You left Esh, dad? Seriously?' Julie was looking at him in disbelief. 'I thought the reason you always wanted me to leave was that you never could?'

'Sure I left. When I was about your age I left for three years, went to Vancouver and then Calgary. I was going to seek my fortune.'

Lan raised an eyebrow.

'My plan was to get rich in the oil patch and I was doing pretty well for a while, working on crews in northern Alberta and making good money, but it isn't something a guy can do for very long, at least not if he wants a proper life. Too much moving around, no roots and physically demanding. If you think I'm a big guy then the guys who work those rigs are built like gorillas. So I decided to use the money I was making to train for something that would support me longer term, a floatplane pilot.'

Julie's eyes opened wide, seeing a side of her father she clearly had no idea was there.

'Got my PPL, the Private Pilot's License, and was just a couple of months short of the first commercial license when your grandmother died and I had to come back to Esh to help your granddad. Never did complete it.'

'That's tragic!' said Lan. 'You mean you gave up your whole career because of your dad?'

Johnny looked a bit sheepish. 'I kept meaning to go back and finish it but one thing after another prevented me. Your granddad was a mess after your grandma died, he couldn't work, the boat was sitting idle, so I decided to take a year off to get him on his feet again, working the boat and keeping the hotel going. But then your mom and I got together and I just decided to stay.'

'But you could have finished your training and worked as a pilot here!'

Johnny wrinkled his nose. 'Trust me, I tried. It wasn't so much finishing the training as where I could work afterwards. I couldn't afford to buy a floatplane and at the time nobody was interested in running a service out of Esh. The best I could have done would have been to have gone flying on contract and returning here every few weeks, but that would have been no better than what I was doing in Alberta. There was no point.'

'Aw, that's so sad!' exclaimed Julie. 'But also romantic…'

'I'm sorry you didn't manage it,' said Lan, 'I'd be using your service for sure. That ferry trip is okay once or twice but if you have to go to Vancouver every week it takes so much time, and money. I don't know how someone like Edward can do it on a regular basis.'

'There's air services between some of the other communities along the coast,' chipped in Aiyana. 'It ought to be viable these days—between say a weekly service to the main places, a taxi service to the smaller ones and tourist trips there has to be enough business, surely? Especially if you could get a contract with some of those fishing lodges, that would bring a lot of regular trips right there.'

Johnny looked at her. 'That last idea is a good one. I have to admit running the *Raven* is getting a bit of a drag, deep-sea fishing is a young man's game. Seeing all of you changing careers is making me envious. I might have to think about this some more...'

- - -

Winter turned to spring and then summer and in late June the *RV Northern Lights* finally set sail with much fanfare, but despite the presence of several TV crews on board it quickly disappeared from the headlines, pushed aside by city riots in the US and a simmering war in the Middle East. The public only had a limited interest in science at the best of times, and a vessel dribbling a steady stream of watery brown liquid into a grey sea was not good TV material, especially when the results would not be known for months.

As summer turned to autumn politics continued to dominate the media, and thanks to Nigel Eddington's downplaying expectations of a success at every chance he got, no TV crews even bothered to come to Esh to wait for the salmon. In Esh itself the rumour had spread that in order to guarantee a non-result the government had not even used iron sulphate, and that the reason they had gone for mixing tanks inside the vessel was to hide the fact that they were just pumping out sea water without anything added. The islanders awaited the salmon run with as much anticipation as every year, but with no great expectation either way whether it would be a good one or not.

The one part of the project that was eventually based in Edenshaw was a small monitoring team of two guys and a girl who went out every morning in a fisheries patrol boat to look for signs of returning salmon, often ending up in Saul's bar. As September turned to October they were starting to be openly confident that the fish weren't coming back.

Aurora had also noticed that Lan was increasingly edgy, not wanting to talk about the project and choosing to shut herself away for days at a time working on her arctic shipping project, which had become a full-time occupation for her. Most stressed of all was Zeb, who had reinvested all of his winnings and then some. This time he'd only been able to get odds of five to one so he'd felt he should put in as much as he could. Only about a quarter of his original punters had taken the wager a second time, and as the days went by he was kicking himself for believing his own sales pitch and letting his enthusiasm get the better of him.

It was in this increasingly tense atmosphere that Lan was having her first coffee and contemplating the fact that she'd been living in Edenshaw for exactly a year without a real job when Gaia walked into Haze one morning with a grin like a Cheshire cat and offered her palm for a high-five.

'Guess what!'

Lan looked at her in disbelief. 'Seriously?'

'I *think* so. I saw some early this morning out by the point, a big shoal. Not as many as the first day last year, but I think I might have caught them a day or two earlier this time.' She leaned forward conspiratorially. 'Perhaps better not tell the others yet but I bet there will be more tomorrow.'

'Maybe,' said Lan, sceptically. 'Seeing one shoal just means the run is starting, it doesn't say much about how big it will be—there are always *some* after all. Have those observers from the Ministry seen them yet?'

'I don't think so. They go out in that patrol boat of theirs every morning about five or ten kilometres out, but I've never seen them close in where the salmon are right now. Another day or two and everyone will notice them though.'

As it turned out it didn't take that long. That evening the Ministry crew were huddled together in the bar looking worried, and the following morning they set off earlier and sailed in the opposite direction than they normally did, spending the whole day around the entrance to the river. Two days later there was no question though, the river was boiling with pink fish and everyone in the village was scrambling to catch them, and Gaia quickly called the TV station to come back and cover it—she wanted to make sure it didn't get buried by the government and that everyone knew.

Despite the lateness of the season Wolf and Johnny had a rush of enquiries for sport fishing boats and accommodation, public awareness of Esh now being much higher thanks to Eddington and Hawthorne's regular press comments on the project. They quickly decided to combine their efforts and hired an additional four ten-metre boats in Vancouver for a month, going down on the overnight ferry with the Manyshots boys to fetch them. Saul splashed out on new sheets and opened up the entire top floor of his hotel for the first time in years, and Haze hired four more staff and started serving in the evenings till late at night. Esh was buzzing.

The days passed and there was still no official

announcement though, and when it did finally come a week later it was simply to confirm that the start of the annual salmon migration had been observed, but that it was too early to estimate numbers yet. It wasn't until another week after that—after more TV crews had descended on Edenshaw and were hyping the story that the 'salmon miracle' had happened again—that the Ministry put out a press release saying that early indications were for a 'larger than average annual salmon run', but with no comment on the linkage to the iron experiment. Nigel Eddington was notably quiet and not giving interviews.

Lan and Aurora had taken a bottle of white wine and were sitting on a log by the river mouth one evening watching the scene, happy.

'Jeez, I feel so relieved!' said Lan. 'I don't think I'd realized how stressed I was by the prospect of it not working.'

'Oh believe me, I did,' replied Aurora dryly. 'You've been very jittery these last few weeks. Not yourself at all.'

'Sorry. I think the consequences of this are only now starting to sink in. For me this is a much bigger deal than the first project, it means that the government now has no case and we're safe from being sued. It also makes the case for it being a reliable technique much stronger—communities could do this on a regular basis to help recover fish stocks and counteract the effects of climate change. It's a first step for communities like ours in adapting to our new warmer world.'

'When you put it like that it sounds quite grand.'

Lan glanced at the half-empty wine bottle beside her. 'Sorry, it must be the alcohol,' she smiled. 'But it is kind of a big deal. If I was still *persona grata* at the university I bet I could easily get funding for repeating it now.' She shrugged. 'Maybe I should try.'

'So they didn't stack the deck by spraying cement powder instead?'

Lan laughed. 'No, I don't think that was ever an option. Too many people watching. They put in slightly less than we did and they dissolved it first, but otherwise very little difference.'

'Except they did proper monitoring of the CO2 uptake, right?'

'Yeah, that's where a lot of the extra cost of the project was. It's public information, so I've asked the lead scientist for a copy of the data. He used to be one of my students.'

Aurora looked thoughtful. 'I'd be interested in that myself,' she said. 'Could I get a copy?'

Two weeks later, in her capacity as CEO of the Echelon Quartet Carbon Offset Company, she put five million dollars' worth of carbon credits up for auction on the Carbon Exchange in London, supported by an impressive package of publically available data.

CHAPTER 30

The Offer

'Hey hon, your boyfriend is on TV!'

'Uh?'

'Craig Cuomo. He's on Jimmy Kimmel.'

Gaia wandered into the living room to see Craig sitting on Jimmy's couch in typical laid-back Cuomo fashion—the twinkling eyes, stone-washed jeans and Ralph Lauren cheesecloth shirt, Converse trainers and casually coiffured white hair—the whole charming sixtysomething package. Jimmy was asking him about his latest film, the one he'd been filming in Tanzania, and like all actors he was smiling and claiming it had been a blast and such a privilege to work with such a great director and actors. Gaia knew that in reality he'd hated every minute of it, the bugs, the delays, the screw-ups.

'But you know the best part Jimmy? It was all those great African kids we got to meet—just amazing kids—they really give you hope for the future of our planet. They have nothing materially, absolutely nothing, but they're really smart and so keen to build a future for themselves. When we had time off from filming I was doing some work with an organization down there that I've been involved with for a while which drills water wells for villages, and they were just so keen to learn how it was done and to do it for themselves. It was really inspirational to watch.'

'Yeah, I can imagine if there was a bunch of kids here in New York watching a drilling rig they'd probably have the tyres off it the moment your head was turned!' joked Kimmel. 'But you're involved in several environmental causes closer to home as well aren't you—whales and climate change and that sort of stuff?'

Cuomo nodded solemnly. 'Global warming is the biggest threat our planet faces, Jimmy. Not just for us humans, but carbon dioxide is acidifying our oceans and killing the marine life. Its impacting the whole food chain.'

'And the oceans have always been pretty close to your heart, haven't they?'

'I've always loved being by the sea, and a few years ago I was fortunate enough to build a house by the ocean, way way up in the Pacific north-west in the Echelon Quartet Islands.'

Gaia nudged Wolf. 'Hey, he's talking about his house!'

'It's isolated—I mean *really* isolated—the only way to get there is by floatplane and it's the only house on this small island off the main island, and even on the main island I don't think there's anyone else living within twenty or thirty miles. Just me and the eagles and the whales. So I just go up there every now and then to meditate and enjoy the nature. It keeps me grounded.'

Gaia laughed. 'Grounded! Jeez, 'detached from reality' would be more like it!'

'I heard you've been involved in some kind of

climate change project up there too?' prompted Kimmel.

'Yeah, climate change has really hit them hard up there. You'd think it would be hard for us humans to mess it up because there's no industry or pollution up there but they've been hit pretty hard. The whole traditional way of life for the First Nations people is based on salmon but climate change has changed the patterns of ocean circulation and the salmon numbers are way way down. When I first started going up there twenty years ago they were abundant and everyone had plenty to eat, but their numbers have been decimated in recent years. Its affected the other wildlife too because they're the main food for the sea eagles and bears, but it's been especially tough on the indigenous communities because the salmon provided both food and jobs for many of them.'

He shrugged modestly. 'So I was talking with some of the folks up there about a year back and they had this crazy idea of trying to do something about it, actually fighting back. They were thinking 'well, this is a man-made problem so let's have a man-made solution' and had this idea that they could attract the salmon back by seeding the ocean with stuff that the plankton grow on. So I invited one of the organizers over to my place and we kicked it around for a couple of days and offered some help and they decided to go ahead.'

'So did it work? Have you seen any salmon yet?' enthused Kimmel.

Cuomo gave his trademark boyish grin. 'Huge success, huge! Last autumn they had the biggest salmon run in their history, I think it was forty or fifty million fish or something. The whole community was involved in bringing in the catch just like in the old days. It was so good the Canadian government actually paid to do the same thing this year and they've just had another bumper salmon harvest.'

'Wow, that's great man! You made a real difference!'

'Well, just a little bit,' he shrugged modestly. 'More encouragement than anything. I was hoping to be more involved in getting the word out, but I was filming in Tanzania most of the time, helping drill those water wells for the kids.'

The show went to a commercial break.

'What an asshole!' she exclaimed, shaking her head in disbelief. 'He made it sound like we couldn't have done it without him.'

'Yeah, he wasn't much help at all really, after suggesting his PR manager could to line things up but then did nothing.'

'Exactly! He was enthusiastic to start with but after we got to his place he was too busy playing pool with Yaz bloody Garcia and entertaining his damn crew he didn't even want to discuss it. And in the morning he basically said he was going to be away filming when the salmon run was likely to happen and wouldn't have the time. He did repost some things I sent him but that was about it, never mentioned it in interviews he gave at the time or anything.'

Wolf shook his head sympathetically. 'Good job you didn't sleep with him then, wasn't it?' he grinned.

Gaia laughed. 'Believe me, that was never on the cards, hon. Your place in my heart and my bed was always safe.'

It was disappointing, but Gaia didn't see any point in contacting Cuomo and complaining. He would probably just say that he'd had to exaggerate his own involvement in order to get the project mentioned at all. She was just glad he hadn't mentioned her name, that would have been embarrassing.

- - -

If there was one thing he'd said that Paul Hawthorne wished he could take back it was the sound-bite that was played over and over by the media in the coming weeks.

Almost a year earlier, when describing the reason for the government's unusual decision to repeat the iron fertilization experiment Hawthorne had claimed that the experiment was designed to prove once and for all whether there was a link between ocean fertilization and salmon numbers, and he had then added that 'if the salmon come back a second time, there can be no doubt fertilization will have caused it'.

At the time it was a throwaway line that he had forgotten almost as soon as he'd said it, but now it was on a dozen news websites. The reason? The government's new position announced just this week was that even two occurrences did not constitute statistically meaningful scientific proof, and that their experts now believed that two large salmon runs in a row—if they proved anything at all—probably indicated changing weather patterns were influencing fishy migration habits. They would not conduct the experiment again but if record salmon numbers were recorded a third year, this time without any fertilization, then *that* would indicate there was no connection between fertilization and salmon numbers. But the endless replaying of the fateful phrase 'there can be no doubt fertilization will have caused it' heavily undermined his and the

Ministry's credibility in the public mind, creating increasing tension between him and his boss.

The tone of the media coverage had changed too. Instead of just playing to the human interest story of the 'little village that could' fighting a losing battle against a government inflexibly defending its UN treaty obligations, there was now a sense of optimism that there might actually exist practical solutions to climate change. In the South Pacific a group of islands threatened by rising sea levels had built a barrier between two islands to drive a series of turbines, powering pumps to keep houses dry. In the Andes a community threatened by an eroding hillside caused by melting glaciers took a lesson from their ancestors and channelled the waters into irrigation channels and fields.

The 'Esh effect' became a byword for finding ingenious ways to benefit from the otherwise destructive effects of man-made climate change. Even Eddington had started to get on the bandwagon by quietly promoting his 'northern power line' idea as a similarly innovative idea to tackle climate change, even though the study that Winter had commissioned had shown that it would be so expensive to build that the electricity it produced would be five times the cost of existing gas-powered generation plants.

It was in this new spirit of optimism that a floatplane landed in the bay one morning, chugged its way across to the pier, and a man in his eighties stepped out. He looked like everyone's favourite grandpa, dressed like a typical tourist in chinos and a sun hat and had a smile on his face as though he'd just landed in Hawaii and liked what he saw. After walking up and down the high street for a while looking at the houses he spotted the café and walked up the pathway to Haze. He sat down at a table and ordered a Coke while continuing to observe the people around him.

'Excuse me. Do you know where I can find Dr Lan Renouf?' he asked Aiyana after a while.

'You the press?'

'No…no, I'd just like to speak with her.'

'I see. I'll let her know you're here,' she replied suspiciously. 'What's your name?'

'Wilbur Brookes.'

If Aiyana recognised the name, she didn't show it. A couple of minutes later she reappeared with Lan, still looking suspicious.

'Ah, Dr Renouf, pleased to meet you,' he half stood up to shake her hand. 'My name is Wilbur Brookes and if you can spare me a few minutes there's something I'd like to discuss with you.'

'*The* Wilbur Brookes?'

The old man chuckled. 'I'm afraid so.'

Wilbur Brookes was a legend in the world of American business. A multi-billionaire, he'd made his money through his unhurried and conservative approach to investments. At eighty-five he had built up a portfolio of household names of American business and simply sat on them while they returned four or five percent, decade after decade. When asked the secret to his investment success he had once joked 'Time. I'm so old even my bad picks came good eventually', but of course the truth was that he rarely made bad picks.

'I'm honoured. How can I help you?'

Mr Brookes sat down again and put his hands together, as if about to tell a child a bedtime story. 'I have been called the least exciting investor in American business because of the long time I hold my investments, although I would prefer to call it 'most long-term investor' rather than 'least exciting'. I've always taken a long-term view of the world and sometimes have had the good fortune to spot new trends before others. Now I want to invest in you.'

Lan couldn't help but laugh. 'Me? I'm flattered, but this place doesn't belong to me. I'm just a house guest.'

For a moment Brookes looked puzzled. 'No, no, I'm not talking about this café. I'm talking about *you*, Dr Renouf. I realize you've been a bit coy about your true involvement but I know you've played a key part in bringing economic fortune back to this community and I think you could help me do the same elsewhere. I'm talking about the business opportunities that are to be had from the tragedy of man-made climate change. I heard what you said in that TV debate and I've come to talk with you about it.'

'Oh!'

She sat down opposite him.

Brookes continued. 'The world is sitting around doing nothing, wringing its hands and seeing nothing but the problem. Don't get me wrong, I'm in no doubt that there are some huge problems facing us—many areas of the globe will become permanently uninhabitable in the coming decades, lost either to drought or to rising seas. But for most places it will be more a matter of adaption. If the predictions are right the American mid-west will become less productive but parts of Canada will become newly viable for agriculture, for example. I want to help mitigate the impact of climate change by helping people better prepare for its worst consequences, and of course one of the better ways of doing that is to motivate them to spot the business opportunities.'

Lan was not sure how to take this. Was it a compassionate gesture, or was the nice old man in front of her who looked like everyone's favourite grandpa just a cold-hearted businessman? Or could he be both?

'Unusual for a businessman to be so altruistic.'

Brookes laughed. 'Oh, I might look like a big softy but I can assure you philanthropy is not my main motivation. Well maybe a bit, but as you yourself said there's a big opportunity here for first-movers. If you can help me identify the opportunities that climate change will create then I can develop solutions, and then I can sell those solutions to the people who didn't have our foresight and find themselves in desperate need of them later on. It's cold business logic I can assure you…mostly anyway.'

'So you want me to work for you as a researcher?' asked Lan, still confused by what exactly he was suggesting.

The old man smiled. 'What I have in mind is to create an institute for climate solutions with you as its Director. Then I want to use that as a vehicle for doing two things: first, to lobby for changes to the international conventions to make it legal to do projects like the one you deny doing, and secondly as a channel to make investments in other groups that have ideas for harnessing climate change for good.' He leaned back and looked out of the window. 'Perhaps it's not just the business side of it…the truth is I'm eighty-five and I want to be remembered for more than building up a nice portfolio of stocks. I'd like to do what I can to leave the planet in better shape than when I arrived. I can afford to take a much longer-term view than any government can, and I want to set in motion something that will achieve something useful over the decades to come. You could probably persuade me to give you whatever you wanted to make it happen. What do you say?'

It was only the desire not to appear too hasty that held Lan back from saying 'yes' immediately, so she spent thirty minutes asking questions about what exactly the institute might do and how big those investments might be before she agreed in principle and they shook hands on it. After a year of looking for a job, she would never have dreamt that the ideal one would come looking for her.

'I think better walking,' announced Brookes after a while, standing up. 'Why don't you give me the tour?'

They took a stroll along the high street to the river and Lan pointed out where the salmon had first been spotted, and they agreed on some basics. The institute, provisionally called the Centre for Climate Change Solutions or C3S for short, would be headquartered in Seattle for tax reasons but would have its operational base in Edenshaw. There was some unused land at the east end of the high street where it could be built, and Brookes thought it important that the building itself be both futuristic in terms of its architectural design and energy efficiency and overlooking the water to which the salmon had returned.

'I'm thinking we'll need a group of technical experts to start finding and assessing ideas,' said Brookes. 'Maybe a dozen to cover the different disciplines? Don't wait to build the building, we can get you legally created within a few weeks and you should get started right away. You can work out of one of my offices in Seattle.'

Lan made a comment about it taking her time to

find the right people. Brookes frowned.

'There's some urgency here Lan, we don't have that much time.'

Lan looked at him questioningly.

'Which part of me being nearly ninety did you not understand?' he replied sarcastically. 'I want to make sure all this gets done as soon as possible. You don't want me dying halfway through and it all getting bogged down in red tape, do you? Besides, I want to see some results while I'm still around to enjoy them. How do you think I'm going to justify all that exotic travel? You're going to have to get busy.'

Brookes also had some more immediate ideas. 'I'm thinking of building a salmon processing plant here to give the community a more solid economic base. I did some research and the unemployment rate here is just awful and a lot of the young people are leaving. If we're going to base C3S here it needs the support of a healthier community, so even if it doesn't make strict financial sense I think it would be sensible to invest in a few things to give it a boost.' He waved vaguely at the houses on the high street. 'And I know this is traditional for the area but if you're going to attract world-class PhD's and climate scientists you're going to need some nicer accommodation too. If we're going to reinvent the future here it needs to look the part.'

Once Brookes left a couple of hours later Lan pinched herself to see if it had all been real. It was a dream job for her, instead of passively monitoring the impact of climate change she could do something about it, but at the same time the enormity of the task felt overwhelming. She returned to the café to gather her thoughts and Julie promptly came down to sit with her, openly curious.

'Sounds like you got a job offer! Spill!' she grinned.

'Huh! Yes you could say that.' She explained the gist of what Wilbur Brookes was proposing, but was apprehensive about how much work it was going to take. 'If I take this on I'm not going to be able to help out here anymore I'm afraid. In fact if I take this on I'm not going to have a life for a while—it's going to be a 24/7 job, especially during the start-up phase.'

Julie was listening with increasing incredulity.

'Are you frigging nuts?! Listen Lan, you have to do this! It sounds like a once-in-a-lifetime opportunity, both for you personally but especially for Esh. If it brings new people here and he's willing to invest in a new fish plant and housing that alone will transform the place. In one go you'll achieve everything and more that Aiyana and I were hoping to do in twenty years.'

She leaned across the table. 'I'm not going to let you say no, more than that, I want in. Let me work with you. I don't know anything about the technical side of it, but I can do a lot on the organizational side and I'm extremely motivated to bring this to Esh. It's going to have a fantastically positive impact on this place in terms of new jobs alone, institute visitors and tourist traffic, not even counting the salmon plant.'

Lan was surprised by her obvious passion. 'What about all this?' she asked, looking around Haze. 'You've achieved so much here, you can't just abandon it.'

'Oh, we're not going to give this up, but Aiyana can run this by herself now. In fact we were actually just talking the other day about hiring two girls to take it over so that Aiyana and I can start up something else. But C3S would be my dream job too, and we also have a couple of other things Aiyana is interested in trying.'

Lan looked reassured. 'As long as you're sure then I

think it would be a great idea to hire you as a sort of operations manager and I'd really appreciate it. It would make my job a lot more manageable, especially if I'm going to have to travel a lot then having someone here to look after all the day-to-day stuff would make a huge difference. It's all very well Mr Brookes offering me his support staff, and I'm sure they're very good, but I don't know them like I know you.'

Julie grinned. 'Let's get to work! No time to waste!'

Lan rolled her eyes. 'Jeez Jules, you're worse than Brookes!'

CHAPTER 31

Change is Coming

To Lan's surprise Wilbur Brookes' proposal was not welcomed by everyone. When she told Aurora about his offer she was lukewarm about his desire to invest in the village.

'I know it sounds generous, and I'm sure it's well-intentioned, but before you get too carried away you need to know some history here. Edenshaw used to have a big cannery back in the eighties, right up until about ten years ago, and for all of that time things were great. It was busy and it employed about two hundred people, almost a third of the village, until the salmon numbers started to drop and profits with them. Then one day out of the blue the American owners just closed it—and not just closed it but dismantled it and shipped it lock, stock and barrel it to some town in Chile. We tried to persuade them to keep it open and we even tried to buy it from them, but they wouldn't listen.'

She shrugged. 'It wasn't just the loss of employment—people could have handled that with a longer notice period—it was more the fact that they had claimed for years that they were supporting the community and then suddenly this completely opposite decision and a refusal to even discuss it. It was a betrayal. It was like dumping someone by text: shitty and cowardly. Because of that bad experience there is a distrust of outside investors here, so you need to understand that if you want to sell your idea to the Council.'

Lan nodded. She understood and thanked Aurora for the warning. Although she hadn't been there long she could of course understand the villager's desire to be in control of their own destiny. It was as natural as not submitting your tax return.

A couple of weeks later, with Julie's support, she pitched the proposal for C3S to a formal meeting of the village council since they would need to give permission for it to be built as well as to sell Brookes the land. Lan made it clear why she wanted it to be located in Edenshaw and the benefits she thought it would bring, but emphasized that the choice was with the villagers. If they didn't want it then C3S would set up in Seattle and Esh would get no benefit.

'But this would really strengthen Esh long-term,' added Julie enthusiastically. 'I think we'd benefit hugely from this. We've been in the news twice recently and have seen some additional tourists as a result but not many, and anyway tourism is very seasonal. If we have the institute housed here it would be bringing in visitors for conferences and meetings on a regular basis, and it would also show to other organizations and businesses that they can relocate here—maybe tech companies who can work from anywhere as long as there's an internet connection.'

'You mean we'd finally get decent wifi?' quipped Johnny.

Lan smiled. 'I wouldn't suggest you do it because of

that, but yes you probably would. More significant would be a few long-term jobs—about a dozen local ones and another dozen specialist roles that would have to be filled by newcomers—and as Julie says a fairly regular stream of publicity and visitors. Also in the immediate term, over say one or two years, there would be the construction of course, which I am guessing might be fifty local jobs.'

Saul frowned. 'How long is Mr Brookes' interest going to last? He might be feeling all philanthropic right now but people's feelings change over time, especially if this ends up being just a cost to him with no revenue.'

'Very good question. As the politicians say, 'I'm glad you asked that'. The idea is that C3S will generate and refine ideas which will lead to profitable businesses, but you're right that those will come much later. Mr Brookes is eighty-five years old and he's anxious that this initiative doesn't die with him—he wants this to be seen as part of his legacy. So to be sure that happens he wants to set up a foundation which will have large capital assets to guarantee that the institute is funded independently of his other businesses and avoiding commercial pressures. I understand that the amount he's planning to put into trust for the foundation is around a hundred million dollars.'

There was an audible gasp around the table.

'Before you get too excited the institute would never touch the principal but only live off the interest. It would have an operating budget of around five million dollars a year. In perpetuity.'

Saul grinned. 'I guess that answers my question. But make sure you get a watertight contract—we don't want his kids coming along later and trying and change it.'

'Don't worry, I will. Now, there's one other thing the Council needs to make a decision about,' continued Lan, 'and I understand this is an emotive topic. Obviously we believe this institute will have a positive effect on Esh for employment and for bringing in new money, but it certainly won't solve all the village's problems and as we all know the village is losing young people. Mr Brookes wants to avoid a situation where the institute flourishes but Edenshaw continues to decline and we end up isolated here, therefore he also wants to make some investments in the community itself in order to strengthen our economy. However these investments would have to be separate from the institute itself, they would be commercial projects run by one of his other companies, and in theory they could be cancelled after his death if they became financially unviable for a significant period. He's willing for them to be neutral in terms of financial return but we shouldn't expect him to be swallowing significant losses year after year.'

Johnny looked around the table. 'I suppose it depends on how much we trust him then, but in principle I think we should view any kind of investment in Esh businesses as a positive thing.'

'The main thing he's thinking of is to build a commercial salmon processing and packing plant.'

Saul stopped smiling. 'Oh. That doesn't sound so good.'

'I know there's been some bad history with the cannery before, but if we've now got a way to sustain the salmon runs through annual ocean fertilization then there's no reason why this plant shouldn't be here for the long term. And I would hope that the plant would be a major contributor to the cost of future fertilization projects, since they'd want to guarantee their supply.'

There was some discussion around the table until eventually Johnny summed up the feeling in the room.

'So we think it's a worthwhile idea, but for something that will have such a big impact on employment we should try and find a way of keeping it under our control and ownership. We should discuss with him about that, maybe make the Council having a fifty-one percent ownership in the processing plant as a condition of setting up the institute?'

Lan frowned, knowing that that idea was not really going to fly. It would be difficult to tie a commercial operation run by one company with a one-time gift of an institute controlled by a different, non-profit, organization. She said as much and the discussion moved back and forth for a while, not finding a solution.

'I might have a solution,' said Aurora after a while. 'Actually I have an announcement of my own to make. I was going to tell you this after Lan had finished her announcement, but now seems like a more appropriate time.' She paused. 'You remember we set up a company to trade in any carbon credits that might result from the original project, which was how we paid for the original project? We couldn't actually sell any credits from that because of questions over whether the project was legal and the lack of measurements of the amount of carbon absorbed by the plankton bloom. But the charter of the company covered *any* iron fertilization project in the northwest Pacific within four hundred kilometres of the coast, so when the government released their data on the second project I decided to list the credits for auction on the exchange which trades these things.'

Everyone leaned forward around the table.

'We made just under five million dollars from selling those credits and the money was credited to our account last week,' she beamed, 'and seventy percent of that money stays with the village council. We could use it for projects such as building a salmon processing plant or paying for future fertilization projects to attract more salmon.'

For a moment there was a stunned silence, before Saul clapped and then stood up and came over and hugged her. 'You're amazing! I'm speechless. I had no idea we could have made so much from something so simple. This changes everything!'

Zeb came over to hug her but paused. 'You're sure we have the money? Where is it, exactly?'

'Oh we have it alright, it's sitting in our bank account earning two-and-a-half percent.'

'But who bought them?' asked Johnny, obviously still incredulous.

'Mostly big European industrial companies, I think there were about a dozen in all. Siemens was one, I remember.'

'But why? I don't get it, what do they get out of it?'

'Oh that's simple,' chipped in Lan. 'They use it as a tax write-off. Or to be specific, they set these credits against the CO2 which their own operations generate so they have less emissions to pay carbon tax on. Most of these countries have quite high carbon taxes now, so buying the CO2 which we've absorbed is cheaper than paying the full tax on the CO2 they've created. It's a win-win situation.'

'Anyway,' continued Aurora, 'the point is that thanks to this we do now have some money that we could use for things like building our own salmon processing plant. I have no idea how much it would cost—and to be honest I would have thought it better to use the money for things like roads and schools—but it is an option.'

Johnny was rocking back in his chair thoughtfully. 'You know folks, all this salmon project stuff is going to change life forever in Esh. Just think about it—we already have millions in the bank, more resources than the village has ever had. We have what looks like a way of getting back to the sort of sustainable salmon harvests we used to have, and now we have someone who's seriously interested in investing more to provide other jobs here that would not be dependent on the salmon. We shouldn't be rushing this or trying to make a decision in one evening.'

- - -

It was Lan's turn to have to be patient, but over the next four weeks the Council came up with a development plan, with considerable informal input from Julie who inserted herself into the process on the grounds that the younger generation needed to be represented if the problem of teenagers leaving the place was going to be addressed properly.

Wilbur Brookes would be offered land for the institute and associated housing on an attractive ninety-nine year lease, on condition that he paid for upgrades to the utilities required to service them. The windfall from the carbon credits would be used for village infrastructure, and the scope of the salmon processing plant was scaled back and Brookes was offered the option of being a forty-nine percent investor, with control over its ownership and operation remaining with the Council.

Johnny was appointed to the newly-created position of Chief Development Officer for Esh, with responsibility to oversee the execution of the village's new development plan. Once he heard about it Edward volunteered to help with the planning aspects since he lived in Victoria, which as the provincial capital was where the regional planning offices were based. Brookes agreed to the terms, although he asked that the plant be delayed by one year until they had a plan in place for a regular fertilization project to provide the salmon, and the institute was legally created a few weeks later.

During the following twelve months Edenshaw was transformed. The eastern end of the village, which for fifty years had been a dumping ground of abandoned cars, allotments and decaying garages, became the site of the institute, and about five hundred metres further twelve small chalet style homes were set back in the trees, including one that Lan was buying herself. The institute building was designed by a firm of Vancouver architects, its interiors all locally sourced wood and the large sloping roof covered entirely in solar panels.

Saul used his five percent from the carbon credits to build some holiday chalets on land he owned at the other edge of the village where the wooded slopes began, and found there was a much stronger interest in them than for his tired first-floor hotel rooms. Once they were built he offered the whole first floor of the hotel to Aiyana and Gaia to turn into a fish-themed restaurant overlooking the harbour specialising in—what else—salmon and local sea food. Aiyana named it Chinook.

With Julie now working for the institute full-time as Operations Director and with Aiyana spending most of her time at Chinook they hired two girls to run Haze, which continued to thrive. The thing that Aurora found most ironic was that Julie, apparently on her own initiative to equip herself better for her new job, quietly enrolled in a distance-learning course in Accounting and Business Administration—precisely the thing she'd sworn she would never do—and genuinely enjoyed it.

Wolf took a bigger role in his sports-fishing boat venture with Johnny, hiring half a dozen local lads to run them year-round and more at peak season, but what he was proudest of was finally finding the missing ingredient for the Echelon Escapes hiking and camping business. It turned out that visitors could not get enough of Edwin Reid's legends, so the three and five day breaks they offered were restructured around the campfire, with Gaia and Aiyana providing the food while Edwin regaled customers with his tales. At the end of every meal he would lead everyone down to the water's edge where they dutifully threw the bones back into the sea, to set the spirits of the salmon free to regenerate. Even the sceptics were taking his theory more seriously since someone had discovered that salmon bones were rich in iron, giving rise to the intriguing possibility that the old legends were rooted in science after all.

Johnny quickly discovered that organizing all the building work necessary for the development of Esh was a full time job so decided to sell his boats, but then changed his mind and hired the Manyshots boys to run them full time, which turned out to be a good judgment call. Widely seen as a couple of layabouts who had been responsible for innumerable dumpster fires and trouble when younger, when challenged to take responsibility for the boats or see them sold and their main source of employment gone, they stepped up and became much more serious about life. Instead of hiring extra crew they had the idea of marketing crew places as adventure holidays and had a steady stream of applicants from rich college kids and stockbrokers 'in search of themselves'.

As for Johnny himself, he needed to travel to Vancouver quite a bit to meet with engineering firms, which started to make him think again about the potential for a regular air service. He decided to finish what he'd started twenty years before and began taking flying lessons again whenever he was in Vancouver, using odd afternoons and extra days. Getting his private pilot's license back was relatively quick, just three months, but the commercial license took another six months and more study than he was expecting.

He'd kept the fact that he was doing this to himself in case it didn't work out, but once he had the license he started renting a floatplane whenever he needed to go to Vancouver and privately advertising places on upcoming trips. All were sold out and he kept getting requests for extra flights, so it wasn't long until he bit the bullet, bought a second-hand six-seater floatplane with his some of his carbon credit windfall, and started regular twice-weekly flights. In the summer evenings he sometimes used it for sightseeing trips for tourists too if there was the demand, which was even more profitable.

But the busiest of all was Lan, who spent the year shuttling between Esh and Seattle, Ottawa, California and television studios, and was spending very little time in Esh. She found herself increasingly glad of the chance to meet up with Edward on her visits to the provincial government offices in Victoria and was full of admiration for the way he quietly got their planning approvals done, on what was after all the largest building project that Esh had ever seen. Applications normally took years to push through but his patience together with being able to drop in on the planning officers several times a week to keep things at the top of the pile produced results. She couldn't help thinking that Johnny's more fiery temperament would not have worked well in that situation. On the other hand Johnny's ability to enthuse others to do their best and get things done showed Lan a whole new side of him too.

Professionally she had become one of the most visible faces on climate change in North America. The media delighted in the fact that she didn't hold back in her criticism of government policy, unlike academic commentators who whenever they were put in the same studio as government representatives suddenly became nervous of losing their funding. Unlike her former self Lan was no longer interested in merely measuring the steadily-warming climate and bemoaning the ineffectiveness of man's attempts to reverse it; thanks to Wilbur Brookes' legal and PR teams lobbying the United Nations and the various international environmental bodies they were well-advanced in bringing real change. The UN was scheduled to vote on an amendment to UNCLOS that would loosen the rules on ocean fertilization experiments and other geoengineering techniques, allowing communities such as Esh to actually do something about their own local problems. The fact that she had achieved in just two years something which successive governments had failed to address in two decades was something not lost on a lot of people.

Even though the physical building was not yet ready the institute already existed legally and Lan had recruited most of her team, working out of Brookes' offices in Seattle. Their remit was to find new solutions to the foreseeable consequences of climate change such as warmer and more variable weather, rising sea levels and increased droughts. Initially they focused on North America but before long were looking further afield, focusing on any technology from which Wilbur Brookes might develop commercially viable solutions.

- - -

One thing nobody was doing that year was repeating the fertilization experiment. Given the government's new position of waiting a further year to see if the salmon run was high anyway without human help, and some legal advice that now that it actually had some money worth suing for the village had more to lose by breaking the law again than it did by doing nothing, the village had decided to follow the government's lead. By not repeating it and waiting to see whether the salmon came back anyway they hoped to get conclusive proof for their iron fertilization argument. Johnny had threatened to go out and scare away any salmon personally but fortunately there was no need—the numbers were dramatically down, but since half the village was employed building the institute and its associated housing it didn't matter so much.

Someone it would turn out to matter to a lot was Paul Hawthorne. By late October it was clear no salmon were coming and the viability of the iron fertilization method was being generally accepted. There was growing public support for 'local solutions' to climate change, something Hawthorne had always been against, and increasing criticism of the Ministry for having gotten it so wrong.

There was a surprising public demand for doing more than merely recycling drinks cartons or changing to LED lights, people actually wanted to feel they were doing something that would make a difference. Eddington was under pressure from the PM to be seen to be more sympathetic to community solutions, something he was not opposed to since it helped create support for his own northern power line idea. And he was enough of a politician to know when he needed to throw someone under the bus to save his own skin. It had also come to his attention that Hawthorne had been working on quite a few things which he hadn't approved, something which pissed him off. Worse, a lot of them just seemed to be a waste of money, random grants to companies, hiring consultants to work on things that weren't even a priority. It made no sense. By Christmas Hawthorne had been quietly reassigned to a different department.

Eddington announced instead that Michael Malik would be joining in the newly created post of Deputy Minister. Even after the second experiment Malik had correctly read the public mood and started speaking out on the issue, pointing out that he had met with the Esh village council to discuss their project almost a year before it took place, and had supported them by helping them apply for grants. Not slow to recognize a passing bandwagon he had even gone out of his way to support the C3S and Lan and to promote the Echelon Islands as a new tourist and sport fishing location. He was the ideal person to give the beleaguered Ministry for Climate Change a new and sympathetic voice, promoting a new positive agenda of community action.

Aurora and Lan smiled and held their tongues, recognizing a common interest and finding Malik more supportive and indeed less litigious than his predecessor. The closest that Malik came to admitting his one hundred and eighty degree change of position was at the opening ceremony for C3S when Lan congratulated him on his new role, and made a joke about how he owed it all to the people of Esh. 'A good politician always listens to his constituents,' he commented serenely.

Adam Winter attended the event too, and congratulated them both on what they had achieved for Esh. 'I'll be honest, two years ago I thought this community was going down the drain. It would have been very easy to see it getting beyond the point of no return, when so many young people had left that it became unviable.'

'Is that something you would have regretted?' asked Aurora. 'I mean, social welfare is not really part of your job, is it?'

'Actually the Ministry's remit covers making plans for communities which will be affected by climate change, but I was just speaking personally. It's always a shame when places with so much history disappear.'

Aurora smiled mischievously. 'And is your concern about Esh getting abandoned something you might have communicated to Judith Altmann by any chance?'

Winter stared at her intently for a few seconds before grinning broadly. 'Obviously I have no idea what you're talking about, but if I did then I would hope that my, purely hypothetical, concerns might stay private?'

Lan looked at the two of them, confused, and looked at Aurora questioningly.

'Oh, you don't want to know, believe me,' smiled Aurora, enigmatically.

For a moment the three of them stood in awkward silence.

'I read somewhere that the Minister's proposal for a wall of wind turbines in the arctic met with some resistance?' said Lan, for the sake of making conversation.

Winter looked at her curiously and sighed. 'Ah, yes, the 'NorPow' project. A victim of the Minister's own unshakable belief in computer models I'm afraid.'

'How come?'

Winter hesitated, picking his words with care. 'Well, one of the curious things I've noticed about climate change is that although most people don't understand the science—which is absolutely fine, it's very complicated—they still accept the models as gospel.'

He paused to wave away a mosquito. 'If I was ever to make any criticism of our excellent Minister it would be that he puts too much faith in our models.'

Lan chuckled. 'But scientists can make models to predict anything!'

'Quite. In our early days we found that if we presented a model that showed the climate was improving, say, then he believed it would really happen. That if we said, for example, that if we closed all coal-fired power stations our carbon emissions would fall to be below our targets, then he would think that all the world's problems were solved.'

'Anyway, long story short, for a long time the Minister was passionately committed to this idea of thousands of wind turbines in the arctic, even though it was clear there would be a myriad of technical problems—but he thought it would all be worth it because they were carbon-free, that they would actually change the climate.'

He stepped back for a moment to let someone pass, the room was crowded. 'So, we started commissioning studies and as part of that someone created a model of how closing the country's coal and gas-fired power stations would affect unemployment. As it turned out those stations are in areas with disproportionately pro-government voters, and closing them all down would create significant job losses which would result in a twelve percent swing towards the opposition at the next election. Once he saw *that* computer model, the Minister lost all interest in the idea.' He smiled.

Lan laughed. 'So nothing to do with the impact on the climate after all? I'd just assumed it was too expensive.' She sipped her wine. 'Good that he shows such concern for people's welfare though.'

'It is, isn't it?' nodded Winter gravely. 'Not all politicians have a human side, but he certainly shows one.'

He looked around the room. 'You know, I have a feeling that people will look back on all of this as a bit of a turning point. At the Ministry we're started to see a lot more grassroots interest in reducing emissions, people eating less beef, thinking twice before flying to Australia on holiday, that sort of thing. The demand for electric vehicles is really accelerating now—I hear Ford is actually thinking of stopping making SUVs altogether. You hear they're making bicycles now?'

Aurora laughed. 'Seriously?'

'Sure, except they've got a fancy name for it.

Instead of SUVs they're now promoting SPVs, 'self-propelled vehicles'. They think there's a market for a commuter bicycle, a bike with a cover to keep the rain off and somewhere to put the shopping, and a battery for the hills.'

Lan shrugged. 'I guess that is one benefit of a warmer climate, it's more realistic to cycle short distances, to work, the shops, that sort of thing.'

Winter leaned forward conspiratorially. 'I even had an executive from one of the big fast food companies in my office the other day basically saying they're thinking of dropping meat entirely.'

'Nice idea, but hard to imagine the public giving up their hamburgers. A no-meat burger? Could there be a future beyond meat?'

'Apparently their sales of burgers has fallen by a third in the last couple of years—so they're thinking about getting ahead of the game and turning it to their advantage. They were asking if they take the plunge and make a big thing about dropping meat entirely, if the government would support them with a public campaign promoting the climate benefits.'

'A Big Mac without beef, who'd-a-thought-it?' mused Lan.

'Did I say it was a Big Mac?' smiled Winter.

'It's the biggest players that have most to lose by being late to the party. Besides, the way things are going beef will be too expensive to put in a hamburger. That's one thing carbon taxes did right, they showed people the real cost of things like cattle ranching.'

'Talking of which, did you hear about that new political party in the US?' chipped in Aurora. 'The Make America Green Again Party. After that series of droughts people are finally realizing that it's things like cattle ranching that are indirectly responsible, and with more and more people living in the cities they reckon there's a lot of people would like to see it banned.'

'Yup, things are finally changing,' agreed Lan.

'Talking of change, I'm leaving Ottawa at the end of next month,' announced Winter. 'I've been offered a job at the new EuroClimate centre in Paris. Thought I'd try out my horrible French on them.'

'Quelle dommage,' said Lan, genuinely pleased for him, 'Our loss. I might come over and hit you up for funding for one of our international projects sometime!'

The three of them touched glasses in congratulations.

'Looks like we've come full circle,' mused Aurora. 'Instead of rooting around in my garage trying to sabotage our project we're all on the same page at last.'

'Which reminds me, you never did tell me where you hid the stuff,' replied Winter, looking curious.

'No, I didn't, did I?' replied Aurora, with a mischievous smile.

CHAPTER 32

Unfinished Business

Aurora was contemplating dietary options for Duncan at the Co-op one afternoon when she heard a familiar voice on the phone in the next aisle.

'...Yeah, it's really good news! I wasn't sure if she'd accept, but she did...'

'...Oh I can tell you it's a big relief for me, sure—I mean we've been talking about this on and off for about a year now—since more or less when Lan and I were working on the first project in fact, but she's always wanted her own space...'

'...I know, I know...'

Aurora found herself transfixed by the conversation. Johnny's voice was getting closer. She decided to stay where she was and engross herself in the sodium content of the tin of dog food she had in her hand.

'...That's the problem when you love someone...'

'...Yup, life will be different that's for sure...'

'...Oh yeah, what's she's achieved is phenomenal, I'm so proud really. Totally transformed life here hasn't it?...'

Eventually Johnny wandered around the corner and into her aisle, still on his phone and giving her a nod as he saw her.

'…I'll let you know when it's official. Don't worry you'll be the first to know!…okay…yup… okay, talk later.'

He greeted Aurora as he ended the call. 'How's things going?'

'Quieter with Lan away so much. How about you?'

'Pretty busy actually with all the development work! It's a full-time job for me now. I wish Lan was around more though, there's a lot we should discuss.'

He looked at his watch. 'Talking of which I need to run! I have a conference call with her and some engineers in ten minutes. Take care, I'll catch up with you later!'

With which he hurried to the check-out, leaving Aurora with a lot of unanswered questions and a can of surprisingly high-fat dog food. No wonder Duncan was a bit out of breath these days.

- - -

In retrospect she might have been a bit hasty making a connection when a few days later Lan announced that she had something she needed to discuss. By that time she had been living at Aurora's house for two years, although admittedly she had hardly been there for much of the past twelve months. It was hard to believe that it had been so long, or that so much had changed in that time. Privately she hoped that Aurora wouldn't mind her leaving, she knew that having her as a lodger had provided her with welcome companionship so she picked a quiet Sunday morning to break the news.

'I heard yesterday that my house is almost ready. I'm going to need to take possession next month.'

Aurora looked at her, knowing that the conversation she'd been putting off for months was finally about to become unavoidable. 'Oh. Well I guess the day had to come, but I hope you'll keep dropping by, you know you're always welcome. I'm so glad you've decided to settle in Edenshaw.'

Lan squeezed her hand. 'I know, and believe me I'll still see lots of you. Probably a lot more once we have C3S operational and I don't have to spend so much time in Seattle.' She paused. 'I want you to know how much I appreciate everything you've done for me Aurora—you've transformed my life. If you hadn't written to me about the salmon project, if you'd picked some other oceanographer, I would never have come here. I'd almost certainly still be in Montreal, although come to think of it I'd probably still have a job.'

They both laughed about that.

'C3S seems to be a lot more satisfying than what you were doing before, so hopefully it's all been worth it in the end.'

'Oh yes, no question,' smiled Lan, putting some cream cheese on a bagel. 'I'd never have met…any of you.'

For a moment they ate silently before Lan continued.

'Actually I won't be the only one from here moving. I was able to allocate one of the new staff houses to Julie, since she's the most senior local employee. And Aiyana is going to move in with her too.'

'It's good that she gets out from under her father,' replied Aurora. 'She's really developed a lot hasn't she? I thought Aiyana had to look after her mother though, she's not in the best of health.'

'They want to live together.'

'Oh. You'd think after working together so closely

for a year they'd want some space,' persisted Aurora. 'I mean you can have too much of someone, can't you?'

Lan sighed. 'They're in love, Aurora.'

'You mean…?'

'Yes.'

Aurora looked surprised. 'Really? Good Lord, that had never occurred to me. I just thought they were good friends!'

'Another first for Esh.'

'Actually not…but the first public ones, I'll grant you that. Things have changed so much around here since all this started.'

'There's something else,' Lan continued, a little nervously. 'I wanted you to be the first to know because it will be common knowledge very soon. When I move into my new house I won't be alone.'

Aurora put up her hand to interrupt her. 'Lan, there's something I need to tell you. Before you go any further. Give me a minute, I need to get something first.'

'But…'

'Please, let me go first,' she said firmly, and went up to her bedroom and took a small framed photo out of her cupboard and returned downstairs.

Aurora took a deep breath.

'There's something I need to tell you, something which in the light of what you are about to say I should have told you earlier.' She was so serious that Lan feared the worst. In a split second she knew what it was. Aurora hadn't looked her best in the last few weeks. She was dying, she didn't want Lan to abandon her in her final months. She…

'There's no easy way of telling you this. I am your mother.'

As if in slow motion Lan felt the handle of her coffee mug swing on her finger, the coffee spilling onto her legs, and was just thinking that it was a good job it was a five minute old cup and not too hot before she felt it bounce off her leg and break on the floor. For a moment neither of them moved.

'Oh! That's my fault! Don't move, I'll get a towel—hang on!'

Lan didn't manage to speak until Aurora was back, patting her wet jeans with a ridiculously large towel.

'What?! You can't be my mother! My mother was Algonquin First Nation,' she spluttered, 'I was born in Montreal.'

Aurora found herself surprisingly composed.

'You're right on the second point, I gave birth to you in Montreal General Hospital, but it's your father who's First Nation, not me.'

Lan was staring at her and Aurora couldn't quite work out whether she was angry or just confused, so decided she'd better just keep going.

'Let me explain. In 1962 I won a scholarship to go to university. I was eighteen years old and it was going to be the first time I left this area and I was the first girl from Esh to ever get a university education. My parents were terribly proud of me, but I was in love—or thought I was in love—with a local boy. There was no way he was ever going to go to university, the educational system was very biased against Natives in those days and in any case he was already a couple of years too old.'

Seeing that Lan was still listening in stunned silence she continued. 'Anyway I was due to go away at the end of the summer and we both knew that that summer was most likely our last together. His parents were pressuring him to marry someone else from the village and I was under no illusions how my parents would react if I tried to marry a non-white, for all their good Christian faith. So one day, a very hot August day without a cloud in the sky, I gave myself to him and we lost our virginity together. On a beach.'

'I remember thinking that I didn't want to leave Esh without having been with him, and I also didn't want to get to Montreal and be the only virgin—it was the sixties after all, and I'd read what student life was like. Unfortunately neither of us really knew what we were doing and three months later I discovered I was pregnant, one month into university. I was terrified. Terrified that I would be thrown out of university, that my parents would disown me, that I wouldn't be able to study, that my whole life was destroyed.'

'Anyway, long story short and I was able to conceal it for a while and then fake illness for long enough to give birth. But all the same I knew that I would be rejected by my family, the village and by your father if I was to come back with a child, and on my own I would have no means to support you. The only option would have been to give up university and try and find some kind of local job, but the quality of life I could have offered you as a single working mom in a big city without any relatives to help would have been pretty poor.

'So I gave you up for adoption,' she sighed heavily. 'I wasn't allowed to know who was going to adopt you and I certainly wasn't allowed to see you again, so I did the only thing I could think of that might give me a way to find you again one day, which was to give you a unique name and insist that it not be changed. I named you after the place you were conceived, Langara

Island.'

Lan gasped. 'What! So that's what it meant! I thought maybe my father was a Spanish footballer,' she said weakly, still looking in shock. 'So, your approaching me about the project was not an accident then?'

For the first time in their conversation Aurora laughed. 'Accident? No, none of this was an accident! Well, except that it worked maybe. Anyway, about a year before I contacted you I heard you talking on a TV documentary about climate change, the name Langara was enough—that had been the idea all along, that it would be completely unique. But I was very reluctant to contact you unless I could be quite sure we had an opportunity to get to know each other first, I didn't want some great embarrassing scene where it was sprung on you and you ran away.

'Then a few weeks before I contacted you I heard of the concept of iron fertilization, so I came up with the idea of the project mainly as a way of reconnecting with you. The fact that it has actually worked has been a complete surprise to me I can tell you, a totally unexpected bonus.'

Lan looked at the floor and gave a short laugh. 'You and me both!' She thought for a moment. 'Are you *sure* about all this?'

'As sure as I can be without us both taking a DNA test. Your birth certificate says you were born in the Montreal General Hospital on the exact same day I gave birth, certainly the only one with the name Langara. And,' she lifted up the photograph that she'd brought downstairs with her, 'you bear a strong resemblance to my own mother. Tall, same nose, same eyes, same cheekbones.'

Lan took the photo and stared at it. She could

hardly believe that after so many years of asking herself where she came from, she finally knew. The resemblance was uncanny.

'I'd like to…' she stopped. 'I was going to say I would like to have a DNA test done so that we can both be sure, but I don't need to. I'm sure you're right but in any case I can't think of anyone else in the world who I'd rather have as my mother.' And with that she burst into tears.

For several minutes they just held each other. Eventually Lan blew her nose. 'Sorry, this is all very emotional, I'd given up looking for you and now this…'

After another minute she had composed herself again. 'So, next question: who's my father?'

Aurora looked at her awkwardly. 'Saul Davidson.'

'Johnny's dad?'

'Johnny's dad.'

Lan stared at the wall. 'Wow. That explains a few things, doesn't it? So Johnny's my half-brother then…all those arguments…' She got up and paced around the room. 'Does he know?'

'Good God no! No one knows. Absolutely no one except you and me.'

Lan was silent, obviously thinking hard. Aurora was surprised she had not reacted more strongly to the news that Johnny was her half-brother.

'So you understand now why I had to tell you first,' added Aurora.

Lan stared at her. 'Well no, actually I don't.'

'Well, because of Johnny, obviously.'

From Lan's blank look it was clear that she had still not made the connection.

'I'm afraid I know about your relationship. About

him moving in with you…'

'Moving in with me? Johnny? Are you crazy?' She burst out laughing.

It was Aurora's turn to look confused.

'What I was about to tell you was that Edward Reid is going to be moving in with me, at least when he's in Esh. I've actually been staying at his place in Victoria whenever I visit there for the last six months or so, so we'll sort of have two homes.'

'Edward?'

Lan nodded, smiling.

'But I thought, oh…I wonder who Johnny was talking about then?' Aurora said, mainly to herself. Then she realized that he must have been referring to Julie's new job and the accommodation that came with it. Of course he loved his daughter, not Lan.

'Edward and I have become close over the past year,' Lan was explaining, 'with him being in Victoria and with my visiting there so much it kind of started there really. It's easier to get to know someone away from all the pressure of village life and all that.'

Once Aurora realized that her revelation about Lan being her daughter as well as Johnny's half-brother was not going to lead to disaster she felt that a weight had been lifted from her. 'I'm really sorry to have sprung this on you, but if you're going to settle down here permanently you had to know the truth. I hope it doesn't change things between us, I don't want it to. I always tried to do what was best for you, even though I didn't know you.'

Lan smiled. 'Actually I couldn't be happier.'

Aurora gave her a hug. 'But what are we going to do about it?'

Lan shrugged. 'Absolutely nothing.'

'Nothing?'

'That's right. People don't need to know, do they? We're not going to tell Saul he has a daughter he didn't know he had or tell Johnny that I'm his half-sister. What good would it do them? Apart from Saul's temper he's a decent man and I'm fine with him being my biological father—as I said it certainly explains a few things—but I don't have any urge to go and hug him. Do you mind?'

'Nothing...' It was Aurora's turn to come to terms with the new situation. 'I guess not, the rest of the village doesn't need to know. It's a secret I've kept for over fifty years, after all.'

'I will tell Edward, obviously. He deserves to know. And it solves a mystery he's been racking his brains about for quite a while, namely my connection with Langara Island.' She went on to explain about her trip there with Edward and the logic that had led them to conclude that she had to be the love-child of a Spanish footballer.

'Never heard of him!' grinned Aurora, 'but I can see why you thought that. I just wanted to give you a name that would be easier for me to trace if I ever wanted to, it didn't occur to me that you would try to go there, or even realize that it was a place.'

After another pause she asked, rather apprehensively 'What about us? What sort of relationship do you want us to have?'

'I'm very happy to know you're my real mother. I'm not sure I'm ever going to get used to calling you 'mom', but I already count you as one of my dearest friends and will still see you all the time.'

'That's a relief.'

'When you think about it, your contacting me was

perfect timing and has had an enormously positive impact on my life,' continued Lan. 'You've actually done more for me, as my mother, than I could ever have hoped for. How many moms help their daughter find both their dream job and their dream partner? Before you came along my career had hit a roadblock, the best I could have hoped for was to spend my last ten years teaching rather than the research I loved. Because of the salmon project I have landed my absolute dream job, way more interesting and influential than I would have ever achieved in the university system.'

'But the salmon project got you fired!' objected Aurora.

'That was my own fault, I shouldn't have shot my mouth off like that. No, your project was the sort of jolt to my system that I needed. And of course I wouldn't have come to live in Esh or met Edward without you either, and I wasn't exactly doing great on the relationships side before. So all in all I'm much better off thanks to your intervention in my life, you shouldn't feel bad about that for a moment.'

'I'm just so relieved you turned out to be such a well-balanced, likeable person. I wouldn't say giving you up for adoption is something I've been feeling guilty about my whole life because I've always believed that it was the best option for you, but what kind of person you became and how you felt about it is something that's been on my mind for a long time, especially the last ten years. I feel whole now. I won't die with regrets.'

Lan looked thoughtful. 'But what would you have done if I hadn't taken on the project? I could easily have not even bothered replying, dismissed it as just a crank idea.'

'Oh, I had a Plan B. And a Plan C too actually, but they weren't nearly so good. I wanted to make sure we had a chance to get to know one another before I told you, I thought that was very important. It wouldn't have been fair just to spring it on you without your having had a chance to get to know what kind of person I was. Besides, if I'd just told you out of the blue it was much more likely you would have just told me to go to hell.'

Lan nodded. 'Go on…'

'Oh, so Plan B…well you'll laugh at this but I was going to enrol as a mature student on your oceanography course. I thought that would bring us into regular contact, but of course it would have been a bit of a one-sided relationship and you wouldn't have had any particular reason to want to get to know me. I guess I could always have deliberately been a poor student so that you'd have felt the need to give me extra tuition though,' she smiled.

'True, although for future reference I try not to get too involved with my student's lives outside of the classroom. And Plan C?'

'That was just to move to Montreal and to live near you and see if I could engineer a friendship that way.'

'A bit risky that one, sounds too much like stalking—and I'm not prone to bonding with old ladies in coffee shops who suddenly want to be my best friend for no reason.'

'Well exactly, but for Plan A I was prepared to have been a lot more pushy to get you involved in the project. I had mentally prepared myself for you to turn me down on the letter and was going to come to Montreal and persuade you in person.'

'And if I'd turned out to be someone you didn't like?'

Aurora frowned. 'Not sure on that one. I guess if you were just a horrible person I might never have told you, just been disappointed and let you get on with your life. What was nice about this way is that we have had a chance to get to know one another for who we really are, not just felt obliged to through a biological relationship.' She stood up. 'Talking of which, I have something that belongs to you.'

She left the room and returned a few seconds later with something bulky by her side.

'My mother made me promise to give this to my daughter, if I ever had one. So I believe it's now yours.' She lifted up the painting she was carrying and placed it on the table. It was a Lawren Harris painting.

'Whoa! You're not serious, this is way too expensive, it's your pension!' replied Lan, almost shocked.

'It's my mother's Harris, the one he gave her. She was always insistent that their two paintings be kept in the family and handed down. You're going to get it sooner or later, you might as well enjoy it right away.'

Lan lifted it up and looked at it in the light.

'Are you sure?' she said doubtfully.

'One condition—you don't sell it until I'm gone. I guess you're not going to have children, at least I hope you're not going to at your age, so it'll be your decision what you do with the three of them eventually.' She looked at the painting wistfully. 'Anyway, I want you to have it and as I said I had actually promised my mother I'd give it to you. She would have liked you I'm sure, and I'm sure in some way she knows all about you.'

Lan took the painting and propped it up over the mantelpiece next to the other one and gave Aurora a hug, then sat down again. They sat for a while in silence looking at the sparkling waters in Edenshaw Sound, mist curling around the mountains on the other side of the water, the subject of the painting.

'So we're cool?'

'We're cool. Mom.'

Also by David Millar

Beyond Dubai: Seeking Lost Cities in the Emirates

Beyond Dubai is a light-hearted journey around the Emirates in search of its past—encountering smugglers, fire-starting genies, loved-up camels, and a mysterious mountain tribe along the way.

In addition to exploring the UAE's lost cities and hidden treasures, it also tells the extraordinary tale of how climate change transformed a once-fertile grassland into the starkly beautiful desert that it is today.

ISBN 978-0-9938321-0-9 (paperback) £9.95 US$12.95
ISBN 978-0-9938321-1-6 (e-book) £1.99 US$2.99

Made in the USA
Monee, IL
11 February 2020

21561365R00238